ALSO BY
EMMA SCOTT

LOST BOYS
The Girl in the Love Song
When You Come Back to Me
The Last Piece of His Heart

FULL TILT DUET
Full Tilt
All In

Little Pieces of Light

EMMA SCOTT

Bloom books

Copyright © 2025 by Emma Scott
Cover and internal design © 2025 by Sourcebooks
Cover design by Antoaneta Lisak/Sourcebooks
Cover images © vinap/Getty Images, fotograzia/
Getty Images, ThomasVogel/Getty Images
Internal art by Neeraj S.

Sourcebooks, Bloom Books, and the colophon are registered trademarks of Sourcebooks.

All rights reserved. No part of this book may be reproduced in any form or by any electronic or mechanical means including information storage and retrieval systems—except in the case of brief quotations embodied in critical articles or reviews—without permission in writing from its publisher, Sourcebooks.

No part of this book may be used or reproduced in any manner for the purpose of training artificial intelligence technologies or systems.

The characters and events portrayed in this book are fictitious or are used fictitiously. Any similarity to real persons, living or dead, is purely coincidental and not intended by the author.

All brand names and product names used in this book are trademarks, registered trademarks, or trade names of their respective holders. Sourcebooks is not associated with any product or vendor in this book.

Published by Bloom Books, an imprint of Sourcebooks
1935 Brookdale RD, Naperville, IL 60563-2773
(630) 961-3900
sourcebooks.com

Cataloging-in-Publication data is on file with the Library of Congress.

The authorized representative in the EEA is Dorling Kindersley Verlag GmbH. Arnulfstr. 124, 80636 Munich, Germany

Manufactured in the UK by Clays and distributed
by Dorling Kindersley Limited, London
001-355613-Oct/25
10 9 8 7 6 5 4 3 2 1

To those who struggle to step out of the shadows and into the light, please never stop sharing your gifts. This one is for you.

PLAYLIST

Sparks // Coldplay
Creep // Radiohead
you should see me in a crown // Billie Eilish
Chop Suey! // System Of A Down
Perfect // Alanis Morissette
Nocturne in E-Flat Major // Frédéric Chopin
Just Friends // Morgan Saint
Superposition // Young the Giant
Please Please Please // Sabrina Carpenter
What Was I Made For? // Billie Eilish
Treat You Better // Shawn Mendes
Variations in B-Flat Major // Franz Schubert
But Daddy I Love Him // Taylor Swift
Follow You // Imagine Dragons
She Will Be Loved // Maroon 5
Supermassive Black Hole // Muse

MEN'S EIGHT ROWING CREW

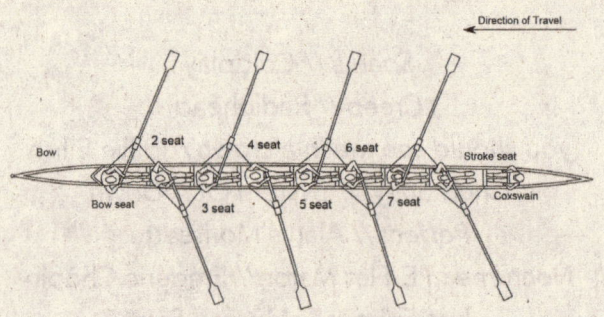

Every one of us is, in the cosmic perspective, precious.

–Carl Sagan

Prologue

XANDER, AGE TEN

IT WAS THE FOURTH OF JULY, AND MY MOTHER WAS walking out on us.

"I'm leaving you."

She said it to my dad, but it was a plural *you* that included me too. The words traveled from Mom's mouth to my heart at the speed of sound (v = 343 meters per second). I thought it must have been faster than that given how hard they punched me in the chest. Faster than the speed of light, even. Einstein's Theory of Special Relativity states that nothing in the universe travels faster than light (c = 186,282 miles per second), but surely this was an exception—a bullet in my heart, shattering my insides.

My mind turned the chaotic pain into a manageable equation:

$F - M(Pd) = e^\wedge \infty \, (D + C)$

Whereas, after she had an affair with a Parisian diplomat (Pd), our family (F) had now lost one mother (M), resulting in emotional devastation raised to an infinite power $(e\wedge\infty)$ for both dad (D) and child (C).

In plain English, it meant my mother didn't think her only son was worth sticking around for.

People had told me I'd inherited my genius from my father. But that morning, he was slow to catch on when I'd already done the math.

"Oh, come on, Sharon," Dad said wearily. "Not this again. It's just one week."

Every summer, we'd drive the six hours from our little home in Gaithersburg, Maryland, to Dad's family house in Castle Hill, Rhode Island. Mom hated these trips. The Rhode Island house was too small, too dark, too full of Dad's books and papers, and crammed with my grandparents' antique furniture Dad inherited after they passed away. Mom would always try to talk Dad out of these trips, then threaten to stay home, then finally give in and complain the entire time.

That morning, my father believed she was keeping to tradition, until he finally analyzed the situation: He and I were packed and ready to go, the Buick loaded with our luggage for the week. A sleek black sedan idled next to said Buick. Mom's luggage was in the front entry. She was dressed up in a dark skirt suit, pink blouse, and heels with her makeup done. Then there were all those hushed phone calls and late nights with her "colleague" at the State Department that past month, hanging over us like a black cloud.

Mom bent and touched her fingertips to my cheek. "It won't be forever."

I stared at her from behind my black, square-framed glasses. What did that mean? She was coming back? When? At some future date between today and forever? It was a statement made of inconclusive data, which was worthless. It was her walking out the door but leaving it cracked behind her, trapping me in a perpetual state of mystery as to when (or if) she'd ever walk back through it.

I sort of hated her for that.

Then she turned to Dad. "I can't do this anymore." Mom shouldered her big bag and took the handle of her rolling suitcase.

Whatever "this" was remained an unknown too; I wouldn't ask, and my father couldn't. He stared at my mother's retreating back as she stepped out the front door and slipped—long-legged and elegant—into the diplomat's waiting sedan and drove away. Then Dad turned to me with a fixed, shell-shocked smile.

"We'd better hit the road if we want to beat traffic."

I hardly felt a minute of the six-hour drive to Castle Hill. Philadelphia flew past me in the west, then New York City in the east, without notice. Next came the green of Connecticut, which gave way to the endless bridges and shorelines of Rhode Island. All those miles slipped out from under me as the shock of my mother's abandonment jolted around my brain, animating thoughts like Frankenstein's monster:

I did this.
It's all my fault.
She doesn't want me.

These were the facts as I saw them, since moms don't leave—but mine did.

"Look, there." Dad pointed out the windshield to a park straight ahead of us where several families were having a Fourth of July party. We'd arrived in Castle Hill. It was the first time he'd spoken in more than an hour. "There're a bunch of kids. How about you go play with them for a while?"

"What…?" My heart that had been thudding with a dull, heavy clang, sped up. "*Now*? Aren't we going to the house?"

"Sure, sure. But I need to go alone for a bit first."

I stared at him. "You're going to leave me here? Dad, I don't know those kids. I can't just walk up and invite myself…"

But he was already pulling the Buick into a parking spot. He rested his pale, long-fingered hands on the top of the steering wheel, his gaze on the party in front of us but not really seeing it. "I need to get some numbers on paper before I lose them. You understand that, right? If I don't write the figures down, they might—whoop!" He made a fluttering motion. "Fly straight out of my head, never to return."

My father was a physicist at the National Institute of

Standards and Technology. This was supposed to be his summer vacation. But I was in the front seat where Mom should have been, so it wasn't a vacation at all.

"What do you say, buddy?" Dad turned to me, almost pleading. "Looks like a fun party. I see some kids your age. Some girls, even. It'll be good for you to practice your social skills in that department before Langdon."

The Langdon School was a private academy for gifted boys that I'd be starting in the fall. It was in Bethesda, a twenty-minute drive from our home and Dad's work at the NIST. But I already knew I'd be taking the bus: With Mom gone, the chances that Dad would pick me up from school every afternoon were infinitesimally small.

I faced forward, swallowing hard. I recognized Brenton Park from past summers. Parents sat at picnic tables while kids, ranging from toddlers to preteens, threw Frisbees, played tag, or ran along the banks of a small pond. I knew there were fish in that pond—catfish, carp, and fathead minnows—and even a few turtles.

"We just got here," I protested weakly. "We've been in the car for more than six hours. I want to go to the house and—"

"Oh, look. Those boys are playing ball." Dad mustered a weak smile. "Doesn't that look fun?"

It did not. How could anything be "fun" ever again?

"They don't know me, Dad," I said. "They're not going to want to play with me."

"You never know until you ask. You could make some new friends."

I doubted that. I had no friends back home. Why would it be different here? I was "a major nerd" and "a freak from another planet." Those would remain constants no matter how many state lines we crossed.

I chewed my bottom lip. Brenton Park was at least a six-mile walk from our house, and there was no bus. "When are you going to come back and get me?"

"I'll be back soon. Before dusk," Dad said. "A few hours, son. That's all I ask."

My father's eyes—blue, like one of mine—were glassy. His lip quavered, reminding me of the neighbor kids back home when they scraped their knees. Dad didn't need to work; he needed to cry about Mom. Fine for him. I wasn't going to give her the satisfaction, even if she never knew it.

I looked straight ahead, jaw clenched. "You'll come and get me at dusk? You won't forget?"

"I won't forget."

"Okay." I climbed out of the car. Dad gave me a little wave, like he was sorry but that he couldn't help it, and drove away.

I put the odds of his coming back on time at sixty-to-one against. It wasn't that he was a bad parent; his mind just didn't work like everyone else's. Mine didn't either, but where I was sharp, organized, and remembered everything, Dad was scattered. Nervous. He could calculate hundreds of probabilities for quantum interactions but couldn't remember to close the garage door. It's part of why Mom left, I knew. I'd heard the fighting.

"If your head wasn't screwed on, Russell, it'd roll right off!"

She didn't say it in a funny way but in an angry way. Over this last year, she'd been angry a lot. I guessed she'd done her own calculations and concluded it wasn't worth it to stay.

It won't be forever.

My mind wouldn't leave her cryptic words alone, turning them over and over, round and round, like a Rubik's Cube but with missing color squares. An equation I couldn't solve, and there was nothing worse than that.

Dusk was coming fast—light's longer wavelengths dominated the sky in shades of red and orange as the sun sank toward the ocean. I figured I had less than an hour to kill until I'd know for sure if Dad forgot me.

Standing alone in the parking lot, I observed the party from a safe distance. In the clearing by the pond, kids were laughing, chasing each other, and throwing bread at the ducks and minnows. From the grill, the humid air trapped the scents of barbecued hamburgers and hot dogs. The grown-up men wore khaki pants and polos (like the uniform I'd wear at Langdon) and the women were in blouses and jeans with designer sandals. Richies of Castle Hill.

Castle Hill was south of Newport on a peninsula shaped like a shoe, where the Atlantic Ocean poured into Narragansett Bay. It was filled with Richies who lived in big houses on the water. They all had luxury cars and yachts, and they all belonged to the Castle Hill Country Club.

Not us.

At the top of the shoe, the land jutted up, then curved back down, like an elbow. The elbow was called the Bend, which was code for "poor." Dad's little house was on the Bend. He may have been a genius—a little famous even, for his work in particle physics and electromagnetic spectroscopy—but Mom was always complaining he didn't publish enough papers in the right journals, so we were always on the "edge of ruin."

I glanced down at my worn shoes and my jeans with the holes in the knees, then pushed my glasses up higher on my nose. I was a Bend kid all the way. No one—certainly not a Richie—was going to let me play with them.

I wouldn't know how anyway.

An anvil-shaped boulder surrounded by weeds and tall, spiky Atlantic manna grass rested near the edge of the parking lot. I sat down on it and waited for dusk while the kids played and the grown-ups drank their wine and grilled their food.

My stomach growled. It had been three hours since the gas stop in Connecticut. The scent of the ocean, the grill, and the sounds of kids laughing carried memories of other, better Fourths of July. Now I was just a boy, sitting on a rock, wondering what I'd done to make my mom leave.

"Hi."

I jerked out of my poor-me thoughts and looked up. My breath caught like I'd been punched in the gut.

It was a girl.

Not just any girl. *The* girl.

I couldn't stop staring. She didn't seem real. She *couldn't* be real; she was too pretty—Alice in Wonderland in a pink dress instead of blue, her thick blond hair curling in long ribbons around puffy sleeves. Big blue-green eyes watched me with curiosity, and her smile included the whole world. It included *me* when I'd never felt more alone in my life.

But she was obviously a Richie, and I was from the Bend. Once she knew that, this perfect girl would walk away. Or I'd drive her away. It only took most kids a few minutes of talking to me to decide I was too freakish to be friends. I'd learned the hard way it was better not to try. Better to be a jerk and save us all the trouble.

"Hey," I answered finally, tearing my eyes off of her and training them on my ratty shoes.

"What are you doing here by yourself?"

The girl's voice was high and sweet, mine full of bitterness.

"Nothing. Sitting. Is that allowed?"

She jerked a thumb to the kids playing behind us. "I saw you from over there. You looked so sad and lonely; I thought I'd say hi."

I scowled. "I'm not sad *or* lonely."

The girl scuffed her shoe in the dirt. "Oh, okay. Sorry."

I felt bad. *She* looked sad and lonely but covered it with her pretty smile. She wasn't dressed for the park in her fancy dress and shiny black shoes, either. More for a family photo or special occasion. She even had something pink and glittery painted on her lips. This girl looked made-up, like a little doll.

Or maybe this is how Richies go to barbecues at the park.

"Sorry," I mumbled. "Bad day."

"Yeah, me too." She brightened and held out her hand. "I'm Emery Wallace."

Slowly, I took her hand, certain my hair was going to stand on end when our skin touched. "Xander Ford."

"Pleased to meet you, Xander."

She gave my hand one strong shake, as if we'd made a business deal. When she let go, I could still feel her touch on my palm. My fingers curled to keep it.

"What are you doing out here, Xander?" Emery smiled. "I like saying your name. Xander with a *Z*."

"With an *X*. It's short for Alexander."

"Oh. Why not go by Alex?"

"Because I don't want to."

She nodded, thinking. "That's smart. Lots of Alexes. I don't know any Xanders. But now I know you!"

The friendliness in her voice hit me right in the chest, warming over the icy cold spot where Mom used to be, just a little bit.

Emery glanced around. "Why are you by the parking lot?"

"I'm waiting for my dad to pick me up."

"Are you here by yourself?"

"Yes."

"Why?"

"My dad and I just got into town, but he had some stuff to do…" I shifted on the rock.

"Do you live around here? I haven't seen you before."

"No," I said. "Well, not permanently. We spend a week or so every summer."

"Oh!" Emery's eyes brightened. "Do you belong to the Club, too?"

She must've thought we had a big vacation house on the water because who in the world—besides my dad—would have a summer home on the Bend?

"No." I sat up straighter. "But my father is very important. He works for the government."

"Really? Like a spy?"

"Umm…no." I peered at her through my glasses. "You sure ask a lot of questions."

"How else am I going to learn anything about you?"

"Why do you want to?"

Emery cocked her head as if the question didn't make sense. "Because that's how you make friends."

A lump grew in my throat. "You want to be my friend?"

"Of course!"

Emery plopped herself next to me on the rock. I froze, and—for once in my life—all thoughts flew out of my head. There was no room for anything but her. She had to be the prettiest girl I'd ever seen, and she smelled like cotton candy. For a short, happy moment, I forgot why I was alone on the rock in the first place or that I was supposed to be trying to make her go away.

I don't want her to go away.

"So…" Emery settled herself beside me and smoothed

her dress. "Your dad works for the government, but he's not a spy."

"He's a physicist. That's what I'm going to be too."

"What does a physi...physicist do?"

She said it with a bunch of *z*'s. *Fizzizzist*.

"Only the most important research in the world. We study why and how the universe is the way it is." I tilted my chin. "It's very complicated. You wouldn't understand it."

That was my usual thing: to make the other person feel stupid so I could feel better about being different. So I could pretend I didn't care if they liked me or not.

Emery wasn't buying it.

She gave me a haughty look. "Is that so?"

"Yep. Like Niels Bohr says, 'Those who are not shocked by quantum theory cannot possibly understand it.'"

"Who the heck is Niels Bohr?"

"He's one of the most famous physicists in history. He won the Nobel Prize for his work applying Max Planck's quantum theories to visualize the world's first atomic structure."

Emery frowned. "How old are you?"

"Ten."

"I'm ten too, but you don't talk like me."

"That's because I'm a genius."

She made the *Is that so?* face again until she saw I wasn't kidding. "Wait, really?"

"Yes, really."

"Does that mean you know everything?"

"Not everything."

She cocked her head. "What grade are you in?"

Here we go. I cleared my throat. "I'm in high school."

Emery's eyes widened. "*High school?*"

A mental countdown began in my head. Any second now, this girl was going to walk away. May as well get it over with.

"I'm leaving the public school for a special high school in the fall. I have two more years, and then I start college. Then I'll go to MIT. Just like my dad."

"But…you're ten!"

"I *know*." I sighed. "It's okay. You don't have to keep talking to me."

She wrinkled her nose. "Why would I stop?"

"Because it's weird."

"It's not weird, it's cool! You're like Sheldon Cooper! Like on that show? *Young Sheldon?*"

I stiffened. I didn't watch TV, but I heard that comparison every day at my high school in Gaithersburg. Mostly, it was the older kids—which was everyone—making fun of me and asking me if I liked trains or *Star Trek*, or if I had something called a Meemaw.

"*No.* I'm not like him."

"He graduated high school when he was eleven."

"I told you I'm not graduating high school. I still have two more years."

Emery swung her legs and scuffed the heels of her shiny black shoes on the rock. "Well, I think that's cool. I wish I could be done in two years. Then I could go right to Rizdy!"

"What's Rizdy?"

"It stands for Rhode Island School of Design. R-I-S-D, but you say it like, 'Rizdy.'"

"Okay. What do you want to design?"

"The inside of houses. I want to be an interior designer and maybe do big events, like weddings. I love drawing and painting and collaging, but more than anything, I love doing makeovers on rooms. You should see my bedroom."

I felt heat creep over the back of my neck. I had no idea what to say to that.

"Soooo…" Emery scooted closer. "What's it like, being a genius?"

"It's…um, okay." I stammered because now our arms were touching. "Some good things, some bad things."

"What are some good things?"

"I can read anything I want," I said. "I can play some piano. I can do math. Really hard math."

Emery made a face. "Math is the *worst*. But I love reading! I love *Wings of Fire,* and *Matilda,* and *The Secret Garden*." She was lit up even brighter now, like a live wire humming with energy. "What are you reading right now?"

"*Meditations* by Marcus Aurelius."

"Huh?"

"Never mind," I said quickly. The last thing I wanted was her to think I was making fun of her.

"Okaaay." Emery cocked her head. "What are the bad things about being a super genius?"

A long list populated in my head. I picked the one at the top. The worst one. "I get lonely."

Geez. I couldn't believe I said that out loud.

Emery's face softened. "You do? Why?"

"Because I don't know how to talk to kids my age." I glanced away. "Never mind. It's dumb."

"It's not dumb. Maybe you just need the practice. If you didn't go to a special school but a regular school, you'd be around more regular kids, right?"

"Yes. But…"

"But regular school is too easy for you?" She grinned. "Do you want to be famous and win a Nobel Prize? Like boring old Niels Bohr? Bohr the Bore."

She giggled and it jumped to me, making me laugh on a day I thought laughing was impossible.

"Yeah…maybe," I said. "Bohr specialized in atomic structure. I want to study black holes, and that's a different kind of physics."

"There are different kinds?"

"Oh yes—"

Emery gasped. "Oh my gosh! Your eyes!"

And before I knew what was happening, she took off my glasses and brushed a lock of brown hair off my forehead. Her face drew closer to mine—so close, our noses were almost touching. My heart beat faster.

"One is dark blue and the other is brown!" she cried. "Or mostly brown. A little bit of blue at the bottom… Wow, that is so cool!"

People had been making a fuss about my heterochromia since I was a small child, teasing me that I'd inherited one eye from my dad and one from my mom. I kind of liked that, but now my mom was gone, and I'd be stuck with the reminder of her forever. Her parting souvenir. But Emery made it seem special again.

"Special" is going to turn into "weirdo" the longer she talks to you. Just you wait.

"Whatever," I said, trying to sound cold and stony. I took my glasses back and put them on. "It's not a big deal."

"Maybe not to you," Emery said. "But I've never seen eyes like yours before."

I'd never seen eyes like hers, either. Not just their blue-green color—a standard color on the spectrum—but how they seemed lit from inside. Bright and warm, but with sadness at the edges.

She'd said she was having a bad day. I should've asked her about herself but didn't know how without sounding like a creep. I had an IQ of 177. I could solve differential equations in my sleep and recite pi to the 1000th digit, but talking about normal things was hard.

Maybe she's right. I just need to practice.

I sucked in a breath to ask about her bad day when the grown-ups at the picnic tables started calling the kids in for dinner.

"Emery!" one of the men shouted, waving a pair of tongs.

"Your dad?" I asked.

"My neighbor." The sadness that had been lurking at the edges of Emery's eyes came out in full. "My dad would never let us do something as fun as a picnic, but…

something bad happened, so he sent Jack and me here for a little while. Jack is my brother. He's eleven."

"What is the bad thing that happened?" I asked, keeping my voice low. "Only if you want to tell me. You don't have to…"

Emery glanced down at her hands in her lap. "My other brother, Grant, is missing. He's almost eighteen, so they think he went up to Newport with some friends." She looked up at me fearfully. "But I think he ran away."

"Why would he do that?"

"My dad is strict. *Very* strict. I heard them arguing this morning in Dad's study. They were shouting about where Grant was going to go to college. Dad has plans for him… He has plans for all of us, but Grant didn't like it." Emery's eyes filled. "When Grant came out, he had a funny look on his face. Then he gave Jack and me big hugs and walked out the door."

He walked out the door. Just like my mother. On the same day.

Emery's pain seemed to be seeping into me. I didn't think I could hurt worse than Mom leaving, but seeing Emery hurt doubled the ache in my heart.

"Maybe he did go to stay with friends," I said awkwardly. "I'll bet he did."

"With no luggage? No nothing?" Then she stuck her smile back on and gave her head a shake. "No, I'm sure you're right. I'm sorry."

"For what?"

"Mom says to always be mindful of how I'm behaving

in front of other people. To always be polite and not make a fuss."

I frowned. "You're not making a fuss. You're worried. It's okay to be worried."

Emery smiled at me, her lower lip quavering, sending new cracks into my heart. The urge to pull her close and protect her somehow came over me. Instead, I awkwardly patted the exact middle of her back. As soon as my palm touched the soft fabric of her dress, she tipped against me as if she were very tired. I froze but let her rest against my shoulder if that was what she needed. I know I did. We sat that way for a few minutes until the dad at the grill called her again.

"Emery! Come get something to eat!"

"Coming!" She wiped her eyes and slipped off the rock. "Are you hungry? Did you have dinner?"

"I'm not hungry," I said. At that moment, my stomach made a loud, embarrassing growl.

Emery's grin came back. "Umm, it kinda sounds like you are."

"I guess I could eat."

"Wait right there!"

A few minutes later, Emery came back with two paper plates containing hot dogs in buns, potato salad, and big wedges of watermelon.

"I couldn't carry drinks," she said, handing me a plate. "Do you want a drink? I can go back…"

"No," I said. Her charity was already too much. But mostly I didn't want her to go away again. "Thank you."

"You're welcome."

For a few moments, there was silence—just me and this girl sitting on a boulder as the sky grew darker, eating our hot dogs and waiting for fireworks.

I already have fireworks.

From a scientific standpoint, it didn't make any sense—I'd just met Emery and we were just kids, but it was true all the same.

Emery finished her hot dog in record time and started on the potato salad. She caught me staring and laughed. "My mother would freak out if she saw me now. But I've been so worried, I haven't eaten anything all day."

"Why would she freak out?"

"She says I have to be careful about my weight." Emery rolled her eyes. "She used to put me in those dumb pageants, and if I didn't fit in a costume just right, she'd get really upset. Like, embarrassed."

I scowled. "You look fine to me." *You're perfect.*

Emery grinned and took a big bite of potato salad. "She's not here to nag me anyway, so I'm going to eat whatever I want."

I put my gaze on my own plate and assessed the data I'd acquired so far:

1. Emery's father didn't want her (or her brother) to attend a fun Fourth of July picnic.
2. He had "plans" for his kids that made them run away.

3. Her mother seemed to be trying to give her an eating disorder.

Emery's parents were either dimming her light on purpose or couldn't even see it, which seemed impossible to me. She was luminous. A Class A1 star, for sure. But that was the kind of observation that got me funny looks and made me zero friends, so I kept it to myself.

"So, Xander," Emery said after a minute, "you're a genius and your dad's a famous scientist who works for the government. What does your mom do?"

The potato salad in my mouth turned to gooey cement. "She works for the government too. The State Department."

"Wow," Emery said. "Where is—?"

"What do your parents do?" I asked, cutting her off before she asked *that* question.

"My dad owns Wallace Industries. It's a big textiles company. And my mom doesn't do anything except hold charity events."

"That sounds nice."

"It's just for show," Emery said. "Mostly she throws dinner parties and stuff like that for Dad's company."

"Oh." I struggled for something else to say and glanced behind us. At the picnic tables, boys shrieked and threw food at each other. "Which one is your brother Jack?"

Emery squinted in the falling light. "Don't see him." Her face fell again. "He didn't want to come here. He wanted to search for Grant. They're best buddies. I'm worried about him too."

My giant IQ rarely failed me, but I was failing Emery. I didn't know what to say to make her feel better. I'd already decided to never speak of my mother ever again, but Emery had told me about her brother. Maybe if I told her about Mom, she'd know that I understood a little of how she was feeling. Wasn't that what friends did? Share the hard stuff so the other didn't feel so alone?

Or she might wonder what was wrong with me that my mom didn't want me.

"My mom…" I cleared my throat. "She left too."

I braced myself for Emery to laugh at me, but she stared at me with a strange expression, almost as if she were scared.

"What do you mean?"

"I mean, she packed up her bags and drove away."

"When?"

"This morning."

"*This morning?*"

Emery's eyes actually filled with tears. Her crying made me want to cry, but I'd made a promise to myself, so I stuffed it down.

"It's no big deal."

"Yes, it is!" Emery cried. "She can't just do that! Where did she go?"

"To Paris, I guess." I sat up stiffly. "I don't know for sure, and I don't care."

"Gosh, Xander, I'm so sorry."

Emery threw her arms around me in a sudden hug, sending her dinner plate into the dirt at our feet. I froze, shocked by the comfort of her soft touch, how her little arms squeezed me as if she were trying to hug all the pain out.

After a moment, she let go and shook her head. "Wow, isn't that weird? My brother and your mom? On the same day?"

I nodded. The odds were improbable, but even more improbable was that, out of all the kids at the park, this girl would choose to sit with me. "I hope your brother comes back, Emery."

She smiled sadly. "I hope your mom comes back, Xander."

"Thanks," I said dully.

I didn't have much hope, but Emery's brother *had* to come back. I didn't want to think about how it would hurt her if he didn't.

"I made a mess," Emery said with a small laugh, glancing at the spilled food on the ground.

"I got it." I jumped down and picked up the watermelon rind, coated in dirt, and used her napkin to get the potato salad.

"You don't have to…"

"Done," I said with a smile and tossed it all in a nearby trash can.

"Thank you," she said.

Now she was on the rock, and I was standing in front of her. I stuffed my hands in the front pockets of my jeans, not sure what to do next. Sit down beside her again? Was that okay with her?

"Umm…" I cleared my throat and rubbed the back of my neck. "Do you want to…feed the pond fish?"

I cringed. A girl like Emery wasn't going to want to get down on her knees in the muck and—

"Yes!" she cried and jumped off the rock. "I'll go get some more hot dog buns."

"Oh, okay." I smiled a little. Maybe I was doing okay at this friend stuff.

Emery raced away, then raced right back. "They wouldn't let me take more than two." She bit her lower lip. "Is that enough? Or maybe I should get something else?"

I frowned. "It's fine."

"Oh. Good. My dad is always telling me I don't know how the world works and that I'd better ask."

"About hot dog buns?"

She shrugged and glanced away.

I added another bit of data to my collection: *4. Emery's dad makes her doubt herself. A lot.*

"Two's perfect."

She beamed and took my hand. "Let's go!"

Hand in hand, we ran to the pond's edge. Emery didn't seem worried about getting dirty and knelt with me as we tossed bits of bread at the minnows and carp. She squealed with delight as a turtle poked its head above the murky surface.

"That's a red-eared slider," I said. "You can tell by the red mark on its head. Lots of people keep them as pets, but they're also considered an invasive species in some areas."

"It's so cute!" Emery looked to me. "How do you know

that? Do you get to automatically know stuff if you're a genius?"

"No," I said. "I don't usually play with anyone when I come to the park, so I learn about the animals and plants and stuff instead."

I expected her to feel sorry for me, but Emery smiled her pretty smile. "I'm so lucky."

"You are?"

She nodded. "Because now I get to learn what you learned while we play together. It's like a whaddyacallit... when more than one thing good happens at the same time?"

"A win-win situation," I murmured, my throat suddenly tight that this girl considered herself lucky to know me.

"Yes!" she cried. "A win-win situation."

"I'm the lucky one, Emery," I said before I could take it back.

Her head whipped to me. "Why?"

"Because..." A hundred options came to mind, but I told the truth. "Because today is one of the worst days of my life and you're making it better. More than better. It's not even the worst day anymore because now it's the day that I met you."

Emery's eyes widened in surprise, and I cursed myself for saying too much. She was going to think I was a creep, but a pink blush came to her cheeks and her smile was prettier than ever.

"Me too," she said. "I mean, I'm still worried about

Grant, but I'm also…happy. Is it bad to feel both at the same time?"

"No," I said. "I'm still sad about my mom, but I'm happy too."

Another small silence fell, but this one felt nice. Warm. Like I could stay in it forever… And then a stinging explosion of water hit me square in the back.

"Get lost, Bender!"

We got to our feet and turned just in time for a second water balloon to hit me in the chest. Water droplets splashed my glasses. I wiped them on my shirt, humiliation burning my skin so hot I thought my clothes would dry in an instant. Two boys—one blond and big, one dark-haired and skinny—were standing twenty feet away, laughing.

Emery stomped her foot. "Stop it, you guys!"

"*Stop it, you guys,*" the blond mimicked in a high-pitched voice. He hurled another balloon. I pushed Emery behind me, and the balloon hit my thigh, soaking my jeans.

"Looks like he peed himself," the dark-haired boy sneered. "Did you pee yourself, Bender?"

"You shut up, Rhett!" Emery cried. "Stop it, both of you!"

"Or what?" the blond taunted.

"Or I'll tell my dad," Emery said.

Both boys instantly stopped smiling. They glanced at one another, then hurried away as if Emery had cast a spell.

"Scaredy-cats," she muttered. "One good thing about my dad is everyone's afraid of him, not just me." She glanced at my damp clothes. "Are you okay?"

"Fine," I said quickly. "Just water. No big deal."

"I'm sorry about them. Tucker and Rhett are jerks."

"It's fine."

"It's not fine. Xander—"

"Just forget it, okay?" I bent to pick up the pieces of balloon so I wouldn't have to look her in the eye. "Don't want the turtles to eat the latex…"

Emery knelt down beside me as we hunted for stray strips of balloon. After we'd gathered them all, we took the scraps to the trash can by the rock. Our rock. We sat down on it again and instantly felt better. Because it was our safe place.

"That was sort of cool, what you did," Emery said after a minute.

"What was?" I asked, because as far as I could tell, there was nothing cool about me. Not one thing.

"That one balloon would have hit me, but you stood in front of me, and it hit you instead," she said. "You protected me."

I frowned. I didn't remember doing that. It was just instinct, maybe, to put myself between Emery and something that could hurt her.

"Thank you, Xander," she said, and then I felt the soft touch of her lips on my cheek.

Instantly, a tingle of electricity shot through me, raising the hair on the back of my neck, but in a nice way. The best way. I fought the urge to touch my face so I wouldn't wash away the feel of her little kiss with my grimy hands. I wiped them on my jeans instead and struggled for something to say. But Emery's kiss was a spell too, erasing all the thoughts in my head.

She's like magic.

A slant of headlights cut across the parking lot. Dusk had fallen without my noticing; it was shocking how fast the world had shrunk to just me and Emery. My dad must have remembered me after all, except now the last thing I wanted to do was leave.

But it wasn't Dad's old Buick, it was a sleek black town car. It pulled alongside the far edge of the parking lot. The driver—tall and pale and dressed in black—got out.

"Miss Emery," he called and waved her over.

"That's Colin, Dad's driver. He's early. We're supposed to stay until the fireworks." Her eyes darted to me. "I have a feeling he's here now because of Grant. Maybe bad news."

"Or maybe good," I said, and it felt like a lie.

Emery smiled gratefully, then looked sad again. "We're supposed to go to Italy for the rest of the summer. I guess I won't see you anymore."

"I guess not," I said, and yet another crack formed in my heart. There were so many, it must've been close to falling to pieces.

"I know!" Emery grabbed my arm. "You can write to me. Write to me, and then I'll have your address, and I'll write you back. Can you remember mine if I tell you?"

"Of course."

"Yay! We'll be pen pals! And even though it's a long way away, let's meet here next year. Next Fourth of July. Right on this rock. You want to?"

One year. It may as well have been a thousand, it felt so far away. She'd probably forget all about me, but it was my only chance, so I took it.

"Yes," I said. "I want to."

Emery's face lit up with happiness at the idea of seeing *me* again, and that was the closest I'd come to crying all day.

She told me her address—a big house on the water, no doubt—and I committed it to memory as if it were the answer to the world's most important question on an exam I must not fail.

The driver called her again, this time more urgently.

"Gotta go," Emery said, walking backwards. "Write to me, okay?"

"I will."

She gave me a little wave in the falling dark, then stopped and bent over a tall yellow flower—a daffodil with a bright yellow trumpet. Emery plucked it and ran back to me, breathless.

"You won't forget me, will you, Xander?"

"I won't," I said. "Never."

"Promise?"

"I promise."

Emery's smile stole my breath and my heart right along with it. She pressed the flower's sturdy green stem into my hand. "See you next year."

I watched her go, watched her climb into the waiting car that looked so cold. Today had been cold and raw too, but Emery…she was everything warm and good, and I knew I'd remember her forever.

———

EMERY, AGE THIRTEEN

He forgot me.

It was the only explanation. I'd been coming to Brenton Park every year for three years. To the rock. *Our* rock. And for three years, Xander was never here. This was the third year. The last year.

I can't do this anymore.

I shifted on the hard stone. My butt was numb; I'd been sitting for hours—since this morning—because I didn't want to risk missing him. But now the sun was sinking, and it was obvious that Xander wasn't coming. Again.

I looked west to the ocean. The paper in my hand was getting wrinkled, the ink stained with my tears, the writing smudged. It wasn't a letter from Xander. He hadn't written me either, like he promised. Not once. Empty mailboxes for years. And each time there was no letter, some little piece of me that had been soft and warm grew hard and cold.

I wasn't supposed to go in Grant's room—no one was.

It was sealed off like an exhibit in a museum. But I snuck in there sometimes. Jack did too, probably more than me. He didn't even bother to sneak, though. When our parents or Belinda—the housekeeper—caught him, he yelled and cursed. He told them to fuck off. That they were insane. That he hated them.

He didn't yell that at Belinda, just our parents.

I didn't yell. I never yelled. Never made a fuss or talked back. I'd just sneak in and cry on Grant's pillow, which hadn't been used in three years and would never be used again.

"He was up in Providence, crossing the train tracks with his headphones on," my father had told Jack and me on that Fourth of July three years ago. After the park. After I sat on the rock with Xander. Dad had gathered us in the sitting room, his tone the same as though he were giving a presentation. "Grant's music was too loud and he didn't hear the train coming. It was a tragic, tragic accident."

I had thought my heart was going to explode. Surely Dad was lying, to say something that horrible. I'd looked to Mom. She sat by the gas fireplace, which was on even though it was summer. One manicured hand covered her eyes. In the other was a glass of ice cubes soaking in amber liquid. She almost always had one of those now.

"Mommy?" I whispered.

She'd said nothing. Not a sound. I wanted to scream and cry but that wasn't what "polite young ladies" did. I'd been trained better than that.

Jack had made enough noise for all of us.

He crumpled to the floor as if someone had shot him. He wailed and screamed and cried. He clawed at the carpet, his eyes wild, until my dad nodded at Belinda and Colin to take him to bed. The next day, they told us Grant's room was off-limits. A shrine where no one was allowed to go. All of his stuff, every photo with him in it—even the memory of him—was locked behind a closed door.

We weren't even allowed to say his name.

Grant had lots of books. Whenever I snuck in, I'd peruse his bookshelves and take something to read. I always expected an alarm to go off, like what would happen if you touched an artifact in a museum.

The other day, I'd taken a book called *A Prayer for Owen Meany*. It was well-worn and dog-eared, with lots of Grant's notes in the margins. He had wanted to be a writer. Dad had wanted him to go to business school and take over the family textile business. They'd had lots of battles about that—a war where both sides lost.

Owen Meany wasn't easy to read at first; it looked like it was going to be a religious book. There was nothing religious or spiritual in the House of Wallace—my parents knelt at the altar of money, status, and prestige. But I kept going and I was glad I did. The book was more about faith and fate, and I was a big believer in fate. Like Xander and me. Like how his mother and my brother left on the same day.

That had to mean something, didn't it?

Even though Xander had never written me—not one

letter—and even though he never met me at our rock, I still hoped. A lot. I had a lot of feelings about him, and they seemed to grow bigger and more complicated as the years went by. So, the other night, I wrote them down. I wrote like how *Owen Meany* starts but changed it to fit Xander.

> *I'm doomed to remember a boy with mismatched eyes—not because of his eyes, or because he was the smartest person I ever knew, but because he is the reason I believe in true love. I'm a hopeless romantic because of Xander Ford.*

It was mushy and girly but so was I. A romantic at heart. I loved love stories. My books had to have one or forget it. And I meant what I wrote. I think I fell in love with Xander when I was ten years old and didn't know it. I knew it now. But he obviously didn't feel the same. He'd broken his promise.

He forgot me.

The sky was growing dark. The fireworks would be starting soon, and he wasn't here. He hadn't written, and now I knew love stories were just pretty lies. The only thing to do was to forget Xander too. It hurt too much, and I was already hurting. My father was strict as ever. My mother was a ghost. Jack was a stranger now. I was the only one trying to make it all better. To obey all the rules and be what they wanted me to be. To make them proud. Because if I did that, maybe they'd finally be happy.

But I couldn't do that and hold on to Xander too.

To the right of our rock was the trash can where Xander had once cleaned up the food I'd dropped after I hugged him…but no. I had to push away all those memories and feelings. Push away the sense that we'd known each other forever and had just been apart for a little while. I had to shove it all into a secret room in my heart and lock the door.

Except I wouldn't sneak into this room. I would keep it locked until Xander Ford was less than a memory. That's what my parents were doing with Grant. I didn't think it would work—how can you erase a whole person? But it was worth a try.

I tore the paper into shreds and put the pieces in the trash can, careful to let not even one word escape, and then I walked away.

Part I

Life is like riding a bicycle. To keep your balance, you must keep moving.
—Albert Einstein

Chapter 1

XANDER, AGE SEVENTEEN

PRESENT DAY

"Hey, Dad, we're here," I said, pulling the Buick onto the driveway that led to the little house. What was once smooth cement was now bursting at the seams with weeds. I grimaced as our car—already overburdened by the U-Haul container attached to the roof—hit a pothole.

But neither my words nor the jolt shook my dad out of his thoughts. Or stupor. Or wherever he'd gone—deeper into the intricate, twisting tunnels of his own mind. The entire drive up from Maryland, he'd stared out the passenger window, muttering to himself. Figures, mostly, for an equation that had no end.

He's not getting better.

I faced forward, observing the house through the grimy, insect-splattered windshield. It looked smaller and more run-down than it had seven years ago. The area was pretty, at least.

Our house was tucked into a corner of forest along the bend in the land that created the Bend. The Bend was an entire neighborhood, but you wouldn't know it. The forest, the road, the silence...it felt as if no one were around for miles. Which was good. There was no one to see how the house was falling apart.

Our only house now. The last stop.

I glanced over at Dad, who had yet to realize the car was no longer moving and sighed.

Mom's leaving wasn't a Big Bang that created a brand-new reality. Instead, it had opened a wormhole to an altered version of the same universe. The same reality on the surface, saturated with all the same painful memories. But if you dug just a little deeper, you'd find an alien landscape.

Dad and I'd become reluctant explorers, discovering little artifacts of Mom's absence every day. Here is the first breakfast she's not here to make. Here is my first day at Langdon School with no one to kiss my cheek in the morning. Here is an empty house after the bus drops me off in the afternoon. Here is Dad, alone in his bedroom, alone in his study, alone at the dinner table while I cleaned up remnants of TV dinners or takeout. Alone, alone, alone.

Mom said it wouldn't be forever, but it'd been seven years. My childhood was all but finished. So was Dad's career. She wasn't going to come back, and if she did, it'd be too late.

Dad was still waiting.

He talked frequently about himself and Mom in their early days. "We were in grad school when I first laid eyes on her," he'd tell me, his eyes distant. "I fell helplessly in love with her in that first moment, but she left me anyway."

I knew exactly how he felt.

Seven years after Mom left, things fell apart. Without her salary, Dad had to work full time with no breaks. We were no longer able to spend summers in Rhode Island, and all that sadness had taken its toll. I'd witnessed the slow erosion of his mind long before a pair of his supervisors from the NIST paid a visit a few weeks ago.

"He's had a breakdown, son," one of the suits had told me in our house in Gaithersburg. "He's increasingly forgetful. Long stretches of blankness…" He cleared his throat. "It's necessary that he retire and begin collecting his pension."

The other suit had been more direct. "We think he might benefit from a therapeutic setting."

I read between the lines.

"Don't let them put me away," Dad had pleaded that night. "I'm onto something. Something big, and they're jealous. They've always been jealous."

"They want to help, Dad."

"I don't need help." He offered a small, heartbreaking chuckle. "Don't put your old man out to pasture just yet. I'm not that far gone. Quite the contrary. My mind has never been sharper. Never have I felt this clarity." He clutched my shoulders. "I'm close, Xander. I'm so close."

Dad insisted he was on the brink of accomplishing what every physicist on the planet was striving to accomplish: to reconcile quantum theory with general relativity and arrive at a unified Theory of Everything.

"I just need to work alone, without all the noise and interference. We could go back to Rhode Island!" Dad cried, hope flaring in his eyes. "You can go to school in Castle Hill and be a regular kid for a change. Go to a normal high school and do all the things normal kids do. Trust me, Xander, you want that. Stay safe a little while longer, because once you get into the field, they'll try to tear you apart."

I *wanted* to be in the field, to keep my brain occupied with practical facts instead of impractical feelings. But Dad needed to be in the Rhode Island house more.

It was decided I'd do a senior year of high school at Castle Hill Academy. A gap year, in which my father would either recover or fall into the cracks of his own mind. He'd spend his days working on his equations and I'd play pretend at the high school. CHA had a robust program of academics, STEM classes, arts, and "elite" sports: gymnastics, lacrosse, water polo, and row. They were even magnanimous enough to allow poor Bend kids to attend.

I already had three degrees from the University of Maryland; the last thing I needed—or wanted—was more high school, but the rowing team was a selling point. I'd been on the Langdon crew, and the physical exertion saved me from drowning in my mother's abandonment and all those empty mailboxes.

The downside to this grand plan was the high probability that Emery Wallace would also be attending the Academy. Unless she'd moved away. That might explain her silence, but I doubted it.

For years, I'd written to Emery. A humiliating and pathetic number of letters, considering that every single one went unanswered. Like my mother, it seemed Emery had changed her mind about wanting to know me. Two years ago, I'd sent the final letter. A confession straight from the heart that left no mystery as to how I felt about her.

No answer.

I'd given up on whatever we might have been. But even so...

Even so, sitting in the drive of our ramshackle house seven years later, my heart thudded at the idea of seeing Emery again. How beautiful she must be now that she'd grown up...

I cleared my mind that wanted to populate with images of Emery. Years of pouring my thoughts and feelings into letters she never bothered to answer had carved the wound in my heart even deeper. A canyon now, a canyon that echoed with emptiness because there was zero probability I'd ever let anyone in again.

"Come on, Dad," I said, gently nudging him back to reality. "We're home."

Dad rushed into the living room like a little kid on

Christmas morning. The house was too small for a proper office, so years ago he'd made a workstation out of an old rollaway desk in one corner of the living room, now almost entirely buried under books and papers.

"Yesss," he sighed, sinking happily into the creaky chair. "I'll finally be able to do some real work."

I let the duffel bags—mine and his—drop to the shag carpet and glanced around. The house was 1,500 square feet of clutter, only now all that clutter was covered in seven years' worth of dust and cobwebs and sprinkled with rat droppings. The front door faced a set of stairs that went up one floor, a ratty maroon couch and chipped wooden coffee table were positioned in front of a stone fireplace, and under the front window sat an old piano. Dad had been pretty good back in the day, and I'd taken lessons. We used to play duets—the one thing that Mom seemed to enjoy—but I couldn't imagine either of us playing again.

Every inch of it—except for my loft—was cluttered with mess. Not filth, just *stuff*. Too much stuff, and now I could see it through my mother's eyes. A claustrophobia-inducing wreck of a house presided over by a wreck of a man and his bitter son.

No wonder she left.

I dismissed the excuse. She had her reasons—maybe a hundred of them, big and small, but all of them had been more important than me.

When the first day of school arrived two weeks later, I rode my bike—it was less embarrassing than the Buick—into the student parking lot of Castle Hill Academy. True to its name, the school sat like an ultra-modern castle on a hill—all white planes, sharp angles, and glass. The lot was filled with Mercedes, Teslas, and BMWs with a few junkers sprinkled in. Other Bend kids.

I didn't see any of my people, but plenty of Richies, sitting on hoods or gathered in groups, talking and laughing. Everyone was dressed for the humidity: the girls in short skirts or cut-off shorts and tight, revealing tops. The boys wore jeans that didn't have holes in them like mine did. Their shirts were designer label polos, while mine was a thinning T-shirt bearing a faded image of a Radiohead—my favorite band—logo.

I locked my bike and shouldered my backpack. I felt the stares as I walked past a clutch of students leaning against a Range Rover. Its back window was soaped with the words *Bow down to your SENIORS!!!*

"What's up, Bender?" someone called.

I rolled my eyes behind my glasses and kept walking. "Bender." How original, not that "Richies" was the paragon of creativity. I wondered—not for the first time—why I was subjecting myself to this experiment.

Tell the truth, a voice whispered. *You're here for her.*

I couldn't help it. I had a masochistic urge to see Emery Wallace, to reopen every single scar on my heart by confirming that she was alive and well and had *chosen* to ignore me.

As I crossed the green expanse of grass that fronted the enormous school, every blond head of hair, every girlish laugh, drew my eye and made my heart jump. I'd nearly made it across the lawn, wondering with equal parts dismay and relief, if Emery had moved away.

And then there she was.

Statues of lions—the school mascot—sat regally on short pillars on either side of a white staircase that led up to the school's front doors. Emery Wallace was perched on one of the pillars, next to a lion's paw, surrounded by a group of Richies. She swung her legs like she had when she was a little girl, beside me on our rock. But she was no longer a little girl.

God help me...

Her legs were tanned and muscled like a dancer's or gymnast's. She wore fashionable, chunky white sneakers, ankle socks, and short shorts. So short, they revealed the flawless expanse of her thighs. A tight-fitting top strained to contain the...*evidence* of her maturity.

I dragged my thoughts away from primal, objectifying observations and studied her face. Emery's blue-green eyes were framed by long, dark lashes under a fringe of bangs. Thick, golden hair poured down her back in loose curls. My knees literally weakened. In seven years, she'd gone from beautiful to breathtaking.

Any second, she'd see me. I wanted the light of her recognition and dreaded it. A rejection in the flesh instead of in the silence of unanswered letters.

I was still yards away when a tall, blond hulk of a guy hooked an arm around her waist. He effortlessly lifted her off the pillar and spun her around. When he set her on her feet, I calculated Emery's height to be hardly over five feet. Her boyfriend, by comparison, was a giant.

Then recognition hit.

Tucker.

The bully who'd thrown water balloons at us with his friend while our backs were turned. What more did I need to know about Emery if this guy was now her boyfriend?

Tucker bent to kiss her, and his hand went straight to her ass, grabbing a handful of flesh through her shorts. She broke the kiss and shoved at his chest, laughing. But when he turned away, her smile collapsed like a wave function once it's been observed.

Observed by me and no one else.

But maybe I was only imagining—*hoping for*—her annoyance, because in the next instant, she was smiling again. Haughty. Imperious. No trace of the warmth I'd known. None of her innate, luminous magic that had erased my loneliness for a few, fleeting moments.

Because there was no such thing as magic. Only facts. Logic. Science.

And these were the observable facts: Emery Wallace was queen of the school, surrounded by adoring drones, with a Prom King of a boyfriend, while I was a poor, pathetic Bend kid who'd clung to a single afternoon long after she'd let it go.

I ducked my head and trudged toward the stairs. I was nearly past Emery's group when she brushed a lock of hair from her eyes and her gaze found me. I felt it in my chest, where it struck me like an electric jolt. Emery's eyes widened in shock, and I could have sworn she lit up, her mouth wanting to smile…

But it must've been my imagination, because her full lips formed a grim line—almost a sneer—and she looked away.

It was no more than I expected yet it hurt. We'd shared only a short, golden collection of minutes seven years ago, and it still fucking hurt.

Chapter 2

EMERY

HE'S HERE.

Every drop of blood rushed straight to my heart watching Xander Ford climb the stairs to the school. Why? How? For a few seconds, I was paralyzed by a storm of emotions, the most confusing of which was relief. Our time together had imprinted something on my heart, something I thought I'd torn up and threw away, but now it was back. Xander was back, and he was no longer a little boy.

Tall, fit, with chestnut hair falling over his eyes…those beautiful, mismatched eyes hiding behind boxy black glasses. He was dressed like a Bend kid, but his shabby clothes couldn't conceal how his body had grown up and filled out. Six feet of lean muscle with biceps that strained against the sleeves of his T-shirt. Broad shoulders tapered to a slim waist, and his forearms…my God.

He was a nerd. A science geek. A genius who'd already done high school when he was *ten*. What right did he have coming back now? And looking like *that*? I'd locked him up in my heart. Somehow, he'd made an escape.

My best friend, Elowen Blake, nudged my arm. "Oh, new kid. Fresh blood." She glanced at my slack-jawed expression. "You know him?"

Every minute of my time with Xander seven years ago came back to me in a rush. How comforted and safe I felt with him. How he protected me, made me feel valued. I thought something special had happened between us that day. I thought we'd know each other forever.

I was wrong.

"Why would I know him?" I said, tilting my chin up. "He's a Bender."

"Looks like it. Too bad. Nice bod." Elowen sighed, tossing a lock of ashy blond hair over her shoulder. "What a waste."

"Who're we talking about?"

I glanced up at my boyfriend, Tucker Hill. His gaze was following Xander up the stairs, eyes narrowed. Any second now, he was going to recognize the kid he pelted with water balloons all those years ago.

I jumped in front of Tucker and threw my arms around his neck. "What's your first class? Mine is AP Calc and I'm already dreading it."

Tucker gripped my waist and walked forward, forcing me to walk backward. "So drop it. You don't belong in that class with all the nerds and dorks." He pulled me in tighter, grinding against me. "You're too hot."

I stifled the urge to roll my eyes and disentangled myself so I could walk on my own. But his arm went around me and rested on my hip. At 6'3" and heavily muscled from years of row and water polo, Tucker was a giant and always draped over me like a lead blanket. The alpha male showing his dominance over the pack, marking me as his property.

I scoffed nonchalantly. "My dad is making me take it. You know how he runs my life like one of his businesses."

Tucker *did* know my dad—his family was at our house for dinner frequently, especially with the election coming up in November. Tucker's father was a senator, and my dad *really* wanted him to be reelected. Something to do with pollution regulations. As in, my father's textile plants kept dumping waste into the ocean, and Tucker's father kept letting him. My job was to link our families so that everyone stayed happy. And nothing was more important than making my dad happy so that maybe, someday, he'd tell me he loved me… Pathetic, but that didn't stop me from trying. Trying so hard, I turned myself inside out until I didn't even know who I was anymore.

"Don't stress about calc, girl," Delilah Winslow piped up. She was Zendaya-levels of beautiful and also the biggest gossip in school. "Since when have you not absolutely killed it, whatever you do?"

"Thanks, babe," I said, keeping my poised smile firmly in place, like a mask that was so tight I could hardly breathe. "It's just a waste of time I could be devoting to prom committee or dance team. Speaking of, practice today after school, 3:00 p.m. sharp."

The four girls in our group who were on the Royal Pride dance team answered back. "Yes, captain."

"Friday's pep rally is the most important," I said sternly. "It sets the standard for the rest of the year. It has to be perfect."

I have to be perfect. Always.

More murmured assents as we stepped inside Castle Hill Academy. The bell rang, and Tucker bent down to kiss me. I tolerated his wet, domineering kiss that was too much PDA for a school hallway first thing in the morning until he finally relinquished me.

"Later, babe."

Tucker and his buddies—mostly gymnastics, polo, and crew athletes—strode down the hall. Lords of the school and Tucker their king. My circle of girls—the lionesses of the pride—broke up with promises to meet at lunch.

I navigated the polished, gleaming hallways to the STEM wing of the school. When I was a freshman, it had taken me nearly a month to map out the Academy. It was bigger than some universities, with different departments in each wing and a state-of-the-art gym in the center that looked like an Olympic training ground.

I figured Xander would spend all his time in the STEM wing, and I'd only risk running into him going to and from calculus.

Why is he here?

The question wouldn't leave me. I couldn't get my

racing heart to slow down. I'd been an expert at playing the part of the Perfect Daughter/Student/Girlfriend, and just one glimpse of Xander Ford put cracks in the façade. I felt dragged back in time to a perfect afternoon and the last time I'd felt real instead of plastic. Before I knew that Grant was dead. Before my parents' expectations constricted around me like a straitjacket.

I ducked into a girls' bathroom and, as soon as the door shut, I sagged, bracing myself on the sink. My reflection stared back: makeup flawlessly applied, hair immaculate, delicate necklaces to accentuate my ample cleavage.

Xander is back.

Like a magic mirror, I watched the thought turn me back into that little girl I'd been with him, free of all life's pressures and pain. To a time when I still believed in love stories…

"You were just kids. It didn't mean anything. He forgot you, remember?"

The words rang out hollowly in the empty bathroom. I'd been a silly fool like my dad was always warning me about being, pining after something that wasn't there. I couldn't let Xander's presence turn me back into the softhearted girl I'd been. Soft things bruised easily. Shutting myself up behind a hard, closed door was safer.

Mask firmly back in place, I tossed a lock of hair over my shoulder and went out. I sauntered into the calculus classroom a minute after the bell rang, fashionably late. Most of the seats were filled, and Xander wasn't in any of them. Maybe I'd imagined him. He had to have a dozen PhDs by now.

Maybe he's teaching here…

The thought almost made me smile as I took the only seat left, in the back corner.

"So glad you could join us, Miss Wallace," Mr. Greer said, standing at the head of the class in front of a huge whiteboard. "Welcome, class, to AP Calculus. I'm assuming you all did the assigned prep work this summer? Let's review."

The entire class pulled out their school-issued iPads and took up notebooks and pencils. I watched in dismay as Mr. Greer began filling the whiteboard with numbers, letters, symbols…equations I barely remembered from Algebra II. Math and my brain just didn't get along, no matter how much Dad expected them to. I'd been managing to keep my head above water for years, but five minutes into class, I knew I'd come to the end of the line.

The girl next to me—new to the school and a Bender by the looks of her eccentric clothes—shot me a curious look. My mask had slipped. Indignation flared. She obviously didn't know who I was…

Oh, get over yourself.

Except I had a reputation to maintain. It was superficial and lonely and total bullshit, but it did the trick: It kept people at a distance so they couldn't see the mess right in front of them.

———

By lunchtime on day one, I was exhausted. My course load was heavy enough without calculus weighing it down, but now it was clear I was in big trouble.

And then I spotted Xander. He sat in a corner of the sunlit cafeteria by himself, reading a book. The light turned the tips of his hair golden as it fell over his eyes. A sack lunch sat on the table in front of him. He talked to no one and no one talked to him.

I could talk to him. I could cross all the stupid, invisible social boundaries and say hi. No harm in that.

But that was the opposite of being hard and aloof. He'd broken his promise and made no effort to tell me why. Maybe he found the social boundaries hard to cross too. But there was no one around now. My friends were at a table on the other side of the room. Maybe...

Xander looked up. Our eyes met for a short moment, but it felt like a current of electricity zipped between us. The weight on my shoulders lifted again for just a moment... Then a smug smirk touched his lips, and he went back to his book.

So there's your answer.

"Screw him," I muttered, even though I sort of felt like crying.

That afternoon, I led the Royal Pride dance team through our routine. We'd been rehearsing since August for Friday's pep rally. The dance looked good, and I was happy—mostly because being captain was something my parents approved of. Mom liked it because it kept me fit, code for *so you don't get fat*. Dad said it would look good on my Brown application. To them, my life boiled down to looking the "right" way and going to the "right" school.

Years before, when I'd told my parents I wanted to go to RISD to be an interior designer, Mom sniffed like she'd smelled something rotten while Dad shot the dream dead. He already had plans. I was to go to Brown, not for the education but for the pedigree, as if I were a show dog with good breeding. I would marry someone like Tucker Hill—someone politically advantageous to the family empire—and inherit millions in return.

"It's your duty, Emery," Dad told me countless times. "We all have a role to play, and that is yours. To ensure the business thrives well into the future. You will be rewarded for it in the end."

I wanted to tell him I'd rather be poor and struggling than live the life he planned for me, but I was too scared to step out of line. Not to mention, our family was already falling apart at the seams; if I didn't try to hold us together, who would?

After practice, I drove my BMW S2 Coupe down Ridge Road to our family home. I idled in the driveway, staring at the big house on the water. Narragansett Bay lay behind it, our speedboat docked in the backyard. (The yacht was at the marina, of course.) I should've felt grateful, but being rich wasn't the same as being happy. This house was just a fancy prison.

I parked in the garage. Jack was already home—his beat-up Camaro sat outside, ready for a quick getaway.

Dad's black sedan was there too. He was home early, and I knew why.

I sighed. "Time to meet the warden."

Inside, I passed through the enormous kitchen, which had bay views and was filled with the scents of Belinda's dinner.

"Hello, Miss Emery," she said, stirring a pot of something on the state-of-the-art gas stove. "How was your first day?"

"Fine," I said, offering her a smile. A real smile. "Smells delicious."

She beamed like a grandmother—she was pushing seventy and had been with us since Grant was a baby. Then her smile tightened. "Mr. Wallace would like to see you in his study right away."

My stomach twisted. "I'm sure he does."

"Will you please tell Mr. Jack?" Belinda asked. "I reminded him when he came in, but he muttered something and stormed off."

Probably "Tell Dad to go to hell."

"I'll get him."

I moved through the house, past the dining room, two sitting rooms, and the formal living room, until I reached the stairs leading up to the bedrooms. No trace of Mom's Chanel No. 5 in the air—she must be out at some late luncheon or charity meeting. Whichever one had more vodka.

Jack's and my bedrooms were on the left wing. Very loud, very angry music thumped behind his door.

"Jack?" I knocked. "Dad wants to see us."

I thought he'd ignore me—as usual—but the music went quiet, and Jack threw open the door. His T-shirt and jeans looked slept in and rumpled, his hair long and messy, and his blue eyes were ringed with dark circles.

"Ah yes, our first day of school tradition," he sneered, crowding me away from his door so he could slip out and shut it behind him. "Let's get this over with."

We took the stairs down, Jack just ahead. One year older than me and my total opposite: dark-haired to my blond, tall to my short, angry and rebellious to my obedient and dutiful. Our parents pretended that Grant never existed, so grieving for him was out of the question. I stuffed all my pain down, letting it out in little bits when I couldn't take it anymore, but Jack wore his out in the open.

Our brother's death had torn him apart so badly, he needed to repeat the sixth grade. I thought us both of in the same year would bring us closer together, but every day, Jack grew farther and farther away.

"I didn't see you today," I offered in a friendly tone. "I guess we don't have any classes together."

"Guess not," he muttered.

"Too bad. That would've been kind of fun—"

"Can we not, Emery?" Jack snapped. "I'm not in the mood for your fucking chitchat."

I recoiled at his cold snap. Moments like these reminded me that no matter how hard I tried to push it down, I couldn't help but feel that when Grant died, I lost two brothers.

At Dad's study, Jack knocked on the door but didn't wait for a response before throwing it open and striding inside. Not for the first time, I wondered how he and I could share so much DNA when he was far braver than me. I followed him in and quietly shut the door behind me.

"You beckoned?" Jack drawled.

Two huge windows overlooking the bay bathed the study in amber twilight, but somehow the room still seemed dark. Heavy drapes and floor-to-ceiling bookcases took up almost every wall. A sitting area with a couch, table, and two chairs was in the center of the room, while my father sat behind a large mahogany desk. Behind him, a fireplace, now cold.

Dad didn't look up from his desktop as we entered but typed in his slow, methodical way, his half-moon reading glasses perched at the end of his nose. At nearly sixty, Grayson Wallace was thin and balding, the top of his head gleaming in the lamplight. He wasn't big or imposing; his intimidating aura came from within. A prickly barbed force field surrounded him, and his eyes were like two shards of colorless glass that cut right through you. Like now, as he looked up at my brother and me.

"Have a seat," he said, indicating the leather chairs in front of his desk.

I sat and rested my backpack on my lap. Jack was slower, sliding into the chair and slouching down.

"Jack," Dad stated, fingers poised on the keyboard. "Your class schedule, please."

My brother remained silent for ten excruciating seconds, pretending to examine his fingernails. My skin itched, and I gripped my bag with white knuckles.

Dad peered over his glasses and repeated in the exact same tone, "Your schedule, please."

"Oh, right." Jack made a show of patting himself down and pulled out a crumpled ball of orange paper from the front pocket of his jeans. He tossed it onto the desk. "Here you go."

Dad stared a moment before picking up the paper and unfolding it. He let out a small sigh through his nose.

"This is a tardy slip from today." He placed it in the trash can under his desk. "So soon, Jack? It's only the first day of school, but you're already determined to be a fuckup."

Our father said all this without raising his voice or changing his tone in the slightest. It was exactly that quiet inflexibility that made him so frightening to everyone on the planet. Even to Jack, though Jack was the only one who fought back.

"I stopped to get a coffee and a blowjob from a guy on the pier." He held up his hands. "Guess I lost track of time."

Dad stiffened. I held my breath.

I didn't think Jack was telling the truth. Or maybe he was; it would be a cold day in hell before he confided in me anything about his personal life. But he liked saying or doing shocking things to get a rise out of our parents. Like a few weeks ago, when he celebrated his nineteenth birthday by stealing a credit card from Mom's purse and charging $2,800 worth of drinks at a gay club in Providence with a fake ID. I thought Dad would kick him out of the house for sure—not for being gay but for defying him. To my dad, there was no greater crime than insubordination. Everything else—who we were or what we wanted—was irrelevant.

"You think your education is a joke," Dad said to Jack in his mild-mannered tone. "You, who are already behind an entire year. You won't think it's quite so funny when you're pumping gas at the local Sunoco or flipping burgers at Cassidy's."

Jack shrugged. "Honest work."

My father stared him down. Jack stared back, but I noticed his Adam's apple hitch in his throat.

Then Dad muttered just loud enough for us to hear, "Degenerate."

Jack flinched, and his eyes grew shiny. Our father glanced up, studying my brother's unshed tears and my stricken face.

"Oh, am I making your life hard for you? For either of you? Hm?"

I felt pinned to my chair. Beside me, Jack swallowed hard.

Dad folded his hands. "Is it difficult that I have given you everything you could ever possibly want? Clothes? Cars? A first-class education at the Academy? Is it a tremendous hardship that I'm invested in your education and success?"

"No, Daddy," I whispered.

Jack shot me a hard, fast look.

"Because I can make it all disappear as easily as I've made it happen. You can have everything, or you can have nothing. The choice is yours."

The air felt tight and thick, the entire world narrowing until there was nothing left but my dad's cold blue stare.

Finally, Jack tilted his chin, his voice quavering as he asked, "Are we done here?"

Our father nodded his head. Once. Jack tore out of the chair, out of the study, and slammed the door.

Unbothered, Dad turned to me. "Your schedule, please."

I dug into my bag for the printout of my classes and handed it over. He set it on the desk and copied it into his spreadsheet. Since Jack and I were in middle school, he kept track of every grade, every test score, every average. Anything less than an A-minus, and there were consequences.

I cleared my throat. "Dad, we need to talk about calculus—"

"It will look good on your application to Brown," he said, the digital green of his spreadsheet reflected in his glasses.

"Only if I pass," I said. "Daddy, I'm just not good at math. I barely survived last year. And I don't need calculus to graduate anyway. I've completed all the math requirements. If I take calculus and fail, it's going to bring my whole average down."

"Then you had better not fail."

My fingers gripped my bag until they ached. "Daddy, please. Hear me out. If I drop it, I'll have more time to devote to my other classes. And there's dance and prom committee…"

"I've told you before, prom committee is a waste of time."

I recoiled. Designing the senior prom was the only shot I had at showing him what I was capable of. What my dreams were made of. If I didn't have prom, I had nothing.

"I've made an allowance to that indulgence," he continued. "But if your grades begin to suffer, then that is what you will drop."

Tears stung my eyes, but I fought them back. "What if I replaced calculus with something better for my application? I could volunteer somewhere. Maybe the animal shelter—?"

"And have you come home smelling like unwashed dog?" He shook his head. "Absolutely not."

I don't know why I thought that would work; we'd been begging to get a dog for years, and my dad refused to hear of it.

I heaved a breath and threw out the longest of long shots. "Maybe I could…get a job?"

I said the last part so quietly, it was nearly a squeak. I would quit Royal Pride and maybe even prom committee if I could only earn my own money.

I'd save it up and move far, far away.

Dad kept typing. "You don't need a job. I provide everything you need."

He meant that I had a bank card for an account that he put money into, but all my spending was scrutinized. I had no savings. I wasn't *allowed* to save enough that would take me far, far away. Heck, I'd never make it out of Rhode Island.

"I'm begging you. Let me drop calculus. I can't do it. I—"

My father slammed his palm on the desk, making me jump. "Let me remind you, your PSAT score was a dismal 1100. You need at least a 1470 for Brown to consider you."

"But—"

"I don't want to hear excuses, Emery. You don't know how the world works, but I do. I know what's best for you. And I know that giving up because something is a little bit hard is what losers do. Do you want to be a loser?"

My cheeks grew hot under my dad's hard stare. I knew what he was really asking: *Do you want me to love you?*

"I don't want to be a loser," I managed, my throat thick.

"Smart choice. Jack is hell-bent on throwing his life away. I will not allow you to embarrass this family the way he has. I will *not allow it*." Dad turned back to his screen. "That is all."

I got up on leaden legs and left his study, my heart heavy and with a thousand words piled up and locked behind my teeth. I shut the door behind me and jumped to see Jack lounging against the wall under a portrait of our great uncle Reginald, the first shipping magnate who began the Wallace empire at the turn of the nineteenth century. My brother wore a disgusted look on his face.

"What?" I demanded.

"Why do you always do whatever he says?" he whisper-shouted.

"Like I have a choice," I hissed. "Should I talk back? Get kicked out of the house? And then what?"

Jack glanced away. I took a step closer, softened my tone.

"Jack, I—"

"Forget it."

He pushed off the wall and stormed away. Back to his room. Back to his anger and loud music.

I went to mine just down the hall. My refuge. The one place I'd been allowed to express myself.

At my door, I stopped and took in all the white, pink, and bright blue. Three years ago, I'd designed it to evoke Japanese cherry blossoms in spring: pink-and-white decor with one sky-blue wall where I'd hand-painted a cherry blossom branch. Hopeful and bright but not overdone. Tasteful.

When they saw it, my mother had declared it, "a bit obvious."

My father had said nothing.

Chapter 3

XANDER

Day one of "regular" high school had been uneventful, if mind-numbingly unchallenging. But I'd come home to my father scribbling away at his desk, safe and content, and that was all that mattered.

And Emery...

There had been a moment in the cafeteria when I thought maybe...but no. If she had a good reason for ignoring my letters, she felt no urgency to tell me. The humiliation brought a fresh rush of blood to my face as I thought of how I'd poured my heart out to her. She probably showed my letters to her friends and laughed and laughed...

I was better off focusing on my goals for the year:

1. keep myself mentally stimulated

2. make the rowing crew
3. earn money

The last was imperative. The more I saved from Dad's pension and from selling the Gaithersburg house, the better the facility I could place him in, should it come to that. I needed a job, one that was close to Dad in case he needed me.

I printed up some ads for tutoring services in math and science and put my cell phone number at the bottom. On the following morning, I pinned my flyers to bulletin boards in the Academy hallways.

The halls were relatively empty due to the student-led club fair happening upstairs. I wandered up to the sun-soaked patio on the second level, with views of the Narragansett to the north and the Atlantic to the south. Booths adorned with streamers, lights, and music lined the patio, enticing students to investigate. But one booth had only a simple hand-painted banner:

Do you want the answer to Life, the Universe, and Everything? Join the Math & Physics Club!

One club with both subjects was exactly my wheelhouse, but likely child's play to me. I nearly kept walking, but a little voice whispered that I used my intellectual superiority as an excuse to avoid certain activities. Like talking to people my age. Making friends. Emery's words from seven years ago echoed in my mind.

Maybe you just need the practice.

I stopped at the booth, where a lanky guy sat behind a

foldout table, reading a book. His clothes were similar to mine: plain jeans, plain shirt, old shoes. A "Bender" like me, if I were forced to classify him.

I cleared my throat. "Forty-two."

He blinked up at me with green eyes set in an angular face. "Huh?"

"The answer to Life, the Universe, and Everything." I pointed at his own banner. "*Hitchhiker's Guide to the Galaxy*?"

"Oh, right!" The guy laughed. "Business has been so slow, I almost forgot I'm supposed to be recruiting." He got to his feet and stuck out his hand. "Dean Yearwood, secretary of the Math & Physics Club."

"Xander Ford."

"Pleased to meet you, Xander. You're new here, yeah? Senior?"

I nodded. "From Maryland. Just moved."

"And are you any good at math, Xander from Maryland?" Dean's smile was wide but genuine.

"You could say that," I said dryly, my automatic *I'm smarter than you* program already up and running.

But if Dean was put off by my arrogance, he didn't show it. He laughed. "Oh, I caught a live one!"

A group of students—Richies—passed by. One of the girls waved and blew him a kiss. "Hello, Dean!"

"Hello, Sierra." He pretended to snatch her kiss out of midair and tuck it inside his lightweight jacket. "Save that for later."

She giggled and the group moved on.

"Apologies for the interruption." Dean heaved a dramatic sigh. "It's not easy being this devastatingly handsome and popular."

I chuckled. Bender or not, Dean was self-possessed and charismatic, two things no amount of smarts was ever going to give me.

"So, Xander Ford, we have an application process to join our illustrious club. You must answer me these questions three."

Dean handed me a clipboard and a pencil, and I studied the questions.

1. The solution to $(dy/dx) = e^{(3x-2y)} + x^2 e^{(-2y)}$
2. A 2 kg object is pushed with a force of 10 N across a frictionless surface. What is the object's acceleration?
3. What is the airspeed velocity of an unladen swallow?

Within minutes, I'd solved all three. I handed back the clipboard.

"That was fast!" Dean said and scanned my answers. His smile collapsed.

"Something wrong?" I asked tightly.

"Not exactly. It's just...you answered the third question. With math."

I frowned. "Was I not supposed to?"

Dean chuckled, then saw I was serious. "Question three is a joke. From *Monty Python and the Holy Grail*."

And that, my friends, is how you go from being a genius to a fool in less than a minute.

The back of my neck burned. "Is that a movie? I don't watch TV or movies."

"Hey, no sweat." Dean chucked me on the arm. "Our club does movie nights once a month. We'll get you caught up." He shook his head in awe. "I can't believe you actually answered question three."

"Well, um, I applied the Strouhal number formula for the cruising flights of insects and birds to create the equation. Without exact figures, I had to estimate—"

"Hey, I'm joking." Dean laughed. "You passed the test. In fact, you overshot it by *a lot*. Where did you say you went to school again?"

"I didn't, but it was Langdon School. It's a private academy in Bethesda."

I may have been socially incompetent, but I knew better than to tell him I'd already been to college.

"Never heard of it," Dean said. "I'm guessing you were president, king, and emperor of your math club."

"I was on the row crew, actually. I'm looking to try out for the team here."

He stared. "You're joking."

I glanced around. "Not that I'm aware of…"

"Holy shit!" Dean's face broke out into what I'd soon learn was his customary grin. "If this isn't your lucky day! You happen to be looking at the coxswain for our Royal Pride crew."

"Seriously?"

"Seriously. But crew here is like football in Texas. You gotta be good. You any good?"

"I like to think so."

"Coach Daniels is holding tryouts down at the Academy marina all day Saturday. Meet me at the gym Saturday morning and I'll show you around."

"I'd appreciate that," I said, touched by his kindness. "Thanks, Dean."

He grinned. "What are friends for?"

At home that afternoon, I was practically humming as I walked in the door. Dad was at his desk, scribbling his endless numbers. The remnants of the lunch I'd left for him were on a plate beside his work, mostly eaten.

"How's it going, Dad?" I asked, dropping my backpack onto the couch in our living room, which I'd labored to tidy up before school began.

"Oh, you know how it is," Dad said, squinting at pages and pages of his equations, trying to reconcile a Theory of Everything. It was an impossible task, but miracles do happen: I'd made a friend today.

I helped myself to some orange juice from the fridge. "Any breakthroughs?"

"Alas, only infinities and contradictions." Dad sighed. "Dead ends, all. But I shall not give up hope! For hopelessness is the ultimate dead end."

I leaned against the entry separating the kitchen and living room, juice in hand. "Can I take a look?"

He hugged his papers to his chest. "No, no. It's not ready. Still percolating." He tapped a finger to his forehead. "Still baking in the old noggin."

"Okay, Dad," I said. "I'm going to my room for a bit, and then I'll see about dinner. Sound good?"

But he was already back to work. I took the stairs up, passed his room, and then climbed again—this time on a rickety staircase that was more like a glorified ladder—to my loft over the garage. It had been my dad's room when he was a kid and was more like a small apartment with its own bathroom. I'd set up my desk beneath the triangular window that faced the bay, with the dark green of the trees below. One wall was crammed with books, while another held a shelf for my 1990s-era record player and vinyl collection of alternative music. A Radiohead poster adorned one wall.

Like my dad, I preferred this house to the one I'd grown up in Gaithersburg. That house was an electrostatic field, charged with the tension of my mother's unhappiness.

She mapped escape routes for every room.

Now that I was older, the distance my mother kept from Dad and me was easier to see. His genius was a lot to take: eccentric and scattered. When I began hurdling over milestones, I think my mother worried I'd turn out just like him.

"Maybe I will," I muttered, lying down on my bed and staring at the ceiling. Not for the first time, I wondered if I'd inherited more from my dad than his brilliance. Maybe my fate was to break down at fifty, too. To have a jar crammed with marbles, so to speak, but slowly lose them, one by one.

I brushed the unsettling thoughts away. My second day of what I was now calling the Experiment hadn't been a total disaster. I might even make some friends in Dean's club, row for the crew, and fill in some holes in my childhood experience that my abnormal intellect had stolen from me.

Maybe even go on a date? With an actual girl?

Images of Emery Wallace floated across my vision, and those I couldn't brush away. She might've been my dream, but now she was just a mirage—someone who became less real the closer I got to her.

I put my hand over my aching heart just as my phone chimed a text from an unknown number.

> Hi. I saw you're offering tutoring at CHA? I need help in calculus.

A job offer. This was turning out to be a pretty good day after all.

Happy to help, I typed. What did you have in mind, timewise?

> At least three times a week, starting ASAP. My name is Emery btw.

My heart nearly stopped. I stared at my phone. Another text rolled in. RU still there?

I'm here.

Is this real? You're not some creep, are you?

There's no name on your ad.

I gritted my teeth. Xander.

Another pause, and then my phone lit up with Emery's incoming call. My stupid heart flooded with everything I'd been trying *not* to feel. I dammed it all up and answered with a cool, "Hello?"

"Xander." Her voice was the same sweet tone but now tinged with distrust. "Xander Ford?"

"That's me."

"I thought I saw you yesterday. So. You're back."

"I'm back."

When I offered nothing else—I don't know what she was waiting for me to say anyway; she's the one who owed me an explanation—she made a huffing sound. "Fine, whatever. I need the help. What's your rate?"

"Thirty dollars an hour," I said. It was too high. She was going to tell me to get lost—

"Done," Emery said. "Tomorrow and Saturday at four o'clock? There are study lounges on the third floor, just off the library."

Her imperious tone got my hackles up. Clearly, Emery Wallace was used to the world bending to fit her schedule. "Tomorrow works, but I have row tryouts on Saturday."

"Oh yeah?" she said. "My boyfriend is captain of the crew."

Her boyfriend, Tucker, the bully…

I made my voice stony. "That information has no bearing on my life."

A pause, and I could practically hear the moment when Emery decided *not* to hang up on me.

She scoffed. "Whatever. Tomorrow and Monday, then?"

"I can do that."

"*Great*," she said with sarcasm. "I'll see you tomorrow. Four o'clock."

Tomorrow. After seven years, we'd be face to face. Part of me wanted to step back in time to make it happen yesterday. Part of me feared it'd be like tearing open an old wound and making it bleed again.

"See you tomorrow, Emery," I said quietly.

She gave a tight, "Yep," and the line went dead.

I set my phone down and stared at it for a moment before my gaze wandered to the items on my desk. There weren't many; only the things I used or cared about the most: a photo of Dad and me at the fifth grade science fair, where I won first place for my homemade particle accelerator; my laptop; a can full of pens; a notebook; and the book *Meditations* by Marcus Aurelius.

I opened the book to the middle, to the flower that lay pressed between the pages, where it had been for seven years. The daffodil had dried to a papery consistency and had lost much of its bright hue, but in my mind's eye it was still a vibrant yellow. I could still remember the exact moment Emery put it in my hands. I could still feel her soft kiss on my cheek…

"Don't be stupid," I murmured. "Do not. Be. Stupid."

Like every night for the past seven years, I contemplated throwing it away, and just like every night for the past seven years, I put the flower safely back in the book and returned it to its place.

Chapter 4

EMERY

IN CALCULUS THE NEXT MORNING, MR. GREER SCRIBBLED endlessly on the whiteboard. For the rest of the students, it seemed to make sense, but the figures and symbols were like hieroglyphics to me. I was hopelessly lost and completely distracted by the fact I had Xander Ford's number sitting in my phone. In a few short hours, we'd be face to face. Or sitting right next to each other, like we had on the rock like we did when we were kids...

Only we weren't little kids anymore. Xander certainly wasn't. His voice on the phone yesterday, for instance. Hearing it for the first time in seven years was like vertigo. And not the bad kind. His voice had deepened, but it was still *him*.

Whatever that meant. As if I knew Xander anymore. Or ever. My heart was still claiming ownership because I thought I'd been in love with him, but that was obviously a stupid, silly thing to believe.

He's going to save my ass in math. A tutor. That's all he is.

"Miss Wallace?"

I jerked out of my thoughts to see the entire room watching me.

"Sorry, what?"

"I was wondering if you could explain to the class the difference between a definite integral and an indefinite integral?"

I froze. My notes were no help, just doodles. I lifted my chin. "I don't know," I stated, as if I could make being unprepared seem cool.

Glances were exchanged and muffled laughs swept through the students; no doubt they were all wondering why an airhead like me was in AP Calculus.

Mr. Greer frowned. "It's an honest answer, anyway. Miss Bennett? Care to give it a try?"

The eclectic girl next to me nodded. Today she wore a patchwork denim skirt, black tights, and an orange patterned top. "A definite integral has upper and lower limits. An indefinite integral has no limits."

"Correct. Take note, Miss Wallace," Mr. Greer said, and went back to the board.

I gave my best *whatever* eye roll, but my cheeks burned.

The girl leaned toward me and whispered, "Hi, I'm Harper. If you ever need help—?"

"I'm good, thanks," I snapped with a fake-sweet smile.

Harper recoiled and I bit the inside of my cheek to keep

from tearing up. For some annoying reason, I cried when I was angry. Which only made me angrier. I was pissed at my father for making me take this class and pissed at myself for being a bitch to Harper…

And at Xander for abandoning me.

Blinking furiously, I copied everything Mr. Greer wrote on the board, even if I didn't understand a thing. Even if I just wanted to run out the door and not stop…

Class ended and we all filed out. Harper Bennett walked in front of me. Her dark hair was in a messy braid, but when I looked closer, I could see it was intricately woven and messy on purpose. Her whole style was deliberate and original. A Bend girl, but so what? I was a Richie, and my life was a mess. If I had someone to talk to, a real friend, maybe I could—

"Hey, girl!"

Sierra Hart, Aria Kingston, Delilah Winslow, and Elowen Blake, were all waiting for me. My crew was all dressed in tight-fitting tops and baggy, designer pants, wore perfect hair and makeup, and carried with them a cloud of expensive perfume. I joined them, and we made our way through the brightly lit halls to our next classes.

"Who's the fashionista?" Aria—with large, dark eyes and raven hair—asked with a snide smile and a nod for Harper walking just ahead.

"She's new. A Bender," Delilah said with authority.

Sierra, pretty, with auburn ringlets, giggled. "Did she make her outfit herself?"

"Probably," I scoffed automatically, as if I were a character in a movie and it was my line.

Harper flinched but kept walking—shoulders straight, head high, until she turned down a separate corridor, away from us vultures.

Shame burned my cheeks. "But I kind of like it. She has interesting style."

"You're joking, right?" Elowen said. "Don't tell me you're growing a soft spot for the Bend kids."

"Let's maintain *some* standards," Aria, the meanest of the mean girls, put in. "This school would be perfect if they kept out the charity cases."

I stared at my "friends," wondering if they believed half of what they were saying or if it was all for show. Like me.

Elowen caught my expression. "You okay?"

She was technically my best friend, but I'd always suspected that if I were to get hit by a bus, she'd send me flowers and steal my boyfriend on the same day.

"My period arrived early," I lied. "Cramps from hell."

"Ah, gotcha," she said. "You do look a little pale."

"Oh my God, speaking of newbies, did you see the new guy in our class this year?" Delilah exclaimed. "Another Bender. His dad was a big-time scientist or something until he had a nervous breakdown, and his mom walked out."

I blinked. "How do you know that?"

Delilah shrugged one shoulder and smiled coyly. "I have my ways."

"His name is Xander something," Aria said. "He's in my debate class, and he's so above it all, you'd think he *invented* arguing. The teacher has no clue what to do with him."

"I think he's kind of hot."

All eyes turned on Sierra. I felt a stab of something sharp in my stomach, worse than a cramp. Something like jealousy. Jealous that she had the guts to say it and jealous because Xander was mine.

Stop it.

Sierra looked up from twirling a lock of hair to see all of us staring, and she giggled. "Please, I would *never*. Where would he take me on a date? McDonald's?"

"On his bike," Delilah said with a knowing nod. "He doesn't even have a car."

Elowen arched a perfect brow at Sierra. "You want to take a ride on his bike?"

The group burst out in laughter.

"Oh my God, *stop*," Sierra said. "I'm just saying he's kind of…built?"

"It's all that bike riding," said Aria, and the laughs came again, ringing out in the halls, loud and sharp.

"Sierra has a soft spot for the poors," Delilah said. "Like Dean Yearwood."

"Everyone knows Dean is special. He gets a pass," Sierra said, and sighed dreamily. "What can I say? I'm a sucker for the lean muscly-type, even if it's wasted on a Bender."

"Wow," Aria said dryly. "Our very own Mother Theresa."

Yet another peal of derisive mirth. Elowen noticed I wasn't joining in and frowned, her eyes narrowing with suspicion. "Are you sure you're okay?"

"Fine," I said, forcing a small smile. "Waiting for the Advil to kick in."

"Mmkay, it's just that we saw the new guy yesterday and you looked like you'd seen a ghost."

All eyes turned to me.

"You know him, Em?" Delilah arched a brow. "Have you taken a ride on his bike?"

I couldn't tell them that I'd met Xander once upon a lifetime ago for one perfect afternoon. Or that I knew he was built from rowing, because he'd mentioned it on the phone last night. Hell, given this conversation, it was obvious I couldn't even let them know he was tutoring me.

I put on an incredulous expression. "How could I possibly know him?"

Elowen shrugged. "Tucker might have some thoughts if he catches you ogling the new guy."

"Right?" Aria chimed in. "He'd set some *boundaries* with Xander. With his fists."

"He would not. Tucker's not a complete Neanderthal," I said, not entirely sure I believed it.

"He's protective of his woman," Sierra said. "You're so lucky, Em. You have a boyfriend who would fucking kill for you."

My stomach roiled. The idea of Tucker beating the shit out of a guy because of jealousy wasn't romantic; it was scary and disturbing. And another reason to keep anything with Xander to myself.

But this was the pot I'd been stewing in for years, and only now did I realize it was boiling over. It had only taken one glimpse of Xander Ford to rekindle all the feelings I'd had when I was with him on that rock. Comfort and safety and being myself. Like I'd forgotten those feelings existed in the world. Like maybe I could have them again if I were brave enough…

"Em? You coming?"

I'd fallen behind. My crew was waiting.

I adjusted my imaginary crown and fell back in step, wondering what they would think if they knew that my heart was secretly counting down the minutes until I could be alone with Xander.

The bike-riding Bender who invented debate…

But I had a whole day to get through first.

My next class was AP English with Ms. Alvarez. She was new to the Academy, and though this was only the second day in her class, she was already my favorite teacher. Mid-thirties, with a long dark braid down her back, she had a relaxed, friendly vibe. She reminded me of Harper Bennett with her earthy clothes and funky jewelry…and then I saw Harper sitting toward the back. Students had shuffled seats and now the only available desk was beside hers next to the only available seat. A flush of heat crept over my face at what my friends had said about her. What *I* had said.

Whatever. What do you care what she thinks?

But that was the bitch of being popular—we all pretended we didn't care what anyone thought, when we actually cared what *everyone* thought.

I took the empty seat. Harper kept her eyes straight ahead, chin up, hands folded neatly on her notebook. Ms. Alvarez moved to the front of the class and wrote on the whiteboard the word *villanelle*.

"Can anyone tell me what a villanelle is?"

A few hands went up, including Harper's.

Ms. Alvarez smiled. "And, no, I'm not referring to the character in *Killing Eve*."

Hands went down along with some laughs. Harper's remained.

"Yes, Ms. Bennett?"

"It's a poem in which the first and third lines of the first stanza are alternated and repeated throughout."

"Very good." Ms. Alvarez returned to the board and wrote as she spoke. "To expand, a villanelle is a nineteen-line poem comprised of five tercets, or three-line stanzas, and one quatrain, or four-line stanza. It has a very specific rhyme scheme and, as Ms. Bennett said, repeating refrains. The most famous villanelle is Dylan Thomas's *Do Not Go Gentle into That Goodnight*, but it's not my favorite. *This* is my favorite."

She turned to the class with a smile and tapped the whiteboard, where she had somehow written out an entire villanelle while explaining a villanelle.

"Sylvia Plath's *Mad Girl's Love Song*," she said. "Is anyone familiar with Plath?"

Hannah Greenway raised her hand. "Didn't she kill herself by sticking her head in an oven?"

Ms. Alvarez's smile tensed. "She did. That's the sensational, unfortunate detail that overshadows her many achievements. But Plath was a prolific writer of scores of letters, journals, short stories, and a novel, and she won the Pulitzer-Prize for poetry—all before the age of thirty." She stepped aside. "Please take a moment to yourselves to read *Mad Girl's Love Song*."

I did and it felt like the poem had slapped me in the face, each line screaming Xander Ford's name. Now that he was back, there was no escaping him. He was everywhere I turned, even in the words of a poet who died more than sixty years ago.

"Would anyone like to tell me about this poem?" Ms. Alvarez asked. "Not only what you think it means, but how it makes you feel?"

My hand rose, almost as if pulled by a string.

"Ms. Wallace?"

"I think the poem is a girl writing about a boy who went away. He said he'd come back but he didn't, and so she waited and waited. She waited so long that now she wonders if everything that happened between them was only in her imagination. Like, maybe she made him up inside her head."

"Very good," Ms. Alvarez said gently. "And how does it make you feel?"

"Sad," I said. "And lonely. Like true love is a delusion. It isn't real. Like it breaks promises and doesn't come back."

The class went silent until a few murmurs broke me out of whatever crazy spell had come over me. Two senior girls—not in my group—whispered and made boo-hoo faces at me. My cheeks burned.

Ms. Alvarez smiled. "Well done, Emery. Thank you for sharing." She turned back to the board. "Our first unit is going to be poetry, where we will be studying the works of Sylvia Plath, Gwendolyn Brooks, and Mary Oliver, among others. You can find our first unit's reading on your iPad. Please click on the link…"

Ms. Alvarez continued with classroom business, assignments, and her expectations for the year while I stared at the poem on the whiteboard. It was as if Sylvia had written it just for me.

Harper leaned and whispered, "That was really good."

"Thanks—"

"Too bad you're a total fake."

She offered a sweet smile—her version of the one I had given her in calculus—and turned her attention back to our teacher.

Indignation made my face hot, but then I realized it was actually just shame. Harper was right. I was a complete fraud. I had a million things I wanted to say that were true and real, but no one to say them to. Because of the façade I'd built to my parents' expectations. A pretty house on the outside and a total mess on the inside that I kept designing in my mind to make it better. If I didn't keep up appearances, the whole thing would come crashing down. What would happen to me then?

LITTLE PIECES OF LIGHT

A strange thought infiltrated my mind.
I'd be free.

Chapter 5

XANDER

I'm in Room 9.

I read Emery's text, and my stomach tightened. One long wall of the Academy's massive library was lined with study rooms: small, windowed offices, each with a whiteboard, round table, and chairs for six. Emery had chosen the last room, tucked in the corner, though every other room was empty.

Because she doesn't want to be seen with me.

Day three of this high school experiment hadn't gone as well as the previous two. Word had somehow gotten out about Dad's breakdown and my mom walking out on us. I caught groups of students whispering and shooting me glances as I passed by.

Fuck them. My father had made groundbreaking

discoveries in structures of molecular orbitals using ultraviolet photoelectron spectroscopy. None of these rich pricks would ever accomplish a fraction of what Dad had—never mind understand it—no matter how much money their parents threw at them.

I'd been stewing in different versions of those acidic thoughts all day, so that by the time my tutoring session with Emery arrived, I was in a foul mood. Her secrecy was a nice touch.

She's probably been gossiping too, yet desperate for my help.

I leaned in the door of study room nine, my armor fully locked into place. "Hey."

Emery had her study materials out, her pencil tapping impatiently. Her eyes rose to meet mine, and I could've sworn her cheeks flushed, her glossy lips lifted ever so slightly.

"Hey," she said, almost a whisper. She cleared her throat. "Are you just going to stand in the door all day?"

"Depends," I said. "Does this school have an underground bunker where you'd feel more comfortable? Or we could take the ferry to Connecticut. Pretty sure no one will see us there."

She rolled her eyes. "Look, it's just better if we keep our business private. For multiple reasons."

"If you insist."

I stepped inside, closing the door behind me. I felt her gaze on me as I set down my backpack and busied myself with retrieving my notebook, pencil, and graphing calculator. But this close to Emery, her flowery perfume was intoxicating, and my gaze was transfixed by the way her hair fell around her shoulders…

Cut it out.

I took the chair beside her. "Where are you struggling?"

"Where am I not?" She pushed her notebook to me, showing a page scrawled with notes. "From this morning. I don't understand any of it."

"Can I ask what might seem like an obvious question?"

"Why am I taking calculus in the first place?" She sighed. "Because my father insists that I take it. To pad my application to Brown."

Without thinking, I blurted, "Brown? I thought you were going to RISD."

Pronounced like Rizdy, she'd said seven years ago, her face lit up with excitement. It had been her dream…

Emery's eyes flared with shock. I hadn't meant to touch that conversation, but it was too late now. "Well? Isn't that what you told me?"

On that perfect afternoon that you evidently forgot all about.

"I told you a lot of things that day," Emery said, her voice stony. "But no, I'm not going to RISD. My father won't allow it, and since he's the one paying for college, I don't have a choice. There. All caught up? Can we get back to the math, please?"

"Fine. But this isn't helpful." I slid her notebook back to her. "Math is like a bridge, and each stepping stone is an essential component. We have to go back to the place where you were doing well and start there, filling in the gaps until you're caught up."

"I don't know that I was ever doing well. I memorized a lot of trigonometry in order to get by, but it's all flown out of my head. I barely passed last year with an A-minus."

"That's more than 'barely passed.'"

"A-minus is my dad's bare minimum."

Emery peered up to see me looking at her. She was punching holes in my armor: Her father was still as strict as ever, denying her her dream school. Stealing her light. My gaze softened and then so did hers, taking in my heterochromic eyes. I didn't miss how that anomaly thrilled her all over again. The moment caught and held. She and I, back where we'd been…

Emery gave her head a shake, breaking the spell. "Anyway, I guess we could start at the end of trig."

I pushed in my chair. "Be right back."

The library had an entire section of classroom textbooks. I found the one I wanted and returned to the study room. Together, Emery and I flipped through the last chapters until we found where she'd gone astray.

"Here," she said. "Honestly, I don't remember most of this stuff, but this is where things got really shaky."

"Inverse trigonometric functions."

"Yes. God, I hate functions," Emery said. "The *worst*."

"Okay, let's see where you're at." I grabbed my pencil and paper and created sample problems not found in the book. I felt her eyes on me again.

"I forgot how good you are at this," she said. "My turn

to ask the obvious question. Why are you here? I'd have thought you'd have a bunch of degrees by now."

"Three," I said, not pausing my work.

"You have *three* degrees?"

I nodded. "Biotechnology, physics, and philosophy from the University of Maryland. MIT is waiting for me to do my postgrad."

"Then why—?"

"Because after my mother walked out, my father needed to be here, and I needed something to do," I said, setting my pencil down with a snap. "And that's all anyone needs to know."

I hated speaking harshly to Emery; it felt counter to every impulse of my heart. But being this close to her… The old hurt was trying to swamp me, and I couldn't let it. Emery recoiled, and I watched her tighten her armor too.

"Fine. Shall I?"

I pushed the sample problems to her, and Emery got to work while I scrolled my phone as if I had texts from friends or any kind of social media to speak of. Silence filled the room for a few minutes until Emery tossed her pencil down.

"I can't do this," she said.

"Sure, you can. It's an arbitrary value—"

"Not the stupid math. This. Us." She turned in her chair to glare at me. "Are we not going to talk about what happened?"

Here we go.

"You're referring to our first encounter, seven years ago."

"When you broke your promise?" she blurted. The mask of imperiousness fell for a moment, and real hurt touched her eyes. But she bottled it back up. "Never mind. It was just stupid kid stuff. Forget it."

Another silence fell in which she wrote furiously to solve the equation, making at least three errors. I should've let it go. It *was* kid stuff. We were ten. Nothing ten-year-olds say should be binding for life, but something happened between us that day and we both knew it.

"I didn't break my promise," I said quietly.

Emery's head whipped up, her eyes blazing for a fight. "You sure about that?"

"*Yes*. I'm sure."

"You never came back to meet me at the park, and I never got any letters. So?" She shrugged as if to say *case closed*.

"My mother left, so Dad had to work constantly to keep up. Coming back for vacation was impossible. And what do you mean, you didn't get any letters?"

"Just that. I never got one letter from you." She crossed her arms. "Are you saying you wrote to me?"

"I wrote to you," I said. "A lot. And you never wrote me back."

"No, you didn't. Wait…you did? How many is a lot?"

"Enough."

Too many.

The pain of my mother leaving was tangled up in the relief of meeting Emery—a bright spot in a vast field of black. But that tiny scrap of happiness withered and died with every passing day I didn't hear from her. I was not about to chalk up seven years of heartache to an issue with the postal service. It could *not* be that trivial. I needed someone to blame.

Emery must've had similar thoughts because she remained just as guarded. "Yeah, well, I never got any."

"I wonder..." I tapped my chin, my voice dripping with sarcasm. "Do you think, perhaps, your authoritarian father might've had something to do with their mysterious disappearance?"

Emery's eyes flared with indignation. "*No*. I asked every day—*every day*—if I had any letters. Then every week. The answer was always no."

The image of a ten-year-old Emery came to me: blond hair gleaming in the sun as she skipped to the mailbox, only to discover it empty yet again. But I'd upheld my end of the deal. I wrote to her and then I waited and waited...

"And of course, he wasn't *lying*," I said snidely. "That would be out of character for a strict, ubercontrolling father who chooses which college his daughter will attend for her."

"Yes, it would be out of character," Emery said, her chin quivering. "Because my father wouldn't bother lying. If he didn't want me corresponding with you, he'd have made sure *everyone* knew it. He'd have sent your letters back. Or burned them while I watched. You'd have received a cease-and-desist if you really wrote me as often as you claim."

"As I *claim*? I poured my fucking—" I bit off my words. "Why didn't you look me up?"

"*How?*"

"I told you my dad worked for the NIST. You could have—"

"You never said that. You said he worked for 'the government.' Not a lot to go on, Xander, especially for a ten-year-old. I didn't even know where you lived."

"Maryland," I said stupidly.

"Gee, that narrows it down," Emery retorted. "You're the genius. Why didn't you think to look *me* up?"

"I did. Once. To double check that the *dozens* of letters I'd sent were going to the right address. And they were."

"You checked *once?*"

"My father was having a prolonged mental breakdown," I said, my voice rising. "I'm sorry I didn't think to follow you on Instagram, but I was a little busy picking up the pieces of our lives after *my mother walked out*."

"So you don't know."

"Know what?"

Emery heaved a shaky breath. "About my brother, Grant, who went missing that day. He…died."

Every muscle in my body seized up. "Oh fuck. Emery…"

"He was in Providence. They said he had his headphones on." She swallowed hard and her voice grew small. "He didn't hear the train."

My heart dropped to the floor and took all of my bullshit and self-pity with it. "Jesus. No, I didn't know." I started to reach for her, then pulled my hand back. "I'm sorry, Emery. I'm so sorry."

She tossed a lock of hair over her shoulder, but her eyes were still shiny, her jaw set against tears. "It's fine. Whatever."

"It's not fine," I said. "You're right about everything. I wrote some things in those letters, and when I didn't hear back…" I ran a hand through my hair. "I get in the habit of thinking I always have the right answers. I thought you were ignoring me, and that's the story I told myself to the exclusion of all other possibilities. But I was wrong, and I'm sorry. I'm so sorry about your brother, Emery."

"Thank you," she said. "I'm sorry too. And your dad? Is he…okay?"

"He's okay. For now." I managed a small smile. "He likes it here. That's why we came back."

She glanced up at me through lowered lids. "So, what…um, did you write in your letters?"

"Nothing," I said quickly. "Nothing important. Kid stuff. I hardly remember."

"Oh." She looked away, then heaved a shaky sigh. "Well, I don't know what happened to them, but I guess it's good we cleared the air."

"Agreed."

"It's kind of a silly thing to argue about, right?" Emery laughed nervously. "So many *big feelings* over nothing."

"Nothing. Right."

"I mean, why are we being so dramatic about something that happened when we were ten?"

"No clue."

A small silence followed. Now that we were done

turning a monumental and consequential incident into something trivial and childish, I supposed we could go back to being virtual strangers.

Emery looked to me uncertainly. "Will you still tutor me?"

I should've said no. My stupid heart wanted to go back to the beginning and pick up where we left off, but that was impossible, and that impossibility was going to be torture. But if I didn't help Emery, her father was going to torture her in his own way, and that I could not stand.

"Of course, I will."

Emery eased a sigh. Relieved but sad too.

"Thank you." She glanced down at her work. "I can't concentrate any more today. Save it for next time?"

"Next time," I said and gathered my stuff, needing to get away too. To sort out this afternoon's revelations that had rewritten the past seven years.

I was at the door of the study room when her soft voice stopped me. "Xander?"

"Yeah?"

She made to speak, then changed her mind. "Nothing."

Chapter 6

EMERY

I'VE MISSED YOU.

I nearly said it; it'd been on the tip of my tongue, but I locked it behind my teeth. What did it even mean, anyway? I had to constantly remind myself that Xander and I didn't actually *know* each other. How could I miss what I never had?

I miss him because I never had him. But I could have had him, all this time...

I'd started to gather my things, but my hands fell away from my bag, and I sank back into the chair. Xander said he'd written to me, and I could feel it in my bones he'd been telling the truth. And that changed everything. My heart had been broken, and now it broke again, imagining him as a little boy, writing to me over and over and never hearing anything back. Now that we'd let all that defensive anger out, I could just be sad. Sad that we'd both wanted to stay in touch, but something had gotten in the way.

He's right. It has to be my dad.

But what I'd said had been true too: My father never resorted to secrecy or mystery. If he didn't want something to happen, it didn't happen, and he made damn sure everyone knew why.

I inhaled a shaky breath. "Only one way to know for sure."

———

Dinner that night was Belinda's pot roast, my favorite. But my food grew cold as my stomach twisted in knots at the thought of confronting my dad.

My mother sat at one end of our long dining table, my father at the other. She'd hardly touched her food either; since Grant died, she'd become sticklike and pale, her thin fingers always wrapped around the stem of a wine glass. Jack sat across from me, shoveling his food so he could be excused as fast as possible. The entire room was loud with silence and thick with the tension of a broken family going through the motions.

Not that my dad seemed to notice any of it. He ate leisurely, sipped his wine, and complimented Belinda on the meal when she brought in a basket of rolls, fresh from the oven.

"Apologies for the delay," she said, setting the fragrant basket down. "I got too busy with the roast."

I reached for a roll, and my mother cleared her

throat and gave me a warning glance. My hand froze in midair and then I snatched it back. Belinda hurried out, mumbling something about turning off the oven.

"Jesus, Mom," Jack snarled. He took two rolls from the basket and tossed one across the table to me.

"*Jack*," Dad said. "That is hardly appropriate table manners."

"She should be allowed to eat her fucking dinner," my brother snapped.

"That language is inappropriate, as well," Dad said in that deadly calm tone of his. "One more outburst and you start losing privileges. Such as participating in any upcoming social events."

There were a ton of back-to-school activities coming up, including the annual bonfire party on the beach down at Castle Hill Lighthouse this weekend, a party that no one at school wanted to miss. Not even Jack.

"I'm nineteen," Jack said. "You can't tell me where I can and can't go."

"So long as you're living under my roof, eating my food, and sleeping in the bed I provide for you, I certainly can."

Jack snapped his mouth shut and glowered at me and my untouched dinner roll. Mom went back to her wine. The silence grew unbearable, as it usually did. I felt its weight on my shoulders. If I didn't say something, no one would.

"I've hired a tutor to help me with math," I said. "We had our first meeting today."

"That's wise," Dad intoned, "considering how you struggle with the subject."

"But I'll need money for it. He's thirty dollars an hour."

He frowned. "That seems high."

"Yes, but he's the best. A genius," I said, hearing the pride in my voice, as if I needed to defend Xander.

You don't need to defend him; you need to protect him.

"This tutor is a student? Do I know him?"

"No. He's new."

"I'll need his name and address if you plan to be at his home," Dad said, dabbing butter onto his dinner roll.

"We'll study at school."

My father peered down at me over his glasses. "His name, Emery."

It was a command, not a question. And ridiculous anyway, considering he never seemed to care where I went or what I did on my dates with Tucker.

"Xander Ford," I said, and watched my dad's face for a spark of recognition or any hint that he'd seen the name before on an envelope—many envelopes—years ago. But his expression remained impassive.

"Ford," Dad mused. "Do I know his parents? Are they members?"

Are they members? was code for *Are they one of us?* If they didn't own a yacht or play tennis at the Castle Hill Country Club with its $50,000 annual membership fee, they weren't worth knowing.

"No," I said, trying to keep the impatience out of my voice. "His dad is a scientist who used to work for the government. In Maryland."

Mom drained her glass and stood up. "I have a

headache," she said, almost a whisper. "I'm going to bed."

"Another headache," Dad mused, annoyance coloring his voice. "Seems to be an epidemic lately."

"Don't trouble yourself about it, Grayson," she muttered tiredly, smoothing a lock of silvery blond hair. "Tomorrow is another day."

"Whatever that means. Goodnight, then."

Mom slipped away to her bedroom—separate from Dad's; they hadn't shared a room in seven years. She walked carefully, stiffly, as if she were delicate and the slightest bump could break her apart.

"Well, I'm impressed to see you taking initiative, Emery." Dad pointed his butter knife at Jack. "You would do well to emulate your sister on that front."

I cringed and averted my gaze from my brother's cold stare, ashamed to admit that I gobbled up the tiny bit of praise like a starving dog who'd been tossed a scrap at the dinner table.

"Can I be excused?" Jack asked. "I *also* have a headache."

"Go," Dad said, waving him away as if he were a fly.

My brother tore out of his chair and stormed up to his room.

Just another Thursday night in the Wallace household.

I wanted to escape to my room too. Every molecule in my body recoiled at the idea of asking my father about Xander's letters. He didn't seem to recognize the name and now he was irritated. Best to leave it alone. But Xander's words came back to me.

I didn't break my promise.

His beautiful, mismatched eyes had been as heavy as his voice. I thought he'd forgotten about me, and that hurt. But he thought I'd forgotten him too, and somehow, that hurt even more. For both our sake, I had to know.

"Daddy?" My voice was a croak. I cleared it and tried again. "I was wondering, do you remember a few summers back when I asked you if I'd gotten any letters?"

"I recall you pestering me about this a long time ago," he said. "My answer is the same now as it was then: No, I don't recall. Why? Who was allegedly writing to you?"

His pale blue eyes felt like X-rays straight to my heart.

"No one," I said quickly. "We're studying Sylvia Plath in English class. She wrote a lot of letters. It made me think of that, is all."

It was a terrible explanation that didn't even make sense, but confronting my father always did that to me—turned my thoughts to mush so that I never said what I'd planned to say.

Dad's lips turned down. "Can't say I approve of your teacher using Plath in her curriculum."

"Why? Sylvia was an amazing poet. She—"

"She was a weak-willed basket case. Life comes with pressure. Glorifying someone for caving into that pressure is not a proper use of school material. I'll be having a word with your teacher."

"Daddy, please don't—"

He slammed his fork down. "Maybe you'd like to stay home from this weekend's activities, too?"

"No," I said in a small voice. "I'm sorry."

He stared at me a moment longer, pinning me down with his eyes. Then he tossed his napkin on his empty bowl and stood up. "I'll put the money into your account for this tutor, but I'd better see results."

He walked out, leaving me alone in the dining room. Marooned, like a survivor after a shipwreck. With Dad's tyranny and Mom's remoteness, we'd already been a dysfunctional family, but Grant's death had smashed us to bits, and I don't know why I still hoped we could be put back together.

Belinda came in to clear the plates, smiling at me pityingly. I wondered, too, why she stayed. How she could stand it.

"Goodnight, Belinda," I said, and got up from the table.

"Goodnight, Miss Emery." She slipped a roll into my hand.

I smiled gratefully and turned to go, then stopped. "Belinda?"

"Yes, dear?"

"What do you do with the mail when you bring it in?"

"I put it directly on your father's desk, every afternoon, as I have for years."

"Did you ever happen to see any personal letters for me?"

"No, dear. But I would never look through the mail." She lowered her voice. "Your father would find that inappropriate."

"Okay, thanks."

I headed upstairs, but instead of going to my room, I made a right and stood in front of Grant's closed door. After pausing to make sure the coast was clear, I stepped inside.

It was just as he'd left it—there were even dirty clothes in the hamper and a UI sweatshirt on the floor. He'd gotten into the University of Iowa, home to the famous Iowa Writers' Workshop, and planned on majoring in creative writing. An amazing accomplishment...and our father couldn't see it.

I turned to his bookshelf and grabbed *A Prayer for Owen Meany*. It had been some years since I'd looked at it. Since Xander disappeared. But as I flipped open the first page, what I'd written about him came back to me.

I'm doomed to remember a boy with mismatched eyes...

Only I didn't have to remember him anymore. He was back.

And he'd kept his promise.

Chapter 7

XANDER

ON FRIDAY MORNING, THE STUDENTS WERE DIVERTED from their first period classes and funneled into a huge auditorium for a pep rally. By the time I arrived, the place was packed, everyone stomping their feet and shouting about Royal Pride—the school's mantra and guiding ethos. Bleachers had been unfolded from both walls, and the seats were filled with students, about a thousand in all.

The cacophony was enough to make me turn around and leave, but then I heard my name. Dean Yearwood sat on the upper level of one side and waved me over. In the interest of the Experiment and putting effort into making friends, I braved the noise and joined him.

Dean gestured at the small group around him—two guys and one girl.

"Xander, I'd like you to meet Kevin Huang,

president of our Math & Physics Club, and Jasper Reed, treasurer."

Sitting one riser below was a girl wearing an eclectic outfit of contrasting styles, with a cloud of brown curls and a pale, delicate face. Shrewd brown eyes observed me.

"This is Harper Bennett," Dean said. "She's new, like you, and a recent addition to our little gang. You'll meet the rest next Wednesday at our first meeting…all two of them."

"Hello," I said with a wave that encompassed them all. "Thank you for having me."

"Our pleasure," Kevin said with a warm smile. He was a skinny guy in a windbreaker, khakis, and nice shoes. Not a Bender, then. My father liked to say you can always read a man's situation by his shoes. "Dean tells me you aced our little quiz."

"I suppose so."

Dean thumped my back. "So modest. I have a feeling that was only a taste of what Xander is capable of."

"No, no, I—"

"Whoa!" Dean exclaimed suddenly, staring at me. "I didn't notice before, but…holy shit! You have two different colored eyes!"

"Not entirely, but…yes." I said as everyone—including Harper—peered at me closely.

"That is the coolest thing ever!" Dean cried.

Jasper nodded. "Typically, one doesn't see such drastic chromatic differences. Intriguing."

"Right." I rubbed the back of my neck. Aside from the

reminder of my mother staring at me in the mirror every morning, the color differential was one more thing to attract too much attention when I just wanted to blend in.

I caught Harper's gaze lingering before she looked away.

"What are your plans after graduation, Xander?" Kevin asked. "MIT? Caltech?"

I wondered if it was okay to tell them MIT was holding a place for me. When I was a kid, my genius was something of a novelty. Now that I was among friendly people my own age, I feared it would seem more like arrogance.

"Yes, MIT," I said carefully. "I'm going to pursue a career in astrophysics."

"Oh!" Jasper exclaimed, brushing a lock of coppery-red hair off his face. Also, not a Bender, judging by the fact he wore an actual suit, including jacket, slacks, and a tie. "An interesting realm. What drew you to that field?"

Just answer honestly. Be yourself. That's how to make friends.

"Well, if we're hoping to uncover a unified theory of quantum gravity, I feel black holes are the best places to look," I said. "Specifically, I'd like to join the Event Horizon Telescope Collaboration observatory team to confirm the existence of Hawking radiation and use interferometry to image direct evidence of a black hole singularity, though I'm acutely aware of how difficult those discoveries might be in my lifetime."

Silent, stunned faces stared at me. So much for being myself.

But then Jasper nodded, seemingly impressed, and Kevin gave a low whistle. Harper smiled but said nothing, still watching me as if she hadn't decided what to make of me.

Dean laughed loud and long. "What did I tell you? This guy's the real deal. Like father, like son."

I instantly tensed up. "You know my dad?"

"The Math & Physics Club religiously studies every edition of *Scientific American*. Last year, we read your father's article on laboratory spectrography and its implications for aquatic pollution monitoring." Kevin beamed. "Fascinating stuff."

Jasper was shaking his head in awe. "The son of Russell Ford in our very own club."

I stared, sure that they were toying with me. "I thought certain rumors had preceded us."

"It's not uncommon for great minds to become overwhelmed and need a break from the pressures of the scientific community," Jasper said. "Quite understandable."

Dean nodded. "In other words, we don't listen to gossipy bullshit."

"Not to be forward but..." Kevin leaned in. "Do you think we could meet him sometime?"

Suddenly, my eyes stung, and my throat felt tight. By all accounts, my father had come to the end of the line, reputationally and professionally. Even in my own mind. To know that his achievements hadn't been wiped away by the wide brush of stigma touched me more than I could say.

"You want to meet my dad?"

"Only if you think he'd be up to it," Dean said quickly, shooting Kevin a stern look. "If he wants his privacy, we understand."

I cleared the emotion out of my throat. "No, I think he would like that. I think he would like that a lot."

The guys seemed thrilled by the idea as we all faced forward to listen to Vice President Newman give a welcoming speech. Harper's gaze lingered on me a moment more, and then she faced forward too.

Mr. Newman spoke at length about the excellence expected of us as Lions on every Royal Pride team and how the Academy prepped its students for bright futures at prestigious universities. Every sentence was met with wild enthusiasm.

Dean read my tight expression and laughed. "Loud enough for ya? School spirit is a big deal here."

"I noticed."

"In a normal school, it would lead up to homecoming, with a football game and a dance," Dean said. "But we don't have a football team. Instead, we have this pep rally to promote the different sports teams and get out the word for tryouts. The 'big game' is our crew's first regatta in about a month, because we're astronomically bougie like that."

"Bougie…?"

"There's a big bonfire party Saturday night at the

lighthouse," Dean continued. "But the first dance isn't until the end of October."

"That would be the Halloween Festival," Kevin put in. "It's a huge deal. Costumes, games, carnival stuff. It's pretty fun."

"You both should come to the bonfire," Dean said.

"Maybe," Harper said. The first word she'd spoken all morning.

"I'll take it," Dean said with a laugh. "How about you, Ford? You'll want to blow off steam after crew tryouts, for sure."

"You're going for crew?" Kevin gave another low whistle. "In addition to our beloved Dean, all the beefed-up jocks are on the rowing crew. Tucker Hill, for instance…"

He pointed at the rows of bleachers on our side of the auditorium, toward the middle front, where a bunch of "beefed-up jocks" sat. Tucker was taller, louder, and bigger than every guy around him, exuding the kind of chest-beating alpha-male superiority that bordered on psychopathy.

Speaking of superiority, why are you being a judgmental prick? He might have changed since that day at the park.

I doubted that. Moreover, I suspected the fact he was Emery's boyfriend had something to do with my dark thoughts, but I chose not to investigate further.

"Last year, Tucker was captain of the row *and* water polo teams, as a *junior*," Kevin said. "And if you didn't know that, he'd be happy to remind you."

"Don't listen to him," Dean said. "Tucker can get a

little hotheaded, for sure, but he's a hell of an athlete and a great team player. You'll see."

Mr. Newman finally wound up his speech. "And now, to kick off what is sure to be another exceptional year, please welcome your Royal Pride dance team!"

The auditorium burst into cheers and applause a split second before being drowned out by loud, thumping, music—a mix of hip-hop and electronic genres. Twelve girls came on stage wearing short shorts and midriff-baring tank tops in the Academy colors—black and gold—with Emery at the front, her hair pulled up in a high ponytail.

The routine was impossibly fast, yet the dancers moved in perfect unison. It was provocative and athletic, sexy and gymnastic. The routine had a hundred moving parts, but all I could see was Emery; my nerves lit up when she performed a run of gymnastic handsprings on the hard floor.

Someone nudged my elbow. Dean was grinning at me and shaking his head. "Not that one, my friend. Literally anyone but her."

"Oh, I wasn't... I mean—"

"I get it. Emery Wallace is a goddess. That is a fact."

Harper turned around and gave us a dark look.

Dean held up his hands. "Don't kill me. I'm just pointing out the obvious." He turned to me and shouted above the pounding beat, "I want you on my crew, Xander, preferably in one piece, so I'm warning you now. She's Tucker Hill's girl. Off. Limits."

His words chafed me—Emery shouldn't *belong* to

anyone—but I felt protective of her myself. That instinctual urge to keep her safe hadn't diminished in seven years, be it from water balloons, tyrannical fathers, or anything else. It was irrational. Unscientific. But her well-being was my responsibility, and no amount of logic could change that feeling.

The dance ended to riotous applause. Emery ran to the bleachers, where Tucker grabbed her and spun her around. My stomach burned with an unpleasant sensation as he kissed her. After what felt like an eternity, he let her go, raised a fist and bellowed, "Royal pride, let's go!"

The auditorium answered with more cheers, the band struck up a march, and everyone joined in on what I surmised was the school's fight song. And Emery...

Emery Wallace was brutally beautiful—exhilarated, flushed, and still out of breath; her skin glistened with a thin sheen of sweat. While everyone around her laughed and sang, her blue-green gaze scanned the crowd. I didn't know who she could be looking for; her friends and boyfriend were beside her...

And then she found me.

At least, I think it was me. She was halfway across the auditorium, but I felt as if her gaze was locked on mine. Her smile dropped, replaced by an expression I couldn't read; her lips parted, and her chest rose with a sharp breath. Her hand drifted to her delicate gold necklace, and she toyed with its charm absently. Then her little finger lifted and curled—twice. Two tiny motions, and I was paralyzed.

Is she waving at me? Do I wave back? Is she even waving at all...?

A girl grabbed Emery's arm and swung her around, laughing and talking in her ear, breaking the spell. I jerked out of the warm, hazy moment into the loud reality of the auditorium and felt another pair of eyes on me. Harper Bennett had one eyebrow raised, amused, and a strange smile on her lips.

"It's sort of like Schrödinger's pinky wave, isn't it?" Harper said, gathering her stuff. "She was both waving at you and not waving at you. The only way to know is to ask her."

I stammered, feeling like I should explain myself, as if I were guilty of some crime. But then the pep rally was over, and Dean was jostling me to get going. By the time I got my backpack on, Harper was gone.

Chapter 8

EMERY

AFTER MIDMORNING BREAK, I HEADED TO ENGLISH CLASS and took a seat beside Harper Bennett toward the back. In calculus, she hadn't said a word to me, not that I blamed her. I'd been a total bitch the other day, and she had every right to ignore me. But I was aching for a real friend to talk to. Someone I could share my thoughts and feelings with and not worry they'd be whispered all over the halls the next day. Someone to talk to about my parents and Jack...

And Xander...

With major effort, I shoved Xander Ford out of my thoughts. We'd gotten things sorted out from a billion years ago, and he was my tutor. End of story.

Except you're keeping a mental countdown until you see him today, but...sure.

While Ms. Alvarez rifled through papers on her desk, I studied Harper. She wore a corduroy jumper skirt over a black long-sleeved top, brown Doc Martens, and earrings in the shape of little yellow airplanes.

"Can I help you?" she asked without looking at me.

"I'm sorry."

"For?"

"You know what for," I said.

She arched a brow, expectant and calm. Not letting me off the hook. I kind of loved that.

"I'm sorry for talking shit yesterday," I said. "And for not speaking up when my friends talked shit."

Harper nodded. "Apology accepted."

"Do you want to hang out sometime?"

She gave me a double-take. "Are you being serious?"

"One hundred percent. Maybe we could go to a movie or grab a coffee milk. I mean…if you want. No big deal."

"Why?"

The question stung like a bee. I faced forward. "Never mind. Forget it."

"No, I mean, why do *you* want to hang out with *me*?" She raised a brow. "You don't have enough friends?"

My friends suck, I nearly said. "You seem…cool."

"I'm very cool," Harper said. "I'm so cool, in fact, that I go all the way off the charts and come back around to uncool." She looked almost shy for a second. "But…yeah."

"Great," I said, and felt a lightness in my chest for all of ten seconds until Ms. Alvarez addressed the class.

"We have some changes to our curriculum," she said

stiffly. "We will no longer be studying Sylvia Plath. There have been…some complaints."

Oh, my fucking God, he didn't…

My face went hot, and I wanted to sink into the floor.

"Complaints from who?" someone asked.

"The details aren't important," Ms. Alvarez said, her gaze grazing me for one second. "Except to say that I'm disappointed, and I encourage everyone to read Plath's work on their own time. We'll be shifting focus to Elizabeth Bishop. You'll find the link to the new syllabus on your iPads."

Harper leaned over to whisper, "I wonder which asshole parent got their panties in a twist over Sylvia."

"I wonder," I murmured, though I knew exactly which asshole parent was responsible. And when class was over, it didn't shock me in the slightest that Ms. Alvarez asked me to stay behind.

"Emery, I wanted to talk to you about something," she said after the last student had filed out. She sat on the edge of her desk while I hugged my notebook in front of me.

"I'm sorry, Ms. Alvarez," I said. "I know it was my dad, but I swear, I—"

"It's okay," she said. "After your beautiful thoughts on the Plath poem last week, I have no doubts this wasn't your idea. Your father had some very strong aversions to Plath. Not her work, but her personal life. *Very* strong aversions."

"I'm sorry he got involved."

She smiled gently. "Can I ask, how are things at home?"

Such a simple question and suddenly, I was on the verge of tears. I swallowed hard. "Things are…fine. My dad is pretty strict. But I'm sure most parents are."

Ms. Alvarez didn't agree or disagree, though I felt like she was seeing right through me. I wished she would tell me everything she saw. I wish she'd tell me what to *do*.

"I'm presuming you have your college plans sorted out?"

"Brown," I said automatically. Like a program installed in me years ago. Then I thought about Grant, and my terrible father and vacant mother, and how we couldn't study Sylvia Plath anymore, and I blurted, "But I don't want to go there."

"No? What is your dream school?"

"Well, it was RISD, to be an interior designer," I said, and the words sounded old and covered in dust. "But now, honestly, I think…" My voice dropped to a whisper. "I think I'd like to move far away from here."

Ms. Alvarez nodded as if she had suspicions that were now confirmed. "UCLA has a wonderful design program. My sister-in-law has a degree in graphic arts from there."

The idea of moving to sunny California, clear across the country from my parents, and having my life all to myself, lit me up from inside. A second later, reality came down like a shroud.

"I can't."

"Why not?"

"My dad is paying for college. I can't get financial aid while I'm stuck to his income, and he won't let me get a job. I'm kind of…trapped."

Tears threatened again, and I blinked them away. I knew what I must've sounded like: poor little rich girl complaining about the Ivy League when college was a luxury for a lot of kids.

Ms. Alvarez's brows knit together. "I see. Well, there are scholarships available—"

"For the daughter of a billionaire?" I tried not to scoff. "I'm going to be late for my next class, Ms. Alvarez. Can I go?"

"Yes, but I want you to know that I'm here for you. Even if it's just to talk. Okay?"

"Sure. Thanks."

"And Emery..." she said when I was at the door. "I know it sounds cheesy, but if you have a dream, don't give up on it. And if you need anything...help with applications for instance, don't hesitate to ask. Okay?"

"Okay," I said. For her sake. Because she was being so nice. It wasn't her fault; she just didn't know my father.

But at the end of the day, Ms. Alvarez's suggestion was still rattling around in my head, filling my mind with maybes. Maybe my dad would have a change of heart and let me apply somewhere besides Brown. Maybe it was possible I could find my way out of Rhode Island on my own. Maybe my prom design plan would actually work. Maybe...

The chances of my father changing his mind were slim, but for the first time in a long time, I was daring to dream. Even if it was just a little sliver of hope, it was still hope.

Because Xander is back.

Maybe it wasn't very feminist of me, but it wasn't a coincidence that all the plastic, suffocating airlessness of my life became unbearable the second I saw him on the first day of school. Seven years ago, he'd made me feel less alone. Now, I felt as if I had someone on my side. Stronger, somehow, like I could be myself.

After my last class, I practically ran to the library for my tutoring session with Xander. Every study room was filled, and he'd taken one in full view of the rest of the library.

"Hey," he said as I stepped inside. "I know this isn't your preferred location, but they're getting crowded already."

"It's okay," I said, ashamed for making him self-conscious. "But maybe we should have an off-campus backup plan. I have a quiz coming up on power functions, and I am *so* unprepared."

"Okay," Xander said, then paused, looking uncomfortable. "Before we begin, I just wanted to say that I hope everything is copacetic between us after the other day."

"Of course. Why wouldn't it be?"

"No reason," he said in the same casual tone.

Because we weren't anything to each other. Not really. We knew personal stuff about each other but also didn't know each other at all. We were stuck somewhere between *stranger* and *friend*.

I didn't like it, but the clock was ticking. If I failed that quiz, I'd be screwed right out of the gate.

Xander pulled out a notebook and pencil from his worn-out backpack. He wore a plain black T-shirt, and I found my gaze wandering over his arms, watching them move. His hands were squarish and strong, one striated with a vein that snaked around his perfect forearm…

"Emery?"

"Right. Power functions. Let the fun begin."

Xander was a patient tutor, and I tried my best, but it was all gibberish. My heart just wasn't in it. My attention kept wandering away from the incomprehensible math—that Xander understood as if it were his native language—to Xander himself. His eyes were filled with thoughts and figures. A genius mind working in overdrive behind his glasses.

He's kind of extraordinary.

Xander tapped the paper with his pencil. "You change the form of the graph by changing the values of k and n. See?"

"If you say so." I rested my cheek in my palm. "What would you be doing if you were at MIT already?"

"Oh, um…where do I start?"

"How about, what made you get into science in the first place? Because of your dad?"

Xander stiffened slightly. "In a manner of speaking. I grew up with my dad talking about physics, and I became fascinated by those concepts that changed our fundamental understanding of the universe."

"So you wanted to follow in his footsteps…?"

"Yes and no. I'm just as interested as he is in finding

a unified Theory of Everything. He worked at it through particle physics at the NIST and is still working on it at home as we speak. But I want to come at it through the study of black holes."

"What exactly is a black hole, anyway?" I shrugged at Xander's quizzical glance. "I honestly want to know."

"Okay, well, they're what happens when a large star dies and collapses under its own gravity, compressing its mass into a dense region where nothing—not even light—can escape. They remain one of the greatest mysteries in physics. It was only a few years ago that scientists captured an image of one."

"What makes them so mysterious?"

Xander gave me another perplexed smile. "Shouldn't we get back to the math?"

"Later. Right now, I'm learning about black holes."

He chuckled and pushed his glasses higher up on his nose, which looked both sexy and adorable at the same time.

"Okay, so everything we thought we knew about physics, from Newton's First Law to Einstein's relativity, breaks down at the singularity—the place inside a black hole where the mass is concentrated, and where space-time curvature becomes theoretically infinite."

"How do you know all that if you guys saw a black hole for the first time only a few years ago?"

"Math," Xander said. "Theories are explored via mathematical equations to see if they pan out."

"Ohhh. Is that what you mean when you say your dad

is working on a unified theory? He's actually just doing math? I imagined you had some sort of lab at your house."

"No, just pencil and paper."

"I feel stupid."

"Please don't," Xander said. "The equations needed to understand things like black hole singularities are beyond most people."

"But you understand it," I said. "And your dad understands it."

"He understands it for *now*."

"What do you mean?"

Xander looked at me cautiously, as if unsure how much to share. Or if he could trust me.

I smiled. "What happens in the study lounge stays in the study lounge."

He smiled back but it faded fast. "I told you my dad had a breakdown and needed some time off. But they think it might be something worse. Something progressive. He might be losing…everything. And it fucking kills me because he's a brilliant scientist, yet he's only going to be remembered for how it all slipped away. It's up to me to sustain his legacy. I'll go to MIT like he did and carry on the Ford name so that all he accomplished wasn't in vain."

I nodded and let his words settle because it seemed like he'd needed to get them out. After a moment, I said, "It's very honorable, Xander, to take care of him like you do. I hope you know that."

He looked at me with something like surprise and gratitude because I suspected he *didn't* know that.

I told a genius something he didn't know.

The moment held, thick and warm, and then Xander gave his head a shake.

"But they might all be wrong about my dad. He's still working on a unified theory, and he says he's close. It seems impossible, but if he solved it, it would change physics forever."

"Why?"

"It would fill in the massive gaps in our knowledge. Like what is actually happening in a black hole's singularity. Or—at the quantum level—how the photons that make up light aren't waves or particles but can exist in a superposition of both states until observed."

"I can't help you with any of that, but that last part sounds like Schrödinger and his dead cat in a box. You know, where you don't know if it's alive or dead until you take a look?"

Xander made a sour face.

"Am I wrong?"

"You're absolutely correct, but Erwin Schrödinger was a Nobel Prize–winning physicist who devised one of the most beautiful and perfect equations in all of science, and all anyone associates him with is a dead cat in a box."

I suppressed a giggle. *He's so cute when he gets his science feelings hurt.* "Awfully touchy about it," I teased.

"I suppose so," Xander admitted with a small smile. "But likely that's because I'm named after him."

"*Erwin?*"

"Erwin Rudolf Josef Alexander Schrödinger. My

father wanted to name me Erwin, but my mother vetoed it. They compromised on Alexander."

"You dodged a bullet, my friend," I said. "And sorry to break it to you, but your namesake is super famous for his 'dead cat in a box.'"

Xander nodded thoughtfully. "Speaking of, I was going to ask if…" He coughed and cleared his throat. "Never mind."

"What? Tell me."

"No, it's stupid. Anyway, I don't want to bore you with this stuff."

"It's not boring, it's fascinating. And I love hearing you talk about what you're passionate about. I like talking to you, period. It feels easy and…real. Like how it did when we were kids." I glanced away. "I mean…would it be so terrible if we were friends?"

"I don't know," Xander said heavily. "Given everything, maybe we should keep it to getting you through calculus."

"What is *everything*?"

"I've been told your boyfriend is the jealous type, for one. I don't want to cause trouble for you, Emery. Or for me. I'm committed to helping you, but after everything that's happened, I feel like staying neutral is better. Safer, maybe."

"Neutral," I said flatly. The word made no sense when it came to him and me, and it hurt more than I wanted to say. "Okay. Sure. Neutral it is."

Xander nodded, but he didn't look any happier than I felt.

"Actually, no," I blurted. *We've been apart for so long. I don't want any more distance.* "That doesn't work for me. I don't want to be neutral, Xander. I've been neutral my whole life, letting life happen around me, and I'm tired of it."

"But Emery—"

"Don't you see? We're like Schrödinger's cat, too. We know too much about each other from way-back-when to be strangers, and we don't actually know each other at all, so we're not quite friends. We're sort of both and yet neither at the same time. And I don't like it."

"You don't?"

"Do you?" I countered. "Look, it sucks that your letters went missing, and we both thought we'd been ghosted but…we have this year. Before you go to MIT and I escape to California—"

Xander looked up sharply. "You're not staying on the East Coast?"

"I don't know. A teacher suggested UCLA today and that felt like something perfect falling into place." My smile collapsed. "It's stupid to hope. There's no way my dad would let me go, and I can't pay for it myself. But it's nice to have something to dream about, right?"

Xander watched me for a long moment, his eyes full of thoughts I couldn't read.

"Okay," he said finally.

"Okay…?"

"I'd like it if we were friends."

"You sure about that?" I grinned. "I'd hate to violate Xander's First Law of Neutrality."

"I'll make an exception. But maybe we should stay in a superposition. We're friends until Tucker observes us, then we become strangers."

"Don't worry about him. He's all talk. And there's nothing wrong with us being friends, right? It's not like we're... I mean, we're just friends."

"Right," Xander said. "Just friends."

"Good," I said with a smile. "Glad we got that settled."

Happy now? You and your "friend" with the super sexy arms can get back to work.

"Shit," Xander said, checking his watch—an old Casio. "I'm afraid I used up our time talking about quantum mechanics, and you have that test coming up. You don't have to pay me for this hour."

"Of course, I will," I said. "We still have next time. I'll probably remember it better if it's fresh, anyway." I gave my old/new friend a little pinky wave. "Bye, Xander."

His eyes widened and the blush returned to his cheeks. "Bye, Emery."

Chapter 9

XANDER

Saturday morning, I dressed in sweatpants and a T-shirt. Underneath, I wore my old athletic tech shorts and tank top that I'd worn for training with my last crew. I'd been too young to row for University of Maryland and had had to find a junior league to keep my skills honed after Langdon.

Dean was waiting for me in the parking lot, where he leaned against the side of an old white Toyota Camry. The September sun was gold and bright, and there was a light breeze. Perfect conditions for being on the water.

"Thanks for meeting me." I clasped Dean's hand. "It's not going to come off as favoritism, will it?"

He snorted a laugh. "You haven't met Coach Daniels. Poseidon himself could have sent you to row for us, and Coach'd say, *I need to see his stroke.* How is your stroke, by the way?" he asked as we headed toward the Academy. "And which position are you *pulling for*? See what I did there?"

"Bow seat," I said with an answering grin. "I like to think I'm pretty good. Our crew won a few titles."

"Sweet!" Dean said. "If I may pour on some more Greek mythology, bow seat is Coach Daniels's Achilles heel. It requires a special skill set, and he's always complaining he can never fill it properly."

"I'll do my best," I said as we stepped onto campus. The Academy rose up around us like a white-winged spaceship—enormous and sleek and reeking of wealth. "Rhode Island—and Castle Hill especially—is tiny. Where does the school get all its money?"

"The Richies set up a foundation that pays for everything," Dean said. "But it's mostly a few families who make it all happen. We call them the Big Five: Hill, Wallace, Winslow, Foster, and Mercer."

My mind instantly sparked at hearing Emery's family name, but I ignored it.

"It feels…extravagant. So many resources for such a small town."

"Au contraire," Dean said. "You didn't know this was a boarding school too? Richies from all over the country send their spawn to live here year-round. International students too." He pointed to a rambling building behind the admin that resembled a castle. "Behold: Atlas Hall. The most outrageous parties happen there. Lots of music, drugs, sex." He grinned. "It's not my scene, but you know how it is."

I did not, in fact, know how it is. I'd never been to a party, but Dean didn't need to know that. He was friendly now, but I was certain there was a limit to the amount of weirdness he'd tolerate.

We headed toward the center of the Academy and into the gym complex through a set of double doors. Dean grinned. "Prepare to be amazed."

Castle Hill Academy's affluence was obvious, but walking into the gym, I realized it was on a whole other level. My jaw dropped.

Dean laughed. "This fucking school, right?"

The gymnasium was shaped like a hexagon, with signage indicating coaches' offices off the lower sides, and girls' and boys' locker rooms off the middle. In the center of the hexagon, a professional-grade gymnastics floor surrounded by equipment: horizontal and uneven bars, pommel horse, balance beam, rings, vault, and various pits filled with Styrofoam blocks for tumbling practice. Beyond that, a wall of glass revealed a huge weight room that looked as if it had every piece of exercise equipment known to mankind.

"It gets better," Dean said and pointed to a passage marked POOLS.

"*Pools*, plural?"

"Yep. One for racing and one for water polo. Not to mention ice baths, a hot tub, and a sauna. Past the pools, you'll find the lacrosse field, and beyond *that*, the path that will take us to the marina and our own little clubhouse. Just for crew."

"Holy shit."

"Holy shit is right. Aren't we lucky?" Dean chucked me on the arm. "Come on. Let's introduce you to Coach Daniels."

Back outside in the brilliant sunshine, we took the walk down to the Academy marina on Narragansett Bay. Tryouts for pairs, fours, and singles would be tomorrow. Today was just for the eights. A bunch of guys were already there, broken into distinct groups: sixteen hopefuls (including me) and four veterans—Tucker Hill among them—who'd likely had been on last year's team. The veterans talked, laughed, and gave each other shit. The newbies stood loosely clumped and silent. All in all, there were twenty of us competing for first string on the eight-man team.

Dean pointed to a tall, thin man in a windbreaker and visor with a whistle hanging from his neck. "That's Coach Daniels."

But there was no time for introductions. The coach, standing with another portlier man, caught sight of Dean and waved him over.

"Yearwood, there you are. A word, please."

"Break a leg," Dean said and jogged away.

I joined the hopefuls, and after a moment, Coach clapped his hands and addressed the group.

"All right everyone, let's get lined up. I'm your head coach, Bruce Daniels. This is assistant coach, Alan Wright, and this is your cox, Dean Yearwood. I'll keep this short. I care about two things: teamwork and excellence. Every man standing here, regardless of their status last year, has an equal shot at a seat this year."

I glanced at Tucker and his friends, arms crossed, nudging each other with their elbows and looking smug. Now that they were seniors, they clearly felt the statement didn't apply to them.

"Show of hands," Coach said. "How many of you have never rowed before?"

Of the sixteen newbies, four raised their hands.

Coach frowned. "I sincerely hope you four didn't decide to give row a try because you thought it might be 'fun' without ever having set an oar in the water."

Judging by the chagrined expressions, that's exactly what they thought.

Coach went down the line with his clipboard, starting with me. "Name and position?"

"Xander Ford. Bow seat."

Coach's eyebrows rose slightly. He moved on while I caught Tucker exchange glances with a lean guy on the team. Likely, the current bow seat—a role that was less brawn and more technical skill, charged with balance and stability. They both turned their glare on me. The implication was clear: If I got the job, I'd be kicking his friend off the team.

Off to a great start already.

Coach Daniels finished taking inventory of his hopefuls and addressed the group.

"For those of you who are new to row, I'm going to give you a real quick rundown, and I mean, real quick.

Once the season gets rolling, we'll get into mechanics, technique, et cetera. But today, I'm going to be shouting a bunch of commands, and you need to know what the hell I'm talking about and react accordingly. Make sense?"

Nervous, murmured assents from the four newbies.

"Good. The boat is called a *shell*. The head of your oar is called a *blade*. How you rotate the oar is called *feathering*. The *catch* is when the blade goes into the water. I want to see clean catches. No flailing around. *Drive* is pulling the oar through the water. *Layback* is how far you lean while you drive. Got all that? If I call out any adjustments to these terms and you don't make them, we're going to have problems. All right, let's go."

I frowned. For the guys here who'd never rowed before, this tryout was over before it began. It was clear that—like everything else at Castle Hill Academy—the only goal was to win. "Having fun" wasn't on the agenda.

An eight-man shell was tied to the dock, with four oars to a side. Coach called out names and seats to form a team, each man sitting with their backs to the front (the bow) of the shell, while Dean hunkered down in the stern with his megaphone, facing forward. It was the job of the coxswain to set the pace, give encouragement, and relay instructions from the coach on race days. Dean Yearwood—who moved fluidly between social groups—seemed put on this planet to be a coxswain.

The first team, comprised of newbies and veterans, shoved off while the rest of us waited our turn. Coach and the assistant puttered alongside the shell in a motorboat, shouting orders and corrections.

A guy beside me—a veteran—crossed his arms and shook his head. He looked as if he'd stepped out of a magazine: exceedingly handsome with light brown skin and dark eyes and dressed in expensive warm-up gear.

"What a bloody shit show," he muttered in a British accent.

I nodded. "Agreed."

It was not going well. Even from the dock, it was clear that the chemistry of the eight guys was completely off. Some of them couldn't control their oars, never mind pull in unison. One actually smacked the guy behind him. Coach Daniels ordered everyone back to the dock and even watching that laborious journey was painful.

"That was the sloppiest bunch of bladework I've ever seen," Coach said. "Let's hope the next group does better. Sakes alive, it can *only* be better than that."

He started calling names for the next group, including mine and the guy beside me, Orion Mercer.

Orion held out his hand. "That's me."

"Xander Ford," I said, shaking it.

"Let's give 'em hell, eh, mate?"

I took my seat at the bow of the shell, my back to the open water. Orion took the number two seat, his back to me. Tucker Hill and some of the other bigger guys took seats three through six—the "engine room," from which much of the power and speed was generated. Once seats seven and eight were filled, Dean put the megaphone to his mouth.

"Let's do this, gentlemen. Nice and easy."

Once we'd pulled away from the dock, Dean gave the word. Blades went into the water, and we all drove back, pushing with our legs against the foot stretchers under the seats in front of us. Within a few strokes, we'd found our rhythm, moving in time to a digital metronome that Dean controlled to keep us in unison. No longer eight men, we became a unit, inhaling into the drive, exhaling through the recovery, over and over. I kept my focus on the middle of Orion's back, my oar to the left, his to the right. The water glided under us at an impressive speed.

"That's it," Coach called from alongside us. "Rhett, watch your layback. You're leaning too far. Good timing, Knox. Nice form, Orion."

Rhett...

I hadn't recognized him, nor he I, but apparently, I was sharing a shell with the other water balloon bully. Awesome.

The water was smooth but made rougher by the coach's boat swells—likely on purpose, to see what we could handle. I braced my legs, feet pressing hard into the stretchers, thighs screaming as I pulled to keep the boat set.

"Excellent work, Xander," Coach called. "Just excellent. Okay, that's it. I've seen enough. Next group."

Two hours later, after rowing bow seat with various combinations of guys, it was clear no one was better than my first group. Back on land, Coach gathered us around again.

"Some changes coming. I'll post the final team roster on the gym bulletin on Monday morning. If you're on it, you'll get an email with further instructions, such as how to order uniforms, the practice and workout schedule, regatta dates, and the like. Okay? That's all, gentlemen."

Then the coaches and Dean huddled, but not before Dean shot me a surreptitious thumbs up.

"Bloody good show," Orion said, clasping my hand.

"Thanks, but I don't think the rest of the crew agrees." I nodded to where Tucker, Rhett—tall and pale with wicked black eyes—and a few of their buddies stood off to the side, muttering to themselves. All of them shot me dark looks.

Orion waved a hand. "We're the best bow pair of the lot, and they know it. They'll come around." He grinned, flashing perfect white teeth. "See you at first practice."

He joined Tucker and the other guys while I pulled on my sweats and gathered my bag. The guys walked past me, one jostling my shoulder. Hard.

"Don't worry, Brent," Tucker said loudly. "Your position is safe. Ford here won't be able to afford the race goggles, never mind the uniform."

The group laughed and moved on; I overhead Orion telling them to ease off.

"Teamwork makes the dream work," I muttered and shouldered my bag, just as Dean jogged to catch up to me.

"Xander, my man! That was the best bow seat action we've seen in years. Is there anything you can't do?"

"Fit in on my own crew?"

Dean slapped my back. "Nah, Tucker'll come around."

I doubted it. Because the other thing I couldn't do was stop thinking about his girlfriend.

Chapter 10

EMERY

Saturday night. The sun hadn't sunk yet, but once it did, most of the Academy students would head over to the west side, to the abandoned lighthouse. It had once guided ships into the Narragansett a hundred years ago. The bonfire party was an unofficial back-to-school tradition—dancing, drinking, and hooking up.

Going to Cassidy's—the burger place on the north side of Castle Hill near the Bend—was a bonfire night tradition too. The guys wanted to fill up on burgers and fries to soak up all the beer and Jägerbombs. The diner was bustling, with servers in 1950s-era uniforms crisscrossing the black-and-white checkered floor to oldies songs.

Our booth was packed with the seven of us: Tucker and me; Aria Kingston and Rhett Calloway, who'd been together since the eighth grade; Gideon Foster, a gymnast who always seemed to run solo; Orion Mercer; and Elowen. She sat as close to Orion as she could without seeming obvious. Not that I blamed her. Orion was probably one of the best-looking guys in school but had a rep for being a manwhore. Elowen had told me this was the year she'd wear him down and make a boyfriend out of him. That didn't sound very romantic, but then again, my own boyfriend's idea of romance was a date crammed with other people and greasy food, followed by fooling around in the cab of his truck.

Tucker sat beside me, his arm slung across the back of the booth, manspreading under the table so I was squashed between him and Gideon. The conversation meandered around the usual stuff: gossip, who was already hooking up with who, and the upcoming Halloween Festival and dance.

"Everyone got their costumes?" Elowen asked. She glanced up at Orion. "You'd make a fantastic Alfie."

Orion frowned. "Who's that, love?"

"From the show, *Emily in Paris*?" Elowen said, and I didn't miss how her eyes brightened at being called "love."

"Never seen it." Orion grinned. "I already have a costume, anyway. I'm going as Mr. Universe, and this"—he gestured to himself—"is my costume."

Elowen gave him a playful little shove that he completely ignored.

"We got our costumes," Tucker said. "Em and I are going as Ken and Barbie...from the movie."

"Oh my God, perfect," Aria said. "Emery, you're literally Barbie."

"Thanks." *Especially if you mean a girl in a box who doesn't know if she can be herself or was made for someone else to play with.*

I gave my head a shake. "Anyway, Tucker just wants an excuse to go shirtless."

"Damn straight." Tucker laughed and lifted a corner of his T-shirt to show the tight six-pack of his abs. "But also, come on. Me in that fur coat and Em wearing… basically anything? We're a shoo-in for Best Couple."

I suppressed the urge to roll my eyes, but no one disagreed.

"How's the crew looking?" Gideon asked. He was blond and big like Tucker, a specialist on the bar for the men's gymnastics team. "Tryouts earlier today, yeah?"

I sat up straighter and listened intently without looking like I was listening intently. I'd been wondering all day how it had gone for Xander.

Because he's my friend. That's what friends do.

"It was alright," Tucker said. "I think Coach is going to shit-can one of our guys and replace him with a Bender. That new guy, Xander Ford."

My pulse kicked up ten notches and a strange pride filled me, as if I could take credit for Xander. As if his very presence at the school was somehow my doing.

I was dying to hear more, but the waitress appeared. She was middle-aged and tired-looking but offered a warm smile.

"Here you go. Four coffee cabinets and three Diet Cokes." She set the milkshakes in front of the guys, the sodas in front of us girls. "Your food will be right out."

"Thank you *so much*," Rhett said. He was beautiful with his jet-black hair and cheery smile, but his eyes were full of malice. He reminded me of a snake or a shark. When the waitress had gone, he leaned back in his seat. "I'll bet that's Ford's mom."

I stiffened as if someone had kicked me in the stomach while Elowen and Tucker burst out laughing.

"Probably," Tucker said. "We should make sure to tip her extra. If he makes the crew, he'll need the cash."

Rhett keeled into Aria who wore a sly smile while Gideon rolled his eyes with an uneasy chuckle.

"Bloody hell," Orion said with a tight laugh. "You're monsters, the lot of you."

"Or maybe we shouldn't tip her," Tucker said, growing serious. "Maybe it'll keep him from stealing Brent's seat."

"I humbly dissent," Orion said. "As two seat, I can tell you Ford is loads better than Brent. Xander's good. He's stable and smart. I could feel the difference, having him at my back."

"Traitor," Rhett said. "I'm going to tell Brent you said that."

"The fuck do I care?" Orion said. "Do you want to win, or do you want to defend your boyfriend?"

Under the table, Gideon's leg jumped, but no one felt it but me. Rhett laughed and tossed a packet of salt at Orion who deflected it back with a grin.

"So he's good?" Elowen asked, her gaze grazing me on the way up to Orion. "He's a major nerd, from all accounts. Not a jock."

Orion shrugged. "He can't be both? And yes, he's bloody good." He waved a hand at Tucker and Rhett. "And both of these knobs know it."

"We'll see," Tucker said. "The roster isn't finalized, anyway."

The waitress came back and set down baskets of fries, onion rings, burgers, and salads. "Can I bring you anything else?"

Tucker tilted his chin. "Yeah. Tell your son to stick to playing *Dungeons & Dragons* or some shit—ow!" He gripped his side, where I'd elbowed him. Hard.

The waitress wore a perplexed smile. "I'm sorry?"

"Nothing," Aria said with syrupy sweetness. "You may go now."

Rhett was laughing into his napkin while Gideon shook his head and focused on his burger.

"Damn, Em." Tucker rubbed his side. "I'm just playing."

Elowen's clear green eyes were like sharpened knives. "Are you okay, Emery? You seem so on edge lately. Not yourself."

All focus turned to me. I threw a lock of hair over my shoulder. "Nothing's wrong with me. I just think there's no reason to be complete assholes to our waitress," I said, deflecting from defending Xander to defending her. "It's barbaric."

"Here, here," Orion said. "Monsters, I tell you."

Tucker chuckled and gave me a jostling hug. "That's my girl. Always looking out for the little people."

The others laughed, but I didn't miss Aria and Elowen exchanging glances as we dug into our food—the boys with bacon cheeseburgers, the girls with their salads but pinching a fry from the guys now and then.

The conversation turned to Gideon's gymnastics team, and my thoughts wandered to last spring. Five months ago. To the afternoon my dad called me into his study to discuss November's election. If Senator Jerome Hill were reelected, he would consider striking down some environmental regulations that would make Wallace Industries hundreds of millions of dollars richer.

"It'd be beneficial for us to foster good relations with the Hills," Dad had said. "I believe his son, Tucker, is in your class."

By that time, Tucker had been circling me for weeks, cajoling me to let him take me out. He was too loud, too full of himself, too much of everything I didn't want in a boyfriend. But I understood the assignment.

And one night late last spring, I told my father, "I'm going to junior prom with Tucker Hill."

His head snapped up, and something happened that was so rare, so unexpected, it stole my breath. Like a comet that only comes around once in a decade or dawn breaking after the longest, coldest night.

"Emery..." He came around the desk and took my face in his hands. "My girl," he said, and patted my cheek. "Family first, yes? I'm so proud of you."

And then he smiled. At me. My father smiled at me, and it was like the sun coming out...

I still remembered how secure it had felt, basking in the warmth of his approval. His love. Or his version of love. And also how sad it was that I needed to beg for what should have come unconditionally.

Then Tucker nudged me, and I blinked out of the memory. "Hey, Em? You ready? Let's roll." He slapped hands with Rhett and Gideon. "Let's get our drink on."

Our group scooted out of the booth. The boys had left a mess, the girls had hardly touched their salads, and there was no tip. I fished two twenties out of my purse and slipped them under the ketchup bottle.

The waitress was just arriving to clean up. "Thank you," she said quietly.

I smiled back but it wasn't like I'd done anything spectacular; showing basic decency didn't deserve awards. It wasn't even my money, anyway, but what my dad put into my account.

Nothing I'd earned.

But in the parking lot, Tucker held open the door of his black Ford F150, an expectant grin on his face, so maybe I'd earned it after all.

We parked at a lookout spot close to the lighthouse. The sun had sunk away, leaving the truck cab dark and stifling, the windows fogged so that I couldn't see the ocean in front of us. Tucker's hands were all over me—along my thighs in my skinny jeans, up my shirt, then in my hair, then at the back of my head, pushing me toward his lap.

I'd done this dozens of times, but that night, his touch made me want to scream, as if I were trapped and suffocating in my own skin.

I shoved him away and sat up. "I'm not in the mood."

Tucker threw up his hands, then brought them down onto the steering wheel. "Oh, come on, Em. I'm on the brink." He turned on a winning grin. "Don't leave me hanging."

I faced him. "Aren't you tired of this?"

"Tired of only getting head? Yes."

"I meant, this." I gestured around the cab. "The same thing, every weekend. Cassidy's with the gang. Then we park somewhere, you get off, and we call it a night."

He frowned. "You haven't complained before."

"Well, I'm complaining now," I snapped and cursed Xander Ford.

One thing I'd managed to remember from math class was the concept of a shared property—something multiple situations had in common. Over the past few days, situations that had been normal in my world were suddenly flipped upside down, and Xander was why. I'd all but forced myself to forget about him, and now, suddenly, he was a default setting—the place my mind and heart went to first.

Ridiculous. We were ten years old. Why does it feel like so much?

"So…what?" Tucker was asking. "You want romance? I told you, babe, it's not my thing." He reached out and brushed his knuckles against my cheek. "But I'll always take care of you. No matter what."

"I can take care of myself."

He burst out laughing, then coughed. "Sure, you can."

My eyes flashed. "You don't believe me?"

"Princess—"

"Don't call me that."

"*Emery.* Be real. You are, like, the perfect woman. Perfect face, perfect tits, perfect ass…you're the whole package. You don't have to *do* anything because you already *have* everything. Why not just enjoy it?"

He leaned in to try to kiss me, but I pulled away, arms crossed.

Tucker sat back, facing forward. A muscle ticked in his jaw. "Your dad loves me, you know."

"So?"

"I'm just saying, if you're holding out on me because you think he'd be pissed, he won't." He glanced at me sideways. "Unless there's some weird purity thing going on?"

"Ugh, gross. Can we please just go?"

Tucker hit the ignition and spoke over the roar of the truck. "I'm just saying, Em. I have needs. A guy can be happy with appetizers only for so long before he needs a real meal. That's just science."

Science. The word instantly conjured Xander Ford. Because of course it did. My default setting. I should be my own default setting, and yet…

Tucker was frustrated, but so was I. Xander Ford was frustrating as hell, in ways I couldn't explain, even to myself. Thinking about him made me mad and warm and irritated and like I wanted to laugh, all at the same time.

We're just friends, I thought, trying to hold onto the irritation. But I had to turn my face to the window so Tucker wouldn't see my smile.

Castle Hill Lighthouse perched on the western tip of the peninsula—the toe of the boot—and was abandoned a long time ago. The lighthouse keeper's house had taken on a mythical, haunted status, and many people had tried and failed over the years to break in and climb up the tower. I don't know who started it, but building a ginormous bonfire became the tradition: a new beacon of light while the old one stood rotting.

By the time Tucker pulled into the beach parking lot, the fire was roaring. A burst of orange and yellow against a dark sky full of stars, with the ocean beyond. A fat moon hung low in the sky, leaving a golden trail in the black water. At least a hundred students were camped on the grassy dunes of coarse, white sand, some with chairs and blankets, others standing in groups. Others, mostly guys, threw broken crates, driftwood, and beer packaging into the flames.

Tucker spotted some friends near the fire. "There's Brent and Rory. Be right back, babe," he said and jogged to greet his bros. I saw Delilah and Sierra talking with some people. I contemplated letting loose and getting wasted; there were coolers full of hard tea and beer on the side of the bonfire. But I wasn't much of a drinker, and I'd hardly had anything to eat. If I got wasted, Tucker would get lucky. At least mostly.

I wasn't hung up on sex, no matter what he might've thought. I just wanted…something more.

Something more was fast becoming my motto for this school year.

Instead of heading for Delilah and Sierra, I wandered among the groups, chatting briefly with a few people but still looking, though I wasn't sure who or what I was looking for.

And then I found Xander.

He stood with Dean Yearwood and Harper on the outer edge of the bonfire. They were all holding bottles of beer, and Dean was regaling them with some story that made them laugh. Harper and Xander looked good together. They made sense. Not like him and me, which was ridiculous anyway. He was a genius, and I was going to be Barbie for Halloween.

I turned up the hood of my pink sweatshirt and kept wandering until I found myself at the side of the lighthouse keeper's house—boarded and locked up. I sat down on a bench that faced the ocean and took it in. Students walked by now and then, but mostly people left me alone. It felt nice being alone. Thoughts of Grant came to me. I wondered if he'd ever sat here during his senior year. If he worried about how to break away from Dad's plans and be himself too. He must have, I thought, listening to the ocean's little roars and hisses and missing him.

After a while, Xander appeared, beer bottle still in hand. He wore jeans, an old jacket, and ratty Converse, his tall frame lean with muscle. But then, everyone was tall to me.

"Am I interrupting?" he asked in a quiet tone.

"Not at all," I said, smiling because I realized I came to this bench to be alone, and Xander was the only person I wanted to be alone with.

"Would you like something to drink? I can get you a beer or something."

"No, thank you." I nodded at the vast black ocean under the vast black sky. "It's pretty out here, isn't it?" I scooted over on the bench. "Here. Sit."

"Thanks." Xander sat down next to me.

Like being on our rock with him again...

The bench was small, and our arms touched along the lengths of his jacket and my sweatshirt. His denim-clad thigh brushed mine. Little tingles and shivers ran over my skin at all those junctures, but I told myself I was just cold.

"I heard you kicked ass at the row tryouts," I said.

"Yeah, but I don't think I made any friends, your boyfriend among them."

"Why not?"

"Because I'm going to take his buddy's seat on the crew."

"Quite confident about that, aren't you?" I teased.

Xander shrugged one shoulder. "The coach seems to know what he's doing; it would be stupid not to give it to me. Orion and I make a good bow pair."

"What's a bow pair?"

"First and second seat on the shell, responsible for stability and…" He waved a hand. "We don't have to talk about rowing."

"I think it's interesting," I said. "You're good at rowing, but you're also good at math and physics and everything else."

"I wouldn't say everything else," Xander said. "All of the social stuff still feels alien."

"You're doing all right."

"Am I? There's a common perception that people with extremely high IQs struggle with social connection."

"But it's not true?"

"No, it's completely true."

I laughed and nudged his arm. "Be serious."

"It's true in my case, anyway." He turned his gaze to me. "But someone once told me I just needed to practice at a regular school." He took a sip of beer. "What about you? How is your senior year going?"

I smiled dryly. "You mean aside from needing constant math tutoring so my dad doesn't disown me? Great."

"And if you pass calculus?"

"I'll go to Brown. That will make him happy."

Xander frowned. "What about what makes *you* happy? Imagine you're on a precipice, looking out over your future. What do you see?"

I made a face. "You're awfully philosophical for a scientist."

"Physics is founded on philosophy. Before there were labs or telescopes or calculus classes, there were ideas."

"Oh, that's right. It's one of your *three* degrees," I teased.

"Yes, but we're talking about you, remember?" he said gently.

My smile faded. "There's not much to say. When I look out over the precipice, so to speak, I just see the future my dad has planned for me. It's like a cold, gray canyon filled with all the luxury and security I could possibly want, but I don't see myself in it anywhere." I gave Xander a look. "Didn't we talk about this the other day?"

"Yes, but I wonder if..."

"What?"

"No, it's too personal," he said. "Or...rude. I don't know how to be anything but blunt and direct."

"Just the facts, eh? Go ahead. I can take it."

Xander heaved a breath. "This is your life, Emery. I wonder if maybe you don't know that it belongs to you and not to your father."

A defensive retort came to my lips but then died. I turned and faced the ocean. "My entire life, I've been trained to know my place in the family and to do what's expected of me. To go to the college Dad wants and date the boy he needs me to date... I mean, I go out with Tucker, and I don't even question it. I just...*obey*, and at the same time, I'm desperate to make my dad proud and to hear, just once, that he loves me." I glanced up. "That's pretty pathetic, isn't it?"

"It's not pathetic. It's all you've known," he said. "And it's daunting to break out of rigid family structures."

"It's downright terrifying," I said. "If you met my dad, you'd see why."

Xander grimaced, almost angry. "Maybe it would help to spend some time visualizing what you want instead."

"Like, manifesting?" I grinned. "How unscientific of you."

"More like counterprogramming," he said. "Pretend for a minute that that future doesn't exist and you get to make one yourself. What does it look like?"

I inhaled the cold salt air and closed my eyes. "I see myself far away from my house. Far from Rhode Island. At UCLA, like my teacher suggested. I see a sunny drafting room and me sketching and designing and making someone's home beautiful. And not super-wealthy megahouses but cozy, safe spaces. Homes."

I looked up to see Xander watching me with an intensity in his eyes that I couldn't describe. A feeling came with that gaze, like a channel from him to me, that made me feel heard. And safe. The atmosphere I wanted to build for others, Xander was making it for me, right there on that bench under the moonlight.

With maximum effort, I tore my eyes away. Because I couldn't stay on this bench with him forever, just like I couldn't stay at the park with him seven years ago. I had to leave his warmth and return to the cold prison of my life. Breaking free... My stomach twisted at the thought, so I pushed it away and put on a smile.

"Anyway, I'm going to design the senior prom and show them what I'm capable of. I'm hoping that once they see that it's what I love and that maybe I'm good at it, they might give me a shot."

"Emery—"

"Please, Xander," I whispered. "I don't want to talk about it anymore. Okay?"

Xander seemed to wrestle with his thoughts, then nodded. "Okay."

After a few silent minutes, things grew easy between us again. Xander took a pull from his beer, which was still nearly full. He made a sour expression that was kind of adorable, scrunching his nose under his glasses.

I grinned. "Not a fan?"

"Not really, but I thought I'd give it a try, and now it's warm." He peered over his shoulder at the bonfire. "This is a public beach. How is everyone getting away with the underage drinking?"

"The cops know the tradition," I said. "Certain families take care of them—financially—to ensure that we all get home safe. Just another perk of this totally-normal-but-not-normal school. Speaking of, how is that going? Even the AP-est of AP classes must be so easy for you."

"It's fine."

I nudged him again. "Come on. Don't start bullshitting me now. You must be so bored."

"To be honest, yes. Imagine if you went back to first grade…" He shook his head. "Sorry, that sounds insulting—"

"*Xander*. Stop apologizing for being smart. Tell me."

"Okay, well, I had thought coming here—my

Experiment, as I like to call it—would be good for me socially. And good for my dad, because it makes him happy to be here. But my brain is going a thousand miles an hour, and it's all just…passing me by."

"What is?"

"All that's out there to be known." Xander turned his head up to the sky, and I imagined he was encompassing the entire galaxy in his eyes, trying to make sense of it all. "I don't like mystery."

I frowned. "That seems weird for someone in your line of work."

"I love working toward solving that which is mysterious, but I hate sitting in it, unprepared or…undefended. I want to measure and calculate and predict so that I'm never…"

"Never what?"

Xander turned to me. "Never caught off guard again."

I nodded, hearing the day his mother left him behind his words.

"What about love?" I asked, not quite looking at him. Not quite sure why I asked in the first place.

"What about it?" he asked slowly.

"Love is mysterious and unpredictable. It can't be measured, it just…is. It's forever."

"Not always," Xander said, his expression growing dark. "My father has told me a hundred times that my mother was 'the one' from the moment he saw her. Felt it in his bones, he said. And she still left him. She left me. A mother's love is supposed to be a constant in the universe.

Unconditional. They lift cars and move mountains for their kids. They're not supposed to leave. They're not supposed to say they'll come back and then not come back."

"Like a broken promise," I said softly, realizing he'd likely felt that too when he thought I'd been ignoring his letters.

Xander nodded. He seemed so sad, and I felt it in my own heart. As if I'd lost something too because he did.

"So you don't believe in true love?"

"I don't believe it's forever," he said. "I believe it exists in finite moments, not infinite waves."

I met his eyes. "I used to think that way too until..."

"Until what?"

You came back.

My face flushed at the sudden, wild thought, and I had to look away. "Well...my brother, for instance. Grant is gone, but my love for him is infinite. It's never going to go away, even if he did." I brightened and nudged his arm again, steering us into safer territory. "And anyway, isn't it the not-knowing that makes it risky? And thrilling?"

He gave me a hesitant grin. "Are we talking about love or science?"

"Both."

"In science, there is no greater thrill than a breakthrough. But love has only ever hurt."

A heavy silence fell, where I itched to comfort him the way he comforted me. To send a wave of safety to him so he wouldn't feel so alone either.

"Wow," I said. "We always seem to get into stuff deep, don't we?"

"Yeah, we do."

"I'm just trying to keep your supersharp mind from being so bored. Is it working?"

"Yes, you're very good at being interesting."

I grinned. "I'm *interesting*?"

He looked shy. "To say the least. Anyway, I signed up for this, so I shouldn't complain. Plus, MIT is sending me course materials, and I'm doing Feynman equations in my spare time."

"I'm not even going to ask what those are. And hey, you're doing calculus with me."

"That helps too."

I suspected he was just saying that to make me feel better, but I took it. "Just doing my part to keep things *interesting*," I said with a smile. "But I hope being here isn't a total bust."

He smiled back. "It's been…adequate."

"What would it take to make it more than adequate?"

Xander's gaze lingered on me a moment more, then settled on the ocean. "Ask me again another time."

I frowned at his strange answer and huddled deeper into my sweatshirt as a sudden shiver ran through me, pleasant and tingly. The autumn wind bit at my skin but felt nice against my flushed cheeks.

For a while, neither of us spoke. The silence didn't need filling. We just sat together, watching the black waves, their white crests glowing under the silver moon.

It was perfect, and like that one day seven years ago, I felt safe with him. I'd felt like I could tell him anything and his touch could keep me from harm. Now, though, Xander was nearly a man.

The moonlight etched his face in silver and shadow, showing off his features—his defined jaw, pointed nose, and full lips. His eyes, though, with their blue and brown, framed by stylish square glasses, were the most beautiful part of his face. His thick brown hair fell over his left eye, as if to hide the ways he stood out, just like he hid his genius: You'd notice eventually, but he'd never draw attention to it.

I'll bet he's smarter than I can imagine.

The thought sent a tingle through me, and I actually had to press my thighs together. I shifted, our hands brushed, and the sensation intensified. This was exactly how we'd been sitting together when we were ten…and exactly not.

Something more…

The warm, safe energy was still there but tinged with heat too. Electricity. Xander probably knew a name for how thick and buzzy the air suddenly felt, but I didn't dare ask him.

I broke his heart, even if I didn't mean to. And he's too smart for me, anyway. I'd eventually bore him too. I belong with someone like Tucker. The Prom King and the Queen Bee. Ken and Barbie.

The thought made me sad down to my bones and killed the buzz instantly. Tucker was who my dad wanted for me. He would never let me have someone like Xander. A Bend kid—even a genius headed to MIT—wasn't going to cut it. No connections, no wealth. Nothing to bring to the table.

Because while I saw all the ways Xander was rich in things that had nothing to do with money, my dad would only see that he wasn't enough.

Chapter 11

XANDER

I'M IN BIG TROUBLE.

Listening to Emery talk about her dreams and aspirations under the moonlight...she was a pretty girl, but her inner beauty was almost physically painful to behold. It transcended all standard conventions and became something else. Something more. This girl possessed an intrinsic luminosity, the absolute magnitude of which was apparent only to me in that moment, sitting beside her. Instead of reflecting another source of illumination, she *was* the illumination.

Stop. That way lies pain...

"The stars are *so* beautiful," Emery said, breaking me from my thoughts. She peered at me from under the thick fringe of her bangs. "That's your brand of physics. Stars and gravity and black holes."

"Astrophysics, yes."

Emery nodded. "Grant's death was like a black hole opening in our family. All that light, just…gone."

I nodded, my heart heavy for her. "I know it's not the same thing, but I think of my mother leaving in similar terms. An impenetrable absence."

Emery turned to me with a wan smile. "I love that—not what it is, but how you describe it." Her hands twisted in her lap. "I think it's worse for my brother, Jack. He was closer to Grant than I was."

I waited while she watched the ocean swell and crash, over and over.

"Our parents had Grant, then seven years later had Jack, then me. Jack says he was insurance in case Grant didn't do what my dad wanted and that they kept going until they got a girl."

"That sounds…coldly pragmatic," I said.

"For my dad, everyone is either an asset or commodity, a profit or a loss." Her voice fell to a whisper. "Grant was a loss."

"I'm so very sorry about Grant," I said. "I could say it a million more times, and I know it wouldn't help anything, but—"

"It helps that you say his name. We're not allowed to say his name," she whispered, as if afraid of being overheard. Her eyes glistened with unshed tears. "We're not allowed to talk about him or tell stories or even look at photos."

My hand rested near hers, and I fought the urge to

touch her. Seven years ago, she'd rested her head on my shoulder. If she did that again, I would wrap my arms around her and hold her. Even though I wasn't allowed to. Even if it was the exact opposite of keeping my heart safe. If I touched her now, I wouldn't let go.

"Xander?"

I swallowed hard. "Yeah?"

Emery turned her face up to mine. "Do you think…?"

"What?"

"I was going to ask if you thought it was possible to break away from the ideas people have of you. The expectations?"

"I don't know," I said. "Maybe it depends on one's escape velocity."

"What's that?"

"In astrophysics, escape velocity is the minimum speed an object must achieve to break free from the gravitational pull of a planet or star."

She nodded. "So maybe in real life, the velocity is how hard someone tries. The harder they try, the better the chance of breaking free."

Emery was looking at me like she was asking for help. For someone to be on her fucking side and tell her she was luminous and alive, instead of stealing her light and making her doubt herself.

"I think that's exactly right," I said fiercely.

"But what if it's not a planet or sun you're trying to break free from? What if it's a black hole that sucks all the light out of you? What then?"

"I think the person needs to keep trying," I said in a low voice. "No matter what. So that their light never goes out."

Her smile was beautiful and delicate, laced with tears she quickly blinked away. "There we go again, getting all deep and stuff." She put her hand on mine. "Thank you."

I swallowed hard, and before I could stop myself, my fingers entwined with hers. The moment lingered. In this moonlight, Emery had a fragile beauty that belied the strength she had in her. More than she even knew. I wanted to pluck it out and show her. Because for all her hurt and doubt, her heart was still open, while mine was shut and locked.

But maybe…

Emery pressed her palm fully into mine, and without moving, I could feel myself lean into her and her into me. Her breath was warm and sweet—it would take nothing to close the short distance between us…

Male voices cut through the moment, ruining it. We snatched our hands back as Tucker and two of his buddies rounded the corner. One was Brent, the soon-to-be-former bow seat.

"Emery! There's my baby doll. I've been looking all over for you. We're going on a packy run, and we need someone to drive—" Tucker stopped short, blinking glassy eyes. "What's going on?"

Emery seemed at a loss. "Oh. I was just… We were…"

"I'm tutoring Emery in calculus," I said smoothly.

"Uh huh." Tucker addressed Emery but his eyes were on me. "You never said anything about any tutoring, Em."

"That's because it's not a big deal." Emery got to her feet. "You know how my dad is about math. Xander's going to help me." She took his arm. "Let's go."

He didn't move; her pushing at him was like pushing against a tree trunk.

Tucker pinned me with a hard, flat stare. "Now, hold on. There's something about this little scene that I don't like."

I wondered if he really could see that there was something more going on, but Tucker was drunk, and his brain's temporal lobe was likely overcrowded with all of the individual Bend kids he'd tormented over the years.

"It's *nothing*," Emery was telling him.

He ignored her and took a step toward me. I stood up, gripping my beer bottle tightly. Tucker had three inches and thirty pounds on me—an uneven match-up without factoring in his buddies.

"I get that you're tutoring my girlfriend, but what is happening right now? Like, under the stars and shit. The two of you all cozy on the bench."

"Tucker, leave it," Emery said.

"We just happened to run into each other," I said. "We're working out our tutoring schedule."

"How complicated is a fucking schedule?"

"I wanted Emery to be prepared for some adjustments." I smiled flatly. "My afternoons will change once I'm added to the crew."

Brent's eyes flared. "Fuck you, asshole! You're not making shit—"

Tucker shoved Brent back, his eyes on me. "Pretty fucking cocky, Ford."

I shrugged. "It's just science."

Emery let out a strange, sudden laugh, then swallowed it down. "Come on, Tucker. Let's go."

Tucker let himself be led away but leveled a finger at me. "I'm on to you, dude. Just know, I'm watching you."

"Duly noted."

As they walked off, Brent flipped me the bird. I let out a shaky breath, my heart pounding for narrowly avoiding having the shit kicked out of me by a factor of three. I would've lost, but I wouldn't have gone down easily. Not when Tucker and his meathead friends ruined what had almost been a perfect moment…

Then Emery glanced over her shoulder, her eyes soft and apologetic. She curled her finger at me, twice, and suddenly, the night didn't feel so ruined.

Until I heard her scream.

Chapter 12

EMERY

I walked away from Xander with Tucker and his friends, each step more painful than the last, and arrived at the bonfire just in time to see my brother pull his hand out of the flames.

What am I looking at...?

It felt like a dream—or a nightmare. Jack held up his smoldering fist as if he were holding a torch. But the torch was his own hand. Then he fell to his knees and began to laugh.

A scream tore out of my throat. I shoved people aside as I rushed to my brother and fell to my knees beside him. Immediately, two sensations flooded my senses: the smell of burnt flesh and the sound of Jack's moans. His skin was blackened in some places, angry red in others, and his hand locked in a tight clench.

I put my arm around his waist, and he held his injured arm out of the way so it wouldn't touch anything. "Jack, what happened?"

His answer was a strangled cry of agony. Murmurs and whispers came from all sides.

"Did anyone see it?"

"I think he fell in."

"I think he was pushed…"

I glared up at Tucker, standing stupidly, mouth hanging open.

"Do something!" I screamed at him and the onlookers. "Someone call an ambulance!"

"I'll drive him to the hospital," Dean Yearwood said, he and Harper appearing by my side. "It's faster than waiting."

I nodded mutely as Dean took hold of Jack from the other side. The two of us dragged my brother across the sand, then the asphalt. Harper jogged in front of us, pushing through students to create a path. It took all three of us to get Jack into the back seat of Dean's car. Immediately the stench of the burn—sickly sweet—mixed with the scent of alcohol from Jack's breath filled the interior. I was glad he was drunk. Maybe it kept him from feeling all of the pain. Jack moaned a constant keening wail, but I had to wonder how much was for his hand and how much was for his heart.

Because he kept talking about Grant.

"It's all bullshit, Emery," he said, half crying, his head lolling on the back of the seat. "For years, they tell us…

But it's lies, you know? They killed Grant. They killed him…"

"Shh, it's okay, Jack," I whispered. "Everything's going to be okay."

But looking at his hand, that felt like the worst lie.

Dean dove into the driver's seat, and Harper sat on the other side of Jack. The two of us sandwiched him in, holding him steady while Dean tore out of the parking lot. Castle Hill didn't have a real hospital, only a medical center, and it was closed for the night. Dean sped north, to Newport. I held Jack and talk soothingly into his ear, hoping to take his mind off the pain and charred nightmare of his fist.

Finally, Dean screeched up to the hospital's emergency room entrance. He threw the car into park and jumped out. "Help us! Someone help us, please," he cried, waving his arms.

Medical personnel came pouring outside.

"What happened?" a doctor asked while carefully extracting my brother from the car.

"We were at a bonfire at the Castle Hill Lighthouse," Dean said, shooting me a glance. "I think he fell. He's pretty drunk."

The doctor nodded grimly as they loaded Jack onto a stretcher. Once he was secure, the team hustled him inside, and then he was gone.

In the waiting room, I sagged against the wall. The adrenaline that had been coursing through my veins bottomed out, and a flood of tears swamped me. Dean and Harper helped me to a chair.

"You want us to call your mom or dad?" Dean asked.

"I'll do it." I pulled out my cell phone, and it fell out of my shaking hands. Harper picked it up and handed it back to me.

"Emery," Dean said before I could dial. "I didn't know what to tell the doctor, or if Jack might get in trouble or something, but you should know. He didn't fall."

Harper nodded. "He said something about a train and then he reached into the fire."

My eyes fell shut and I thought I was going to be sick all over again.

Oh, Jack.

"Okay," I whispered. "Okay. Let me just…I'll tell them."

Dean and Harper moved away to let me call my dad.

He answered on the second ring with a curt, "Yes?"

"I'm at Newport Hospital. It's Jack."

"What happened?" Dad asked with a slight tinge of urgency in his tone.

"His hand… We were at the bonfire and…he burned his hand. It's pretty bad. He needs help, Daddy. He needs—"

"Was he drunk?"

"What—? Daddy, just come, please. Newport Hospital."

"Calm down, Emery, and don't say anything to anyone. I'll be right there."

The line went quiet, and I let the phone fall to my lap. Harper sat with me while Dean talked to the nurses at the front desk.

"Do you want some water?" Harper asked. "Coffee?"

"Water, please," I rasped. I felt as if I'd been lost in a desert. Harper returned quickly with a paper cup. "Thank you for helping tonight."

"Of course."

She and Dean sat on either side of me as we waited. Finally, my father arrived with Colin, his driver and unofficial bodyguard.

I rushed to him, then stopped when I saw no one else was with them. "Where's Mom?"

"She's indisposed," Dad said tightly, glancing between Dean and Harper, who flanked me. To them, he said, "This is a family matter. You may go."

"Daddy!" I cried, mortified. "If it weren't for Dean, we'd still be at the beach waiting for an ambulance."

My father offered Dean his hand. "I appreciate your quick thinking, son, but this issue is a private one."

"Sure, sure," Dean said, and glanced at me. "Keep us posted, okay?"

I nodded as Harper gave my hand a squeeze, and then they headed out.

Dad glanced around. "Who is the doctor in charge?"

"I don't know. They're working on Jack. They took him back somewhere and told us to wait."

Grayson Wallace was not about to wait. He went to the nurse's station with Colin and started making demands. I sank back into my chair and waited for what felt like an eternity before a doctor appeared.

"Wallace family?"

I jumped up. "Yes."

My father indicated a quiet corner where we should talk. "What's the situation?" he asked once we were out of earshot.

"I'm not going to beat around the bush," the doctor said. His badge read *Baker*. "Jack has sustained second- and third-degree burns over approximately eighty percent of his left hand and wrist."

My dad stiffened. "What does that mean? Does he keep his hand?"

Oh God...

The doctor nodded. "He will. It's a matter of how much damage—if any—was done to his tendons, nerves, and muscles. I estimate he's facing at least one skin graft surgery and rehabilitation. The burn specialist, Dr. O'Connell, will do a thorough assessment tomorrow morning."

"How is Jack?" I asked in a small voice.

"He's sedated and resting with painkillers." Dr. Baker turned to my dad. "I have to tell you, sir, his blood alcohol content was .15 percent, which is extremely high and extraordinarily dangerous."

My father's lips made a thin line. "So he fell. He fell into the fire like a drunkard."

I started to protest. "That's not—"

"Accidents like this happen when one is that careless," he snapped.

Dr. Baker's eyes went between us, and he cleared his throat. "Yes, well, we have him on antibiotics to prevent infection, but I think he has a long road ahead of him."

"Fine, thank you. Let's go, Emery."

I stared. "We're *leaving*?"

"You heard the doctor. We can't see him right now. He's unconscious or sleeping it off. We'll come back in the morning at a reasonable hour."

I stared helplessly at Dr. Baker, who shot me sympathetic look. "He's sedated," he told me gently. "He'll be better suited for visitors tomorrow."

"Thank you," I said, because he was giving me permission to leave without being eaten alive by guilt.

I followed my dad to the parking lot. Colin held open the door to the sedan, and we climbed inside.

"Daddy," I said into the quiet before Colin started the car. "I heard that maybe…maybe it wasn't an accident. He didn't fall. I think Jack…" I swallowed hard, my voice shaky. "I think he needs help. Since Grant died, he needs—"

"We do not speak of that," my father replied. "But yes, I agree. Your brother needs help. Perhaps at a rehab facility or boarding school or military academy, where he can get his head on straight."

"No, Daddy. I meant—"

"Be silent, Emery. I've had enough for one evening."

I snapped my mouth shut, anger flaring. *He's* had enough? He didn't see Jack's charred hand. He didn't smell the burnt flesh or…

I squeezed my eyes shut and vowed to be at the hospital first thing in the morning, with or without my dad.

My phone buzzed with a text; it had been buzzing all

night. I had at least twenty missed messages. Each was more disgusting than the last—just people eager for gossip and drama.

Except for one. Xander.

> You don't have to answer, but I hope Jack is okay.
> And that you are too.

I smiled and turned away from my father, toward the window, where the night was as black as ever, and typed a reply.

> It's not good. Probably needs skin grafts. We'll know more tomorrow.

Xander's follow-up text was instant. How can I help?
I smiled. You just did. Just being there helps.

> Do you want to talk?

I glanced at my dad. Can't now. But thank you.
The rolling dots came and went. Then again. Xander was wrestling with what to say. Finally, a new text popped up.

> I wish I'd been there for you tonight.

My vision blurred as tears filled my eyes. Before I could reply, he sent another.

> I wish I'd been there for you so many nights. I probably shouldn't say that, but I feel like we lost seven years.

I quickly replied, "I do too."
My dad heard my sniffling and glanced my way.

> I have to go. Goodnight, Xander.
> Goodnight, Emery.

And before I knew what I was doing, I sent a red heart emoji and then tucked my phone away.

Sunday morning, I was awake before dawn. I was still dressed in my jeans and sweatshirt from the night before. I wouldn't have cared, but the sweatshirt smelled like smoke. I changed my shirt, brushed my hair and teeth, and ran downstairs. Jack may have acted like he hated me these past few years, but the thought of him waking up alone made me sick.

Muffled voices met me as I neared the kitchen. I peeked inside to see my mother, still in her nightgown and robe, sitting on a stool at the island and my father leaning against the counter opposite her. He wore a scowl while she glared back at him through bleary eyes.

"Enough is enough, Grayson," she hissed. "What more do you want? We've already lost—"

"Don't say it," he cut her off with a slashing motion.

Mom slid off the stool and tightened her robe around her. "I'm saying no. I know you don't like that, but for once, I'm saying it. He stays. He stays before you run him out the door too."

My heart thudded in my chest, and I stepped into the kitchen as my mother made her way out. She stopped short to see me. "Emery…"

"We're going to the hospital now, right?" I looked between her and my dad's red face and angry glare. "To see Jack?"

Mom nodded. "In a bit. I need to get dressed. I need to…prepare."

She stepped past me, and I looked to Dad. "Well?"

He gritted his teeth, arms crossed in quiet fury for having been told "no." I guessed he'd told her his plan to send Jack somewhere terrible and she'd vetoed it. A first, as far as I knew.

"Daddy…?"

"Not now, Emery," he snapped and walked past me. "I have some things to wrap up. I'll be along shortly."

I stood alone in the big kitchen, listening to the silence and feeling time ticking away. Then I grabbed my keys and headed out.

―

At Newport Hospital, I gave Jack's name and received directions to the fourth floor burn ward. His private room, purchased for him by our father, looked more like a suite. Not because our dad wanted him to have the best, but because he wanted to keep the news of this incident from spreading.

A doctor—a middle-aged woman with reddish hair—was just stepping out. She looked relieved to see me.

"Oh, hello. Are you family?"

"I'm Jack's sister, Emery."

"Hi Emery, I'm Dr. O'Connell. I'm in charge of your brother's care while he's here."

"How is he? I mean, how bad is it?"

"What we're seeing is encouraging, actually," she said. "Initial assessments last night were grim, but after careful evaluation and preliminary treatment, I'm happy to report that the damage wasn't as severe as we'd thought."

I breathed a sigh of relief. "Oh, thank God."

"To be clear, Jack has sustained serious burns that will require him to wear special dressings for weeks to prevent infection. That he clenched his hand into a fist likely saved his fingers, and there's no underlying damage to fascia or tissues, which means I think he can avoid surgery. We'll keep him here a few more days and keep a close eye."

"That all sounds really good," I said. "Can I see him?"

Dr. O'Connell's gaze flickered over my shoulder, looking for the parents that were surely racing down the hall to their son… Seeing no one else, her brow furrowed, and she gave me a smile.

"Go on in. He's awake, but the painkillers are strong. He might not be himself."

I nodded as if I knew what Jack was like as himself. He'd hardly spoken to me in years.

The doctor left, and I knocked. "Jack?"

"Go away," came a tired voice.

I stepped inside anyway. Jack was lying in the bed, the head elevated, staring out the window at the parking lot below. His left hand was wrapped in a strange, gauzy-looking glove, and he had IV lines trailing out of his elbow. His face was pale against his dark hair, but he looked okay. Better than I'd expected, just like the doctor had said.

"Hey," I said, slowly drawing closer. "How are you feeling?"

"Great. Never better."

"Jack—"

"What do you want, Emery?" he snapped, his clear blue eyes—eyes like Dad's—turning to glare daggers at me.

"Why are you so mad at me? Why are you *always* so mad at me?" I waved a hand. "Never mind. I don't want to argue. I just wanted to see you and make sure you're okay."

"It's a little late for that," he muttered.

I took a seat beside his bed. Closer, I could see gel smeared down the skin of his forearm below the gauzy mitt. I wished Mom were here to smooth his hair and tell him she'd take care of him. And that Dad would sit beside him and vow to help him through whatever he might be struggling with that made him do such a thing…

But those were fantasy parents. All he had right then was me.

"Jack," I said, trying again. "*Why?*"

My brother's gaze moved to the ceiling, shining with tears. "Because I had to get it out."

"Get what out?"

"All this pain," he said, his voice a whisper. "For Grant. I feel like I'm going to explode because Mom and Dad don't…" He swallowed hard, and a tear slid down his cheek. "So my brilliant drunk idea was to force it out. Just…reach into the fire and grab it and show them."

Tears flooded my vision. "Oh, Jack."

He sniffed and wiped his eyes with his good hand. "But whatever. They don't care."

"Mom is coming," I said quickly. "She's just slow and Dad said—"

"Ah, there it is. The Emery Excuse Express, right on schedule."

"What? No, I'm just—"

"You want to know why I'm pissed at you, Emery? Because you do this every time. Make excuses for them. Defend them."

"I'm not defending them. I just wanted you to know they're coming soon—"

"Oh, thank fucking God, they're coming *soon*." Jack rolled his eyes, his voice thick with bitter sarcasm. "Good to know. Next time I'll stick my head in the fireplace and see if that gets them to pick up the pace."

The image sent a cold shiver down my spine. "Don't say that. I'm not making excuses. I just…"

I don't want you to feel so alone.

But he was right. We were both alone in this and on opposite sides of the field. "I feel like if I don't keep trying, it will all fall apart," I said in a small voice.

Jack sighed. "It fell apart a long time ago, Em. When Grant died."

I glanced at the door and leaned closer. "Last night you said some things. I don't know if you remember. About Grant. You said…you said they killed him."

Jack stared at me for a long moment, conflicted, a hundred thoughts behind his eyes, as if he were struggling between what to say and what to keep to himself.

"I'm tired, Emery," he said finally, turning away. "I'm so tired. I want to sleep now."

"Jack…"

"Go back to your pep rallies and your boyfriend and your dances."

I bit back tears. "That's not fair."

"No, I mean it," he said, his eyes fluttering shut. "You're better off. It's better if you…"

But he took whatever he was going to say into sleep. I sat with him for a while, wiping my tears, and then I left.

Chapter 13

XANDER

I jerked awake, having dreamt I was in a symphony hall listening to a jangling rendition of one of Chopin's nocturnes, then realized it was coming from our rickety old piano downstairs. It was dark still; my digital clock radio on the bedside table read 4:14 a.m.

I shuffled downstairs in my sweats and T-shirt. Dad was at the piano in his pajamas, hair askew.

"Xander!" he cried, still playing. "Not bad, eh? Your old man still has it. Come play with me. Let's duet like we used to."

"Dad, it's four in the morning."

"Come. Sit." He stopped playing to pat the bench beside him. "What shall it be? A little Mozart? Perhaps some Schubert?"

I rubbed my eyes and glanced over at his desk, strewn

with papers, each covered with equations. I bent to get a closer look.

"*No!*" Dad tore from the piano, grabbed his papers, and bunched them protectively to his chest. "Not yet. I can't share this with anyone. Not even my own precious son. If the information got into the wrong hands, God knows what untold horrors might be unleashed upon the planet."

Paranoia. This is new.

My stomach twisted. "What do you mean?"

"I mean, Xander, that I'm close. So close."

"To a unified theory?"

"Indeed, my boy. Complete and utter comprehension of the world." Dad's eyes were wide and alight from within. "Newton thought he had it. Einstein too, then he lost it. Then came Heisenberg with his uncertainties, who said it must remain unknowable, and then Schrödinger with his wave functions, who said it was not. But they were all missing one piece of the puzzle. Like the very paradoxical nature of particle-wave duality itself, they were all correct and yet all wrong at the same time!"

"And you think you've found the last piece?" I asked dubiously, yet my pulse quickened just the same. My dad was a genius, very nearly on par with the greats he just named. Was it possible…?

"It's there, Xander," Dad said, taking a seat at his desk and rifling through his papers. "Just outside of my reach but *right there*. I can feel it."

I stepped back, uncertainty swirling in my gut that

perhaps my dad was afflicted with his own kind of duality—that he was telling the truth but that unlocking such a discovery might come at the cost of his own mind.

"Okay, Dad, I'll leave you to it."

"Thank you, my boy. Thank you…"

In our little kitchen, I made coffee and set one mug down beside my father—already back at work, scribbling away—and took another upstairs. I still had hours to go before school. I sat at my own desk, spartan and clean, and watched the morning light creep over the surrounding greenery from my window. The queasiness in my stomach didn't abate, and the black coffee wasn't helping. With trepidation, I let my fingers hover over the keys of my laptop. Finally, I opened the search engine and started typing.

Warning signs of dementia

A list populated, and I scanned it quickly.

Bouts of forgetfulness, blankness, mood changes, withdrawal…

My stomach clenched harder. He'd exhibited mild signs of all those symptoms and hadn't stepped foot outside the house in a week. It was merely Dad's zeal for the science, I reasoned. He wasn't forgetful, he was preoccupied with the work and obsessed with finishing.

Every great physicist has a little bit of madness in him, he'd once told me.

"Not yet," I murmured. "Please, just not yet."

I turned my concentration to today's tutoring session with Emery. Helping her pass calculus was a worthy challenge, at least, to keep her tyrannical father off her back. I concocted a dozen practice equations—more than she could do in an hour—and then grabbed my phone for the hundredth time since Saturday night. I reread our text exchange over and over.

I wish I'd been there for you tonight.

I'd failed Emery, arriving at the bonfire in time to see Dean and Harper help her and her brother to Dean's car. And I'd failed her over the past seven years. It wasn't my fault that my letters had gone missing, but I could have tried harder to connect. Instead, my wounded pride and more wounded heart kept me from trying again. Who knows what might have happened for Emery had I just made the effort to find her? To tell her…

"There's nothing more to say," I declared to no one.

Feelings my ten-year-old self had nurtured were trying to grow back after I'd mercilessly yanked them out. If I let them take root in the empty places where my mother had been, I'd suffer a different version of the same colossal hurt all over again. Abandonment. Rejection. And even if I threw caution to the wind, the odds of something happening between a girl like Emery and a guy like me were statistically negligible. I had nothing to offer her but math equations and quantum theory.

My father had taken that route, and where did it

get him? He'd offered his heart to my mother with both hands, and she'd left him with nothing.

Because loving someone wasn't enough to make them stay.

At the Academy, I headed straight to the gym. A group of guys who'd tried out for row crew surrounded a bulletin in the glass case outside. Some were fist-bumping, but most muttered dejectedly. I hung back, watching, as Brent let out a curse and punched the wall. A few of his buddies led him away, patting him on the back.

"My father's going to *kill* me," he said, and suddenly my shit-talking felt petty and small.

When the group had moved on, I stepped up to read the roster, scrolling past the single, pairs, and fours, straight to the eight-man sweep.

Eights:
Coxswain: Dean Yearwood
Stroke Seat: Rhett Calloway
Seven Seat: Henry Moore
Six and Five Seats: Knox Whitman and Tucker Hill (captain)
Four and Three Seats: Justin Wu and Kai Thornton
Two Seat: Orion Mercer
Bow Seat: Xander Ford

I let out a breath. For all my braggadocio, I hadn't

been entirely certain Coach Daniels would take me on. My small smile vanished when a voice came from behind.

"Congrats, Ford."

I turned. Tucker loomed behind me with Rhett Calloway beside him. Just like seven years ago, though I wasn't the scrawny kid they'd pelted with water balloons anymore.

"I guess we'll see what you got," Tucker said. "But Coach doesn't fuck around and neither do I. We want to win. End of."

"I can imagine," I said before I could stop myself. "Considering how you blew it last season."

Apparently, one aspect of my little Experiment was the development of a death wish.

Tucker's eyes flared. "What the fuck do you know about it?"

"New Haven Prep beat you in the five thousand and the two thousand meters in two separate regattas." I shrugged. "Given the glaring weaknesses in their crew, both should've been easy wins."

Rhett chuckled darkly. "I'm starting to like this guy."

"Whatever." Tucker puffed his chest. "Pull your weight, Ford, and we won't have any problems. But if I see you looking at my girlfriend the way you looked at her on Saturday night, I'm going to take an oar and smash every bone in your face."

"Informing me is premeditation. A bold choice."

Tucker smirked. "My father is a senator. I can do whatever the fuck I want. You on the other hand…your mom bolted, and your father is a washed-up loser whose brains are turning to oatmeal as we speak."

A jolt of white-hot rage flooded me, and my hands balled into fists.

Tucker's smirk became a satisfied smile. "Enjoy your smart mouth while you can, Ford," he said, walking away with Rhett. "Everyone knows that *batshit crazy* runs in the family."

"You okay?" Dean asked as we walked through the halls after midmorning break. "You made the crew! That's huge! So why do you look like someone pissed in your Cheerios?"

"Part of Tucker's little welcome-to-the-crew speech included a few comments about my dad." I gave him a hard look. "I thought you said he's a good captain."

"He is so long as he doesn't have a personal beef with you." Dean's eyebrows rose meaningfully. "Does he have a personal beef with you?"

"No. He has no reason to worry, believe me."

Emery and I are just friends. I'd been repeating that over and over in my mind like a yogi's mantra, but it wasn't bringing me any peace.

"Mmkay," Dean said. "Just keep it that way. For your sake."

"Hey, Dean," I asked after a moment. "How does everyone know my father had some…health issues in Maryland?"

And that my mom walked out. Don't forget that little tidbit.

"My money is on Delilah Winslow," he said. "Her mom works for the Pembroke Science Institute at Brown. Delilah must've heard it from her."

"Fucking hell."

"Sorry, man. They smell weakness like a shark in the water. But don't let it get you down. Russell Ford is a legend." He chucked my shoulder and grinned. "See you at practice tomorrow, my friend."

I nodded absently. Tucker's threats of physical violence aside, I was looking forward to getting into a shell and rowing out some of my stagnant energy. Nothing was better than being in the fresh air, out on the water.

Well, almost nothing…

Emery Wallace walked down the hall a dozen yards ahead of me. Her long blond hair hung in thick ribbons down the back of a dress that showed the luscious curves and valleys of her hourglass figure. She was Marilyn Monroe remade in a modern era—with the same kind of intangible charisma that made people gravitate to her. And like Marilyn, Emery's beauty was as far as most people got.

Not me. I knew the heart that beat in her chest and her warmth and her light. I'd told Emery that love was finite, and of course, she disagreed. Her capacity to love and trust and hope seemed bottomless.

But I knew the jagged rocks were down there; I'd been smashed on them before. To ignore the risk was stupid, something I strove to never be.

I continued to my speech and debate class, which was as simple to me as finger painting and served to remind me that the Experiment meant nothing. It was just a time-out before going to MIT, to follow in Dad's footsteps. If he didn't solve for a unified theory, I'd finish what he started.

Everything—and everyone—else was just a distraction.

Chapter 14

EMERY

After the Weekend from Hell, I'd arrived at school Monday morning just in time to duck into calculus. But I couldn't avoid my friends at midmorning break. I reluctantly joined them at our spot—a little courtyard off the cafeteria with wrought iron tables and chairs—and braced myself for questions about Jack. It was obvious they'd all been talking about him; the whole school was talking about him. There was even a video going around that someone had taken with their phone, but I didn't want to know who.

So I don't go and claw their eyes out.

"Jack's going to be okay," I announced to my friends impatiently, as if I were already bored of the subject. "He got wasted and tripped. It's not a big deal. He'll be back at school in a week or two."

I took a seat beside Tucker, hoping my little act was the end of it. But clearly, I didn't know my friends very well. They surrounded me immediately, asking questions. Most with sympathy. Others—like Aria, Rhett, and Elowen—not so much.

"We're glad he's okay, Em," Elowen said, as if speaking for the whole school. "But you weren't there. A bunch of people saw him put his hand in the fire. Like...*deliberately*."

My stomach clenched, and I fought to keep my face neutral. "Yeah, because he was *drunk*. Like I said, it's not a big deal."

Glances were exchanged, like birds darting through the air all around me.

"It's just that we're worried about him," Aria said with a sweet smile that didn't touch her eyes in the slightest. "He seemed like he was in a bad way, and he was talking about your brother. The one who died—"

"All right, that's bloody well enough," Orion cut in. "He's going to be okay, and that's the long and short of it, eh?"

"Thank you," I said, then glared at Tucker.

He glanced back with a stupid "What did I do?" look on his face.

The conversation moved on to other subjects, but I knew it'd swing right back to Jack as soon as I was out of earshot. Every single one of us at CHA had pressure to excel, so seeing someone else crack was almost motivating. Like reassurance that they might have it hard, but hey, at least they weren't sticking their hands into a raging fire.

They killed him…

Jack's words haunted me. I was too scared to look at them, but my parents' neglect of Jack was bad enough. Mom had eventually visited him, maybe staying five minutes, and my dad lectured him the entire time about "family image" and "media scrutiny."

Neither had asked him why he'd done it.

I have to get out.

At lunch, I went directly to the library, pulled up UCLA's webpage, and printed the application forms. I filled them out and took them with shaking hands to Ms. Alvarez's class. She looked up from her desk, where she was eating a sandwich and grading papers.

"Hello, Emery. What brings you…are you all right? You look pale."

I set the application forms on her desk. "I can't send this from my house, and I can't receive any responses there either. And I have no way to pay for this college. Not while being attached to my parents' money, which I will be until I'm twenty-four. So basically, this is probably a waste of time, but…here we are."

Ms. Alvarez scanned the forms. A small smile touched her lips, then was dampened by concern. "Are you in danger, Emery? I have to ask."

"No, nothing like that," I said automatically. Then I thought of Grant walking out the front door to meet that train and Jack's burnt fist. "I have to get away from here, Ms. Alvarez. The farther away, the better."

"I see." Ms. Alvarez looked grave. "Well, I can use my

mailing address, though it might jeopardize my job if your father interferes like he did with my curriculum."

"Oh, God. I didn't think of that. No, forget it…"

I started to reach for the papers, but Ms. Alvarez was faster.

"A PO Box will do the trick. And as for the financial aid, it might prove difficult, given your family's wealth. I would suggest applying for any scholarships available to you and maybe even private loans." She pursed her lips. "Although I don't like that you should be buried in college debt when your family has all the means in the world."

"I have to get in first."

She smiled. "I think UCLA would love to have you. But it says here the application fee is ninety-five dollars."

"I know, and I don't have it. They watch my money. Every cent. But I have these really expensive boots I've hardly worn and a few other things. I'll sell them and pay you back. I promise."

"I'm going to hold you to that, Emery, only because I want you to do this on your own. To have as much authority and autonomy over your decisions as you can. Okay?"

My head bobbed in a nod. "Thank you, Ms. A. Thank you so much."

"You're welcome, sweetheart. I don't know exactly what your situation is, but you're not the first student to sit across from me this year already crumpling under the weight of their parents' expectations."

"That's exactly how it feels," I said. "Sometimes I can hardly breathe."

Ms. Alvarez reached over and took my hand in hers. "It's a big step, and I'm proud of you." She cocked her head. "They don't tell you that, do they?"

I shook my head, blinking away tears.

My teacher gave my hand a final pat. "You'd better get to your next class. I'll take care of this and let you know when I hear back."

I let out a shaky sigh and got to my feet. "Holy crap. It's real, isn't it? I'm really doing this?"

Ms. Alvarez smiled. "It's scary to break free of all that's familiar—and financially secure—and jump into the unknown. You're a brave girl, Emery. Don't forget that."

"I'll try not to."

But as soon as I got back home—into the tense, suffocating dome of my house—all my bravado fled.

Holy shit, what have I done?

At the dinner table, I could hardly move, paralyzed by fear. Any second now, my father would look at my face and see the defiance painted all over it.

"So, Emery," he said. "Anything interesting happen at school today?"

I swallowed hard. "Nope, nothing."

"We'll be formalizing your application to Brown soon." He salted his mashed potatoes. "I presume your tutoring sessions are going well. No surprises?"

I nearly dropped my fork. "Um, no. No surprises."

"Good. Given how often you spend tutoring with that boy, not to mention the cost, I expect straight As."

"Yes," I said stupidly, my brain in panic mode. "In

fact, I have homework I should get a jump on. May I be excused?"

My father frowned. "I suppose so."

I practically ran up to my room. Safely inside, I sat on my four-poster bed and grabbed my sketchpad to take refuge in my art. The first prom committee meeting was coming up, and I wanted to get a jump on the theme. To make it beautiful. To show my dad what I could do. That way, I wouldn't have to run all the way to California, and Dad would never have to know that I'd made an escape plan.

You think your dad's suddenly going to become impressed with your art and let you walk away from his plans?

"Maybe he will," I said in a small voice. I hated how my courage drained out the second I stepped foot in my house. I wanted to feel how I felt when I was with Xander. How life felt open and full of possibilities, instead of cold and shuttered.

"So make it real."

I picked up my phone and texted him.

I applied to UCLA.

Xander's reply came a moment later. You did?

I did. I have no way of paying for it, but it felt nice to try. Even a little.

No reply.

It's all your fault, really, I sent after a minute. All that talk about escape velocity…;-)

Nothing.

The hopeful buoyancy deflated out of me, and I tried not to feel as hurt as I did. "Okay, good talk."

I turned my phone face down and tried to focus on my prom design, but I'd lost my spark. I went to shut off the light and dive into sleep when my phone chimed a text from Xander.

In order to attend UCLA and be eligible for financial aid, free from your parents' income, you must qualify as an independent student. The criteria for which—in part—are as follows:

1. You're homeless or about to become homeless
2. You're emancipated
3. You're married

I stared at his orderly, formal text. Like a message coming from far away—a shooting star that landed in my lap.

Then another text followed.

If you can't get emancipated I'll marry you.

"Oh my God…" My shaking fingers hit *call*.

Xander's voice was low and quiet when he answered. "Hi, Emery."

"You'll *what?*"

"It's strictly for practical purposes. You'll be able to break free of your dad's money and have more access to aid."

"I…I don't know what to say."

"We both have to be eighteen," he continued, all business. "My birthday is on November tenth. Yours?"

"March fifth. But Xander—"

"I have nothing, Emery. Only a pension that's going to go to my dad's care when he needs to be institutionalized. You might still incur massive debt for the rest of your life—"

"When you put it that way…"

"But you'd be free."

Tears stung my eyes and clogged my throat. "You would…do that for me?"

"Yeah, Em, I would."

"But you're going to MIT." *Thousands of miles away…*

"Yes, but that won't matter," he said. "It would be a pretend marriage. No expectations. Nothing permanent"

"I…" I shook my head. "No, this is crazy. I can't get married unless it's…real."

For love…

"It would be real," Xander said. "A real piece of paper that gets you out of Rhode Island. Nothing more."

I nodded, though I wasn't sure that made me feel better. "Right. Just a piece of paper. We wouldn't actually call each other husband or wife or use it against each other somehow."

"Never."

"Okay. It's not going to come to that, anyway," I said quickly. "I still have my prom idea. I'm still holding out hope that my dad sees what I can do and supports me."

"He might," Xander said, doubt lacing his words. "This is just for backup."

"In case of emergency, get married?" I sniffed a laugh.

"Something like that." A pause fell and then he said, "Anyway, I wanted you to know that you have options."

"I don't know what to say. Thank you, Xander," I said. "Thank you so much."

I heard him hesitate, heard his throat click as he swallowed hard. "Goodnight, Emery."

The line went quiet. I lay back on my pillow, my phone on my chest. Tears blurred my vision, my heart full imagining Xander in his room, researching how to help my dreams come true.

Marriage was an extreme option—a total break from my family. Exile. I wasn't sure I was strong enough to make that leap or even go through with UCLA in the first place. Suddenly, I didn't feel so alone. I felt like I did back on that rock, seven years ago, with Xander's hand on my back, gentle and hesitant, but letting me know he was there.

Chapter 15

XANDER

I rested my phone on my chest and stared at the ceiling, wondering what the hell I'd done.

"Because she's my friend."

Einstein called the speed of light a universal speed limit. Nothing was faster, and that gave the universe some order. I could consider my marriage "proposal" on the same order of magnitude. The distance between Emery and me would be a protective boundary—her in California, me in Massachusetts. We almost couldn't get farther apart and still be in the same country. That incontrovertible fact would bring order to my universe, where right now there was only the chaos of my heart reaching for what I knew it could never really have.

Helping to make her dreams come true was nonnegotiable. I'd do whatever it took—even marrying her if I had to—to let her escape her terrible father and live her own life.

Another paradox: Sacrificing my happiness for hers would be the hardest thing I could do, and yet there was nothing easier.

Part II

Science cannot solve the ultimate mystery of nature. And that is because, in the last analysis, we ourselves are a part of the mystery that we are trying to solve.
—Max Planck

Chapter 16

XANDER

MID-OCTOBER

"All right, gentlemen." Coach Daniels clapped his hands. "Time to get in the water."

The Royal Pride row crew gathered in the gym gave a collective but tired cheer. We hadn't been on the water since tryouts. Instead, Coach worked us to the point of exhaustion on form and fitness three afternoons per week and most Saturday mornings. The Academy gym had a whole set of ergometers, and we spent our time on the specialized row machines or lifting weights to get into prime racing shape.

Dean let loose a piercing whistle. "You heard the man. Get suited up!"

In the locker room, we changed from our workout clothes into the Academy-sanctioned practice gear: a short-sleeved and short-legged unisuit in black and gold (even our practice gear bore the Academy colors). I threw on a windbreaker and shoes over my row socks—both also team issue.

"Wow, Ford, I'm impressed," Rhett Calloway sneered from across the row of lockers. "How did you manage to pay for all the gear?" He pretended to have an epiphany. "Oh, that's right. Tucker's girlfriend is paying for it with 'tutoring.'" He made air quotes, his dark eyes glinting with malevolence.

Tucker glowered at me instead of his friend. "Nah, I'll bet he had to fill out the financial hardship form. Isn't that right, Ford?"

They were both wrong. I had contemplated using the Academy scholarship system that helped Bend kids pay for the myriad of technology and equipment required to participate in school activities. For row alone, this meant $1,250 worth of practice clothes, two sets of race-day uniforms, a sweat suit, and goggles, as well as a formal suit, jacket, and tie for the yearbook photo and post-regatta galas and award ceremonies. But my father was doing well—working hard and happy—and in a fit of optimism, I paid for the entire package out of our account.

Not that Rhett or Tucker needed to know any of that. Using facts on people who'd already made up their minds was usually a losing proposition.

As for Emery…her revealing that I tutored her three times a week was both good and bad. Good, because we had nothing to hide, and bad, because we had nothing to hide. Because we were friends.

You proposed to your friend.

I nearly clocked my head on my open locker as the thought snuck in and made me jump. I had to remind myself—for the millionth time since that conversation six weeks ago—that it was for business purposes only.

But facts were also wasted on a heart that had already made up its mind.

"Leave him be," Orion said, pulling on his unisuit. "What bloody business is it of ours? He's our teammate, yeah?"

I gave Orion a nod in thanks. He had clout with the guys, because Tucker and Rhett left me alone, and we headed down to the dock.

"I probably sound like a broken record by now," Coach said next to the choppy water under a cloudy sky. "We have the Narragansett Bay Club Regatta coming up, and then the cold weather is going to shut us down until March. This is our shot to show the clubs what they can look forward to competing against in spring."

Assistant Coach Wright stepped up. "Today on the docket, pause drills. Dean is going to call out a hold so we can see where you're at in both individual form and as a unit. Okay, let's go."

The shell was tethered parallel to the dock. We all climbed in, me at the bow and Dean as cox all the way on the other end closest to Rhett, who pulled in the stroke seat.

Over the past few weeks, I'd spent more time on an ergometer than I could possibly want. Despite the chill in the air, it felt good to get on the water. Once the team was in, Tucker, from the five seat, shifted into captain mode.

"All right, guys, let's show Coach what we can do. Nice and clean at every pause. We got this."

Orion turned to look at me over his left shoulder, grinning. "Hear that? We got this."

I grinned back. "Where are we taking it?"

He cackled. "You're a madman, Ford."

At the opposite end of the shell, Dean adjusted his mic'd headset. "Ready? And…pull."

My back to the open water, I pulled along with my team, and the shell glided away from the dock. Coach's boat puttered alongside us, and he put a megaphone to his mouth.

"Up first, I want to see a hold on the finish," he said. "Smooth drive, then clean finish. Legs, body, arms…in that order. Go ahead, Dean."

"On it," Dean said, his voice amplified over the wind. We all rowed in unison, pulling at our oars, but even before Dean called for the pause, I knew we weren't synced.

"Ready…and…hold!"

We all stopped in the leaned-back position, oars pulled up to our chests.

"Rhett, your oar is nearly up to your chin," Coach complained. "You look like your elbows are coming out of your goddamn neck. Good, Knox. Good, Kai. Excellent, Xander."

Again and again, at different parts of the stroke, Dean called for a hold, and Coach assessed our form and then complained about it. He was especially hard on Rhett and excruciatingly complimentary of me.

"I wish you could all turn around and watch Ford's stroke. He's textbook at every single pause, and the only one who looks like he knows what the hell he's doing."

My face went red, and the other guys turned around to glance at me—Rhett, Tucker, and Justin with grimaces; Kai, Henry, and Knox with approval. Orion flashed me a brilliant smile and a thumbs up.

"Let's go again," Coach said. "This time, hold on the catch. I want to see clean catches, no smashing. Smooth."

"Row," Dean called, and we began. After a few strokes, he called a hold on the catch.

"Christ, Calloway, look at your blade," Coach bellowed into the megaphone. "No, hold it," he snapped when Rhett tried to fix his angle. "You're shallow as hell and about to wash out. Go again."

The drills went on for two hours, until finally we were allowed to dock. Every part of my body was on fire with exertion as we stood in a row, Coach pacing up and down our line. He gave us his general feedback—none of it good—then stopped in front of Rhett.

"You're around six feet, right? What do you weigh?"

"About one-seventy, Coach," Rhett said in a low, wary tone.

Without breaking eye contact, Coach called out to me at the other end of the line. "Ford. Height and weight."

"Six feet, one-sixty-nine," I said, having weighed in prior to practice as required.

"Calloway, I don't know what the hell you've been doing since last year," Coach said, "but I'll remind you that stroke seat isn't just a position, it's a responsibility. The entire crew is relying on you for pace. For rhythm. For technical precision. If you can't hack it, I'm going to switch you and Ford, you got me?"

My eyes fell shut. *Fuck me.*

"I want to see serious improvement by next practice, okay? That's it, gentlemen."

The team broke up and we headed to the clubhouse to change. I could feel Rhett's black gaze, like icy daggers in my back.

In the clubhouse, I'd just pulled my jacket over my aching shoulders when I felt a presence behind me. I tensed, bracing myself, and turned around. Rhett's pale skin, dark eyes, and mirthless smile brought to mind a vampire.

"Sounds like you're really good, Ford," he said. "Do you want to trade seats with me, so the whole team can see how fucking *textbook* you are?"

"I'm happy where I am, thanks."

Rhett didn't move but stared at me with that odd, maniacal grin. I stared back, unwilling to blink first. From my periphery, I could see the whole team watching. Tucker, Orion, and Dean moved closer.

"Hey." Rhett leaned in, his head cocked. "What's wrong with your eyes?"

I knew we'd be on the water with goggles, so I was wearing contacts. I had no glasses to act as a shield that could often make people believe the chromatic difference was just a trick of the light.

Before I could answer, Rhett chuckled. "Let me guess. One is from your crazy dad and the other from your mom. To remember her by. You know...because she walked out on you."

The blood in my veins went cold, and my hands balled into fists. Rhett read my reaction, and his eyes widened in glee.

"I'm right, aren't I? Which is which?" He pointed his finger at my left eye. "I'm guessing brown is Mommy."

I smacked his hand away. "Fuck off, Rhett."

Shocked, he snarled and shoved me in the chest. "Fuck *you*, Ford."

I shoved him back, and a full-blown altercation would have ensued if not for Dean moving to stand between us.

"Okay, that's *enough*."

To my shock, Tucker pulled Rhett aside. "Let him be."

"Whatever, freak," Rhett snarled, and he and Tucker moved off.

"You good?" Dean asked.

It took me a second to tear my gaze off Rhett. "Sure. Never better."

I finished getting dressed, and Dean and I walked out. At the door, Orion stopped me to clasp hands.

"You deserve all the good shit Coach says about you, all right?" He leaned in, his brown eyes glinting. "Just don't take Rhett's seat. I don't want that bloody bastard behind me."

I smiled a little. "Thanks, man."

"What's Rhett's deal?" I asked Dean as we headed to the parking lot on the other side of campus. "He seems… sadistic."

"Nah." Dean waved a hand. "His dad is in the music industry. Rhett gets to rub elbows with celebrities on the regular. I think it inflates his ego. Not that that excuses him talking shit like that to you. He's a tremendous asshole, for sure."

I nodded, though I wasn't sure I agreed it was only a matter of ego. There'd been something in Rhett's eyes that set my hair on end. Like looking into twin black holes where no light escaped, only infinite darkness.

I told myself I was being dramatic but also vowed to watch my back.

"You have plans for the Halloween Festival?" Dean asked. "Only a week to get your costume together."

"I'm not going."

"You have to go! The costume contest alone is worth it, with big prizes for the winners. Everyone goes all out."

"I wouldn't have the first clue what to be."

"I hate to be obvious, but…Einstein?" Dean said with a grin. "And when you get on stage for the contest, you can give that lecture on nonsymmetric field theory like you did at our club meeting last week. You're a sure win, even if no one knows what the hell you're talking about."

"I'd rather not stand out. What's your costume?"

"Ferris Bueller."

I stared at him blankly.

"Dude, we have *got* to get you caught up," Dean said. "Okay, next order of business. Who are you taking?"

"I'm not taking anyone," I said, trying and failing to keep the image of Emery and Tucker dancing together from parading across my eyes. "Who are you taking? Harper?"

Dean looked confused. "No, I can't get a read on her. But if I had to guess, I think she likes you."

"Me?"

"Yeah, man. She's always looking at you during club meetings. You should ask her. But quick, before someone beats you to it."

"But not you?"

"Nah," Dean said. "I like to keep my options open."

We arrived at the parking lot, him to his Camry, me to my bike.

"See you Monday, Xander," he said, leaning against his open door. "And hey, good job today. Orion's right—your form is top-notch, and if Rhett doesn't get his shit together, I think you'd make a great stroke seat." He wagged his brows. "Then you'd be right in front of me on the boat. We could stare meaningfully into each other's eyes."

I chuckled as I climbed on my bike. "See you, man."

Though Dean was joking, I wondered if he hadn't asked Harper to the dance for a particular reason. I tried to picture them together and couldn't. But when I tried to picture Dean with a guy, that didn't work, either. He was just…Dean. The guy everyone liked, who was always surrounded by people but always alone too.

In any case, it was none of my business who he liked or didn't like. I had enough problems of my own. Namely, I was counting down the seconds to my next tutoring session with Emery.

My fiancée.

I ground my teeth together. Apparently, my intrusive thoughts had a sense of humor.

At home, my father was at his desk, staring at the wall.

"Hey, Dad?" No answer. I drew closer and put my hand on his shoulder. "Dad?"

He jolted out of his reverie. "Eh? Oh, Xander. Hi."

I eased a sigh of relief. "I'm sorry if I broke your concentration."

It was four in the afternoon, but he was still in his pajamas, and his dark hair—graying at the temples—stuck up in all directions.

Dad stood and took hold of my shoulders. "Xander. We need to start packing. We have to get back to Maryland."

My stomach clenched. "No, Dad, we live here now. Since August."

"Oh no, no, no, son. Your mother would never agree to live here."

"Dad…Mom left us. She walked out seven years ago. Remember?"

Please remember…

Fear gnawed my insides. I'd heard him in the kitchen a couple of nights recently and came down to find him disoriented. I always told myself he was just tired.

Sleepwalking, maybe. But the instances of him *going away* seemed to be happening more frequently.

"Hm?" Dad blinked as if he were coming out of a trance.

"Mom's not here anymore."

He scoffed. "Yes, I know that. She's living it up in Paris." He smiled. "It's too bad she can't see you now. She'd be so proud of the man you've become."

I nodded, pushing down a lump of emotion. I didn't allow thoughts of my mother to infiltrate my mind. Ever. "Dad, are you okay?"

"Me? Never better!" He returned to his desk. "I'm about ready for dinner, though. Unraveling the secrets of the universe is hungry work. Let's order a pizza!"

"Sure."

When the pizza arrived, I put on a movie, something I'd started doing recently to keep up with Dean's references. But I couldn't focus; I had one eye on *Ferris Bueller's Day Off* and one on my dad. He chuckled at the funny parts, ate pizza, then popcorn, and all seemed well… But later that night I woke to pots and pans banging in the kitchen. Dad was making breakfast at 3:00 a.m.

On Monday morning, I called the Academy front office and told them I'd be late, then made the phone call I'd been dreading but couldn't put off any longer.

———

"This is ridiculous," my father said in an exam room at a

medical clinic in Newport. "And it's taking valuable time away from my work."

"I know," I said. "But a checkup can't hurt, right?"

Dad shot me a hard look. "Don't tell me you're suddenly believing what they said about me at the NIST," he said. "Is that what this is about? That I'm losing my mind?"

"I'm not *suddenly* believing anything, Dad. I'm worried about you."

He said nothing, and then the doctor arrived with a balding head and friendly demeanor.

"Hello, I'm Dr. Mandel," he said. "You're Xander, here with your dad, Mr. Ford?"

"Dr. Ford," I said quickly. "He has PhDs in philosophy, particle physics, and applied mathematics."

Don't let him lose it all, please.

"Impressive."

Dr. Mandel turned to my father, who looked less like a thrice-degreed scientist and more like a petulant child on the exam table. "And what brings you here today, Dr. Ford?"

Dad jerked a thumb at me sullenly. "Ask him."

"I think," I said slowly, "we should address some of my dad's recent episodes with forgetfulness."

"I don't know what he's talking about," Dad grumbled.

With a pain in my heart, I told the doctor about his breakdown in Bethesda, his restless nights, and his episodes of confusion and blankness. Dad looked at me the entire time, wounded. As if I'd betrayed him.

Dr. Mandel nodded. "Xander, would you mind giving me a moment with your dad?"

I gladly stepped outside and sat in the waiting room, chewing on my thumbnail.

Twenty minutes later, the doctor came out, alone. "Your father is just using the restroom, but I wanted to tell you, I have some concerns."

"Okay," I said warily.

"He's in wonderful physical health," he said, taking a seat opposite mine. "But cognitively, I am seeing a few warning signs."

"Warning signs of?"

"Early onset dementia. Possibly Lewy body dementia."

My heart dropped to my stomach and clanged a heavy beat.

"I've seen my share of cases, but I'm no specialist," Dr. Mandel added. "I would suggest taking him to see a neurologist for a concrete diagnosis and treatment plan. In the meantime, I'm prescribing donepezil, a common medication for someone in your father's condition."

His condition. Losing his memories, his education, his sense of himself...

"He's only fifty-eight," I said thickly. "He's so young,"

Dr. Mandel leaned over his knees. "I'm so sorry, Xander. Do you have anyone at home to provide support?"

"No," I said darkly. "But this medication will help?"

Dr. Mandel nodded. "Have him take it right before bed. It should alleviate nighttime wandering and slow down the cognitive decline, but it's not a cure. Again, I recommend a specialist—"

"I'm ready to go," my dad said, appearing behind the doctor. He mustered a weak smile. "Come on, son. Let's blow this joint."

Dr. Mandel shook our hands. "Don't hesitate to call if you have questions."

In the car, my normally jovial dad was sullen and quiet.

"I don't need a specialist," he said finally as I drove the Buick back to Castle Hill.

"Dad—"

"You're seventeen years old. I'm still the adult here. I get to decide what to do, and I say I'm just fine. I'll take the medicine, but that's it. If—*if*—things get…harder, then we can reassess."

"I can stay home," I said. "I'll quit school. It's stupid to go anyway—"

"You'll stay home and do what?" Dad asked, shaking his head. "I have work to do, and I don't need you hovering over my shoulder while I do it."

"But Dad—"

"Don't do that, Alexander," he said gravely. "Don't act like it's over."

We'd come to a red light. I looked over at my father and saw the fear in his eyes. His brilliant eyes, through which he had delved deep into the quantum realm and shared what he found there. Whatever genius I possessed was only a fraction of his, and to think he might be losing everything…

"I'm not ready yet, son," he said. "Not yet. Okay?"

I swallowed the tears down, like a hard lump in my throat. "Okay, Dad," I said. "Okay."

He smiled and gave my cheek a pat. The light changed, and we drove on. He seemed happy again. Like himself.

Because he's still himself. He's still here.

"So!" he said after a minute. "Given any thought about a Halloween costume this year?"

"I have actually. I'm going as one of the world's greatest physicists."

"Oh yeah?" Dad rubbed his chin. "Hmm, let me guess. Heisenberg? Feynman? Or your namesake, good ole Erwin?" He chuckled.

"Nope," I said.

"Who, then?"

"You."

Chapter 17

EMERY

"Remind me why we're out here again?" Harper asked, bundled in her puffy coat that went all the way down to her fuzzy boots and had probably been in style in the 1980s. She narrowed her eyes against the bracing wind that came across the Narragansett.

We sat on the aluminum bleachers that had been set up for the inaugural regatta next week after the Halloween Festival. The rowing crew was out of sight, around a bend in the Bend. Their coaches stood on the dock several yards ahead of us, stopwatches in hand, as they watched and waited.

"We're here to support my boyfriend and our friend," I said, shielding my eyes and looking out over the bay. "It'll be Tucker's first regatta as a senior and Xander's first for CHA. It's a big deal."

"Hm," Harper said noncommittally.

"You mean to tell me you aren't having fun, wasting your afternoon freezing your booty off out here with me?"

She laughed and rolled her eyes. "More fun than I can handle. And don't worry, your secret is safe with me."

"What secret?"

"That the glamorous Emery Wallace is actually kind of a dork."

I giggled and gave her a playful nudge. I'd been hanging out with Harper a lot over the past six weeks, and it shamed me to admit that it had taken nearly all of those six weeks to not feel self-conscious about it. As if it were a crime against humanity to be friendly with a Bend kid. Not just friendly but friends. A mismatched sort of friendship: she was slow to share too many personal details, while I spilled my guts at the least provocation.

"Speaking of wasting afternoons," Harper said, "shouldn't you be studying for your calc midterm?"

"Ugh. Buzzkill, Bennett."

She smirked. "You have three tutoring sessions per week with Xander. He has to know what he's doing; he probably learned this stuff in kindergarten."

In another bold step toward being a better human, I stopped hiding that Xander was tutoring me. I wanted to walk away from all the usual peer-pressure bullshit and be my own person. Baby steps, for sure, but it was better than standing still.

"Is he a bad teacher?" Harper was saying. She gave

me a sly look. "Or are you using your tutoring time for something else…?"

"What? No," I said quickly. "We do the math. Or we try. I just like talking to him more."

"What happens if you fail?" she asked, huddling deeper in her coat against the late October chill.

"I don't want to think about it," I said, and gave a shiver that had nothing to do with the cold air.

"I don't like it, Em," Harper said. "There has to be something you can do to go to the school you want, where you want, instead of whatever terrible plans your dad has for you. From everything you've told me, he sounds…"

"Like a tyrant?" I smiled wryly. "You're not wrong. And there is a way out. Maybe."

"Let's hear it."

I glanced at her sideways. Harper was trustworthy. She could've spilled the tea about Jack's bonfire incident and never did.

"Xander said he'd marry me."

Harper's eyelids fluttered. "I beg your pardon."

I told Harper about how I'd applied to UCLA on the sly weeks ago and the text and conversation with Xander that followed.

"It wouldn't be a real marriage. Just to detach from my parents' money. Detach from them altogether maybe." The thought was a perfect blend of euphoria, sadness, and fear. I bit my lip. "No, no, it's crazy… right?"

Harper cocked her head. "Is it, though? Desperate

times call for desperate measures." Her brown eyes twinkled. "So what did you say when Xander asked you to marry him?"

I glared at her and ignored the flock of butterflies that took off in my stomach at her particular choice of words. "He didn't *propose*. He just offered it as an option."

"That's generous of him."

"It's more than generous. It's so sweet that he'd be willing to do that for me."

"But…?"

"I can't get *married*, Harper. For one thing, I don't turn eighteen until March. That's a long way away."

"But not too late for financial aid applications."

"And for *another thing*," I said pointedly, "I don't think I could go through with it. I don't want to get married unless I mean it. Not until I'm older and can actually do it right. It's important to me."

Because I believe that love is infinite…

Inexplicably, tears sprang to my eyes. I blinked them away quickly, mentally blaming the wind. "And anyway, if I go through with all this, my dad will disown me for sure. I wouldn't have a family."

"Are they really worth keeping?" Harper asked gently. "I know that sounds terrible, and I don't pretend to know what it's like to have the kind of pressure they're putting on you. But if our own family is no good for us, it's okay to build a new one from scratch."

"Easier said than done."

Harper blew out a breath. "Can I be honest?"

"Because you've been so timid and reserved up until now?" I teased.

She didn't smile. "I think if you really believed your prom idea would work, you wouldn't have applied to UCLA."

"Maybe," I said. "But can you blame me for trying? I'd rather have my parents see me for who I am and appreciate my dreams and talents than to have to sneak around or do something dramatic like get married."

"I get that." Harper put her hand on mine. "And I imagine defying your father is terrifying. But I believe in you. Xander believes in you, or he wouldn't have made that offer. And I think, deep down, you believe in you."

My throat tightened, and I smiled gratefully at my friend. "I'm trying." I huffed a breath. "In any case, I don't have to worry about it right now."

"Emery—"

"So!" I said brightly. "Who's your date to the Halloween Festival?"

Harper looked as if she'd protest, then let it go. "As of right now, no one."

"Any prospects?"

"I'm waiting for a particular someone to ask me," she said, and her face softened. A pink blush came to her pale cheeks.

"Oooh, who? Tell me! Someone I know?"

"No, forget it," she said. "It's not going to happen. Not in my lifetime."

"Okay, how about Dean?"

"We're just friends."

Just friends. Like me and Xander. And friends wanted what was best for each other, right? To make each other happy.

"What about Xander?" I blurted.

She gave me a strange look. "You think I should go with Xander. Your fiancé."

"Oh my God, stop. And why not? You're in the math club together. You're both super smart. I think you'd make a cute couple."

Harper stared at me like I'd grown a second head. "You do?"

"Of course!" I said, my smile fixed. "You're both my friends, and I want my friends to be happy."

Harper studied me for a long moment, eyes narrowed. Finally, she nodded. "Sure. I'd go with Xander if he asked me."

My stomach twanged, like the way it feels when you bump your funny bone—tingling and kind of awful at the same time.

"Great," I said faintly. "I'll talk to him tomorrow."

"If you insist."

"I do."

She gave me a final, strange look just as Aria, Sierra, Delilah, and Elowen approached. She noticed them and then instantly gathered her stuff and slid off the bleachers. "See you, Em."

"Oh, okay. Bye." I gave her a little wave.

"*Rude*," Aria said. "You'd think we had the bubonic

plague, the way she acts. Honestly, Em, I don't know why you bother with the Benders. First Xander and now her."

"She's smart and funny and nice."

And real.

Elowen rolled her eyes. "Whatever."

The girls settled around me to watch for the crew. Aria was there for her boyfriend, Rhett. Elowen was there in her never-ending quest to get Orion's attention. I was there for Tucker.

Theoretically, I thought, and—like every science word in the English language—it made me think of Xander. Though nowadays, nothing was needed to make me think of Xander, because I was already always thinking about him.

Harper had been right; over the past six weeks, we had our tutoring sessions, but when Xander wasn't cramming calculus theorems into my brain, we talked about everything. It was so cute that he could rattle off the most complicated facts about quantum mechanics yet had never seen a single episode of *Friends*. He was adorable in so many ways but also just plain hot. And he had no idea how it drove me nuts when he pushed his glasses up higher on his nose or rolled up a sleeve to reveal one of his perfect forearms.

But it would only be a matter of time before he got bored with me—if he wasn't already. Harper was smart and talented. They made more sense. Hence, my grand plan to pair them up. But it was shockingly painful that she agreed, proving I was a dummy after all.

"I feel like I haven't seen you in forever, Em," Delilah piped up from my right. "You've been so absent lately. Spending all your time being *tutored*."

I sighed. I'd been avoiding this conversation that I knew had been brewing. "That's because I need the help."

"Poor Tucker," Elowen said from my left. "He's going to get lonely without you."

"Careful, Em," Aria said from behind. "If Orion doesn't come around, Elowen might just snatch your man out of sheer neglect."

Elowen snorted delicately. "Please. I would *never* do that to Em, and she would never do that to Tucker."

"Exactly right," I said.

But that was a lie. There was nothing between Tucker and me and never had been. Only my desire to please my dad.

I should just break up with him. Now. Today. Another baby step toward living my own life.

The thought gave me an actual shiver of fear at what my dad would do if I caused that kind of "turbulence" right before the election that was now just around the corner.

"Here they come," Sierra said, sitting up eagerly.

The boys' boat was coming around the Bend. My gaze latched on to the first seat, the bow seat, to find Xander. But though the guys were dressed identically in their long-sleeved practice unisuits with matching goggles— the small, iridescent kind that swimmers wore—I could tell immediately it wasn't him. He was at the stern of the boat, facing Dean. The rest of the crew were lined up behind him.

"Ugh, Rhett was right," Aria groused. "The coach switched him and Xander. Now Rhett's the bow and Xander has the stroke seat, which is only *the most important* seat on the crew."

I suppressed a smile that was full of pride, conscious that Delilah was beside me, taking mental notes on everything like a reporter for TMZ.

"Oh my God, I can see why you guys are so into crew," Sierra said. "How sexy is *that*?"

We all shut up and watched as the guys came speeding through the water, the boat cutting the dark blue like a knife. They rowed in exact unison, arm muscles perfectly cut under the tight latex, shoulders and biceps flexing, their faces each wearing the same grimace of determination.

They're so fast. They've never been this fast…until Xander. My fiancé.

A crazed laugh nearly burst out of me, but I caught it in time.

"I mean, look at the way they move," Sierra said, then bit her lip.

"Right?" Elowen said, her gaze on Orion, no doubt. "All that back-and-forth…imagine that in bed." She gave me a nudge. "You don't have to imagine. You get Tucker whenever you want."

I barely heard her, my eyes drinking in Xander, who was all sleek lines and lean muscle, rowing with speed and fluidity. As stroke seat, he set the pace, which meant everyone behind him had to keep up.

"Em?"

"Yep, sure," I said absently, my gaze stubbornly refusing to let go of Xander. He was rowing like a man possessed, his teeth bared, pulling and then pushing… It was the easiest leap of the imagination—like mental Photoshop—to put myself underneath him, to be the recipient of that heated exertion…

As the boat drew closer, the coaches on the dock were grabbing at each other like excited kids on Christmas morning. The guys gave it their all, Dean shouting at them through his mic'd headset to *pull, goddammit.* His voice laden with commanding authority I'd never heard from him before.

Finally, the boat arrowed across some finish line only they could see. The guys immediately slumped in sheer exhaustion while their coaches jumped up and down.

"Six minutes, forty-eight seconds!" the coach shouted. "*Six-forty-eight,* you magnificent bastards!"

"Holy shit," Aria said. "For a two thousand meter, that's insanely fast."

I nodded, unable to keep my grin from breaking ear to ear as the guys cheered tiredly, landing heavy thumps on each other's backs. Dean leaned forward to grab Xander by the shoulders and shake him, laughing. Then the guy behind Xander, Henry Moore, took a turn grabbing his shoulders and giving him an awkward from behind hug.

Orion, at the other end of the boat, pumped his fist, and even Tucker looked ecstatic.

Only Rhett at the bow wasn't cheering. He looked downright murderous.

"Fucking Bender," Aria said and stood up with a huff.

"That was hot," Sierra said. "Dean Yearwood can tell me how hard to pull anytime he wants."

The rest of us busted out laughing as we all went down to greet the guys at the dock.

Tucker enveloped me in a quick embrace, then went right back to celebrating with the guys and talking shit about New Haven Prep in the upcoming regatta.

Xander looked tired but satisfied, surrounded by the coaches and Dean, who were making a big deal about "stroke rates" and his "punishing pace" and thumping him on the back. He was clearly their hero. He took it all in with a quiet dignity that was sexy as hell. Sexier than all the chest puffing and loud bravado around him.

Until he saw me. Then his expression lifted into surprise and something like happiness.

I crooked my little finger at him and smiled. He smiled back...just as Tucker grabbed me and spun me around. The guilt hit me; this was his win too, and I was supposed to be happy for him, but I didn't feel anything at all.

That night, Jack came down to dinner wearing all black. Black jeans and a long-sleeved black shirt with a black armband around his right bicep. Even the fingerless burn glove that he wore over his left hand was black. His hand was nearly healed, but I knew under that glove, his skin was terribly scarred and would be for the rest of his life.

My brother took his seat across from me with more energy and enthusiasm than I'd seen in a long time, digging into his dinner with a strange, bright smile. My stomach clenched, as the air suddenly felt electric.

And not in a good way.

"Is this a preview of your Halloween costume for Saturday?" my father asked mildly.

"Nope."

"Then what is it, Jack?" my mother put in before taking a sip of wine, as if she needed to fortify herself before hearing the answer.

"Well," Jack said conversationally. "I learned something very interesting in history class last week." He cut into his steak and took a bite. "Did you know that Victorians had detailed rituals for mourning deceased family members?"

Mom stared at Jack with wide eyes while my dad set his fork down with deliberate slowness.

"Jack…"

"It's quite fascinating," Jack said in a jovial tone, talking around a mouthful of steak. "A widower, for example, would be expected to wear black for one year, but a widow wore black for two full two years. Fucking patriarchy, am I right?"

My mouth went dry as my mother covered her eyes with one hand, her other gripping the stem of her wine glass.

"*Jack*," my father said. "That kind of language is unacceptable—"

"But the point was," Jack continued, unbothered, "to demonstrate to the world that they were grieving. To wear their grief openly, out in public. So that *everyone knew* they lost someone."

Mom made a strangled sound, like a whimper.

Dad tossed his napkin on the table, seething now. "Are you satisfied? You've upset your mother."

Jack ignored him and forked a green bean. "So I got to thinking. As a kind of project for history class—extra credit, if you will—I'll wear black for an entire year. Because even though it was seven years ago and I'm not a widower, it's never too late to do the right thing. You know?"

My father stood up now, his eyes black, and leveled a finger at Jack. "You shut your mouth. You shut your goddamn mouth. I'm warning you…"

"Not to mention, Dia de los Muertos is just around the corner. Another tradition in which the living honor the dead, because it's the *right thing to do*."

I sat frozen, watching as my dad moved toward Jack's chair. Jack jumped up and skirted behind Mom. My father and brother stared each other down, circling the table.

"I'm going to wear black for an entire year," Jack said loudly, all traces of humor gone, his eyes shining now. "And people will ask me why."

"*Jack*," Dad bellowed, chasing my brother as he moved behind my chair.

I flinched, my heart clanging.

"And you know what I'll say, Dad?" Jack cried. "I'll say, 'I'm in mourning for my brother, Grant.' I'll say his name! I'll scream it from the fucking rooftops! His name was Grant Nathaniel Wallace, and he was here! *He was fucking here!*"

I watched in a kind of detached horror as my brother knocked over my dad's chair to create a roadblock and then raced upstairs. My dad stopped as the slam of Jack's bedroom door reverberated so hard, the delicate plates in the china cabinet rattled.

Slowly, with measured breaths, Dad righted his chair and sat back down. He smoothed his napkin over his lap and resumed his meal. My mother, still covering her eyes, lifted her wine glass to her mouth with a shaky hand.

"Emery," Dad said, jolting me from my shock. "I'm sending your application to Brown this week and putting in for a conditional acceptance. This means we should hear back much sooner."

I struggled to find my voice, dizzy with the change of subject. "But I haven't…I haven't written the application letter."

"I've taken the liberty of doing it for you. I know what they want to hear and what they'll be expecting. I also don't trust that you will show the proper enthusiasm." He turned his gaze to me. "I understand you have a calculus midterm coming up?"

I nodded.

"And SATs are in a few weeks. Given the number of

tutoring sessions you've had with that Xander person, I expect nothing less than stellar results on both. Am I clear?"

"Yes," I said, barely a whisper.

"And how are things with Tucker?"

My head shot up. "Um, okay, I guess. Why?"

"Because the election is in a few days, and we need to keep a united front with the Hill family. No turbulence."

"And what if…?"

"Don't mumble, Emery," Dad said. "What if what?"

"What if I don't want to be with him anymore?" I managed. "What if I don't have feelings for him…at all?"

What if I never did?

Before he could answer, my mother abruptly pushed her chair back and stood up. "I'm going to bed."

When she was gone, my father stared straight ahead to my mother's empty chair. "Jack's upset her greatly," he said. "Your brother is treading on thin ice. Very thin ice."

"I think he's just in pain, Dad," I said quietly.

We all are.

"Is that so?" he mused and resumed eating his dinner. "He doesn't know what pain is."

I couldn't tell if that was a statement or a threat. But I did know that it would take nothing at all for Dad to decide I was on thin ice as well. One crack, with Tucker or math or anything else, and I'd fall right in.

Chapter 18

XANDER

I READ THE TEXT FROM EMERY AND STOPPED ON MY WAY to the library.

> All the study rooms are full. We have to meet at my house. Do you have the address?

I texted back, Yes.

It'd been emblazoned on my mind for seven years, and I'd handwritten it on more letters than I cared to count.

Her reply came fast. Oh, right. See you soon.

I rode my bike through Castle Hill, toward the coast and along Ridge Road, with every muscle in my body screaming from yesterday's row practice. I'd dreaded being moved to stroke seat but accepted the challenge, and it paid off. Six minutes, forty-eight seconds was elite-level speed for a two thousand meter, and CHA hadn't come close to touching it in years. Even Tucker gave me a grudging nod of approval in the clubhouse. Rhett's expression promised murder at a future date.

He'll push me off that bridge when we come to it.

I pedaled down Emery's long driveway, where she was checking her phone as she leaned against her white BMW. With the sun peeking through the clouds, the strands of her blond hair glowed golden. She wore tight jeans and a soft, white sweater. All of her looked soft and warm and…

Luscious.

"Stop it," I muttered under my breath as I approached, walking my bike. "Hey."

"Hey," she said, then looked pained. "God, I forgot you don't drive. I'm sorry, I should have given you a ride, but I'm not thinking clearly. Sort of panicking about that midterm."

"It's fine," I said, glancing up at the huge white house. Ten of mine could fit in hers. The cars in the circular drive were luxury vehicles—not one rusted Buick. Everything about her house felt like a reflection of what I didn't have.

"Are you sure it's okay that I'm here?" I asked as I parked my bike.

Emery walked us through a side entrance. "Of course," she said. "My parents know you tutor me."

We'd come into a large, stainless steel and white marble kitchen where a portly older woman was preparing dinner.

"Hello, Miss Emery." She smiled at me warmly, if curiously. "And who is your friend?"

"Hi, Belinda. This is Xander," Emery said, rummaging in the pantry. She grabbed a bag of chips and two bananas and dumped them in my arms. "Something to drink?"

"Uh, just water, thanks."

She retrieved two bottles of water from the fridge. "Bye, Belinda."

"Bye, Miss Emery," Belinda said and went back to her carrot-chopping with a small smile.

Emery led me through her immense, immaculate house. A house filled with everything one could possibly want, yet it felt oddly empty. And cold. We were halfway up the stairs when a woman started down.

"Hi, Mom," Emery said. "This is Xander Ford. He's the math tutor I told you guys about."

"Pleased to meet you, Mrs. Wallace," I said, noting that I'd been downgraded from *friend* to *tutor* in the presence of her mother.

Emery's mom was beautiful, with blond hair and the same blue-green eyes as her daughter, but she seemed wraithlike. Almost hollow. As if she were made of paper and the slightest breeze would blow her away. She didn't reply but stared at me with something like alarm on her face.

"Mom?" Emery said warily. "You okay?"

Her mother blinked and tore her gaze from me. "Emery, your father will be home at five o'clock."

"I know."

"*Five o'clock*, Emery." She gave me a final, hard glance, then continued past us down the stairs, leaving a trail of perfume and a faint whiff of alcohol in her wake.

"Sorry about her," Emery said, looking away. "She's... not feeling well."

"It's okay," I said. "I'll make sure I'm gone before five."

She smiled at me gratefully and led me down a hallway toward her room. She caught me glancing to the right, to the other wing of bedrooms.

"Grant's room is the one on the left," Emery whispered. "I sneak in there sometimes. To visit him. Don't tell anyone."

"I never would."

She smiled again, and I followed her into her room. Unlike the rest of the house, Emery's space was warm and brightly lit, and everything about it was *her*.

Her room was at least three times the size of my loft and furnished like a living room as much as a bedroom. A pink reclining chair sat in one corner, a white desk stood under the window that overlooked the bay, and a fluffy pink throw rug lay over the carpet.

The dominant color was white with tasteful pink accents, little vases of flowers, and blank walls—except for two. One wall was completely covered in collages. Squares of paper populated with clusters of photos or images or sketches that ran along distinct themes: the 1940s, French provincial countryside, Art Deco glamour... All of them saturated with taste and style. This wasn't just a hobby but professional-level artistry, like design blueprints for all the rooms Emery would never get to touch thanks to her father's oppression.

But the wall behind Emery's bed made me catch my

breath. Electric blue with a cherry blossom branch laden with little pink flowers arching down from the right corner, shedding petals here and there. At first, I thought it must be wallpaper, but upon closer inspection—as close as I dared get to Emery's queen-sized bed—I realized it was hand-painted.

"You made this?"

Emery was at her desk, gathering chopped up magazines and printouts for a work-in-progress. "Yep. I convinced my parents to let me decorate my room. I thought it would help show them what I was capable of but...nope." She smiled sadly and held up a printout. "Prom ideas. My last chance."

Aside from marrying me, came the thought, but I pushed it away. Of all the things we talked about over the past six weeks, my "proposal" wasn't one of them. We'd both shelved it out of sight, stuffed it in a closet until—if—she needed it.

"Emery...your room is incredible."

She glanced away, smiling. "Thank you."

Anger swept through me that her parents could look at what she'd done to this room—transforming it into a safe, warm space that reflected Emery exactly—and not put her on the first bus to RISD.

She removed a decorative throw pillow from a chair in the corner, then dragged the chair beside the one already at her desk. She giggled at me standing there like a dope, my arms laden with bananas and chips. "Oh my gosh, you can put those here."

We sat together as the late October clouds rolled over the Narragansett, and I felt as if I'd been lured into a trap. Being in Emery's bedroom was dangerous. It was suffused with *her:* her warmth and softness, her artistry—but heat too. An electricity or energy that made the air feel combustible. Radioactive. It didn't help either, the way she sipped her drink, touching her tongue to her lips afterward, or the way she glanced up at me from under her bangs, as if we shared a secret only the two of us knew.

This was a bad idea.

The radiant energy of Emery's room, her nearness, herself… decayed the walls I'd put up to protect myself until they were flimsy and paper-thin. I didn't trust I'd remember how to chew food, so I drank water for my throat, which had gone dry. Eventually, we pulled out the study materials, and Emery assumed her usual position: elbow on table, cheek propped in her palm, pencil tapping idly in her other hand.

"The midterm is going to cover hyperbolic functions, right?" I said, flipping open the math text, seeking refuge in the safety of cold, sterile numbers. "So let's start here…"

"How's your dad doing?" Emery asked. "Still working on the unified theory?"

I smiled at her gentle concern and the fact she would do literally anything besides math.

"Yeah, he is," I said. "But it's a struggle. His equations keep running into infinities, especially when they come up against phenomena like entanglement."

Emery arched a brow. "English, please."

I chuckled. "He's using super hard math—the kind that makes this stuff look like basic arithmetic—to try to make sense of entangled particles."

"What are those?"

I frowned. "Don't you think we should study? You're paying me for this time…"

She waved a hand. "In a minute. Please continue."

Emery's eyes were bright and curious. Expectant.

Not to mention, it's impossible for me to say no to her.

"Well, if quantum particles have previously interacted, they can become intrinsically linked. Whatever happens to one particle instantaneously happens to the other, no matter how far apart they are. Light-years even. That's called entanglement."

Emery wore a small smile. "Sounds like you and me."

My heart suddenly skipped a beat—her words like an alarm that had woken it up. "What do you mean?"

"We met for the first time when we were ten. Maybe that 'previous interaction' bound us together, even after you moved away. And maybe that's why you moved back to Castle Hill and why I needed tutoring. We're linked." She toyed with her pencil, not looking at me, her cheeks dusted with a faint blush. "Entangled."

I should've told her that was silly, romantic nonsense and not at all how particle physics worked, but I swallowed it all down. Because that's sort of exactly how it worked. And because she was right. Meeting her had changed me forever.

"Right, well…we should get back to it."

She heaved a sigh. "If you insist."

As with nearly all of our tutoring sessions, it only took a few minutes of actual work before Emery stopped paying attention to the math. Again. I felt her gaze on me and cleared my throat. "Emery…"

"You're dressed like your eyes."

"Sorry?"

"Blue sweater, brown pants." She grinned. "Did you color-coordinate on purpose?"

"Um, no. I don't ever think about my eyes."

"Really?" Emery gushed. "Because I just *can't* with them."

"You can't…what?"

She laughed. "Get over how amazing they are. As someone obsessed with color palettes, I need to take a closer look. Can I?"

"Um…sure."

Emery took off my glasses and brushed the hair off my brow. Her hand lingered on my temple, pressing my hair away, her nose inches from mine. Identical actions as those seven years ago when she first discovered the anomaly. I shifted in my chair as my groin tightened.

"Your right eye is a beautiful slate blue. Like the sky just after the sun drops out of sight. Your left eye is a rich brown, like gingerbread, with a wedge of that same blue as your right. If your eye was a clock, it'd be all brown but five to eight would be blue."

"Technically, both my eyes are blue with the left having a segment of brown from eight to five," I said, not missing that she used the word *beautiful*. "It's called sectoral heterochromia."

"I read about that," Emery said, releasing me from her gentle touch. "I looked it up after you came back to Castle Hill. They say people with heterochromia possess special gifts or have a destiny that sets them apart from others. That definitely sounds like you."

"Or it's merely a genetic anomaly caused by variations in the amount and distribution of melanin in my iris."

She rolled her eyes with a grin. "Don't be boring. Too much science and not enough imagination isn't good for the soul."

Emery meant it as a tease, but I bristled. I didn't want to be boring. Not for her. But I was all science and math, barricading myself behind its exactness. No surprises. My mother's sudden absence had been surprise enough, and the discoloration of my left eye was a never-ending reminder of her.

I'd once read on some silly astrological website that nonhomogeneous eye color symbolized opposing forces within. I'd dismissed it immediately, but maybe there was something to it. With Emery, I felt a storm of conflicting feelings. Impossibilities. We couldn't be more different. I was too rigid where she was fluid, too closed where she was open and brave.

She's so much braver than me.

"Anyway, you should show your eyes off more," Emery said, pulling me from my thoughts. "You could wear contacts and keep your hair off your face." She laid her cheek in her hand with a sad smile. "I'd bet you'd get all the girls if you did that."

I don't want all the girls…

"We should get back to the math…"

"Are you going to the Halloween Festival?" she asked suddenly.

"I think so," I said, glancing away. "I might ask Harper."

"Oh. Oh!" Emery exclaimed, sitting up. "Yes, good! I was…um, I was going to suggest that, actually."

"You were?"

"Yeah. She's becoming a good friend. And you're a good friend. So…perfect, right?"

Emery smiled the smile I'd come to recognize as the one she wore when she was trying to take whatever was in front of her and turn it into something good.

I rolled the pencil over my knuckles. "I guess you're going with Tucker?"

"Yep," she said and toyed with the edge of her textbook.

"How long have you two been together?" In all our talks, we'd never spoken about him. I'd never wanted to; it felt like willingly chugging gasoline.

"About six months," she said. "His dad is a senator, and my dad is counting on him to be reelected in a few days. Senator Hill will pass some laws that allow Wallace Industries to keep making their textiles however they want without worrying about the environment. Pretty terrible, right?"

It was certainly terrible that her father was using her

to further his own ends. I suddenly doubted that dating Tucker had been her idea. "What happens if Hill loses the election?"

Emery shrugged. "Not sure. But maybe..."

"Maybe...?"

Maybe she breaks up with Tucker and then what? She chooses you with your broken house and your broken father and your broken heart that's too afraid of getting broken some more?

"Tucker's not a bad guy," she said. "And anyway, he and I make sense."

"What does that mean, you make sense?"

"Well, we do," she said uncertainly. "The Prom King and the Queen Bee—"

"That's not all you are, Emery." I gestured to her room. "Look around. You're so talented. A real artist. And more than that you're..."

"What?" she asked, leaning in ever so slightly.

My jaw worked but nothing came out, my mind warring with my heart, which wanted to tell her she was a luminous star shining in the vast darkness that wanted to swallow her up. A diamond clenched in the hand of her ruthless father, who didn't realize how bright she could shine if he just let her go.

Emery mistook my hesitation. "Sorry, I don't mean to put you on the spot. My parents don't ask Jack or me how we are, or what we're thinking or feeling..."

"I think you're extraordinary," I blurted.

Emery froze, her eyes wide. "What? No..."

"You are, and you should never reduce yourself to any one thing when you are multitudes."

She let out a shaky little breath. "You're too nice to me. I can't compare to you and your genius. You're the extraordinary one, Xander." She smiled shyly. "I'm simple. I like pretty things. You can calculate black hole singularities, while I can't even get through high school math and—where are you going?"

I jumped up and went to her wall of collages, searching until I found the perfect one for my purpose.

"Can I?"

Before she could answer, I carefully unpinned it from the wall and brought it to the desk. The collage was all her own artistry in different mediums—sketches, watercolor, oil—and evoked a scene in winter: a cabin by a snowy lake; an icy waterfall—frozen—its water trapped in crystalline icicles; a grandfather clock with no numbers on its face, but a cold moon instead. The entire collage spoke of a world instantly frozen in time. What had once been green and vibrant, now icy and still.

I grabbed my pencil and a sheet of paper and wrote: $y(x,t) = A\sin(kx - \omega t + \Phi)$

"Do you know what that is?"

Emery gave me a look. "What do you think?"

"When I think about the motion of a wave, this is what I see," I said, tapping the equation. Then I pointed at her collage, where the lake's small wave crashed on the icy shore. "This is what you see."

Emery looked to the beauty of the wave, then to me, confused, but I was already scribbling.

$T(t) = T_s + (T_0 - T_s)e^{-kt}$

"This is Newton's Law of Cooling," I said. "It's what I see when I consider water turning to ice." I indicated her collage's frozen waterfall. "This is what you see. This is what you *create*."

"Xander..."

I wrote another equation. $T = 2\pi\sqrt{L/g}$

"This is a sinusoidal function for one swing of a pendulum." I tapped my equation and then her grandfather clock. "This is yours."

She looked to me, stunned to be hearing what someone should have been telling her her whole life.

"You have something I will never have, Emery," I said. "You have the ability to see through the building blocks of something—the matter and the particles and the unbending calculus of it all—to its heart." I turned to her delicate rendering of the cherry blossom tree. "I can model the branching structures of trees with fractal geometry, but I could never make one come alive on a plain white wall. There is nothing simple about you, Emery. Not one thing."

I looked back to see her eyes were full. She swallowed, and the motion loosened a tear from her lash. It spilled down her cheek.

"Thank you, Xander," she whispered.

For once in my life, I acted without thinking. I reached out my hand and cupped her cheek. It fit so easily there, as if I were made to hold her. My thumb swept across her soft, warm skin, taking the tear with it. Absorbing it into me, like I wanted to do with everything that hurt her.

Because we're entangled.

Emery swallowed hard and pressed herself into my touch. Her eyes, still shining, dropped to my mouth for the shortest of seconds and her own lips parted. My heart pounded against my ribs, as if it were about to be set free, and for one short moment, I allowed myself to believe I could have this. This beautiful, perfect girl I'd wanted since I was ten years old.

I inclined my head toward her, a gravitational pull I was helpless to resist. Emery's chin tilted up ever so slightly, her breath warm and sweet on my lips…

"What are you doing?" came a voice from the door.

The words pelted us like bullets. Emery and I jumped up with comical sameness, and stepped apart from each other, our faces wearing identical flushes, our eyes wide with the same shock.

"Daddy…" Emery stammered, breathing hard. "You're home early."

A man stood in the doorway of her room—a door he'd opened without knocking. I'd pictured Emery's father as a golem—a giant, petrified statue of a man, with no blood in his veins. Instead, Grayson Wallace was slight, shorter than me, and balding. He wore slacks, a white button-down, and a cardigan. Plain. Bland. In a crowd, my gaze would pass right over him. But his eyes…his eyes were like chips of ice, and I suddenly felt as cold as the scene in Emery's collage.

"Daddy, this is Xander," Emery said with forced cheer. "My…um, tutor."

"Nice to meet you, sir."

Her father's gaze sized me up and down, from my old shoes to the worn-out sweater I wore over my worn-out T-shirt. I was examined, analyzed, and rejected, all in an instant.

"Xander Ford," he said. "Your father is Russell Ford."

"Yes," I said, muscles tensing all over my body.

"His father is a famous physicist," Emery said. "In fact, he—"

"Hush up, Emery," Grayson Wallace said calmly, not looking at her. "Russell Ford's laboratory work paved the way for new methods of detecting pollutants in large bodies of water."

I tilted my chin. "Yes, it did."

"The ramifications of which cost me twenty million dollars in regulatory fines last year."

"Daddy…"

"*Be silent*, Emery."

White-hot rage swept through me at how he spoke to her. He stared me down, but I stared back…and then he shrugged.

"I hear your father has suffered some health issues lately. Send him my best, will you?" He turned to Emery. "Get dressed. We have dinner tonight with the Hills."

Emery's gaze darted between us, distraught. Her father didn't move from the door. I gathered my things and shouldered my backpack.

"I'll walk you down, Xander," she said.

"No need. I'll see our guest out," her father countered.

Emery shot me a fearful, apologetic look as I strode out. I followed Grayson Wallace through his house while he chatted with me conversationally the entire time.

"It's not easy, running a multinational corporation *and* a household such as mine, as I'm sure you can imagine," he said.

"No, sir."

"There are so many moving parts," Grayson said, ushering me to the side entrance by the garage. "Plates spinning, if you will. And I cannot let a single one fall. It could start a chain reaction, and before I know it, the whole thing is in shambles."

He opened the door, and I stepped out into the cold while he stood inside his enormous white house, arms crossed.

"So, you see, Xander, if something were to try to disrupt the plates that I've spun into a fortune large enough to take care of my daughter for the rest of her life, I'd be very angry. I did not work this hard for her to piss it away on something—or someone—so far beneath her. After all, why would she choose a handful of pennies when I'm offering her a mountain of gold?"

I clenched my teeth from spitting something back. Something that would only make things worse for Emery.

Grayson's bland tone hardened slightly. "She's impressionable, my daughter. Easily led astray. With the wrong influences, she might make poor choices, and then I'd be forced to seek alternative methods of correction. Permanent grounding, perhaps. No dance, no prom committee, and no charity cases who don't belong anywhere near her or this house."

He turned his back on me before I could say a word, before I could catch the breath in my throat.

"Your tutoring services will no longer be needed. Good evening."

Then he shut the door in my face.

Chapter 19

EMERY

Halloween night was strangely warm, which boded well for Tucker and his Mojo Dojo Casa House Ken costume. When he'd picked me up to take me to the festival, I had to bite my cheek to keep from laughing as he *yes, sir'd* and *no, sir'd* my dad while wearing a full-length faux fur coat and no shirt.

But in Tucker's truck, my humor faded. I sat in the passenger seat in my pink gingham dress watching Castle Hill zip past in the dark. Although I hadn't been thrilled about going as Barbie, I never did anything halfway. My costume was spot-on, right down to the white jewelry and pink pumps, while Tucker was the perfect Ken. We had a good shot at Best Couple, which was probably why he was so excited.

Tucker hummed along to a song on the radio, tapping

the wheel and nodding his head. We hardly spoke—certainly never had conversations like Xander and I have.

Had, I corrected. *Xander isn't speaking to me anymore.*

After Dad ushered Xander out of the house a few days ago, he informed me that our tutoring sessions were over. Now Xander avoided me at school. Whatever my father had said had done the trick. Something disgusting about Dr. Ford, maybe, that couldn't be taken back.

So be it. I'll keep doing what my dad wants, and he'll love me, and we'll be a happy family. No turbulence.

I sounded out-of-control in my own head. I *felt* out-of-control. Like whatever mental fortitude I'd been using to survive my own household was starting to unravel.

I turned to Tucker. "What are your hopes and dreams?"

His brows furrowed under the black-and-white bandana around his forehead. "What do you mean?"

"Just what I said. What do you hope for your future? What do you want to do?"

"Well, I want to go 3-and-0 in the regattas this season, grab a championship in water polo, make Prom King with you as my hot Queen, and then I'll go to Columbia. Get into politics."

"Do you see yourself as a senator, too?"

Tucker glanced at me sideways. "Why all the questions? Did Grayson put you up to this?"

"No, I genuinely want to know."

He shrugged. "Maybe I'll run for office. Don't know yet."

I waited, arms crossed. "Now, you're supposed to ask

me about my hopes and dreams. Not that I'm allowed to have any."

Tucker frowned. "You're acting weird."

"It's not weird to want to talk, Tucker. Talking is what boyfriends and girlfriends do. Otherwise, it isn't a real relationship."

"How are we not real? We're together, aren't we?"

"But why? What do you like about me?"

He grinned. "For one thing, you're the hottest girl in school."

"Try again."

"I don't know. You're a good dancer, and you're…hot."

"You said that already."

"What's gotten into you, Em? You've changed since Ford's been 'tutoring' you," he said, emphasizing *tutoring* with air quotes. "Just what the hell is going on with you two?"

"Nothing's going on, and he's not my tutor anymore."

"Good," Tucker said. "Ford's a killer stroke seat, I'll give him that, but he's aiming pretty fucking high if he thinks he's good enough for you." He frowned at me when I turned away. "Jesus, Em, that was a compliment. You're awfully touchy about a guy who supposedly doesn't mean anything to you."

I couldn't have said it better myself, I thought, and tried not to burst into tears.

Tucker pulled his truck into the lot at Bennington Farm. It was a rustically elegant estate on twelve acres that held weddings, balls, and parties of all kinds. Its expansive backyard could serve as a beautiful place for a reception or, like tonight, be transformed into a Halloween festival with hay, pumpkins, and wagon wheel decor. Lights were strung up between booths that offered popcorn, caramel apples, hot dogs, and cotton candy.

Tucker led me across the hay-strewn grounds to find our group. Along the way, he signed us up for the costume contest, and then we hit a photo booth where a professional photographer took our picture.

At the edge of the dance floor, we joined my friends along with Tucker's athlete buddies, including some of the row crew, his water polo teammates, and a few guys from the gymnastics team. Big, blond Gideon Foster was dressed as a gladiator. Orion Mercer was elegantly handsome as a 1920s gangster. Elowen, a sexy pirate, stuck to his side like glue. He ignored her and seemed to be scanning the crowd for someone else.

I kept my eyes to myself, not wanting to see Xander and Harper together. Not wanting to see Xander at all. I could still feel his hand on my cheek, his thumb brushing away my tear. He'd wanted to kiss me; I'd felt it vibrating off of him like a current. And God, I wanted it too, and I hadn't known how badly until it was happening. As if what had begun seven years ago was finally coming full circle.

Like coming home…

He doesn't want to kiss me anymore. He won't even talk to me.

If my father had been truly cruel to him, I couldn't blame Xander for wanting nothing more to do with me.

I just wasn't prepared for how much it hurt or how much more suffocating my life had become. It felt like I could barely breathe.

"Em! Tucker!" Aria waved as she and Rhett joined us. "What do you think?" she said, showing off their costumes, which, like most Richies', were professional quality down to the wig and makeup. He was dressed as Gomez Addams, she as a sexy Wednesday. "We just might give you and Tucker a run for Best Couple."

"Bloody hell." Orion snorted a laugh. "You realize Gomez is Wednesday's *father*, right?"

Aria sniffed. "They're *fictional*, Orion. No one's going to care."

"If you say so." He shot me a private *Can you believe this shit?* glance and I managed a smile in return.

I noticed Tucker and some guys already passing around a flask; he'd be wasted by ten o'clock. I felt drunk too, in my own way. A strange energy ramping up inside me, trying to break free. Like I wanted to scream or cry or run and not stop until I arrived somewhere else. Until I could *be* someone else.

Delilah and Sierra bounced over, Sierra a white swan ballerina and Delilah her twin in black.

"You look ah-mazing, Emery," Sierra said.

"Thanks. You guys look great, too. From *The Black Swan*, right?"

"Yes!" Sierra said. "Before and after the madness."

"You okay?" Delilah asked, scrutinizing. "You're the saddest Barbie I've ever seen."

"I can't imagine why," I muttered. "I have everything I could possibly want."

They exchanged glances, and Delilah touched my arm. "You want something to drink, Em? I'll get you some water—"

But before I could answer, Tucker was there, pulling at my hand. "Come on, babe. Let's dance."

On the dance floor, he wrapped his arms around my waist, his groin grinding against me as the DJ played Sabrina Carpenter's "Please Please Please."

"You want to know what I like about you?" Tucker growled in my ear, his breath tinged with whiskey. "You're fucking perfect. No girl comes close."

"It's not a competition," I muttered.

"Huh?"

"Nothing."

I ringed my arms around Tucker's neck; if not for my heels, I might not have reached. I wanted to hold and be held, but he led with his crotch, his hands massaging my waist, then slipping lower, over my ass.

"I can't wait to get you into the truck later," he said. "We can celebrate our costume win. Whaddya say, Em?" He held me tighter so I could feel his erection through his leather pants. "You make me so hard. I don't want to wait anymore. Let's just do it." He put his mouth to my ear. "Let's fuck."

Why not? What was I holding out for? I didn't believe in that archaic nonsense about "giving away" my virginity. I only wanted to feel comfortable and respected. I wanted to *want* to do it, not to just get it over with. The first time and every time.

But it didn't matter what I wanted, anyway, or who I wanted it with. My father had taught me that, and suddenly I felt like if I didn't say something true and real, I was going to explode. So I did.

"I don't think we should see each other anymore."

Tucker's eyes widened; he was just as shocked as me. "What did you say?"

"I said, I don't think we should be together."

"What the fuck? Em…are you breaking up with me?"

"I think so," I said, my heart pounding. "Maybe. No, yes, I—"

"Maybe?" he scoffed darkly. "Oh, I get it. *Maybe*, if my dad loses the election. *Maybe not*, if he wins. Whatever it takes to keep Grayson Wallace happy."

"He'll never be happy," I said as the force of what I'd done hit me. "I need some water."

I pushed through the crowd to a long table set up with refreshments. My hands trembled as I poured myself some water.

What did I just do?

Something my father would think was wrong but that felt exactly right. A paradox or a superposition or something that was both things at the same time. I tossed the water back like it was a shot of booze, then reached in my clutch for my phone to call an Uber to take me home.

But the costume contest was beginning. Tucker found me again.

"Come on, babe." He took me by the arm and guided me to the stage on the dance floor. "Don't be like that. Let's go win this and then we can talk, if that's what you want so badly."

We lined up with the other contestants to wait until it was our turn to parade across the stage. The winners would be determined by whomever the crowd cheered for the loudest. The Scariest and Most Original winners were picked, and Dean Yearwood easily took Best Costume for his Ferris Bueller—not only because his leather jacket and leopard-print vest were spot-on, but also because, like Ferris, everyone loved him.

Then it was time for Best Couples Costume.

The pairs moved to the front of the stage: Tucker and me, the Joker and Harley Quinn, Coraline and Wybie, and then Rhett and Aria as Gomez and Wednesday. I had to suppress a smile as some faces in the audience were clearly disturbed by the father/daughter pairing.

"It's okay, Em," Tucker said in my ear, his breath reeking of liquor. "I came on too strong. I get that. But we're perfect together, and you know it."

"No. I can't do this anymore."

"Come on, babe. The election is in a few days. Let's not do any crazy shit until then."

"Tucker, it's *over*," I said, but my words were drowned out by the DJ moving to stand behind us.

"And now we have...Ken and Barbie!"

Tucker fist pumped and pointed at his friends. I smiled my pretty smile and waited for it to be over, so I could go home to my bed and cry forever.

We started to get off the stage when someone from the crowd shouted, "Wait! What about Barbenheimer?"

"Barbenheimer!" someone echoed.

Others took up the call, and soon enough, a guy in a suit and an old-timey hat was being pushed to the stage.

Xander…

He'd put in contacts and his hair was tucked under the hat, revealing more of his handsome face than usual. Just like I'd suggested.

"Hold on, Barbie," the DJ said. "Looks like we have another contender. Oppenheimer, come on up!"

Tucker glared murderous daggers but restrained himself from making a scene and stepped aside as Xander joined me. Xander looked like a deer in headlights, clearly uncomfortable with the attention.

"For your consideration," the DJ bellowed, "Barbenheimer!"

The crowd went wild—mostly girls who were really seeing Xander for the first time. To me, his glasses didn't make him less attractive, but now his handsomeness was plainly obvious—beautiful angular features, those eyes, and even his clothes. Six feet of lean hotness in a plain suit.

I felt a certain happiness that the crowd loved him, but my heart cracked again too. It was tradition for the winners to dance together, like newlyweds at their wedding. A wild laugh nearly burst out of me. Or maybe it was a sob.

"The audience has spoken! Barbenheimer it is!" The DJ returned to his booth. "And for this special couple, their own special song."

The rest of the hopefuls left the stage, Tucker dragged off by Rhett and Orion and pacified with the flask. For now.

"What is happening right now?" Xander asked me.

"I'm Barbie, you're Oppenheimer. Barbenheimer. The two movies came out on the same day, so it became a thing for people to see both."

"My costume isn't J. Robert Oppenheimer. I'm dressed as my dad. This is the suit and hat he wore when he gave his dissertation at MIT."

"They don't know that, and now we're the Best Couple." I took his hand, that wild, reckless energy still coursing through my veins. "Come on. It's time for our dance. It's tradition."

I led him to the center of the dance floor. A spotlight fell on us as Billie Eilish's "What Was I Made For?" played over the sound system.

I moved to put my arms around his neck, but Xander took my right hand in his left, the old-fashioned way. My left went around his shoulder while his other hand found my waist. From the edge of the dance floor, Tucker and Rhett were talking with heads bowed, eyes on us, while my friends whispered and murmured.

But then, at the sensation of being held by Xander, the entire world faded out, and all that remained was his hand holding mine, his arm around me, his nearness. The out-of-control feeling didn't go away but mellowed from something hot and fiery into something molten and warm.

"I'm sorry," Xander said, his gaze darting over the crowd watching us. "I didn't mean for this to happen."

My eyes filled again. "Do you mean this dance? Or when you touched my face the other day? Or the way you're looking at me right now?"

"Emery..."

His expression was a mix of pain and want. Desire. I could see it plain as day because I felt it too.

"I broke up with Tucker," I blurted.

Xander's eyes flared. "You did? When?"

"Just now. My dad will kill me, and I'm terrified and happy and maybe going a little bit crazy all at the same time."

Xander stared at me, a hundred thoughts behind his eyes.

Tell me I did the right thing. Tell me that you're happy too...

"Em, you have to be careful. Your father—"

"Isn't here right now," I said. "Please, Xander. Let's have this dance."

Looking torn, he gave me a single nod, and that was enough. I rested my cheek on Xander's chest with my head tucked under his chin. I fit perfectly there. He pulled our joined hands in, laid our clasped fingers over his heart. His arm tightened around me, and our bodies pressed together, touching in a hundred places.

And I wanted to stay there, always.

"Emery." Xander's voice was soft, his mouth by my ear. "Why are you crying?"

I shook my head against his chest, my shoulders shaking. "Because this feels so perfect. Like how it's supposed to be, and we've been pretending we're just friends."

"I know," he said quietly.

"You haven't called or texted or said hello at school…"

"Because I…I thought it would be best to give you some space," he said. "And…Emery, we *should* stay friends. Because I—"

"You want to stay neutral," I said. "You don't believe in love."

"It's not that simple."

"You're right, it's not. Love is messy and complicated and doesn't always work out in some neat equation."

Xander turned me slowly, held me tighter. I could feel his heart thump against my cheek, fast and hard. "Why are you saying all this?"

"I don't know what I'm saying," I said. "I don't know how I'm *supposed* to feel, but I know how I *do* feel, and it's all bursting out of me. Since you came back, everything changed. I feel like I've been waiting for you all this time…"

"Emery, don't," he said in a low warning tone. "Please, don't."

I lifted my head from the warm dark of Xander's embrace to the glaring light of the dance floor and the hundreds of pairs of eyes on us—then to his stricken expression as he shook his head at me.

He doesn't want this…

With a muffled cry, I slipped out of his arms and ran off the dance floor, pushing wildly through the crowd. I sprinted through the festival, turning corners around booths and food trucks until I found a quiet place behind a small wagon filled with hay. I sagged against it and caught my breath.

Moments later, Xander turned the corner.

"You should go," I said. "If Tucker finds you here, he'll kill you."

"I don't care. We need to have this out." He tossed his hat aside and ran his hand over his eyes. "Look, I'm sorry, but we can't do this."

"We can't do what?" I said, crossing my arms, shaking, holding myself together. "I need to hear you say it."

"You know what," he said, his voice low and quavering. "There is only one way this ends. Me at MIT, and you in California. Because I am going to help make that happen for you, Emery, if it's the last fucking thing I do."

"I thought…the other day, in my room…"

"That was a mistake," Xander said, even if his eyes were telling me—screaming at me—that it wasn't.

"That's not true," I said. "I was there. I—"

"Emery, look…" Xander shoved his fingers through his hair, frustrated. "We got caught up in a moment when we were ten years old and romanticized it. We made it into something it's not."

His words hit me straight in the heart like a hammer. "Is that what we did?"

"Yes. So now we have all this…built-up expectation, maybe, when the fact is, we were just kids."

"That is the *fact*. But the feelings? They all meant nothing?"

"Not nothing," Xander said in a pained whisper. "They just can't mean everything."

I stared, willing back tears. A desperate, panicky feeling lit me up from the inside, because the best thing in my airless, closed-up life was slipping away.

He read the despair on my face and shook his head. "Fuck, Emery, I'm so sorry, but—"

"For what, Xander? You've figured it all out with your facts and logic and equations—"

"That's right because I have to keep you safe," he said, his voice rising now. "And me too. I told myself I would never get into this situation—"

"Oh, I see," I shot back. "I'm a *situation*."

"No, you don't see—"

"But you can hold me like that and nearly kiss me—"

"I refuse to lose one more person I love!" Xander shouted, then froze, his eyes wide. "Never mind. Forget it."

Too late. A sudden feeling of warmth and shock flooded me, making me stumble back. My heart felt full and on the verge of shattering, both at the same time.

"Don't you think I know how impossible it is?" I whispered. "I do. And I'm scared too, but—"

"There is no 'but,' Emery," Xander said. "There are no exceptions to the rule. I am going to MIT. I am going to finish what my father started. And you have to go to California. You have to follow your dreams and get as far away from that psychopath as you can."

"That doesn't mean we can't…*be* something to each other. Even far apart."

"How?" he demanded. "People leave, Emery. And they don't come back, even when they say they will."

"It wouldn't be like that, I promise…"

The word made him wince. "I've heard that before."

His cold tone hurt; he sounded like my dad. Tears threatened. "So that's it then? There's nothing else to talk about?"

"I said everything I wanted to say in those letters, and you never answered me back—"

"I never got the letters!" I cried, fresh tears spilling over.

"I'm not saying it's your fault. I'm saying, I have… limits." He shook his head, hands on his hips. "I lost my mom, and I'm losing my dad now too. Slowly, but it's happening." Xander's handsome face was etched with so much pain, his voice heavy with it. "I shouldn't be kissing you, Emery. I should be trying to save you."

"Save me?"

"Yes. To keep that light of yours from going out. I don't want to hurt you. The last thing on this fucking planet I want to do is hurt you. But it will only get worse. For both of us."

I heard his unspoken words, an echo of what he'd said the other night about love. Because he'd been hurt so badly before. His heart broken by his mother who should have loved him forever and instead taught him that love had limits.

"Okay," I whispered. "If that's what you want."

He met my eyes head on. "That's what I want."

And then my heart broke, too.

Silence, and then footsteps. Dean and Harper slowly came around the corner.

"Hey, guys," Dean said slowly. "Everything cool?"

"I need to go home," I managed.

"I'll take you." Harper offered me the puffy sleeve of her arm—she was dressed as a suffragette—and I took it. Xander gave me a final pained glance, and then I couldn't see through my tears.

Harper hustled me through the crowd, so I didn't have to see or talk to anybody. In her car, an old Prius, I slumped in the passenger seat and cried.

"Oh, babe," Harper said, pulling me in for a hug. "Is now a bad time to say I knew it all along?"

"What did you know?"

"You and Xander—"

"There is no me and Xander." I looked up at her through my tears. "Please, Harper. Take me home."

———

Harper dropped me off, and I trudged up the drive to the house. It was late, after eleven, and I headed straight through the quiet dark toward my room. I was almost at the stairs when my father's voice—soft and calm—made me freeze.

"Emery. Come here a moment."

The door to Dad's study was open, and a faint glow of yellow light reached the hall. I stepped inside. He had a fire going—the flames burning behind him and casting him in shadow. The small green Tiffany lamp on his desk cast more shadows against his sharp nose and gleamed over his balding head, which was bent over some papers.

"Sit."

I obeyed, sinking into the seat across from him, my hands folded in the lap of my dress, every muscle in my body tense, my heart still aching from the conversation with Xander. After several long moments, my father set his pen down and regarded me.

"Did you win?"

I blinked. "Win…?"

"The costume contest. Tucker seemed quite confident you two would win Best Couple."

"Oh. Uh, no. We didn't win."

My heart was pounding now under my dad's scrutiny, as if he knew. As if he could see it on my face that I *had* won, just not with his golden boy. I'd won Best Couple with the boy who didn't want me…

"That's a shame," Dad said. "You're home early. I'd have thought you and Tucker would have stayed later at the party."

"I…I'm not feeling well."

Dad nodded. "We never talked after that Xander fellow left the other day."

My hands made fists in my lap. "He didn't *leave*,

Daddy," I said slowly, feeling like I was poking a rattlesnake but was unable to help myself. "You kicked him out."

"I know what I saw, Emery," Dad said. "And I didn't like it."

He let the words hang in the air between us, thick with disapproval and unspoken warning. Just when I thought I'd shatter with the tension, he leaned back in his chair.

"The Narragansett Bay Regatta is coming up. The same night as the election, as it happens. Until that time, we need to keep a united front with the Hills. You'll attend the election watch party with Tucker, of course."

"I don't want to be with Tucker anymore," I said, hardly a whisper. "I broke up with him—"

My father got up from his chair and came around desktop my side, speaking as if he hadn't heard me. Or chose not to.

"Duty to family, Emery. There's nothing more important." He sat on the edge of his desk, looming over me. "I know that you know that, which is why I'm so proud of you."

I could hardly believe what I was hearing. "You are?"

"Of course. It's natural to have a slip up now and then. But one must never lose sight of the goal."

He took my hands and drew me to my feet.

"Never forget, Emery, infatuations come and go. At times, we're led by our hearts, but hearts are foolish. Impractical. What the heart wants usually leads to pain and will rarely keep a roof over our heads. You're smarter than that. You have every advantage in the world, and I know you won't throw it away over a soft moment or two, will you?"

I stared. Everything he was saying was at war with what I felt, but he was right—my own heart had led me straight to pain. And why was that? Because of a "soft moment" seven years ago that Xander himself said didn't mean to him what it did to me. A small part of me screamed not to listen to either of them, to hold on to the truth in my heart, but where would it get me? Out on the street. In the cold.

I shook my head. "No, Daddy."

"Of course not. Because that's something only stupid people do. Are you stupid?"

My throat went dry. "No."

He smiled then, so proud. Pleased. Happy with me.

"That's right."

And then to my utter shock, he wrapped his arms around me in a warm hug. It was over before I could move or think and was followed by a pat on my cheek.

"It's late. Get some sleep."

He returned to his desk, bent over his papers, and got back to work without another word.

I left his study and headed upstairs feeling numb, hollowed out. Before I found my door, my mother opened hers.

"Emery…" She was dressed in her silk pajamas, her eyes shadowed but clear. "I thought I heard you come in. Is everything all right?"

"Yes, Mom. Everything's fine. I'm just…tired." I managed a smile. "It's been a long day."

"Did Tucker drop you off?"

"No, my friend. Harper."

"And things are good with you and…him?"

"Great," I managed weakly. "Our costumes were a big hit."

"Emery." She took a step closer. "Does he…treat you well?"

It was the first time she'd ever asked me something like that.

I swallowed hard. "Sure. He's fine."

"And that other boy? Xander?"

"He's just a friend. Actually, I don't know if he's even that anymore," I said, fighting back tears. "You don't have to worry, Mom. You won't see him here again. I promise."

My mother's brows came together, and she wore an expression I couldn't read in the dim light. "Oh. Okay, then."

"Goodnight," I said, and hurried into my room.

I shut the door, kicked off my shoes, and crawled into bed. For a long while, I lay still, staring at the ceiling until the numbness thawed, and then I cried until there was nothing left.

Chapter 20

XANDER

I sagged against the wagon, the memory of Emery's tears battering my heart.

Because you broke hers.

"Fuck." I gave the hard wood a sharp jab with my elbow, but the pain wasn't nearly enough.

"You want to talk?" Dean offered gently. "Before Tucker finds you and smashes your teeth in? Sorry. Bad joke."

"It'd be no less than I deserve. But no, I'm good."

"Love you, man," Dean said, giving me a hug. "And whatever just happened with Emery, it'll work itself out. The best things always do."

He left, and I was alone. Distantly, the party was still going. Any second now, Tucker was going to show up with fists swinging. Because I'd held Emery in front of the whole school like she was mine. Like she was precious to me…

But no one came, so I left.

Harper and I had arrived at the festival separately; when I'd asked her to accompany me—as friends only—she'd given me a knowing look. "As friends only," she'd repeated. "Love triangles aren't my thing."

I found my bike, which I'd chained to a fence far from the entrance to Bennington Farm, and jumped on. I pedaled hard through the late fall chill that would only get colder as we headed into a snowy winter. The cold fell away as my blood heated at the sense memory of Emery's body pressed to mine, how she felt in my arms, how perfect and *right* it had been. And how fucking radiant she looked, baring her heart to me…

Even so, I'd lied to her. I'd lied when I said what happened when we were kids wasn't one of the most impactful moments of my life. And then more lies of omission because I didn't tell her that some part of me *recognized* her, this beautiful girl who made me feel like I belonged somewhere in the world.

There was no logic behind such a feeling. Nothing to be gained but pain, so I held back. I kept my feelings locked away because I'd written them to her in letters, but the letters were lost, and I wasn't willing to speak them aloud a second time and tell her…

That I'm in love with her.

My bike nearly careened off the road as the thought announced itself in my mind, body, and soul like a sonic boom. I pulled over and rested one foot on the ground.

"*Fuck.*"

My heart banged against my ribs, and my breath came short as I finally admitted what I knew seven years ago. The feelings I'd tried to kill during the years of silence came back with a vengeance the minute I'd laid eyes on Emery on the first day of school. My mother's abandonment had taught my mind to keep itself protected, but apparently my stupid fucking heart had never learned the lesson.

But my father's mind was deteriorating, and I wouldn't abandon him or his reputation. I had to stay here and take care of them both, while Emery had to get to California. I couldn't start something with her only to watch her leave and then suffer through years of long distance…of waiting for her to tell me she couldn't do it anymore.

I got home and let my bike crash against the wall of the house. Inside, it was dark and quiet. I ran upstairs to my loft and straight to my desk. I grabbed *Meditations* and opened it to the page where Emery's daffodil lay pressed. A symbol of my hypocrisy. I'd told her it meant nothing and yet…

The delicate, papery flower trembled in my grasp. My fingers were ready to crush it and throw it away. To let her go…

…and then I laid it back between the pages and shut the book. I folded my arms on the desk and buried my face in them as the jangling sound of our old piano rose up from the first floor, discordant and loud.

"Xander, my boy!" my father called above the tumult. "Come down and play with your old man. Your mother wants to hear the Schubert!"

I squeezed my eyes shut in the blackness.

"Xander? Are you there?"

"I'm here, Dad," I called back. "I'm right here."

The morning of the Narragansett Bay Regatta dawned bleak and windy. Thick, gray nimbostratus clouds hung in the sky, promising rain. As I pulled up to the Academy marina in our Buick, I saw that the waters were churning and whitecapped.

"Should make for interesting races, eh?" Orion Mercer said, falling into step beside me in the student parking lot. "But hey, check out the crowd." He jerked his chin to where the bleachers were full of spectators offsetting the gray sky with their colorful banners. A huge black and gold sign read LET'S GO LIONS!

Orion chucked me on the shoulder. "Let's give 'em a bloody good show."

I barely heard him. The Royal Pride dance team was set to be at the regatta to support our crew, which meant Emery would be watching. Pain squeezed my chest.

Too late now, jackass. You ruined everything. Royally.

In the clubhouse, the crews put on our racing gear: black, long-sleeved unisuits with gold trim and our last names printed across the back. I expected Tucker to give me hell, but both he and Rhett were surprisingly relaxed. Almost friendly.

Coach Daniels gathered us around as he took a knee.

"The water's going to be shit; I'm not going to lie," he said. "Like a big pot of boiling stew that'll freeze your nuts off."

"This is already one helluva pep talk, Coach," Dean said, and everyone laughed.

Despite the poor weather conditions, morale was high. Our two thousand meter had been under seven minutes the other day; even Coach was smiling.

He gave advice to our fours, pairs, and to Cassian Thorne, who rowed single, then turned to my eight-man crew. "You've been working hard, and I have no doubt we're going to give New Haven Prep a different Royal Pride crew to contend with this season. What do you say?"

He put his hand in the center, and we all followed suit.

"Royal Pride on three," Tucker bellowed. "One, two, three!"

"*Royal Pride!*"

The circle broke up to a lot of backslapping and shit-talking of our Connecticut opponents. Even Tucker gave me an encouraging nod.

Outside in the cold, the crews from the various schools around the Eastern Seaboard—some coming all the way from Massachusetts—were on the dock, stretching and pinwheeling their arms. Our nemesis, New Haven Prep, wore green and yellow. They looked smug and confident; no doubt last season's victories were dancing in their heads. I found my competitive edge that only came out when rowing. With my team, I was no longer an isolated individual, separated by my intellect or anything else. On the water, in that shell, I belonged.

Dean slapped both hands on my shoulders. "You good, stroke seat?"

"Losing builds character," I said. "They'll thank us later."

A slow smile spread over his lips. "We're going to win. Oh, shit, we are *so* going to win."

I grinned, but then my bravado slipped when I caught site of the Royal Pride dance team. The girls were huddled near the bleachers that were packed with spectators bundled against the oncoming storm. My gaze went to Emery automatically. When she was around, nothing and no one else registered.

She stood with her team in black leggings and a black sweater with a gold lion on the front. Her hair was pulled into a high ponytail, and her arms were crossed against the cold. Our eyes met—an instantaneous exchange of electricity that went straight to the center of me. Her expression tightened, as if she'd flinched, and then she looked away.

I expected nothing less. It was for the best. It was what I wanted; I'd told her that myself. But that didn't stop my chest from feeling as if it had caved in.

I averted my eyes and fought to regain my focus.

The crews—eight in all, each with their own eights, fours, pairs, and singles—lined up in rows on the dock, our hands clasped behind our backs. The president of the Narragansett Bay Row Association made a speech, welcoming the other teams to our waters and encouraging us all to have a clean race. The singles, pairs, and fours were up first, right in front of the bleachers.

We watched from the dock, cheering our guys on. Our pairs came in second, our four-man took a disappointing fifth, but our single, Cassian Thorne, pulled off a win. Then it was our turn to race. Every eight-man crew boarded schooners that would take us to the starting line so that we'd finish the two thousand meter race in front of the bleachers.

At another smaller dock around the Bend, eight shells were tethered, and officials from the regatta association watched us closely to ensure a clean race. Teams climbed in and readied their oars. Our shell had an outside lane closest to shore, with New Haven Prep on our port side.

When I rowed bow, my oar had been to my left. As stroke seat, it was to the right. I'd thought it'd be a difficult adjustment, but I found I had more strength and control on the right. I gripped the oar with both hands, my every muscle tensed like a coiled spring ready to release.

The eight-man shells moved to the starting line in choppy water. From the dock, someone raised an air horn.

"We got this, team," Tucker said from the five seat. "Let's show those New Haven fucks and everyone else what we're made of."

Murmured assents from behind me, while directly in front of me, Dean adjusted his headset and readied his digital metronome. "Nice and easy, guys. We need that clean starting burst. Remember, high twenty right off the horn."

He shot me a confirming glance, and I nodded. High twenty meant the first strokes would be twenty high-powered bursts to get to maximum speed and establish racing pace.

Our team grew still. Ready. On my port side, the New Haven Prep team did the same, each rower gripping his oar and waiting.

The air horn broke the silence—a match to a fuse deep inside me, flaring into action. I pulled, and the crew—lined up behind me—pulled with me. It was my job to set the pace, matching every *tick* of Dean's metronome with my drive so that the sound and the movement became one.

Within minutes, my shoulders, abs, and quads burned, and the cold air stung my lungs. Two thousand meters was going to feel like miles, but I turned off my thinking mind and channeled the energy into my body, synapses firing in obeisance to that *tick tick tick*....

"Wind-up!" Dean called.

The metronome got faster and so did I. Out of my periphery, I saw nothing but green and yellow. We were neck-and-neck with New Haven Prep.

Not good enough.

My shoulders screamed. The grunts of my teammates echoed mine. The other crews were slipping away into obscurity. Insignificance. Only New Haven Prep mattered, and they were losing ground. Soon enough, I was parallel to their bow seat—a red-haired guy, puffing his cheeks with every exhale. I attuned my focus to Dean's metronome to keep my pace steady but turned my head enough so that the bow seat knew I was staring straight at him. He couldn't see my eyes; we both wore the same style of reflective sunglasses, but there was no mistaking my intent.

Dean covered his mic. "Dude, what are you doing?"

"I'm saying hi," I gritted out between breaths.

New Haven's bow seat caught sight of me staring at him and did a double-take. It wasn't much but enough to cause a short break in rhythm. And because Dean Yearwood was the best damn cox I'd ever rowed with, he saw our opponent's fault and instantly pounced.

"Winding up in three, two…go!"

I turned away from New Haven again, giving everything I had to the new pace. A few more strokes and we were surrounded by nothing but open water.

"That's it, that's it," Dean shouted, all traces of his usual happy-go-lucky natured erased. "Come on, fucking pull!"

We pulled like nothing else mattered. Not the choppy water, nor the sky that was going to break open at any second. Just our team working in perfect mechanical harmony: legs, body, arms, then arms, body, legs, carving our way through turbulent water as one entity, inhaling with the drive, as if we were sucking energy out of the wind and channeling it through our oars.

To my starboard, I saw the curve of the land—a riot of color as spectators rose from their chairs—but we kept pulling toward the finish. New Haven Prep was making a valiant effort, but we were a length up, and there wasn't enough water to catch up.

The bell rang from the docks, signaling that we'd crossed the finish line, and then Dean was gripping my shoulders and shaking me.

"Holy shit, Xander! We won. We *won!*"

I wanted to smile, but I didn't have the strength. The oar fell out of my slack hand and fatigue swooped in. I sucked in deep breaths, each inhale of cold air scraping against my throat, while my lungs burned as if on fire. From behind, Henry thumped my shoulders. With heavy limbs, I turned to congratulate him. My team wore identical masks of exhaustion, breathing hard through wide, victorious smiles.

We'd won. I should've been ecstatic. Instead, race over, my mind went straight to thoughts of Emery.

On dry ground, we lined up to shake hands with the other crews, earning grudging nods of respect from New Haven Prep. Afterward, we changed into our black and gold tracksuits for the awards presentation, where the association president put a crystal trophy in Tucker's hands. There were more speeches, and then they released us.

Family and friends rushed the crew, and girlfriends hugged boyfriends. Aria embraced Rhett while Kai Thornton's girlfriend leaped into his arms. Dean was congratulated by Coach and a few officials. Tucker high-fived his friends with loud cheers and whoops, then lifted Emery off the ground and spun her around. He tried to kiss her, but she turned her head away, so he only got her cheek. Her expression was blank. Resigned. Defeated. My stomach clenched with guilt. I'd vowed to save her from anyone who tried to dim her light, and then I'd dimmed it myself.

In our clubhouse, Coach gathered us around again. "Gentlemen, you did good. Your time was impressive, given those conditions, and you should be proud of yourselves. We'll do a postrace debriefing at next practice, but now it's time to celebrate!"

We went to our lockers to change into street clothes. As I swapped out my contacts and put on my glasses, Orion and Dean appeared at my side.

"Bloody hell, Ford. I nearly put out my shoulder trying to match your pace. Good on ya, mate!" He jostled Dean. "And Yearwood, no one's a better coxy than you."

"Nah," Dean said. "You should've seen the shit Xander pulled with their bow seat."

"Which you jumped on and used to our advantage," I put in. "Orion's right. You're the best, my friend."

"Aw, shucks," Dean said, grinning ear to ear. "You guys do the hard work. I just sit and yell at you. Oh, and steer the boat, but that's not important."

"I hear the Castle Hill Country Club is going all out for this party," Orion said. "You're both coming, yeah?"

"Is pi an irrational number?" Dean grinned.

"Huh?"

"That would be a *yes*."

Orion rolled his eyes with a laugh. "Dorks, the lot of you. Ford?"

"I'm not going."

I couldn't leave my dad alone for so long to go to some fancy party and watch Emery be beautiful all night. Let alone if she reconciled with Tucker or found someone else. Someone who wouldn't drop her heart when she handed it to them with both hands.

Orion frowned. "You have to come. It wouldn't be the same without you!"

"I'll think about it," I said, though it was a lie.

"That's the spirit!"

He chucked my arm and joined other guys, whooping and hollering our victory.

"You good?" Dean asked, looking concerned.

"Yep. Just…not feeling well."

He lowered his voice after making sure Tucker wasn't listening. "Look, the election's today. Emery will be with Tucker at his dad's watch party, so you should come. Celebrate with the guys."

"I'm just not up to it," I said. "But go. Have fun, and I'll see you at school."

The locker room emptied. I was moving slowly, my arms like lead, when suddenly a heavy hand clamped my shoulder and spun me around. I had half a second to register Tucker's left fist before he buried it in my gut, pushing the air out of me. It bent me double, and then his right fist smashed my cheek, sending me reeling and my glasses skittering across the floor.

I slumped to the clubhouse floor, knees to my chest, struggling to catch my breath. Without my glasses, the world became an airless, blurry place with two hazy figures looming over me.

"That's for Halloween," Tucker said. "Because I warned you, Ford. I fucking warned you to stay away from Emery."

"You sure showed me," I choked out. "Waiting until after the race to coldcock me like a fucking coward."

He shrugged. "I wanted the win."

Rhett bent down to my level, hands on his knees, grinning a sunny grin that somehow made his eyes even blacker.

"Hey, Ford. Want to hear a joke? What's the difference between Amelia Earhart and your mom?"

"Fuck you."

"Nothing! They both left, never to be found again."

His and Tucker's booming laughter filled the clubhouse as they walked off, Tucker crushing my glasses under his shoe along the way.

I pushed myself up to sitting and slumped against the lockers, my face throbbing and my breath coming short. I hurt, but it wasn't anything compared to the ache in my heart.

When I had recovered my breath and the pain in my face dulled, I gathered my things and headed out, but no sooner had I stepped outside than the skies broke open and the rain came down.

Chapter 21

EMERY

"I WANT TO GO HOME," I MUTTERED, MY WORDS DROWNED out in the chatter of a hundred conversations, clinking glasses, and the blaring of cable news channels from at least six different flat-screen TVs mounted on the walls of Newport's private club, the Regency.

The mood among Senator Hill's election watch party guests—his family, friends, and donors—was muted. The numbers coming in weren't good; Jerome Hill was likely going to lose.

Why am I here?

The answer, of course, was simple: My father had demanded it.

He and Mom were set to come together, but Tucker had picked me up—business as usual. It didn't matter that I'd already broken up with him. Not to him or my father.

I'd tried to claim some agency over my own life, yet I was still steamrolled into coming here. A final show of support for the Hills from the Wallaces, just in case the numbers turned around.

Because Dad himself hadn't even shown up.

He must've gotten wind of the early returns and decided to make a clean break, leaving me to do the dirty work of pretty smiles and goodbyes in my little red cocktail dress. What the heck was I supposed to say?

Hi, Senator Hill. You're no longer useful to my dad but thanks for the nice party?

But an uglier, more insidious thought twisted my insides. My father had used Jerome Hill, just as I'd been his tool. His pawn. Taught to obey. Never make waves. Jack made waves and look where that got him. Cast outside the circle of my dad's approval.

Now I know why Grant walked out the door.

Outside, the rain came down in buckets, spattering the tall glass windows that overlooked the bay. Just south, the Regatta Gala would be in full swing at the Castle Hill Country Club. Xander would be there, celebrating their win. Maybe I could escape this terrible party and go to him…

Just the thought of being with Xander chased some of the sadness away. But he'd told me what he wanted, and it wasn't me. He'd torn down our day at the park seven years ago and reduced it to rubble, even if his eyes had told a different story—that he was protecting himself from more hurt, more rejection, by making us into nothing.

"He can't do that," I murmured, still standing alone at the window. "We're entangled."

A commotion erupted at one of the TVs, and a man hushed the crowd. "This is it," he said, and everyone quieted to listen to the cable news host.

"CNN is now making the call: in a stunning upset, Rhode Island's incumbent Senator Jerome Hill has lost his bid for reelection to media mogul and billionaire Charles Harrington. Analysts point to Harrington's aggressive media campaign and widespread financial backing as key factors to his success…"

The atmosphere in the room deflated, then a round of applause went up for Senator Hill, and toasts were made to soften the blow of defeat.

It was over. I was officially free. Now my little defiance didn't mean anything. It wasn't even mine anymore.

Anger flared, burning away some of the fear that had lived in me since I was a kid—the constant stress of trying to please my dad and the terror of what would happen when I didn't. I set my water glass down and headed for the coat check. I'd just put on my black peacoat when Tucker found me.

"Babe, there you are." His eyes were shadowed and glassy.

"I'm going home."

"I'll give you a ride."

"No, I'm calling an Uber."

"What? Why?"

"*Why?*" I spat, incredulous. "Can no one hear me when I speak? Do I have any voice at all?"

"What the hell are you talking about? I hear you just fine—"

"Tucker, *we are not together anymore*."

His expression hardened. "Because my dad lost, right? He's no longer useful to Grayson, so fuckity-bye-bye, is that it?"

"I'm sorry about the election, but I told you on Halloween night that we were over."

He exhaled through his nose and ran a hand through his blond hair. "Look, Em. It's been a crappy night. Just let me take you home and we can talk shit out, or whatever. Please?"

I bit my lip. My dad used me, but he'd used Tucker too. And now Tucker's dad had lost his job. "Fine. But straight home."

I waited in the lobby of the Regency, sheltered from the pouring rain, while Tucker fetched his truck and picked me up. He pulled onto the road, and a minute later, withdrew a flask from inside his blazer pocket.

"Tucker, it's a fucking hurricane out there. You shouldn't be drinking. You shouldn't ever be drinking and driving, but especially—"

"Like it matters," he said. "The cops will give me a pass for one more night before word gets out that I'm not the son of a senator anymore."

"You're a lot more than that, Tucker. Nobody is only one thing," I said, my heart aching to repeat Xander's words. "But you need to stop driving. It's too dangerous."

Tucker ignored me, taking a long pull from his flask as

he drove into the black night with rain coming down so hard, the windshield wipers could barely keep up. Soon, I'd lost all sense of where we were.

"Tucker, stop the truck. You're scaring me."

"You want me to stop the truck? Sure, no problem."

He drove on for what felt like another mile and then abruptly pulled off onto a shoulder. Through the truck's headlights, I saw nothing but trees, muddy road, and slants of rain coming down like bullets to pelt the cab.

He took another shot from the flask—whiskey, by the scent of it—then turned to look at me. He was much drunker than I'd realized, his bleary gaze grazing me up and down from my short dress to my ample cleavage. I tightened my coat around me.

"You wanted to talk," I said, my heart pounding. "Let's talk."

"Nah, changed my mind." He slowly put the cap on his flask, set it on the dash, and turned to me. "I'm tired of talking. I'm tired of being used. You used me, Emery, same way your dad used my family."

"I know, Tucker, and I'm sorry. But that doesn't mean—"

"I don't want to hear any more Wallace bullshit," he said, moving toward me. "I completed my service. Now it's time I got paid."

He took my chin in one hand, wrenching my mouth open for a kiss while his other hand slid up my thigh.

"No...stop it!" I cried, twisting and turning, pushing at his chest. It was like pushing on a brick wall. "Tucker, don't..."

"Come on, Em," he said, his breath stinking of whiskey, his huge body crowding me against the door. He undid my seatbelt and then reached for my thigh again. "Let's have one good fuck before calling it quits."

"*No!*" I stopped pushing at him long enough to bring my right hand around in a stinging slap that caught him full on the cheek.

"Fuck!" He reared back, holding his face. "Goddammit, Em…"

"I told you no," I said, my voice shockingly steady. "Now take me home."

He sat back, considering. "No. I don't think I will. Get out."

"What?"

"You heard me." He reached across me and opened my door, giving it a shove. "Get the fuck out."

"I…I don't know where we are. And the rain…"

"Not my problem." Tucker took a long drink from his flask, then glared at me. "Well? You're letting water into my truck."

"Tucker…"

"Get. The fuck. Out." He cocked his head. "Or you can pay up. The choice is yours."

I felt tears sting my eyes, but I gathered my coat around me and stepped into the downpour. The night was black with no streetlights. Tucker yanked the door closed and tore off in a muddy spray, his headlights revealing an oak tree in the distance.

I hurried for the tree, the mud soaking my shoes,

the cold rain drenching me to the bone, plastering my hair to my cheeks and making me shiver until I thought my teeth would shatter. Under the relative shelter of the branches, I pulled out my phone to check my location. I was somewhere in the Bend, too far to walk home in the storm.

I called Harper. No answer.

With trembling fingers, I found the number I wanted first anyway—the only person I wanted—and pushed *call*.

Chapter 22

XANDER

Dad was playing the piano again, clunky chords on our rickety piano...

I came groggily out of sleep, then realized the sound wasn't coming from downstairs but from my phone on the bedside table. The clock radio said it was nearly one in the morning, and outside my window, the rain was coming down in torrents. I fumbled for my spare glasses and instantly sat upright when I saw who was calling.

I slid the answer bar. "Emery? What's wrong?"

Because I knew instinctively something had happened. Something bad.

"Xander," she said tearfully, over the sound of the driving rain. "I need you. Can you...can you help me?"

"Where are you?"

"I...I don't know. He just left me."

"Who? What happened?" I jumped out of bed and wrestled my jeans on with one hand. "Never mind, tell me where you are."

"I'm on a road somewhere. In the Bend, I think."

My head whipped to the window streaked with rain. "You're *outside*?" I threw on a shirt and fought for calm. "Emery, drop me a pin. Okay?"

"O-okay."

She was shivering. Teeth chattering.

He just left me…

Tucker.

Fury boiled in me and a red haze descended over my eyes, but the *ping* of a dropped pin brought me back. She was in my neighborhood, maybe a three-minute drive, but the houses were spread out and she was in the dark, in the pouring rain…

"Emery, I see you. I'm really close, okay? I'll be right there."

"Okay," she said, her voice small.

"Don't hang up. I'm putting you on speaker." I tossed my phone on the bed, so I could pull on my sweatshirt and shoes.

"Thank you, Xander."

Jesus Christ, I thought my insides were going to combust from the mix of fear and rage.

He'd better have only left her in the rain. If he touched her…if he hurt her in any way…

Then I was going to jail, end of story.

"Emery, you still there?" I asked and ran down

the stairs. The house was quiet, thank God, my dad sleeping.

"I-I'm here."

I grabbed my keys, then stopped at what made for a linen closet off the kitchen and grabbed an old camping blanket.

"I'm coming, Em." I rushed into the garage. "Three minutes."

"Okay."

I threw the car into reverse and pulled out of the garage. Immediately, the windshield was doused, as if someone had thrown a bucket of water onto it.

"Fucking Christ."

I drove into the night, into a downpour that showed no signs of letting up but was nothing compared to the storm boiling inside me.

He left her in this. He left her. I left her…

I'd left Emery.

If anything had happened to her that couldn't be taken back, I'd never forgive myself. Not in this life or the next, or in any of the infinite possible lifetimes that might await me in the cold, black universe.

It took everything I had not to drive like a maniac. The only thing slowing me down was the thought that she'd be stranded if I skidded in the rain and wrapped the Buick around a tree.

After what felt like an eternity, my headlights splashed over a lone figure pressed against the trunk of a huge, white oak. She wore a black coat over a red dress, both clinging to her as if she'd swam in them.

Dammit to hell.

I pulled over, threw the car in park but left the engine running. With the blanket in my arms, I raced out of the car and was instantly drenched. When I reached Emery, I threw the blanket over her, wrapping her in a cocoon. Her hair was plastered around her face, her eye makeup streaking her cheeks in black tears.

"How long have you been out here?" I shouted over the rain.

"I-I don't know," she cried. "Not long, but…"

"Long enough. God, Em." I wrapped her in my arms in a fierce embrace. She clung to me tightly, and for a long moment, I just held her.

I'm not letting go. Never again…

"Come on," I said gruffly, my voice thick. "I'll take you home."

I reached for the passenger door, but she tugged my hand. "I'm not going to my house tonight. I can't stand the fucking thought of it."

"But, Em…"

"Take me to your house, Xander. Please."

Embarrassment at the idea of showing her my shabby little house flashed through me, but I was only going to do what she wanted.

I hustled her into the front seat of the car and came to take the wheel. Inside, water dripped from my hair and spotted my glasses so I could hardly see. I shut the door and cranked the heat all the way up while the rain pelted the roof and hood like stones.

"What happened?" I asked, my voice dangerously low. I took off my glasses and tried to dry the lenses on my sodden sweatshirt. "What did he do? It was Tucker, right?"

She nodded.

My jaw clenched as I turned the car around and headed back to my house. "Tell me."

Emery started to speak, then peered closer. "Wait, what happened to your face? Your cheek is puffy…"

"Doesn't matter. I deserve worse if…" I bit off my words. "Tell me everything."

She faced forward, warming her hands on the heater, and told me what happened as I navigated the darkened streets through the rain-splattered windshield. She told me about the party, Senator Hill's loss, and how Tucker was upset and wanted to take her home. To talk.

I listened with mounting anger, my sore muscles tensing with every word.

"Tucker was drunk, but I didn't see how badly until it was too late. Instead of taking me home, he drove me here. He said he was tired of being used. Then he pulled the truck over and said that it was time I paid up."

"What does that mean?" I asked, my heart thudding in my chest like a jackhammer.

"God, it's so humiliating," she said, shaking her head miserably. "He wanted me to have sex with him, and I said no. And he didn't want to hear no. Nothing happened," she added quickly as a strangled sound escaped me. "I slapped him, and it sobered him a little. He told me to get out of the truck. So I did."

My house appeared in front of us. I pulled into the garage and shut off the engine, then gripped the steering wheel.

"Nothing happened?" I asked, my voice stony. "He didn't…? Because I swear to God, Emery, if he hurt you…"

"He didn't hurt me, I promise. And it's all my fault anyway—"

"*It's not your fault*," I said, practically shouting. "It's not your fault. Not one fucking thing that happened tonight was your fault."

Emery nodded, though I don't know that she believed me. I tried to feel relieved that Tucker hadn't forced himself on her, but she wouldn't have been in that situation in the first place if I'd been there for her.

I pushed out of the car and went around to her side. Wrapping an arm around her, I guided her through the dark house and up the stairs to my loft, lit by the yellow glow of my desk lamp.

"We have to get you warm," I said. "Wait here."

In my bathroom, I flipped on the light. The fluorescent glare revealed its plainness, but at least it was clean. I started the shower and hurried back to my bedroom, where Emery stood shivering.

I riffled through my dresser and grabbed a pair of drawstring pants and an old Langdon sweatshirt. I set them on the bathroom counter with a clean towel, then went back for Emery. I started to take the blanket from her, but she gripped my wrists. Her blue eyes, streaked with mascara and red with tears, met mine.

"Do you want to know what I thought when you came to get me tonight?" she asked. "When you put this blanket around me? I thought…now I'm where I'm supposed to be."

My eyes fell shut, my heart aching. "I'm sorry, Emery. I'm so sorry."

"You don't have to be. I should never have gotten in that truck."

"And if I'd been there, you wouldn't have." She started to protest but gave up as I guided her to the bathroom. "You're freezing. Get warmed up, and I'll make you some tea, okay?"

She nodded and shut the door behind her.

I sagged as the adrenaline and raw emotion of the night drained away. A shiver reminded me I was soaking wet too. I changed into sweatpants and a T-shirt, then went to the kitchen. The old kettle took forever to heat. When the water was hot enough, I made mint tea and took a steaming mug back to my loft. There, I shut the door and turned to see Emery at my desk. Her face was scrubbed clean, her damp hair glistening like dark gold ribbons. My sweatshirt hung loose on her, and the sleep pants I'd lent her spilled over her small feet.

And in her hand was the dried daffodil.

I froze, my throat tightening and my heart stuttering at her beauty, as the unmistakable, undeniable truth washed over me—as obvious as the flower in her hand.

I'm hers. I've always been hers.

"I didn't mean to pry, but this is the book you were reading when we met."

"Yes," I said thickly. "You remember that?"

"I remember every minute of that day, Xander. Every second."

"So do I."

"Because it meant something, didn't it?" she asked, her eyes so full of love and hope, I could hardly look at her, she was so beautiful.

"Yeah, Em," I whispered. "It meant everything."

Emery smiled softly. Knowingly. And with that smile, the fight went out of me. All the hesitation, the walls of reasons and logic I'd barricaded myself behind...it all came crashing down.

Everything that happened after was as inevitable as my next breath.

I set down the mug of tea on my desk, and she returned the flower to its place. I brushed the hair off her shoulders while she took my glasses off and set them beside the tea. In the next instant, she was in my arms. I pulled her in close and bent to press my forehead to hers, leaving only the smallest, heated space between us.

"Hi," she whispered.

"Hi," I answered gruffly.

"I missed you."

"I missed you, too." I swallowed hard. "Emery..."

"I know you're scared of being hurt. So am I. But I think that what we feel for each other is more powerful than fear. And we can't think about what might happen later." Her hands went to my hair, her fingers threading at my nape. "We have to trust that it will work itself out.

Because you and me...something happened that day seven years ago, and we can't pretend it didn't." She smiled, her lips close to mine. "We're entangled."

I nodded and pulled back to look into her eyes. "Whatever happens to you, happens to me."

Emery made a little sound that was half sob, half laugh, her expression one of pure happiness and want—want of *me*. It illuminated her from the inside out. I bent my head, savoring the smoldering burn a little longer—this first touch would never come again—before lowering my mouth to hers and kissing her.

Our lips met, and I nearly stumbled as raw hunger swept through me, trying to steal my strength. I'd dreamt of this moment countless times, imagining how she'd feel, how she'd taste, and yet, I was unprepared for reality.

Emery's soft mouth parted with a little gasp, as if she too was shocked by the intensity of our connection. We moved apart just a tiny bit, our eyes meeting, before we crashed together again. Our arms tightened, pressing our bodies together—her softness against my hardness. She whimpered as my tongue ventured into her mouth, tasting and touching—gently at first, then with urgency. Making up for lost time. Every kiss we should have had before this night was in this one. Our lost time reclaimed; our lost connection rebuilt. Finally. At last.

Emery responded with soft moans, letting me in, her tongue tangling with mine. Exploring with soft curiosity but heat too. Desire that simmered, wanting to ignite into something more...but not tonight. Tonight was to show her, with this kiss, that she had been right about everything. To infuse this moment with the warmth and satiation of our reunion. Because that's what it was. Not just seven years or seven weeks but lifetimes were in this kiss, bursting forth after lying dormant and waiting.

The notion made no sense; I could only measure its veracity by the force of the need, the sheer relief of this coming together. Emotions that defied logic left my head reeling. Thoughts cleared away to make space for the pure desire I had for this girl. Desire to have her, protect her, and give myself up to her, all at the same time.

All I knew was Emery, and she was all that mattered.

Finally I pulled back to look at her. Take her in. By the yellow light of my lamp, her cheeks were flushed, her lips swollen and full. But the night had exhausted her.

She smiled as her eyes fell shut, and she rested her head on my chest. My arms went around her, holding her tight, my hand stroking her hair.

"My Xander…" she murmured.

"Come on," I said, and kissed her forehead. "You need to sleep." I guided her to the bed and covered her with my comforter. "I'll sleep on the floor."

"Not on your life," she said, her eyes closing as soon as her head touched the pillow.

I chuckled and shut off the light, then climbed into bed beside her. She reached for me at once, and I pulled her in close. Our arms and legs entwined, so that I didn't know where she ended and I began.

I held her until she fell asleep—it took only moments

until her breaths grew deep and even—and then I let myself fall too, wrapped in her.

Entangled.

Chapter 23

EMERY

I woke wrapped in Xander's arms and thought I must be dreaming. He held me tightly. Protectively. I smiled and nestled closer to him, our kiss still alive in my mind, stirring me awake, though it couldn't have been more than a little past dawn. A slant of silvery-gold light fell across the bed. The storm was over.

My cheek lay on Xander's chest, and I listened to the steady *thump* of his heart in my ear, while last night played on repeat.

A tale of two nights, I thought. The first half, dark and cold and miserable. The second, warm and safe and good. Kissing Xander…

It wasn't anything I was prepared for. His mouth on mine, his lips, his tongue…the pull of his kiss drawing me in. Like coming home. A lost part of me that had been wandering alone out in the cold had found itself at last, safe with him. Because he was who I was supposed to be kissing and touching. The one I was supposed to love…

I shouldn't have been thinking like that, but I couldn't help myself. I'd fallen in love with Xander Ford when I was ten years old, and when I tried to tear up that love and throw it away, it came back, all grown up. It was a little bit scary and a whole lot thrilling, how much I felt for him. And when he saw me holding that flower, it'd been written all over his face that he felt the same. He and I, we were inevitable.

Infinite.

The perfect contentment threatened to lull me back to sleep, but reality had other plans. I'd been out all night—on a school night—without telling my parents. If I didn't get home soon, Dad would use his connections at Castle Hill's police department to send out a search party.

I sat up and glanced around. Xander's room was tidy and simple, a desk under the window, a blue comforter on the bed, a Radiohead poster over a bookshelf. Nothing to indicate that a super genius lived here; I'd half expected a periodic table on the wall or a poster of Stephen Hawking.

That's because you've been living in a world of stereotypes and snap judgments.

That was true, but I was working on being a better person. For him but for me, too.

I went to the window, half expecting to see a police cruiser or Dad's black sedan and Colin waiting to steal me away. But outside, everything was glistening from the rain.

Quiet. I was safe here, tucked deep in the forest, away from the world.

I slipped back into bed and curled against Xander—my chest to his warm back, my arm wrapped around him. A big spoon to his little spoon.

Xander stirred, and in a half sleep, he found my hand on his chest and laced his fingers with mine, then cinched me in tighter, so that we were practically melded together. With the purest contentment, I nestled my face into the back of his neck. He had a tiny mole on his pale skin that I hadn't known was there.

But now I know. Now, I can know all of him…

Happiness flooded me, and I planted a kiss on the back of his neck. Because I could do that now, too. I could kiss him whenever I wanted, and that sent tingles down my spine and between my legs. I bit my lip thinking about what else could happen between us now. All the ways he'd touch me…

Xander stirred again and rolled over to face me. The smile that came to his lips when he saw me nearly brought me to tears.

"Don't look at me like that," I said with a sniff. "You're going to make me cry, and I did enough of that last night."

His smile instantly collapsed because he felt responsible. His words from last night sung out in my heart.

What happens to you, happens to me.

"You have to stop blaming yourself for last night," I said. "It wasn't your fault."

"I just hate that Tucker tried something with you. It could have been so much worse."

"But it wasn't." I reached out to touch his bruised cheekbone. "This was him."

"Small price to pay." Xander craned to kiss my lips, my chin, my nose, then pulled me closer.

"So we're really doing this." I traced a heart on his T-shirt with my finger. "I know you have doubts—"

"Not about how I feel for you, Emery. Only what's coming at the end of the year."

"I'm more worried that you'll get bored with me."

"Bored? With *you*?"

"Well, yeah," I said with a small smile. "You *might* have noticed that I'm not as smart as you."

He heaved a long-suffering sigh. "Few people are."

I snorted and gave him a nudge. "I'm being serious."

"Emery, how could I ever be bored with you? You have more vitality than anyone I've ever met. I'm the one who should be worried. I'm always in my head, and you're all heart."

"Maybe that's why we work," I ventured. "Like yin and yang."

"I thought we were entangled particles."

I grinned. "I love that the most, but it's harder to find a Hallmark card for it."

He chuckled, then grew serious. "Whatever we are, I don't want to mess it up."

I moved to prop my chin on my hands, my hands on his chest. "Me neither. But it's going to be hard. Because… God, I can't even say it."

"We need to keep us a secret."

I nodded. "Not because of any bullshit peer pressure at school. But if word were to get back to my dad through Tucker or Delilah, he'll make both our lives impossible."

"He threatened as much the other day." Xander brushed a lock of hair from my eyes. "I don't want to ruin your shot at getting out of here."

"You're not ruining anything. You're making everything better."

I kissed him softly and then traced my finger along his chin. He loosely wrapped a lock of my hair around his finger, and for a few long moments, we stayed that way—me lying over his chest, each taking the other in with little touches, little looks. As if we were getting reacquainted after a long separation.

"Hey, I never congratulated you on your win at the regatta," I said after a minute. "That must've been pretty exciting."

"It was fine."

"Only fine?"

"No racing victory is ever going to come close to how I feel right now."

I buried my face in his neck. "My God, Xander, I can't even with you."

He chuckled and then a loud *bang* erupted from downstairs. We both shot to sitting.

"My dad," he said almost apologetically and climbed out of bed. "He likes to cook breakfast…a lot."

"What if he catches me here…?"

"He won't care. He'll be ecstatic, actually, and make a bunch of really inappropriate jokes."

"I like him already. Can I meet him?"

"I don't think..." Xander stopped. "Actually, yes. You should meet him. Because I shouldn't be embarrassed."

"No," I said with a smile. "You shouldn't."

My dress and coat were still a sodden mess, so I had to stay in Xander's Langdon sweatshirt and pajama pants. He found me a plastic bag for my wet clothes and heels, and then we went down.

In the Fords' small kitchen, Xander's father was humming as he pulled bacon and eggs from the fridge. He had Tim Burton hair—dark but graying and sticking out all over—and wore a maroon bathrobe over his blue pajamas.

"Hey, Dad," Xander said from the entry, his hand clasped with mine. "I'd like you to meet someone."

"Hm?" Dr. Ford turned and stared at me a moment, his eyes—blue like one of Xander's—going between the two of us. Then a sly look came over his angular features. "Well, who is this lovely young lady?"

"Emery, this is my dad, Dr. Russell Ford. Dad, this is Emery Wallace." Xander's face turned red. "She's, uh... she's..."

"I'm his girlfriend," I blurted and then flinched. The words hung in the air, and it was too late to snatch them back, so I started stammering like a madwoman. "I mean...we're not dating anyone else, right? I don't want to be with anyone else...but, maybe it's too soon—?"

Xander glanced down at me; his smile was like the one from earlier—so touched and happy, I wanted to cry. Understanding passed between us. It may have only been one kiss, one night, but that kiss was seven years in the making, and neither of us wanted to waste one more second.

"Yes," he said. "She's my girlfriend."

I'm his girlfriend. It felt so much different than what I'd been with Tucker. *Because this is what it's supposed to feel like.*

"Very pleased to meet you, Emery." Dr. Ford held out his hand for me to shake, and it trembled as if he were cold. I felt Xander tense beside me, while his father stared fearfully. He started to withdraw it, but I was quicker.

"I'm very happy to meet you, Dr. Ford," I said, taking his hand in both of mine. "Xander's told me so much about you."

"Has he?" He beamed as the tension in the room eased. "Only good things, I hope. And please. Call me Russell."

"He tells me you're working on a unified theory, and that you're close to solving it," I said awkwardly, like trying out a foreign language with a native speaker for the first time.

"Could be, could be," Russell said, resuming his breakfast prep. "Are you interested in physics, young lady?"

I'm interested in the physical perfection of your son, I thought and suppressed a giggle. "I think it's fascinating, but I can't hope to understand it."

"Ah, spoken like a true physicist already! It was the

great Richard Feynman who declared that nobody understands quantum mechanics." A mischievous glint came to his eye. "I believe it was also Feynman who said, 'Physics is like sex: Sure, it may give some practical results, but that's not why we do it.' Isn't that right, son?"

"Jesus, Dad," Xander said, mortified, while I shook with laughter.

Russell grinned. "You may have discovered better than I, Miss Emery, that it's very easy to make my boy blush." He reached his trembling hand and fondly patted Xander's cheek, but then his smile fell. "What's this bruise?"

"Rowing accident," Xander said quickly. "Dad, I have to get Emery home. We have school."

"Very well. Lovely to meet you, Miss Emery."

"You too, Dr. Ford—*Russell.*"

We went to the garage, and in the car, Xander's expression was pained. "The tremor is new. It's a symptom of Lewy body dementia, which is like Parkinson's and Alzheimer's all rolled into one."

"I'm so sorry, Xander," I said, taking his hand and entwining my fingers with his. "Your dad is wonderful. It only took a minute to fall in love with him." I smiled gently. "Must run in the family."

Xander kissed the back of my hand. "Thank you. I needed to hear that."

"But *my* dad on the other hand…" I gave myself a shake. "I'm about to go into battle. Before we get to my house, I need to call for reinforcements."

I pulled out my phone—my stomach clenching at all

the texts and missed calls from my parents—and called Harper.

"Emery" she said sleepily. "It's early."

"Harper, I need your help."

I gave her a quick recap of last night and asked if she'd cover for me if my parents called.

"Of course, I will. Tucker, that asshole," she snapped. "Jesus, Em, I'm sorry I missed your call last night. Are you okay?"

I glanced at Xander. "Never better."

"Thank God. And yes, I can *hear* you smile. Tell Xander I said hi, I told you so, and that I'm proud of him for finally getting his head out of his ass."

I grinned. "I'll be sure to do that. Thanks, Harper." I hung up. "You get all that?"

Xander chuckled. "Loud and clear."

———

We arrived at my neighborhood with the sun fully risen. Xander idled the car on the street, out of sight from my house.

"Are you going to be okay?" he asked. "Because I can't let you go up there if it's not safe."

"I'll be okay. I have to stand up for myself, even if it's just one baby step at a time."

"That's more than a lot of people ever do for themselves," Xander said. "You're braver than you know."

"Thank you," I said with a smile. "*I* needed to hear *that*."

He leaned over, his hand cupping my cheek like it had during our last tutoring session and kissed me. I was glad to be sitting down, because just like last night, his kiss made my knees weak. The scent of his soap on his warm skin mingled with the taste of him that was so clean and good. I didn't know how I could want something so badly that was already happening, but that's what kissing Xander felt like. I was there, kissing and being kissed, and still it wasn't enough.

"Call me later," he said.

"I will."

I grabbed the bag carrying my coat, shoes, and ruined dress, and walked up the long drive to the house, barefoot and in Xander's clothes.

Inside, my parents were at the kitchen island, both in their pajamas, my dad on his phone.

"Hold on, officer. She's home. Thank you."

He set his phone on the counter and glared icy daggers at me while my mother's eyes fell closed in relief.

Dad crossed his arms. "Well?"

"*Grayson*," Mom snapped. She turned to me. "Are you all right?"

"I'm fine, Mom."

Her bleary gaze took me in and then sharpened on Xander's sweatshirt, which read Langdon School, Bethesda, Maryland, with the school's seal—a sun breaking from behind a mountain—in the center.

Shit. I had no good excuse for wearing a boy's clothes. My nervousness ratcheted up, making it hard to think.

"Where have you been?" Dad demanded.

"At my friend, Harper's."

"Harper who?"

"She's a new friend. She took me in last night after Tucker left me stranded on a deserted road in the middle of a monsoon."

Mom's hand flew to her throat. "He did what?"

"After the election party, Tucker drove me to a secluded spot, tried to get me to have sex with him, and then kicked me out of his truck when I said no."

My parents stared at me with conflicting expressions—my mom's horrified, my dad's startled and unsure.

"Why didn't you come here?" he asked.

"Because I didn't want to," I said, my lip quavering. "I needed to be with…my friend."

"You could have called or answered one text."

"I was too upset, okay? And we're broken up now, so I don't want to talk about Tucker ever again."

They exchanged glances, my mother glaring at my father.

"And if I call this Harper?" he said.

"Jesus, Grayson," Mom hissed. "Emery's home safe now. What else matters?"

Dad seemed about to let it go; I thought I was home free…and then it was his turn to notice my outfit. "What are you wearing?"

"Harper has a brother," I blurted stupidly, but then the hurt swooped in, giving me courage. "And is that what you care about, Dad? Tucker left me in the freezing rain after trying to…" I clenched my jaw. I would not cry. I would *not*. "But call Harper if it's so important. Go ahead. I'll give you the number."

For the first time in my life, I met my dad's gaze head on. I felt like puking, but he didn't need to know that.

"For God's sake, leave her alone," Mom whispered.

"Fine," Dad said, after the longest moment of my life. "But we have something else to talk about, Emery. Namely, how you earned a C-minus on your calculus midterm."

I eased a breath, loosening my clenched stomach, but anger was still boiling up in me, and there was so much more of it than I thought. Years' worth, and it was all going to come bursting out if I wasn't careful.

"You made me fire my tutor, remember?" I snapped. "You kicked him out of the house, *remember*?"

"Watch your tone, young lady," Dad said. "He 'tutored' you for weeks. You should, at the very least, have a rudimentary understanding of the math."

"I told you, it doesn't stick. It's not what I'm good at or what I'm passionate about. I want to design—"

"Your only job is to get good grades. Your admission to Brown is riding on that. But if you're still struggling, then you need to drop the superfluous nonsense like the prom committee."

"No!" I cried, shocked at my own volume. "I won't do it. I'll drop dance, but I'm working really hard to come up with a theme for prom, and I have so many ideas—"

"Prom committee isn't something that will impress an Ivy League school." He reached for his phone and turned to go. He was going to walk out of the room and that would be the end of it. Frustration and anger raced through my veins, but stupid tears came to my eyes. My thoughts became a jumble, like they always did when confronting him, and I couldn't spit them out.

"That sounds reasonable," Mom said suddenly.

We both stopped to stare at her. She smoothed the sleeve of her silk bathrobe.

"If she *must* drop anything, she can drop dance. You may keep your prom committee commitments, Emery."

A balloon of relief and hope expanded in my chest. "Really?"

Dad bristled. "Now, wait a minute—"

"I presume you have a budget meeting with the Board of Trustees very soon?" Mom asked me. "A sudden change of leadership on the prom committee wouldn't sit well with them. Not to mention, it'd be quite unprofessional for a Wallace to suddenly quit."

I nodded but didn't dare speak.

Mom gave my dad an imperious look—identical to the one I used to wear at school—then slipped off the stool with her coffee mug.

"Then it's settled," she said. "I'm glad you're home safe and that your friend, *Harper*, was such a help. But next time, at least send a text if you're going to be out all night."

Dad and I watched her walk out, leaving us in icy silence. Then he turned to me, his tone as flat as ever. "It would be a mistake to believe you're in the clear, here. Fix your math grade, Emery, or there will be consequences."

He started to go but I couldn't help myself from blurting,

"Aren't you sad for me that I broke up with Tucker? I know how happy you were when we got together."

Oh my God…

I couldn't believe I'd said that—insinuations about the Hills' usefulness to him ringing loud and clear in our spacious, immaculate kitchen.

But Dad was scarily matter-of-fact.

"Tucker's father lost his bid for reelection. He's a loser. We don't associate with losers." He started to go, then stopped, his gaze dropping noticeably to my borrowed sweatshirt. "And Emery, if I were to hear that you broke things off with Tucker only to take up with someone of poor standing in the community, I *will* revoke your prom committee privileges. Is that clear?"

I nodded mutely. When he was gone, I sagged against the island, my legs shaking, then nearly jumped out of my skin at a voice at the door.

"How does it feel?"

Jack leaned in the entry to the kitchen, dressed in a faded black T-shirt and black sweatpants.

"How does what feel?" I asked dully.

"Standing up to the Munsters."

"Pretty terrible," I said. "But also kind of good. Mom defended me, at least."

"Don't get used to it," Jack said, pushing himself off the wall. "She always caves, eventually. Just ask Grant. Oh, that's right," he said bitterly. "We can't."

"What does that mean, Jack? *Jack*…?"

But he'd already walked away.

Chapter 24

XANDER

The rowing season was on hold until spring, but that didn't mean we were allowed to slack off. Coach Daniels set up a punishing schedule with constant weight training and long hours logged on the ergometer.

Monday afternoon, I finished with my classes and headed to the Academy gym. Inside, the men's gymnasts were training, straddling pommel horses and doing insane tumbling runs on the mat. Gideon Foster was on the horizontal bar, Declan McConnell on the rings.

In the weight room, I spotted Tucker doing curls between benches and racks of dumbbells.

My jaw clenched. I wasn't a violent person, but Emery had been left shivering in the dark by the side of the road, and that was un-fucking-acceptable.

I strode up to Tucker and tapped him on the shoulder. "Hill. We need to talk."

"I got nothing to say to you, Ford," he said, grunting with each hammer curl.

"I have something to say to you."

He set down his dumbbells and turned, then jumped back to see me standing not one inch from his face, my arms at my side, still.

"Jesus! The hell?"

"You left her," I said, my voice deadly calm. "You fucking left her in the pouring rain."

For a fraction of a second, remorse flitted across Tucker's features. He glanced around as Rhett and Orion drew closer. Then he sneered. "Back off, Ford, if you know what's good for you."

He pretended to turn away, but I sensed the feint, and this time I was ready. Tucker whipped around, right fist leading. I ducked the blow and brought my left elbow up in a quick jab that struck him squarely on the nose.

Tucker reeled, staggering back as blood seeped from under his cupped hands. He stared at me with wide eyes. "I think you broke my fucking nose."

"I didn't want a physical confrontation," I said. "But there needs to be a reckoning."

"A *what*?" He spat a wad of blood on the floor. "I was drunk that night. I don't remember shit."

"I'll jog your memory," I stated, my eyes locked on his. "There was a torrential downpour, and you left her stranded on a deserted road."

He snorted. "So what? You're here to defend her honor?"

"Yes."

"He's challenging you to a duel," Rhett sneered from beside Tucker. "Did you see *Hamilton* one too many times?"

"Shut the fuck up, Rhett," Orion put in.

Tucker glowered at me. "Pretty fucking bold maneuver, Ford. You know I could kick your ass right now."

"Possibly, given our height and weight differentials, and your amplified propensity for violence," I said. "Regardless, I can't, in good conscience, remain teammates with someone of such low character."

"Low character." Rhett chuckled. "Who does this guy think he is?"

"I said, shut it, Calloway," Orion said from my right.

Tucker read my meaning. "It's cool, Rhett. Can we have a minute?"

Rhett stepped back, and Orion leaned in. "I've got your back," he said before moving a few feet away, arms crossed, watching.

"You'd quit the team over this?" Tucker asked when we were alone, holding his gym towel to his nose. "Don't be stupid. We're set to sweep the regattas."

I shrugged. "I don't give a shit."

"Like hell. Rhett's never been better at bow, and you're the best stroke we've ever had. You fucking love it." He cocked his head. "Oh, but you love her more, is that it?"

I swallowed hard but maintained my merciless eye contact until Tucker relented.

"Fine. You're right. I fucked up. My dad lost his election and Emery's father turned his back on us the same hour. Grayson Wallace looks like a little fucking weasel, but he's got clout in this state. A lot of it. I was pissed off and drunk and I took it out on her."

"You tried to get her to do something she didn't want to do," I said tightly.

"I didn't force myself on her, I swear. She said no and I backed off."

"She had to slap you first." I nodded at his bloody nose. "I'm detecting a pattern."

"Fucking hell, *I backed off*. But I shouldn't have left her in the rain." He glanced down at the bloody towel in his hand. "Is she okay?"

I nodded, once.

Tucker waited for me to say more. "So? We good now? Clean slate?"

"It's not me you need to make things right with."

His glare hardened. "Don't get all uppity on me, Ford. I'm calling a truce. Take it or leave it, but I'm not going to offer twice."

"Apologize to her or I'll quit the team." I arched a brow. "*I'm* not going to offer twice."

"Fuck me," Tucker groused. "Fine, I'll tell her I'm sorry. Happy?"

"No, but it's a start."

Tucker touched the towel to his swollen nose. "Jesus,

Ford," he said with a grudging chuckle. "You've got some balls, I'll give you that. But can I give you some advice? Watch yourself. Her dad is not a good guy."

"I'm well aware."

"I'm serious," Tucker said. "As bad as you think he is, he's a whole lot worse—"

A bone-chilling howl from the main gym suddenly filled the air. Tucker and I froze, then everyone in the weight room rushed inside, where a crowd had gathered around the mat beneath the horizontal bar. Someone was moaning and making strange, hiccupping noises of pure agony. Declan McConnell broke from the group to vomit in a nearby trashcan.

"Gideon," Tucker murmured and pushed through the crowd, then stopped short. "Jesus fucking Christ, someone call an ambulance!"

My own stomach wanted to heave. Gideon Foster was on the mat, deathly pale and covered in a thin sheen of sweat. He was sitting up, both palms flat on the ground, staring in wide-eyed shock at his right leg, which was bent at a ninety-degree angle at the knee, protruding obscenely away from his body.

The gymnastics coach and trainers rushed over, and the school security backed the rest of us away. We were ushered out of the gym as sirens wailed from the parking lot.

"Poor bastard," Orion said from beside me. "He was set to go to World's, then the possibly the Olympics. Guess that's done."

"That's Castle Hill Academy for you," said a guy at my left. "It chews you up and spits you out."

"Yep," Orion agreed. "First it's Jack Wallace at the bonfire, today it's Gideon." He turned and gave me a grim look. "Now we wait."

A shiver went down my spine. "For?"

"Strike three."

Part III

> *We must have perseverance and above all confidence in ourselves. We must believe that we are gifted for something, and that this thing, at whatever cost, must be attained.*
> —Marie Curie

Chapter 25

XANDER

DECEMBER

"Earth to Xander. Come in, Xander."

"Hm?"

I blinked back into the fluorescent starkness of the classroom where I'd been counting down the seconds until later that afternoon when I'd be alone with Emery in the dim quiet of my loft. Six pairs of eyes—the Math & Physics Club—were on me, waiting.

Dean and Harper exchanged amused glances. No one at the school was supposed to know about Emery and me, but they were my best friends, and I'd never had best friends before. Or a girlfriend. Aside from the physical altercations with Tucker Hill, my little Experiment was going pretty well.

"I was asking if you'd given any more thought to hosting our annual Christmas party," Kevin Huang, our president said. "Not to be forward, but it might be the best opportunity for us to meet your father."

Jasper Reed, our VP Elena Clark, and Micah West—another newbie like Harper and me—nodded eagerly.

"It would be an honor, truly," Jasper said in his stiff, formal way.

"I'm dying for him to sign my issue of *Scientific American*," Elena said.

"I think he'd be touched that you want to meet him," I said slowly. "But I have to see if he's up for it."

My dad's illness was like a shadow that followed me around, stealing the light out of the best days. The medication they'd given him was working the same way putty worked to seal a leaking dam—it stemmed the tide of his dementia, but Dr. Mandel had warned me it couldn't hold forever.

I'm going to lose him while he's still here.

"Let's not force the issue," Dean said, jumping up to indicate the meeting—and the subject—was closed. "Until next week."

The group filed out except for Dean, Harper, and me.

"How is he?" Dean asked, checking his phone before tucking it into his back pocket.

"He's hanging in there," I said. "Still working on his theory, and he's still able to play the piano. He's had a run of good days lately too. I have to think that means something."

"Absolutely," Harper said. "And no pressure, okay? If it doesn't work to have the party at your place, we'll find an alternative."

"Thanks, but maybe I should host it. This might be Dad's last chance to…"

Remember his accomplishments.

Meet people who appreciate him.

Have one last good Christmas…

The last thought hit me harder than Tucker ever could. I shouldered my backpack. "I'll ask him about it this afternoon."

Our club meetings ran for a couple hours every Wednesday after the last bell had rung; the three of us stepped into an empty hallway. Outside, under a gray sky, snowdrifts piled along the Academy walkways. Harper put a knit beanie on over her brown curls, and Dean and I bundled into our coats. My friends were quiet, letting me recover from my heavy moment.

"So, how are things with Emery?" Harper asked, eventually. "She gave me a stellar report about you. You're really nailing the whole boyfriend thing."

"Good to know," I said, unable to hide my smile.

Both friends shot me expectant looks as we headed for the student parking lot.

"And?" Dean said, wagging his eyebrows. "How goes it on your end? I haven't had a chance to have some manly man-talk with my best bro in a while."

Harper rolled her eyes.

I laughed. "Things are fine. Perfect, actually, except—"

"Except you can't tell anyone or go anywhere where people will see you," Harper finished.

"Yes, that."

"Her dad is a piece of work," Dean said. "But hey, in a few short months, she'll be eighteen and can tell him to fuck off forever."

I shot Harper a quick glance, and she gave me a short nod of understanding. I hadn't told Dean about my vow to marry Emery as an emergency measure to escape her family. The promise felt oddly delicate. Handled the wrong way, I feared it would break something between us, so I left it alone, even in my mind.

"What about Christmas gifts?" Dean asked. "Last year, we did a white elephant for the club. That was a hit, even if I ended up with a wall hanging of a singing fish."

I chuckled as we arrived at my Buick. "Sounds good. And speaking of gifts, I need to pick out something for Emery. I have an hour to kill before she comes over."

In order to keep her father off her back, I was still secretly trying to help Emery pass her math class, though now instead of her wanting to abandon the equations for chitchat, we struggled to keep our hands off each other. We hadn't slept together—that was waiting for us in the future, until after she turned eighteen, at least, and if/when she desired. I was content with just being with her, absorbing her light.

"Want some help picking out a gift?" Harper asked. "I have an hour to kill before I become Emery's alibi for coming over to your house."

Dean laughed. "Such a tangled web of deceit. I'd be happy to help but alas, I have plans." He chucked me on the shoulder. "We'll have to save our man-talk over brewskies for another time."

"Can't wait," I deadpanned. We laughed and I hugged my friend goodbye, then turned to Harper. "Shall we?"

I drove us to the little village of Castle Hill, which always looked more like a set out of a movie than an actual place. It had a quaint main street with shops, restaurants, boutiques, and a general store that was more like a Whole Foods in disguise. Now, with the recent snowfall and Christmas decor, it resembled a picture postcard for small-town holiday cheer.

"Dean's acting weird," Harper said suddenly as I pulled into a parking space behind a Christmas tree lot.

"How so?"

"He's been jumpy lately. Manic, even. You haven't noticed?"

I frowned and shut off the engine. "No. But like he said, I haven't seen much of him lately."

"There's that too," she said. "He always has 'other plans' and spends a lot of time on his phone. He used to hardly touch it, now it's in his hand constantly."

Guilt sank like a heavy stone in my gut. "I've been so wrapped up with Emery, I haven't been paying attention. Maybe he's stressed about finals?"

"Maybe," Harper said, her gaze forward. "I have a bad feeling."

"Now I do too. He's so private," I said. "He's one of my best friends, and yet I've never been to his house. He's never mentioned his parents or anything about his home life at all."

"Me neither. But I have the feeling he's under a lot of pressure."

"Really? But he's..."

"A Bender?" Harper arched a brow. "So are you. So am I. You don't feel the pressure this school—this entire fucking town—puts on you to be something worthy of walking its hallowed halls?"

"I see your point," I said, though my pressure was different. To salvage my dad's legacy by following him to MIT and ensure he wouldn't be forgotten, even as his disease chewed up every last vestige of what made him great.

But Harper's words were making me scared for Dean. "You and he aren't...?"

"No," she said. "Just friends. And he's the same mix of open and completely closed off with me as he is with you." She turned to me with sudden urgency. "I know you have enough on your plate with your dad, but can you talk to him? Have that 'manly chat,' but for real?"

"Of course," I said. "I'd turn the car around and do it now if I could. I'll make it happen, I promise."

"Thank you. On a more festive note: We need a Christmas gift for the love of your life. Let's do this."

She was teasing, but I didn't bother to correct her. Warmth flooded me, driving out some of the cold fear. That was Emery's specialty—to make everything beautiful. To make even the worst situations feel hopeful.

And what happens in six months...?

I cut that thought off at the pass and followed Harper into a store.

"What's your budget?" she asked in the boutique as we wandered through aisles of Murano glass pieces, ornaments, cards, and jewelry. "Her family has billions, so nothing fancy is going to impress her."

"I can't afford fancy," I said. "I'm aiming for 'thoughtfully touching.'"

"Alexander, my friend, you are one of the good ones." Harper picked up a snow globe and gave it a shake. "How about this?"

But my gaze had already snagged on a jewelry counter. Antique rings, pendants, and earrings were arrayed on black velvet stands and trays.

Harper bent to peer beside me. "Ring shopping for your fiancée?"

"Um, *no*." I coughed, the back of my neck growing hot. "I like that one."

I pointed to a tarnished heart-shaped locket tucked in the corner like a castaway, etched with swirls that resembled flower petals.

"Very pretty," Harper said. "Unique."

I called the salesclerk over. She unlocked the case and set the necklace in my hand. I opened the locket, which was about an inch long and flat, and inspiration struck me like lightning.

"I'll take it."

It was getting dark by the time I dropped Harper back at her car at school, and snow had begun to fall in gentle drifts. I came home to find my dad happily at work at his desk, bent over his mess of papers.

"How's it going, Dad?"

"Never better, son. I believe I'm only a few factors away from cracking it."

"Only a few factors?" I asked, my pulse quickening. "Seriously?"

He chuckled. "Give or take a hundred. You know how it is." He turned to face me. His narrow face was gaunt, and his eyes were shadowed, but his smile was as wide as ever. "One step forward, two steps backward…into infinity."

I smiled faintly. Stepping backward into infinity was exactly what dementia was forcing him to do.

"But even this great work isn't everything," Dad said. "We must remember our Goethe: All theory is gray, but forever green is the tree of life."

"Yeah, speaking of, the Math & Physics Club throws a Christmas party every year. I was thinking we could have it here."

"Here?"

We glanced around the small, dimly lit living area with its shabby furniture and stacks of books on every available surface. It was December fifteenth and no sign of Christmas anywhere. No green tree to speak of.

He rubbed his chin. "Not very merry, is it?"

Shame burned my cheeks. "Fuck, I'm sorry. I've been

so wrapped up with Emery and training for spring row season—"

"Not your fault, my boy. I've been no help, buried in theorems for weeks." His smile fell. "Christmas was always your mother's favorite. She made it so festive."

"*I'll* make it festive," I declared. "I'll ask Emery to help. This is exactly her skill set. She'll make it beautiful, and we'll have a suitable party."

"Wonderful!" Dad said. "Won't that be nice to have your friends over, with food and lights and a tree? You and I will play piano for them, and we'll have music and lots of joy."

"That's exactly right," I said gruffly. "Everyone from the club is eager to meet you."

"Me?" He looked overcome for a moment. "Why that's…unexpected. How lovely. Thank you, Xander."

"Yep." I cleared my throat. "Emery will be here soon. We'll get right on it."

"Wonderful." He smiled and laid a shaking hand on my shoulder. "My eyes are tired. I think I'll take a nap. Give you two some privacy."

I let loose a shaky breath. "Thanks, but getting her through her calculus final is my number one priority."

"Sure, it is," he said. "Use protection!"

"*Dad.*"

"What?" he said innocently. "I'm merely reminding you to safeguard your axioms to *protect* against inconsistencies." He tsk-tsked me with a wink and a grin. "Get your mind out of the gutter, son."

I chuckled and watched him retreat to his room, wondering how I could feel so happy and so sad at the same time.

Chapter 26

EMERY

"Where is everyone?" I asked, glancing around the empty classroom.

Thursday afternoon was our prom committee meeting and the only other person in the room was Delilah Winslow.

"I think it's just you and me now," she said, tucking a few ringlets behind her ear. "Elowen and Sierra have, um…other commitments."

That didn't hurt as much as I thought it would. I was seeing less and less of my old friends and spending more time with Harper, and as many afternoons and weekends with Xander as I could get away with.

"Why are you still here?" I asked. I hadn't forgotten that the Academy's premiere gossip had been responsible for spilling Xander's home situation to the whole school.

"Because I want to be," Delilah said earnestly. "I know how talented you are, and I really want to help make this prom something amazing." Her gaze dropped to her perfectly manicured fingers. "And also…I miss hanging out with you. Sierra's been so busy lately, and Elowen has completely taken over the dance team since you left. She acts like she's queen of the school, and I'm just…I'm tired."

Delilah sounded like how I felt at the start of the year, but that didn't mean I could trust her.

"You shared some pretty private things about…people at this school."

"I know, and I'm sorry," she said, meeting my gaze directly. "It was my way of being valuable to the group. I understand if you don't believe me."

I believed her, though trusting her might take time. But giving people a second chance was a good thing to do. Harper had done it for me.

I gave Delilah a smile and reached for my portfolio. "I'm glad you're still here. Today's kind of a big day."

"I know!" she said, clapping her hands together. "I can't wait to see the theme. Did the board love it?"

Earlier that week, I'd had a meeting with the Board of Trustees to show them my idea for the prom design and get budget approval. It had felt like going in for an important job interview and a Broadway audition all rolled into one. The looks of awe and approval on their faces when I showed them my plans gave me a rush of hope that my parents might feel the same.

"They approved it," I told Delilah. "We are going to throw a Black-and-White Ball."

I pulled out a series of sketches mounted on cardboard stock for what the Castle Hill Country Club ballroom would look like after we were done with it. Round tables would surround the dance floor, draped in white cloth and adorned with glass centerpieces of black-and-white balls, tall black candles, and white flowers. At the ballroom entrance, black balloons would rise from the floor in a narrow cluster, expanding to cover the ceiling like smoke. Clear balloons, tethered with LED-lit strings, would float between tables like crystal bubbles. Over the dance floor, a balloon "chandelier" of black and clear spheres would sparkle with delicate lights.

"Holy shit," Delilah's eyes widened as she flipped through the sketches. "Oh, Emery… It's so beautiful. Just gorgeous, and it's made mostly of balloons?"

"If we get the lighting right, they should look like glass orbs. The board wouldn't let me suspend actual glass from the ceiling," I said with a chuckle. "But they okayed glass in the centerpieces. I think it might turn out really nice."

"Nice?" Delilah shrieked. "This is going to be *epic*. But is the dress code going to be black-and-white? Because I feel like the girlies aren't going to want to be limited when it comes to their dresses."

"Black-and-white attire is optional."

But I already knew I was wearing white and Xander would look devastating in black. Yin and yang…

Or a couple at their wedding.

The thought gave me a jolt, but I shoved it away. Xander was going to be my date to the prom because once my parents saw what I could do, they'd be so happy, nothing else would matter.

I glanced at my sketches and then at Delilah. "This is going to be a lot of work for just the two of us."

She brushed the dark cloud of ringlets from her shoulder and whipped out a clipboard and pen. "We got this. We'll handle the details and hire guys to do the actual… ballooning. Okay, what else do we need?"

We brainstormed for another hour, our to-do list growing longer than a CVS receipt, and by the end, I felt optimistic. We had plenty of time and the trustees had given me an insane budget.

Delilah and I wrapped up the meeting, and she gave me a quick hug before we parted ways.

"Thanks, Em."

"For what?"

"For being friends with me still. When I'm around you, I feel like it's okay to not be performing all the time. To not be so fake, you know?"

I smiled. "I know what you mean."

On my way to the car, I spotted Xander walking with Harper and Dean. He gave the slightest of nods and a smile. My calculus final was tomorrow, and we had one more tutoring session at his place that afternoon to save me from disaster.

I crooked my pinky at him, my heart swelling and skin already tingling, anticipating Xander's hands on me after all the boring math was out of the way, even if he never let it go much further than touching over clothes.

Because he's the best person I know, and we might only have a few months left together on the same side of the country.

The thought brought fast tears to my eyes, but I pushed those down too.

"I have a plan," I told the doubting voices and clutched my portfolio tighter to me. "And it's going to work."

Two hours later, I was at Xander's desk in his loft, watching him grade the practice test he'd made for me. My heart skipped a beat when he frowned at the equations I'd labored over, his expression grim.

I leaned forward, hands twisting. "Well?"

Xander set down his red pen with a sigh and shook his head gravely. "Emery..."

"You have *got* to be kidding me. I felt really good about this one."

"I don't know what happened, but...you got every single one correct."

I froze. "Wait, what?"

Xander grinned, a mischievous glint in his eyes. "You nailed it."

I stared a moment, then swatted his arm. "Oh my God, I am going to kill you!"

He laughed as I shoved all the papers and notebooks aside and climbed onto his lap, straddling him. I took off his glasses and settled against him, ringing my arms around his neck.

"That was mean," he said, his hands running up my jean-clad thighs to my hips. "Do you forgive me?"

"No," I said, all my mock irritation and even relief burning away at his touch. I let my lips hover over his, breathing hotly. "And you're not sorry at all."

"That's true, but I'm proud of you. This stuff isn't easy."

"It's too late for sweet talk." I brushed my lips against his. "I'm mad at you."

He craned up to kiss me, but I moved just out of reach and rolled my hips, grinding against him and eliciting a gruff sound from deep in his chest. "So mad…"

Xander groaned and gripped my hips, pulling me down on him while lifting to meet me. He lunged again, this time capturing my mouth. Taking what he wanted. A soft whimper escaped me, and he took that too, devouring me with biting, sucking kisses that set my blood on fire.

My hand slipped down his chest, over his T-shirt, to his erection straining in his jeans. "You're so hard," I breathed between kisses. "I want you, Xander. I want to…"

"I know," he said gruffly. "I want you so bad sometimes I can barely think."

"That's saying something…"

"But we should wait," Xander said seriously. "I'm eighteen. You're seventeen. Even if you and Tucker have already…" He bit off his words.

"We haven't. We never did."

"Really?"

"Really." My hands were back in Xander's hair, then tracing his jawline with my finger. "I could have a hundred times, but I kept waiting to *want* to. But now, with you, I want to. I think maybe I was waiting for you, even if I didn't know it."

"Me too," he said.

"You've never…?"

"Emery, you're my first girlfriend, my first kiss, my first everything."

I stared. "I was your first *kiss*?"

My mind went back to the rainy night when he kissed me for the first time, the moment taking on a whole new depth I never thought possible.

"I can't believe you've never kissed anyone," I said. "I mean…look at you."

He smiled bashfully. "I could have, once or twice. But I think I was waiting for you too." He glanced down. "So if it's okay with you, I want to wait a little longer. To experience just being with you and being good for you in a bunch of other ways that aren't about sex."

I stared in disbelief. My entire life, my mother put me in pageants and contests, teaching me that being beautiful was the most important thing—that my value lay in how attractive I was to men. Men leered at me, made lewd comments, told me to smile because what I felt inside wasn't nearly as important as giving them something pretty to look at. Hell, Tucker had spent our entire time together assuring me that I was a hot piece of ass, good for one thing and one thing only. And then came Xander…

"No one has ever said something like that to me before."

His expression grew hard. "That's because they've only been looking at you, Emery, instead of seeing you."

My heart felt so full, I could barely stand it. I wrapped my arms around him, buried my face in his neck. "Don't. You're going to make me cry."

His hands held my face, and he leaned back to look at me. His gaze was so intent, so full, it stole my breath and made my heart pound. Xander kissed me then, his lips moving gently over mine, his tongue touching mine softly. With his palm cupping my jaw, his thumb brushed over my lower lip before pressing down, opening my mouth more for him. Just that one movement—that one taking—made me dizzy with want and burned up my tears in heated need.

"And anyway," he said, his voice gruff and thick. "We can do other things."

I gasped as he gripped me under my thighs with both hands and got up from the chair, taking me with him. He carried me to his bed and laid me down, then covered my body with his. We kissed and touched, our hands roaming over our clothes until it wasn't enough. Until we needed skin and heat and to be naked with each other.

I sat up and pulled my sweater over my head, taking my shirt with it and leaving me in my bra. Xander's eyes swept over me, and everywhere they landed, I felt the tingling anticipation of his touch. We'd kept our clothes on before but today was different.

"More this time," I whispered, moving so that we were both kneeling.

He nodded and pulled his shirt off, leaving him bare-chested. I'd felt the hard contours of him before, but now...

"Jesus, Xander." I stared greedily, my fingertips tracing his collarbone, across the planes of his chest, then down to the ridges of his abs. "They need to make rowing a national requirement."

He didn't reply, uninterested in his own perfection, but reached for me. His hands slid into my hair as he kissed me—a hard, thrilling kiss—that was different from his usual. Xander's kisses never failed to ignite every part of me from the inside out, but this time I felt his intentions shift. His need deepen.

He started to undo the clasp of my bra but then paused, checking with me first with a quick glimpse. I nodded and then felt it loosen. Slowly, he pulled it off my arms and tossed it aside, his gaze drinking me in.

"Emery," he breathed. "You're so goddamn beautiful, it hurts to look at you."

His hands slipped down over my breasts, thumbs brushing my nipples in maddeningly soft little touches. I placed my hands on his and pressed them against me, letting him know to squeeze and knead and touch me without restraint. Being topless with him, with his hands on me like this, it felt like our first kiss. A reunion, this time with our bodies, and I could only imagine what it was going to feel like when he was finally inside me.

Xander erased my thoughts with another biting kiss, then he tore away, his forehead bending to touch mine, his breathing coming harder now as he fought for control. I could feel the tension in him, the suppressed want for me that coiled in every taut muscle. His mouth took mine again before moving to my neck, my throat, then down to one nipple. I whimpered as the heated wetness of his tongue swirled over me, as his teeth bit lightly—teasing me—before clamping down and sucking.

I let out a cry, my hands in his hair, gripping the strands and holding him in place while little bolts of electricity radiated from everywhere he touched me, then skimmed down my back and between my legs until I was practically panting.

"Xander…I…"

He came back up for more kisses, his arms sliding around me and holding me close, chest to chest. So much bare skin touching…he was so warm, yet hard against my softness. His hands roamed, returning to my face, to hold me like I was precious and then kissing me like I was the air he needed to breathe. To feel both at once, desired and cherished…to feel how badly he wanted me while never losing himself in his own need, was a kind of consideration I'd never known before.

"Emery," he breathed, his hands slipping down my back, then around the front of my jeans. "I want to touch you."

"Yes," I whispered. "God, yes. Me too."

I tore at his buttons while he worked to undo mine. We came apart to slip off our jeans, then lay side by side in our underwear, his head beside mine on the pillow. We tangled like vines, arms and legs entwined, kissing hard enough that breathing came second to the deep sweeps of our tongues that needed to explore every corner. Below, our hips moved in desperate thrusts, his erection pressing against the center of me again and again.

Just when I thought I couldn't take it another minute, his hand slipped over my breast, my stomach, then lower, leaving little fires along every inch skin he touched. He went between my legs, cupped me over the silk of my underwear, and began rubbing gently. A moan fell out of my mouth at the sensation—a deep ache of pleasure that was begging for release.

I let my hand follow the same path down his magnificent body, honed by God-knew-how-many hours in the gym, trailing over the lean muscles of his torso that tensed under my touch. I slipped lower, under the waistband of his boxer briefs, to find the hard length of him—thick and perfect. I wrapped my fingers around him and stroked him once.

He released a hissing breath. "Fuck, Em…"

"Do you have lotion?"

He nodded at the nightstand behind me. There was a box of tissues there, while in the drawer I found a little bottle of lotion. The image of Xander lying on his back, taking himself in hand and working to make himself come, suddenly flashed across my mind, and the ache between my legs intensified.

I put a few tissues beside me and then a small amount of lotion in my palm before coming back to him. We tangled again immediately, as I slipped my hand inside his underwear to caress him again, this time with smooth frictionless motion, the lotion sliding easily over his erection.

"What do you think about when you do this to yourself?" I breathed against his lips, working him in long, slow strokes and squeezes.

"Can you guess?" he said gruffly. "I think about you." He went between my legs again, to my damp underwear. "I think about being here. Being inside you. Making you come."

Dear God…

A little cry erupted out of me as his fingers slipped beneath the hem of my underwear, to that sensitive little knot of flesh that was already throbbing.

"You're so wet," he breathed, somehow surprised that he'd created this want in me. "Just here, okay?"

I nodded, and he rubbed his fingers over me, the sensation sending licks of fire through me and making me dizzy. We fell into a rhythm, each striving to bring the other higher and higher, my leg locked around his hip, our mouths clashing in messy kisses.

The intensity building at the center of me reached a sudden, shocking peak and Xander's fingers coaxed me over the edge. I gasped, my body going rigid, as the pleasure broke and spilled all through me in shuddering waves. He pressed his fingers harder, moving in slow, rhythmic circles, somehow attuned to my orgasm and making it last.

I let out a final, stuttering breath, every cell in my body feeling as if it were brand new, electrified by him and only him. I kissed Xander with renewed fervor to give him what he'd given me.

"Emery…" he grunted, as I squeezed and stroked the thick length of him again and again. "I'm going to…"

I grabbed the tissues I'd stashed beside me and came back to him, reveling in how his muscles tensed, how his face was a mask of pained ecstasy, and the noises he made—all of it my doing. His pleasure belonged to me, and I took it. I coaxed his release out of him, his body shuddering like mine had, into the tissue.

"Jesus Christ," he gasped.

He lay on his back, breathing hard, and I watched his abs expanding and contracting with pride. With satisfaction. Because all of these reactions and moans and the deep satiation radiating off of him came from me.

Xander tossed the tissue aside, then rolled back to me, hauling me to him and wrapping me in his embrace. He kissed me long and slow, a recovery kiss, to soothe my swollen lips and chafed skin.

His blue and brown eyes searched mine. "Are you good?"

"Are you kidding?" I said softly. "I feel like I'm in a warm bath. Every part of me is humming and happy. *I'm* happy."

Xander smiled. "Me too." He kissed my cheek, my temple, then my hair, inhaling deeply. "Me too, Em."

I basked in him, moved almost to tears again at how considerate he was of me, how he made me feel so safe. Xander held me tightly, protectively, as if he could keep me from the things that would hurt me. Or tear us apart.

I held him just as tightly and fought off the doubt and fear, sure that something that felt this right could only last forever.

Chapter 27

XANDER

Emery seemed aglow with happiness as she studied my living room, her eyes dancing as she envisioned decorations. The winter break from school had begun, her calculus final had gone well, and she was free from math forever. Strangely, her father hadn't insisted on her taking yet another class. Her application to Brown was still pending; I assumed he thought they had enough information to decide to accept her or not.

Watching her standing in my house, making sketches and notes, I harbored a secret, selfish desire that she get into Brown, even if she hated it, because at least then she'd stay. The idea of us going to separate ends of the country chilled me to my bones, fueled by my mother's parting words.

It won't be forever.

But what if it was?

Emery bounded up to me, breaking me from my thoughts by throwing her arms around my neck. "I'm off. Harper is meeting me in town, then we'll be back to get to work."

I pulled her in close. She wore a pale green sweater today and little earrings in the shape of Christmas bows. "I'll pick up the books and take my dad out for supplies for tomorrow's party. How long will you need?"

"A good four or five hours at least. Maybe you could see a movie, too?" She laughed at my sour face. "I know you hate that, but I need the time."

I kissed her nose. "Whatever you need. Speaking of…"

From my wallet, I pulled out three one-hundred-dollar bills. Now it was her turn to make a sour face.

"I hate that I can't contribute," she said. "My family is sitting on a pile of gold and hardly shares a single bit unless there's a tax break in there somewhere."

"You're contributing your artistry," I told her. "That's worth a pile of gold itself."

She beamed and pocketed the money. "I hope this is the tutoring money my dad put in my account. There's some poetic justice in him footing the bill for something he hates."

I smiled but didn't confirm or deny. I hadn't touched that money—more than six hundred dollars—but kept it in my account. I wasn't sure what it was for, but it didn't feel right to spend it, so I left it alone.

I kissed Emery a final time and then she was gone, off

to make a beautiful Christmas and bring it back to my dad. I moved the stacks of books, vacuumed, and dusted until the living room was moderately presentable. Shabby, but clean.

"Dad, you ready to go?" I called, wrapping a scarf around my neck and pulling on my coat. No answer. I leaned into the hallway off the kitchen and called toward his room. "Dad?"

He came downstairs wearing a shirt and sweater over his pajama bottoms and slippers. "Eh, Xander?" he blinked at me, his hair askew. "I feel as though I'm missing something. We were to go somewhere?"

"Yeah, Dad," I said, swallowing hard. "We're going shopping for the Christmas party tomorrow, remember? I thought we'd get some lunch while we're out and see a movie."

"Ah yes. Lovely, lovely." He smoothed the front of his sweater with trembling hands. His left, worse than his right. "A party?"

My heart sank. "The Math & Physics Club is coming over tomorrow night. They all want to meet you. And Emery is going to decorate for us while we're out. We'll have a real Christmas."

He blinked and then looked at me funny. "Of course, I know that, Xander. I've been looking forward to it all week!" He strode toward me, beaming. "I'm ready when you are."

"Um, Dad…pants?"

He glanced down and chuckled. "Oh dear, can't get far like this. Be right back."

I smiled, my stomach tightening because the internal clock in my heart wouldn't stop its countdown to when these spells of forgetting would stretch and stretch until they'd erased him completely.

But when he reemerged from his room, he was dressed, his hair relatively smooth, and his eyes sharp. I tried to let that bolster me, but I'd researched Lewy body dementia and knew that periods of stability were often followed by steep declines.

Not yet.

I drove us to Cassidy's, a little diner downtown popular with Academy students—a fact I remembered just after the waitress took our order. But before he'd departed for home in London, Orion had told me most Richies left Castle Hill for European tours, African safaris, or long ski trips in places like Aspen or the Alps.

The diner was quiet, and we ate burgers and fries, my dad regaling me about the time his thirteen-year-old son, Alexander, met one of his heroes, Andrea Ghez, when the famed astrophysicist came to the NIST to give a speech.

"It was she who discovered the supermassive black hole, Sagittarius A*, at the center of our very own Milky Way galaxy," he said proudly. "You should have seen my boy's face, all lit up, listening to her. He declared right then and there he'd be an astrophysicist too."

I smiled over the ache in my heart. "Yeah, he did."

But at the old, single-screen movie theater, Dad recognized me again as we watched *It's a Wonderful Life*, a movie about a man on the brink of suicide until he's shown what life would be like in his small town if he'd never existed.

I glanced at my dad as the silver light of the old black-and-white movie played over his features. I sent my own prayer to whatever guardian angel might be listening that meeting my friends might do that for him. Maybe show him some appreciation that would stick when the black hole of dementia sucked the memories out of him.

After the movie, we went grocery shopping for party supplies, food, and drink. In the parking lot, my dad slumped against the passenger seat, exhausted.

"I believe I'm ready for a nap," he said sleepily.

"Sure thing." I shot Emery a text. I have to bring him back.

She replied immediately. No problem. All done! Followed by the Christmas tree emoji and the red lipstick emoji.

She's my angel, I thought as I drove through gentle drifts of snow back to our house at the end of the road.

"Isn't that beautiful?" Dad said. "The trees and the sunset…what a thing to see."

The trees surrounding our house were bearded white, and snow carpeted the ground, covered our roof, and piled on our old mailbox. Behind, the sun was setting, lining everything in ribbons of gold.

"Come on," I said gently, taking his arm. "It's cold."

Before we could reach the front door, Emery emerged, her cheeks flushed.

"Emery, my dear!" Dad exclaimed. "What a lovely surprise. What are you doing here?"

She didn't blink but smiled her brilliant smile. "Hello, Russell. I want to show you something."

"Well, all right."

She took his hand and led him inside. I followed and then tried my damndest not to burst into tears like a goddamn baby when I saw what she'd done.

Harper, who was there, straightening and tidying, read my face and nodded at Emery. "It's all her. I just work here."

"No, Harper helped a ton," Emery said, guiding my dad to a seat on the couch.

"Oh, Emery," my dad said, pulling off his winter hat. "Oh, my sweet girl."

Our living room was still our living room. I don't know what I expected—Emery's talents were such that I wouldn't have put it past her to make the place seem brand new even with three hundred bucks. But instead of making it unrecognizable, she somehow made it *more*.

She'd rearranged some of the furniture to take advantage of the space and the light to amplify the cozy hominess I remembered as a kid. As if she'd returned it to a former, happier time when my family—and my father's mind—were still whole.

A Christmas tree covered in white lights and ornaments glowed from beside the fireplace, where green garlands of fir and pine were strung across the mantel. The window wore green too, highlighting the rustic bones of the house, while red-and-green plaid cloths were draped over the piano and the coffee table. Red candles, pinecones, and silver ornaments made a centerpiece on the table. Over the chimney were two stockings, one red and covered in silver stars, the other green with little atomic symbols.

Which don't exist at your local store. She made those.

I'd asked her to help me decorate two days ago, and she managed to make those damn stockings. She made all this happen, including the look of pure delight on my dad's face, and I'd never be able to repay her for that.

"Would you like some eggnog, Russell?" Emery asked.

"My dear, that would be lovely."

She moved to take the grocery bags out of my hands. "I'm assuming you bought eggnog."

I nodded faintly. "Emery…"

"It's nothing," she said softly. "I'm so, so happy to do it. Really."

While Harper and my dad got acquainted and Emery and I headed to the kitchen, a sudden thought jumped into my mind. "His equations…"

"I didn't touch his desk," Emery said. "I figured he might have a system or something, and I wasn't about to mess with it."

A quick glance at Dad's desk showed the same cyclone of paper as usual. In the kitchen, I set down the bags and took her in my arms. "You're an angel."

"It's really not a big deal—" she began, but I shook my head.

"Did you see his face when we came in?" I swallowed

hard. "That was my Christmas present. I couldn't ask for anything more."

"That's very sweet, Xander." She kissed me softly, then her smile turned playful. "But you're still getting a real present."

She laughed and bounded back into the living room, a ball of pure light and energy because what she'd done for my house was what she was meant to do. And the only lone shadow of the afternoon was the certainty that she needed to get far away. To make her dreams come true, and I couldn't let anyone take that from her.

Not even me.

By twilight the following afternoon, with food and drink ready and Christmas carols playing from my phone, which was hooked up to a home device Harper let me borrow, our little party was in full swing.

I'd built a fire in our fireplace for the first time. Dean, Harper, and the rest of the Math & Physics Club—Elena, Jasper, Micah, and Kevin—surrounded my dad on the couch, peppering him with questions. Elena hadn't been kidding about bringing a copy of *Scientific American* with her for him to autograph. She was a small girl with bright eyes and looked like a groupie meeting her idol.

Emery arrived last, needing to extricate herself from her family with some excuse. She threw her arms around my neck and kissed me in front of the whole group.

"I thought we were a secret," I said.

"We are, but Harper and Dean assured me this was a safe space," Emery said.

"She's correct," Kevin said, tipping an imaginary hat to her, while Micah—a freshman—nodded with a big grin.

"Well in that case…" I kissed her again, incurring laughs and hoots.

"Get a room!" Dean bellowed.

I caught Harper's eye, and she raised her brows. I nodded and pulled Dean aside into the kitchen.

"Hey, man. I just wanted to say…" I rubbed the back of my neck. "I'm realizing I'm not very good at this."

"Are you proposing to me, Alexander?" Dean grinned. "After kissing another girl right in front of me?"

I rolled my eyes. "Look, I…I haven't had a friend until this year. Not a real one. Not until you. And, well…I love you."

Dean's angular face softened. "Oh, Dr. Xander Ford has found the *L* word, ladies and gentlemen." He laughed and engulfed me in a hug. "I love you too, man."

"I mean it, Dean. I'm really damn grateful for you."

He made a face. "You think that's a one-way street? Most years, I move around from group to group. The jocks like me because I keep their shit in order. The girls like me because I'm harmless and they know it." He shrugged. "But I'm a little on the smart side—"

"*A lot* on the smart side."

"So, it's nice to have someone to talk shop with. Even if talking to you is sort of like talking to Einstein."

I smirked. "Not even close."

"You know what I mean."

"But Dean, if you need anything or…ever want to talk. I'm here, okay?"

He smiled. "Duly noted, my friend. Thank you."

"So…you're good?"

"Never better. I mean it," he added to my dubious look. "It's been a little tough lately at home, but I'm good. I promise."

"You'd tell me if you weren't?"

"Of course." He hugged me again. "Merry Christmas."

Dean rejoined the group, and I caught Harper's meaningful glance. I nodded and she sighed with relief and mouthed *Thank you*.

But there was nothing to thank me for. Being there for a friend, I realized, wasn't a gift that was given but something you just did, and I made a vow to be better at it.

I relaxed then, into the party and the atmosphere that Emery had created. We ate snacks and cookies and drank eggnog and cider while Dean filled my dad in on my exploits at school.

"We do movie nights once a month," he said. "Mostly for Xander's education…and against his will. Your son is a certifiable genius, Dr. Ford, but completely clueless when it comes to pop culture."

"Here we go," I muttered with a laugh. I sat in the chair by the fire, Emery in my lap, her fingers lazily running through my hair.

Dad chuckled. "Don't I know it. He's had his head in a book since he was two!"

"Even math- or science-related movies don't get a pass," Dean said cackling. "Last week, we watched *A Beautiful Mind*. Or as Xander calls it, *A Terrible Movie*."

"It cheated," I said with a shrug. "You can't just have the guy staring at a wall of light-up numbers and somehow we're supposed to believe he's good at math."

Kevin grinned. "But if they *showed* the math, no one would understand it."

"I would," I said, and they all burst out laughing.

"If you really want to make Xander mad," Emery said, "tell him he's being such a Scorpio."

Elena snickered. "And that there are people who believe the Earth is flat."

I scowled. "That's the most ridiculous thing I've ever heard. The Greeks knew it was spherical two thousand years ago. And how do they explain gravity, or do they not 'believe' in that either?"

Emery laughed and pressed a kiss to my cheek. "We shouldn't get you all worked up. Even if I sort of love you all worked up..."

"Too late for sweet talk," I said, echoing our conversation from the other day. "Now I'm mad."

"Mm, I'll have to make it up to you later."

She laid a soft kiss under my ear as I sipped my cider and watched the party happening around me. My dad looked as happy as I'd seen him in years, wearing the ugly scarf he'd won in the white elephant gift exchange wrapped around his neck.

"Come, Xander!" he said suddenly, getting to his feet. "Let's play for these fine friends of yours."

"Oh, I don't think so…"

Emery nudged my arm. "You play the piano? You never told me!"

"Only a little and I'm not very good," I said. "If we want to hear real piano playing, we should get Harper up there. She's the maestro."

"Oh no, I'm not letting you off the hook," Harper said with a laugh.

"Stop dragging your feet, Alexander, and come play for your friends. Schubert's *Fantasie* in F Minor duet, if you please!"

"He can play *only a little* Schubert." Harper snorted as Emery sat beside her on the floor, cross-legged.

Reluctantly, I joined my dad at the piano.

"Now, this duet is a conversation between the *secondo*—Xander—and the *primo*—myself. He'll be responsible for the technical weight of the piece, while I get to have all the fun." Dad wagged his eyebrows. He gave me a nod and lifted his hands in a flourish, then brought them back down… where they trembled like leaves over the keys. "Oh dear."

He tried a few notes, but his fingers wouldn't cooperate.

"Oh, it's okay, Dad," I said tightly. "Maybe you're just…tired."

He chuckled nervously and clasped his shaking hands together. "That must be it." He turned on the bench to address my friends. "My apologies. Seems I'm having a bit of an episode."

I looked helplessly to Emery and Harper. Emery jumped up to help my dad back to the couch, and Harper slid onto the piano bench and began a rousing rendition of "Twelve Days of Christmas."

Everyone sang along, including my dad, who, within seconds, was cheerful and laughing, as if he'd forgotten all about the incident.

No. *Because* he'd forgotten all about it.

———

Later that night, our friends went home after telling my father over and over what an honor it had been. He went to bed exhausted but happy, and I prayed he'd remember how they talked about his accomplishments and breakthroughs, his legacy while on this earth.

Harper was the last to go, insisting on helping to clean up, and then it was just me and Emery.

"Come on," she said, taking my hand. "Time for your present. Your *real* present."

"Oh, I think the industrial-sized tub of cheese balls I won at the white elephant is gift enough."

She giggled as we went upstairs to my room. "You're just jealous of my pickle-shaped ornament with Nicholas Cage's face on it."

"I tried to get that, actually. Trade?"

"Over my dead body. And you don't even know who Nicholas Cage is." She laughed and pushed me to sit on my bed. "Wait one sec."

I watched as Emery pulled my curtain aside and

retrieved a flat, rectangular gift, about the size of a dinner mat, wrapped in white paper with a red bow.

"I stashed this yesterday when I was decorating." She set it in my lap and sat beside me.

"It's heavy," I said, guessing a photo or painting. I unwrapped the gift and stared, my heart trying to climb out of my throat.

Emery had made me a collage of my life. Sketches, photos, and painted figures meshed together in shades of blue and brown. I took it in as a whole at first, then the individual parts: a rowing crew on smooth water, atomic symbols, stars and galaxies, my heterochromic eyes sketched with astounding precision—there was even a diagram of Schrödinger's thought experiment with the cat in the box. My eyes filled at a sketch of me and my father from my fifth grade science fair. An exact replica of the photo of us on my desk.

But it was the watercolor image in the center that stole my breath. A little blond girl and brown-haired boy, their backs to us, sat on a rock. The girl's head rested on his shoulder, and his hand was on the exact center of her back.

"Do you like it?" Emery asked uncertainly.

"Emery…I…"

I nearly said it. The three words were right there, ready to escape from my heart and into the world, naked and defenseless against the circumstances that wanted to tear us apart.

"Thank you," I said instead. "It's the most incredible thing anyone has ever given me."

Her smile was radiant as she kissed me. "I'm so glad. I wasn't sure…"

"Emery, it's extraordinary."

She blushed. "I was shooting for 'does not suck.'"

"My turn." I went to my desk drawer and pulled out a small box wrapped in shiny green paper and a white ribbon. I handed it to Emery and sat beside her, my heart thumping as she opened it.

"Oh, Xander," she said, lifting the locket from its black velvet box. "It's so beautiful."

"It's kind of old…"

"Which is why I love it. Imagine the stories it can tell." She handed it to me. "Help me put it on."

Emery turned her back to me and lifted her long hair from her neck. I clasped the closure, and she hugged me. "Thank you."

"You didn't look inside."

"Wait, really…?" she whispered, her fingers trembling as she opened the heart on its tiny hinge. Inside, was a little yellow petal, sealed in resin to keep it for all time. "Is this…?"

"From the flower you gave me," I said. "I wanted you to have a piece of it too. Because it's like a relic of that day. A sacred relic from the day that I met you."

"A piece of our story," she whispered.

"Yes, Em. Our story."

Her tears spilled over, and she cried into my neck. I held her and kissed her, all the while too cowardly to tell her how I felt, old hurts reminding me how easy it could be for someone you loved to suddenly walk out the door. Then it was too late; time for her to get home.

I walked her to my front door. The night was black but soft, the front porch light casting a warm yellow glow. We kissed goodbye, and she stepped backward onto the path, grasping the locket in her palm.

"Hey, it's snowing," she said. She held out her hand, her smile radiant as she caught snowflakes on her fingers.

My heart ached to look at her. Her hair flowed in soft gold ribbons around the shoulders of her white cashmere sweater. Her cheeks were flushed pink from the cold. From under her bangs, her blue-green eyes were bright and brilliant. Everything about her was soft and warm, white and gold… I watched as snowflakes dusted her hair. I couldn't understand how all of this beauty—the interior luminosity of her—could possibly be for me.

Tell her. Tell her now…

But the words remained trapped in my throat, restrained by a heart that was scared to declare itself the property of this girl who was, in all likelihood, going to leave. Because she had to. Because her beauty wasn't all for me, but something she needed to share with the world, far away from her father's poison.

Then I let the moment slip out of my hands again. Emery crooked two fingers at me with a smile and stepped into the night.

Part IV

Merciless is the law of nature,
and rapidly and irresistibly
we are drawn to our doom.
—Nikola Tesla

Part IV

Chapter 28

EMERY

MARCH

"Happy birthday, dear Emery..." Delilah and Harper sang very loudly—and badly—at our bench under the willow tree in the quad at midmorning break. "Happy birthday to yoooooou."

Harper handed me a brownie with a candle in it, while Delilah gave me a quick hug. "Make a wish, Em!"

A hundred wishes filled my heart, all of them with Xander's name on them. But his father was slipping away, and my heart broke for them both.

I wish for Dr. Ford to defy the odds and stay with us for a long time.

I blew out the candle, and Delilah gave me a sly look. "I think I can guess what you wished for. You and Xander? At long last...?"

Heat flushed my cheeks, and my fingers went to

the locket over my heart. "I don't have to wish for that."

"Eeep!" She clapped her hands while Harper—on my left—rolled her eyes with a laugh. Letting Delilah Winslow in on the fact that Xander and I were together had been the ultimate test of her trustworthiness, and she'd passed with flying colors.

"Xander's taking me to somewhere secret tomorrow for what he calls 'a big date.'"

"Are you excited? Nervous?"

"Both, maybe. It feels kind of perfect. We waited long enough but also just the right amount of time." I waved a hand. "Anyway, I don't want to get ahead of myself. He says he just wants to be with me in whatever way feels right for both of us."

"That's the sweetest thing I've ever heard," Delilah gushed. "Isn't she lucky?"

"Yes," Harper said with a tilted smile. "The luckiest."

My new-and-improved best friend seemed a little down lately but wouldn't divulge why. She said she'd share when she felt ready, and since I wanted to be a good friend to her, I had to respect her privacy…even if I wanted to hug any hurt right out of her.

I broke off pieces of my birthday brownie for my friends and then took a bite. "So, Delilah, what's the news from the Other Side? No gossip, just good stuff."

Since Christmas, I'd spent all my time with Xander, my new friends, and working on the prom. My old life was starting to feel like it had belonged to someone else, and now I had a new one that was inching closer to the one I wanted.

Delilah hesitated. "Elowen and Tucker are official. You may have noticed."

"Oh, I have," I said with a laugh. "Their PDA is pretty hard to miss. I guess it was like that when we were together, too. My sincere apologies to the class."

"Too little too late, my friend," Harper said, brushing crumbs off her hands.

"You're not mad?" Delilah asked me. "It's kind of low of her to get with your ex without talking to you first."

"Nope," I said. "Tucker and I were not a great fit, to put it mildly. If they're happy, I'm happy."

"Orion's the one who should be happy that Elowen finally found a new hobby." Delilah giggled. "She stuck to him like a barnacle for ages."

Harper stood up, muttering something about throwing her napkin away.

"And speaking of Orion," Delilah continued. "He's throwing a party in Atlas Hall after the Head of the Bay Regatta next weekend. Sounds like it'll be pretty epic."

"Only if they win," I said. "If they lose, it'll be a—"

"A pity party?"

"Nice." I offered my hand for a high-five.

"What are we high-fiving about?" Harper asked, resuming her seat on the bench.

"Delilah's terrible joke," I said. "Also, Orion is throwing a post-regatta rager."

"Ah."

"You guys should come," Delilah said. "Since the entire row crew will be there, you'll have an excuse to party with your man, Em."

I sighed. "I suppose, but I'm tired of hiding us. Xander is amazing in every way, and I hate keeping him like a dirty secret."

"You think your dad would care?" Harper asked. "And who would tell him anyway?"

"Not me," Delilah said quickly.

"He has his ways," I said. "And it's so stupid. I care less and less what he thinks, right up until I have to confront him. Then I'm scared shitless."

"Well, prom is also going to be epic with a capital *E*; that should impress him." Delilah turned to Harper. "You should see what Emery's doing. It's just breathtaking."

Harper smiled. "I'm not surprised."

"*We* are doing it," I corrected. "This whole project wouldn't happen if it weren't for you."

Delilah glanced down, touched. "Thanks, Em. That's nice to hear."

We finished the brownie, and I gave Delilah a hug goodbye when she stood to leave for class, then Harper and I headed to English. Spring was coming early—the air was losing its icy chill and things were turning green again.

"She turned out pretty well." Harper nodded at Delilah's retreating back. "You'd almost think it was possible for people to change," she said bitterly.

I gave her a concerned look. "Referring to anyone in particular?"

"Ignore me," she said. "Hey, you want to see a movie or something tonight?"

"I can't," I said. "My family is doing a big birthday dinner. We might actually have a nice evening together. *That* would be a birthday wish come true." We arrived at Ms. Alvarez's class. "I know I'm a broken record, but if you ever want to talk…"

Harper silenced me with a hug. "You're first on my list."

"I love that so much. Love *you*."

"Love you too."

I glanced around to make sure no one was watching before slipping inside the art supply room. It was as big as most classrooms, with supplies neatly stored in bins and on shelves along the wall and a long table in the center, where Xander was leaning, waiting for me. Our new lunchtime routine: to find a secluded spot and grab a few stolen moments when pretending we weren't together grew unbearable.

I shut the door and flew at him, wrapping him in my arms and kissing him hard. He responded at once, his mouth opening for my tongue to explore and taste, and then he took his turn, pressing in, his hands in my hair, kissing me until we were breathless.

"Hello to you too," he said huskily when we finally came up for air.

"I'm in a good mood," I said. "We're in the final

stretches for prom. I even have my dress picked out." I cocked my head. "Come to think of it, the only thing I don't have is a date."

Xander ringed his arms around my waist. "Me neither. There's someone I want to ask, but I'm not sure if it's allowed."

I grinned. "It's allowed. Prom is where I show my dad everything, right? My artistry, my dreams, and…my love."

I brushed my fingers through Xander's hair. In all the time we'd been together, we'd never said the words that felt like they'd been waiting to be voiced. Both of us too afraid to say them when the end of the year was uncertain.

I watched Xander push his own doubt away and smile. "Your art is extraordinary. I don't see how anyone could deny you anything."

"There you go again, saying all the things that make me melt into a puddle." He hadn't even seen my design; I wanted to surprise him, but his faith in me was a present unto itself.

"Well, in that case," Xander began. "Emery, will you—" He stopped, shaking his head. "Wait, wait, wait. This is your event. Your design, your planning, and your hard work. It doesn't feel right that I ask you to something that belongs to you."

"It doesn't *belong* to me, but…damn you," I said, sniffing a laugh. "You're too much."

He raised his brows expectantly. "Well? I'm waiting."

I laughed and nudged his arm. "Xander Ford, will you go to the prom with me?"

"I'd be honored."

He kissed me then, and I couldn't help but think of his marriage "proposal." We hadn't spoken of it, not once. It was something we didn't touch—a last resort to help me escape. But now that we had feelings for each other, it seemed even more dangerous somehow.

It won't come to that.

Xander pulled away and whispered, "Happy birthday."

"Thank you." I sank my fingers into his hair, my other hand sliding over his chest, feeling every line and contour through his T-shirt. "You know what that means."

His face reddened, but his gaze grew dark and even more heated.

"It doesn't have to mean anything," he said, holding my face gently while his eyes roamed, coming again and again to my mouth. "But if you want to…"

"Oh, I want to," I said. "It's almost torture not to, at this point."

He nodded. "I wish I could be with you tonight."

"Me too," I said gently. "It's going to be hard for him, isn't it? And you."

While I had my birthday dinner with my family, Xander would be driving his father to Boston to check him into a hospital for the weekend. A specialist was going to run a battery of tests to see how likely it was for him to continue living at home.

"He doesn't want to go, but we're coming to the point where there aren't many choices left anymore."

"I'm sorry," I said. "I wish there was something I could do."

"You're already doing it," Xander said, pulling me tighter to him. "You make everything better, just by being you."

"That's the best birthday present already."

"Oh no, I have plans," he said, brightening. "Tomorrow, you're all mine."

"I can't wait," I said and kissed him again. "And I'm all yours right now."

The space immediately grew heated, Xander's eyes dilated. "That's true."

He scooted back on the table and pulled me onto his lap. I straddled him in my leggings. His mouth took mine in a heated kiss while his hand trailed down my shirt, pausing to cup my breast, thumb circling my nipple over my shirt.

"We don't have a lot of time," I said, my heart already pounding. "Only a few minutes."

He took off his glasses and set them beside him with deliberate slowness, his gaze and voice heavy with authority and intention.

"That's all I need."

I got home from school just in time to meet my parents as they were walking out the door. Both were dressed for a gala, my mother in a (real) full-length chinchilla coat over a black cocktail dress, and my father in a tux.

"I didn't realize my birthday dinner was black-tie formal," I said with a weak smile, just as Colin walked past carrying two small pieces of luggage to the car.

"Senator Harrington has invited us to Washington, DC, for a fundraiser at the St. Regis tonight, then as his guests for the weekend," my father said. "It's important we cultivate a good relationship with John and his family, considering he is serving on the Committee on Environment and Public Works."

"Right. Senator Harrington." The man who unseated Tucker's dad and was now Wallace Industries' new favorite person.

"Charles has a son about your age," Dad said. "Colton. He's quite involved in tech, apparently. He's sold two companies for a small fortune, and he's only twenty-four."

"Twenty-four isn't 'about my age,'" I said.

"Don't split hairs, Emery. It's close enough," Dad said, adjusting a cuff link.

Mom touched my chin, her smile watery. "Belinda has made you a wonderful birthday dinner, and we've left your gifts on the table." She frowned and lifted the pendant on its chain around my neck. "This is lovely. Where did you get it?"

I took my gift from Xander off only to shower and usually kept it tucked it under my shirt. I had forgotten to adjust it after lunch in the art room.

"Oh, uh, Harper. For Christmas. It's pretty, right?"

"Yes." Mom smiled wanly and let it rest against my chest. "Very pretty."

"Do you really have to leave for DC tonight?" I said, partially to change the subject but mostly because I was watching my Very Happy Dinner with my Very Happy

Family slide right down the drain. "It couldn't wait one more day?"

"The timing isn't ideal, but we'll make it up to you when we get back." Dad pecked me on the cheek. "Happy Birthday, Emery."

I watched them drive off to Middletown, in Newport, where our private jet awaited. I'd turned down Harper. Delilah had wanted to throw me a party. I could have gone to Boston with Xander and Dr. Ford for moral support. I could have done anything else, but instead I'd foolishly trusted my parents.

Tears of frustration and hurt stung my eyes, but I willed them down. My parents didn't deserve them.

In the dining room, a dozen elegantly wrapped gifts were stacked on one end. Scents of Belinda's pot roast emanated from the kitchen. She came through the double doors, wiping her hands on her apron.

"Happy Birthday, darling!" she exclaimed, though the pity was bright in her eyes. "Your mom and dad…they had a pressing engagement."

"I heard. Where's Jack?"

Her hands twisted. "I haven't seen him, love."

"You probably made a lot of pot roast for just me."

"Oh, it'll keep, it'll keep. Are you hungry?"

"Not really—" I began just as Jack came striding in.

He glanced around, taking weight of the room. "They're not here, are they? Those motherfu—" Jack bit off his words for Belinda's sake. "It's only your eighteenth birthday. Not like it's important or anything."

"Thanks for rubbing it in," I muttered.

"I just meant they're the literal worst." Jack offered a commiserating smile. "They're lucky we don't full Menendez-brothers on them."

"Now, Jack Wallace," Belinda scolded but only half-heartedly, clearly relieved he was here. "Let's have a nice dinner, if you please. You two set the table, and I'll be right back."

She headed to the kitchen, leaving us alone, the years of distance and animosity like ghosts between my brother and me.

"You're in a good mood," I said, crossing my arms. "I don't think you've spoken that many words to me in ages. Must be a *special* occasion." I noticed a Newport Medical Clinic visitor sticker on his shirt, peeking out from under his jacket. "What…um…or who brought about the change of heart?"

"Stuff. Life," he said. "I've been a dick, and I'm sorry. They just make me so fucking angry, and I've been taking it out on you. For years."

"Oh. Okay. Thank you."

"Come here."

To my shock, Jack wrapped me in a hug, his chin resting on my head. I sagged into his brotherly embrace, the first I'd had since Grant died, and held on tight.

"Let's have a nice dinner where you can eat all the bread and cake you want, then open your gifts and decide which to keep and which to sell for escape money."

I stared in shock. "How did you…? I mean, is that what you do?"

"Yep," Jack said, setting the table for three with silverware and plates from our side cabinet. "Other than my camera, I sold everything I own to pay for my new wardrobe"—he gestured at his black jeans and shirt—"with plenty left over. And I got a job."

"Where?" I asked, feeling a stab of jealousy.

"At the single-screen movie theater. I work the box office. I saw your boyfriend there with his dad back in December."

Another jolt of shock. "I-I don't have a boyfriend. I broke up with Tucker ages ago."

"It's okay, Em." Jack set out water glasses from our best crystal. "I won't say a word. He's that super genius, Xander, right? He didn't recognize me. He seemed pretty worried about his dad."

"How did you know we're together?" I said, my heart skipping a dozen beats. "Does *Dad* know?"

"I have my ways," Jack said. "And no. If Dad knew, you'd have heard about it. Where is your man now? We could invite him over, straight into the jackal's den."

"His father has early onset dementia. He's dropping him off with a specialist in Boston for the weekend to run a bunch of tests and won't be back until late tonight."

"I'm sorry to hear that," Jack said just as Belinda arrived, a steaming pot in her mitted hands. "Here, Belinda." He pulled out a chair. "You sit. I'll serve."

Our housekeeper and I exchanged glances. "Do you have a fever, Mr. Jack?" she asked, taking a seat while he went to the kitchen and came back with green beans and bread. "I haven't seen your handsome face wear anything but a scowl in ages."

He shrugged but also looked as if it were impossible to stop smiling, and that made me smile. I recognized that look.

He's in love too.

The three of us sat down to Belinda's dinner and her homemade angel food cake with a side of fresh strawberries. It was the best dinner I'd had at home in ages. After, we cleaned up to give Belinda the night off, and then I took my gifts upstairs.

In my room, I contemplated opening the presents from my parents, but they had "personal shopper" written all over them, and I wasn't in the mood. I'd changed into my pajama pants and sweatshirt, when a knock came at the door.

"Come in."

Jack stepped inside, carrying his laptop. "Hey. I have something for you. A birthday present. Seven years too late," he said, as we sat side by side on my bed. "I'm sorry again for being terrible to you. You're doing the best you can too. But anyway, I made this for you."

Jack opened his laptop and played a video. My breath caught and my eyes flooded with tears almost immediately. It was of Jack, me, and Grant as kids. A film of our childhood. Grant, handsome and lean with dark blond hair and a wide smile, playing on the surf in Barbados. Or skiing in Aspen. Or just the three of us goofing off at home, being kids—set to a soundtrack of soulful piano music. The film was expertly cut together, with the last frame showing Grant, about age sixteen, standing at the door, waving goodbye. He'd been on his way to a party, I remembered—happy and smiling. It was haunting nonetheless.

"Jack, that was beautiful." I wiped my eyes. "You *made* this?"

He nodded and shut the laptop. "It was more compilation than anything else, but yeah. It's what I want to do. To be a filmmaker."

"That's so wonderful. I'm so happy you found what you love. I'm glad we're talking again. I've missed you." I took his left hand, which still wore a neoprene fingerless glove. "How is it?"

"Hideously scarred for life," he said without traces of irony. "My hand modeling career is over before it began." He gave my fingers a squeeze. "I'm getting out of here, Em. I'm going to graduate from the Academy and live my life far away from Grayson and Cassandra Wallace. And you should do the same."

I glanced down at our entwined hands. "I have something like a plan too, but there's a part of me that wants to stay. To keep trying. To show Dad my own art and somehow keep us together. Don't you want that too?"

"He's not going to change, Em. Trust me."

"You know something, don't you? About Grant?"

Jack's blue eyes hardened, becoming as icy as our father's. He rose to go. "I'll send you a link to the video," he said, and went to the door. "If you decide to leave, I'll try to help you however I can. But if you decide to stay, I won't see you after graduation."

"That sounds like goodbye," I said softly.

"It's for my own good." He looked torn, his dark hair falling over his handsome, angular features. "And yours too, Em. If you have a chance to get far away from here, take it."

Chapter 29

EMERY

The following morning, I drove to Xander's house and parked around the side. He greeted me at the door, and I flew into his arms, chased by Jack's ominous words from the night before. "Getting far away" meant living thousands of miles away from Xander. I couldn't stand the thought, so I kissed him instead. I kissed him as if we'd been apart for weeks instead of two days.

"I needed that," he said when we broke our kiss and stepped inside.

"How's your dad?"

"Fine, I guess. The scientist in him wants the data about his condition, but the rest of him is scared shitless. So am I." Xander sighed. "They're going to keep him until Sunday night. Guess we'll know more then. How was your birthday with the family?"

"It was just Jack, me, and Belinda. My parents had a last-minute emergency gala event to attend in Washington, DC. As one does."

Xander's expression grew stormy.

"It was really nice, actually," I said. "Jack apologized for acting like he's hated me for seven years."

"And you forgave him?"

"Of course," I said with a small smile. "I've only got one brother left."

"He's lucky to have you, and so am I." Xander banished his cloudy thoughts and worry for his father. "You're in the clear for the entire day? Because we've got some driving to do."

"My parents are out of town. I have all day…and all night."

Xander pulled me close, his voice rough. "Even better—but not yet."

"You're going to buy me dinner first?" I said with a grin as he grabbed his keys and jacket. I glanced down at my jeans, boots, and white sweater. "Am I dressed for this mystery date?"

"You're perfect."

"Where are we going, anyway?"

Xander gave a tilted smile. "Somewhere we don't have to hide."

Xander drove to our "mystery date," but I knew what he had in mind as soon as the signs for Point Judith came into view.

"Oh my God, I haven't been to Block Island since I was a kid! That's the plan, right?"

"Do you like it?" Xander asked. "I wasn't sure if it would be…enough."

"I love it," I said, and kissed his cheek.

And I love you, Xander.

The words were bursting out of me, but maybe saying that would be too much, so I bit them back.

At Point Judith, the southernmost tip of Rhode Island, Xander parked the car, and we took the ferry to Block Island, a tourist spot that was bustling in summer and more subdued in the winter months. The little town of New Shoreham was busy but not crowded on this brisk, early spring day.

Xander and I strolled hand in hand past shops and restaurants that lined the beach, which was still too chilly for sunbathing but perfect for long walks along the Atlantic, the water stretching out into forever. We kissed whenever we felt like it, not caring who saw us. Any time we stopped to peruse an art gallery or stroll through a boutique, his arm was around me. He'd brush his lips against my forehead just because, while I'd tuck myself into his jacket whenever we paused to take in the view.

It felt so good to love Xander out in the open, I had to tell him. It was going to come bursting out of me sooner or later.

Like now, maybe.

We waited in line at a stand that sold specialty chocolates and hot cocoa. Beside me, Xander pulled out his phone to confirm the dinner reservation he'd made at a swanky seafood restaurant for later that night. As he spoke to the hostess, he absently twisted a lock of my hair around his finger.

I didn't know why, but that little gesture made my heart flutter and my blood heat at the same time—so natural and intimate—even a little possessive in that unassuming way of his.

"Okay, we're all set," he said, ending the call.

I turned to him, the words on my lips, ready to fall, when another call came in on his phone. He frowned at the screen.

"Sorry, Em, it's the specialist calling about my dad."

"Go ahead," I said. "I'll get the drinks."

Xander moved to a nearby bench while I bought us two gourmet hot chocolates and brought them over. I sat down just as he was hanging up.

"They say he's doing well," Xander said. "Cooperating and in high spirits. I couldn't ask for a better report, all things considered."

"I'm so glad," I said, handing him the cup of hot chocolate with whipped cream.

"There's sort of a beautiful, terrible irony in a man struggling with dementia while explaining to his doctors about his quest for a unified theory."

"I know." I gave Xander's hand a squeeze. "But honestly, he should've just asked me. I figured that out ages ago."

Xander started to smile. "Oh yeah?"

"Sure. It's pretty simple, really. No long math problems required."

"Do tell."

I sipped my hot chocolate. "Magic."

"That's it?"

"Yep."

Xander chuckled. "Well, Einstein *did* call it 'spooky,' though not in a complimentary way."

"See? If Einstein agrees with me, then it must be true. So there you go. Theory of Everything, solved. Your dad is free to quote my work in his paper. I don't mind."

Now Xander was laughing, which was exactly my goal in the first place.

"To be honest, there are theories that sound pretty fantastical when it comes to solving this stuff," he said. "Like the many-worlds theory."

"Oh, I like the sound of that. Explain."

"Remember Schrödinger's cat?"

"I remember you get adorably grouchy about it," I teased. "And yes. It's both alive and dead until you look at it."

"Right. A superposition of both states until observed. According to the MWI, or many-worlds interpretation, the particle—or cat—isn't only in a superposition, but also represents the coexistence of multiple outcomes across different universes."

"It does what now?"

"For example, flip a coin. While it's in the air, it's in a superposition of both heads and tails. According to the

MWI, when it lands, the universe splits into two branches: one where it landed on heads and another where it landed on tails. We experience only one outcome because we exist in a single branch of what is actually a vast multiverse."

I gave him a doubtful look. "That's an actual quantum theory?"

"Sure is," Xander said. "You can then extrapolate the coin flip for literally anything that results in an outcome. Meaning, the universe splits any time we make any decision at all."

"So there might be different versions of us in different lifetimes, living out the repercussions of every choice we did or didn't make? Like parallel universes?"

"Theoretically."

"*Theoretically*," I said, "there is a universe in which I received the letters you wrote to me when we were ten. And I wrote you back, and we kept in touch the entire seven years. We shared all of our deepest thoughts and secrets, and maybe we...maybe we even fell in love. So that when you moved to Castle Hill, we didn't waste a second. You were waiting for me on our rock, and I flew at you, and we kissed even though we hadn't seen each other in ages, but it didn't matter because we knew each other and maybe we always have." I inhaled a breath in the cool air. "Is that possible? And don't say theoretically."

"*Hypothetically*, yes," Xander said, smiling. "If you take the MWI theory out of the quantum world and apply it to ours, there are infinite possibilities with infinite iterations of us. But that means millions of versions of us who never found each other—universes where we never met. Or where I didn't write letters. Or I wrote them, and you decided not to reply. Or I never moved to Castle Hill because my dad stayed healthy. Or my mom never left us."

"And Grant never died," I murmured, and shook my head. "It's too much. You could get lost in a maze of *what ifs* that all lead to regret. Wanting what can never be."

Xander nodded. "You could."

I tucked myself around his arm. "Maybe the point of this life—our branch of the universe—is to make the best of what *did* happen and not regret what didn't. We have to hope the other versions of us found happiness too, even the ones where we never reunited."

He brushed a lock of hair from my cheek. "I hope that they did."

I inhaled again, my heart crashing against my chest. "But I refuse to believe that in all the infinite infinities there is even one universe in which we never came together."

"No?"

"No. It was the great physicist, Alexander Ford, who once said, what happens to you, happens to me. Because we're entangled by that mysterious force that cannot be seen, measured, or understood completely, but is very real nonetheless. It's love. And, Xander, I—"

Before I could say another word, Xander kissed me softly, then took my face in his hands that were warm and gentle. "I love you, Emery."

I stared, conscious that a little gasp escaped me. "You do…?"

"Yeah, I do. I almost said it a hundred times, but I was scared. I *am* scared—that the end of the year is going to race toward us and we're going to get smashed. But I had to say it first. I *owed* it to you to say it first. To be brave like you and not leave you waiting or wondering for one more goddamn second."

Tears stung my eyes.

"I love you, Xander," I said. "I love you so much. I almost said it a hundred times too, but I didn't want it to be too much or too soon. But how can it be too soon when it feels like we waited forever to get here?"

"I don't know. But…I feel that too. Something unexplainable that defies any logic or reason." His thumbs brushed my cheek. "But I know I love you, Emery. You make me believe in magic."

―――

Xander took me to a beautiful restaurant overlooking the ocean, all the while a hot, heavy haze of expectation thickening every breath, every word, every bite of food until I felt drunk.

We took the ferry back and drove home into a deepening night. His house was dark and quiet as Xander took me by the hand and led me up the stairs. No sooner had he shut the door to his room than I was in his arms. My back pressed against the door as he kissed me with deep sweeps of his tongue. Demanding. Devouring. And me offering myself willingly. There was no hesitation. Nothing stopping what felt inevitable. A coming together that felt so perfect and right it must've been written in the stars. All I knew was an electric hum of anticipation everywhere he was going to touch me.

We stumbled farther into his room, stripping out of jackets and sweaters. He lifted me onto his desk and moved between the V of my legs, our hands roaming, tugging at clothing, mine carving through his hair, his tangling in mine. All the while, Xander kissed me with a possessive need that stole my breath and ran just as hot as my own.

He took off his glasses and set them beside me so he could bury his face in my neck, kissing the delicate skin beneath my ear and grazing his teeth so that shivers skimmed down my spine. I tugged at his shirt, lifting it up and off, his magnificent torso bare to me in the lone light of his lamp.

I placed my hand on his heart, felt the rapid *thump* of his pulse beating against my palm, then let it drift down, my fingertips grazing his warm skin over the hard lines and ridges of his abdomen. Xander made a sound in his chest as my fingers moved over his jeans to the hard bulge of his erection. I undid the buttons while he moved in, kissing me, one hand cupping my jaw, the other in my hair—a fist, sending tiny licks of pain over my skin to add to the electric tingles that were fast growing into a heavy ache.

He took off my sweater, then the shirt beneath, filling his eyes with my breasts spilling out of my bra. The hunger in his gaze stole my breath.

"Take it off me, Xander," I said, and he complied,

unhooking it at my back, then slowly drawing it off my arms and casting it aside.

"Jesus, Em."

His eyes were hooded, both colors darkened. He took my breasts in his hands before putting his mouth on one nipple, sucking and biting, then kissing the bites with soothing, velvety sweeps of his tongue. Every touch made sparks; every spark added to the burning desire in the center of me—drawing it in tighter, heavier, waiting for Xander's touch in the deepest places to set it loose.

I tugged his jeans off his hips. He moved away from me long enough to strip mine off of me, then came back, his erection straining against my dampened panties as I wrapped my legs around his waist. He ground his hips against mine, plundering my mouth with a kiss, then moving down my throat.

"Please…" I managed. "I need you…"

Xander carried me to the bed, then lay over me, kissing me slowly, deeply. But so much bare skin on bare skin, our bodies aligned and ready, only served to fan the flames higher. Within moments, our hips were rising and falling again, grinding, seeking connection.

"Wait, wait, wait," he breathed, pulling himself away from me with effort and bracing himself on his forearms. "We have to slow down. I don't want to hurt you."

"It's okay," I said. "I trust you."

The way his face softened at those words…his eyes full of love and pain because I knew it hurt him to love this much. And the fact that he did anyway, that he loved *me*…

"I just want it to be perfect for you," he said.

"It's already perfect because it's you." I pushed him onto his back and straddled him. "But this is your night too."

I bent over him, took his lips in mine with a sucking kiss that made him groan. My hair fell down around us, blocking out the rest of the world. I kissed him again, a licking, biting kiss, then took his lower lip. He made a sound deep in his chest, a sexy, pained sound of want, his hips rising, his erection pressing into me.

I moved my mouth over his chin, his neck, then down over the broad plains of his chest. My hot, open mouth kissed the tight lines of his torso, which contracted under my touch. I moved lower, tugged at the hem of his boxer briefs, but he stopped me.

"No," he said, taking hold of my shoulders and rolling me onto my back. "When I come it's going to be inside you. But…I want to make it good for you first. Okay?"

I nodded mutely, my breath catching at a different kind of anticipation. Now it was his turn to drag his mouth over my skin, between my breasts, his hair tickling my chin; I put both hands in the thick softness of it, made fists just tight enough that he grunted and took my nipple between his teeth.

I gasped, arching into him and then he moved lower, sending pleasant shivers dancing across my skin as he got to my navel, then down…

"Can I?"

I nodded breathlessly, watching him as he tugged my

underwear off my hips, down my legs, and tossed it away. Uncertainty found me for the first time. He was right there, and I was naked before him. Nothing left to hide. But Xander's eyes drank me in, his eyes liquid pools of want and lust and love and desire.

"Yes," he murmured. "So fucking beautiful."

I bit my lip then cried out when he put his mouth against me. The sudden pleasure shocked me, like a flare lighting up a black sky, and I gasped, my hips bucking. Xander kissed and sucked and licked, gripping my hips to hold me still as the pleasure crescendoed; now it was an entire sky full of fireworks, him attuned to my every moan and gasp, knowing exactly what to do to bring me up and over the edge… I crashed over, shuddering into the last slow strokes of his tongue before he made his way back up my body, kissing every inch of skin along the way until he lay over me again.

"Hurry," I breathed against his lips. "I need you while I'm feeling like this."

He nodded and reached to his nightstand for a condom. Within seconds he was ready, and then he was propped over me again, his forearms on either side of me, hands holding my face.

"Emery?"

I nodded, tilted my hips and let my legs fall apart enough to reach down between us with my hand to guide him inside. He sucked in a breath. The orgasm he'd given me was still throbbing through me as he slowly moved inside me, inch by inch.

I tensed, a little cry escaping me.

"I'm hurting you."

I shook my head. "Don't stop. Whatever you do, don't stop."

He obeyed, sank in deeper. I slid my hands down the smooth skin of his back, pulling him to me until our hips touched, joined completely.

"Jesus Christ," he said into my neck, his breath gusting heavily. Then he lifted his head to study me. "Are you okay?"

I nodded quickly. "Yes. God, you feel so good."

The hard heaviness of him inside me felt like nothing I could explain with words. A perfect joining of bodies after a long wait. And the look in Xander's eyes told me he felt this moment as much as I did.

Still going slowly, Xander began to move, watching me, studying my face for discomfort, until I kissed him, my lips brushing against his.

"It's okay," I whispered. "I want this. I want this so bad."

My words spurred him. The pain had already faded, and now Xander moved in me a little faster, deeper. I wrapped my legs around his narrow waist, reveling in the undulations of his body, the lean masculinity of him, on top of me and inside me. I felt soft and feminine by comparison, taking him in and bringing him closer to the ecstasy he had brought me.

"Emery…" he said. A choked word, him on the brink.

I nodded. "Yes. Yes…"

With the final strangled cry, his face contorted in that beautiful, painful ecstasy. His last thrusts became erratic and deep. I locked him to me, wanting to take all of it, until he collapsed on top of me, a perfect, heavy blanket of warm skin and muscle, his orgasm shuddering through him until he was spent.

Xander's chest expanded against mine in deep breaths, and I smiled into the dark, my hands in his hair. The years between the day we met and this one had finally disappeared, and he was right where he was supposed to be. In my arms.

Gently, he moved off of me and disposed of the condom, then came right back to gather me to him, my back to his chest, his arms around me, our fingers laced. He kissed my neck, my shoulder, my body growing heavy and drowsy, until finally I drifted down into sleep, taking Xander with me.

Because he's mine. And I'm his. Since always and into forever.

Chapter 30

XANDER

The morning light slanted over the bed, over Emery's golden hair, setting individual strands alight where they spilled over the pillow. We hadn't moved all night; she was wrapped in my arms, our bodies aligned everywhere, our fingers entwined.

I'd woken that morning thinking I'd had the best dream. That it couldn't possibly be real. But she was here, in my bed, and last night…I'd had to move slightly so she wouldn't feel my erection pressing into her backside, but a sobering thought hit me like a cold shower.

I can't keep her.

Emery had the unwavering—baseless—hope that her father would finally see her for who she was and support her dreams. She pinned everything on her designs winning him over. Because she still loved him in the same, desperate and futile way that I still loved my mother. And just like my hope that my mother would return had done nothing but hurt me, I knew Emery's hope was only going to hurt her in the end. She needed to go to California or somewhere else, far away from her parents' toxic brand of love, if she was going to live a life full of the art and joy she wanted. That she deserved.

I shut my eyes and gathered her close to me, burying my face in her hair and inhaling deeply.

Not yet...

Emery sighed contentedly; I hadn't known she was awake. "Xander?"

"Hm?"

"Is it true we're made of stardust?"

"Yes."

"Really? It's not just something poetic Shakespeare once said?"

"Close. Carl Sagan, and it's true," I said, kissing her shoulder. "The atoms that make up our bodies were once part of stars that lived and died billions of years ago."

"I love that." She reached her hand into the slant of light. Dust motes hovered lazily as she wafted her fingers through them, sending them dancing on tiny currents of air. "I love to think we're pieces of the huge stars that light up the universe. They came together to make us, then dissolve away when we die. But we never wink out for good. We just keep going, our little pieces of light, coming together again and again, forever."

I nodded on the pillow we shared, held her tighter, my eyes falling shut at the ache in my heart.

Jesus, I loved this girl, who wasn't just a collection of particles of light, but an entire star unto herself. She took the rigid science of my thinking and broke it down to its realest and richest states. The sense of meaninglessness and loneliness that can come from studying the cosmos like I did—the sense of being an infinitesimal speck in the vastness of space… Emery somehow alchemized it into a feeling of sheer awe and wonder that I, this little speck, existed at all to love her like I did. The love I felt for Emery could not be measured or formulated into an equation. It wasn't a finite particle but an infinite wave that rippled out into forever, because that's how long I would love her.

I'd told her last night she made me believe in magic, but Emery Wallace made me believe in infinity too.

I held her tighter. "I don't want this to end."

She tensed for a second, then nodded. "Me neither."

I waited for her to say more. To tell me she'd give up all her plans and come with me to MIT. To forget trying to fix her awful family, forget her dreams, forget the prom even, and just *be* with me.

Her phone chimed a text. She grabbed it from the nightstand. "It's Jack. He says my parents are on their way home. I have to go."

I pulled on my underwear and jeans, and Emery caught sight of my expression.

"Hey." She stopped, kneeling on my bed, now only in her panties, her hair a tousled mess from having my hands in it. Her lips were swollen from my kisses, and a few spots of blood stained the sheets because I'd been inside her. "I love you."

Because she believed that was enough to make everything right.

"I love you," I said, because I wanted to believe that was enough to keep her.

We dressed, and I walked her down to her car, where she put her arms around my neck and kissed me goodbye. I watched her drive away and then sat on the stoop of my empty house, trying to tell my psyche that Emery leaving wasn't the same. That she'd come back. That we weren't done.

The Academy gym was open, even on a Sunday. There was always some event or competition for one of the elite sports. Far be it for CHA to ever encourage a day of rest.

Such were my bitter thoughts as I climbed onto an ergometer, ready to row myself into a meditative state of pure physical exertion for a few hours before I had to pick up my father from Boston.

No sooner had I sat down on the row machine than a friendly voice hailed me.

"Xander!" Dean exclaimed, coming to clasp hands. "Putting in extra hours for Friday's regatta? Overkill, don't you think? You're already Coach's favorite."

I didn't smile.

Dean pulled a bench over. "Hey. You okay?"

"Not really. What are you doing right now?"

"I was helping Kai on his drive, but he's done for the day. You want some help?"

I nodded, the need to row growing into an urgency. "I want to push the pace as hard as I can."

Dean frowned. "Mmkay, but just remember, the big boys in the engine room aren't going to be as fast as you."

"Tough shit."

"Oooh, spicy. All right, let's work out some of this aggression and then you can tell me what's actually bothering you."

The erg was state-of-the-art with air resistance that would increase based on my effort. Dean set the damper to medium resistance to start, but I shook my head.

"Higher."

"All the way up to eleven, eh? Your funeral."

He pulled out his digital metronome, and I began to pull to the *tick tick tick*. But soon I was outpacing it, and Dean had to keep adjusting.

"Xander, take it easy," he warned, but I ignored him.

I pulled the erg's handle up to my chest, its coiled wires making a zipping sound with every pull, while my thighs worked to move the sliding seat back and forth. I pressed my feet into the footrests, driving against them with everything I had. Within minutes, my shoulders, abs, and quads were screaming, my lungs aching and throat raw. Dean stopped trying to slow me down and watched, wide-eyed, increasing his metronome.

Tickticktick…

Sweat stung my eyes, and I grunted with every pull.

"How long?" Dean asked.

"Fifteen," I managed.

"Dude, *no*."

Fifteen minutes, the length of an elite five thousand meter. I wanted to test my endurance, build stamina for my crew, but mostly I needed the adrenaline and endorphins to shove every hard thought out of my system. I made it to eight minutes at the most punishing pace I'd ever attempted, and then my stomach seized.

I let the handle go with a snap and staggered off the erg to vomit into a dirty towel bin. I heaved until there was nothing left, gasping for breath, and then Dean was there with a clean towel and a bottle of water. He guided me back to the erg to sit and straddled the bench beside me.

"Welp, you're not going to make any friends with the custodial staff," Dean said while I sucked in huge drafts of air and then chugged half the bottle of water. He waited until I'd caught my breath. "Better? Okay, now you want to tell me what's really going on?"

"I told Emery I loved her and spent the night with her, and it was fucking perfect."

Dean sputtered a nervous chuckle. "How is that a bad thing? Did she not say it back?"

"She did."

He glanced around. "Am I being pranked? You're sleeping with Emery Wallace, the most beautiful girl in school and quite possibly the tristate area, and she told you she loves you." He tapped his chin thoughtfully. "Hm, yes, I can see how that'd be rough."

I put the towel over my head. "I'm fucked, Dean."

"Why?" I felt his hand on my shoulder. "I'm here, man."

With a sigh, I stripped off the towel and told him the whole story, including my offer to marry Emery should she need the complete divestiture from her family. Dean's eyes widened and then he gave a low whistle.

"So that…is a lot." He frowned. "Why didn't you tell me all this before?"

"I didn't want to bother you."

"You can't bother me, I'm your friend, remember? I want to hear all this shit. I can't promise I have good advice, but I can try."

"I'll take anything."

"Well, for starters, you need to stop thinking so much. I know that's your thing, but have you considered Occam's razor? The simplest solution is usually the best."

"Which is?"

"You move to California with her." He cocked his head at my expression. "You never considered it?"

"Not seriously," I said. "I've been locked on going to MIT, finishing my father's work, and keeping him close to the house that he loved. I need to put him in a home somewhere he recognizes. To give him something to hold on to."

"Because you're a good son, Xander," Dean said. "But you're also a good guy for Emery. Maybe you don't have to sacrifice one for the other. Just ask your dad what he thinks. Tell him everything." He gave me a wry smile at my dubious expression. "You're in your head a lot, my friend. Put what's in your heart out into the world and see what happens. Maybe Dr. Ford would love nothing better than to get the hell out of dodge and live his golden years sipping piña coladas by a pool in Pasadena. Ha. Say that five times fast…"

I sniffed a laugh. "I don't think he wants that."

"You never know unless you ask."

"I suppose." I smiled gratefully. "I feel stupid."

Dean chuckled. "There's a first time for everything."

"Not for the first time. I'm pretty terrible at thinking outside of my usual systems."

"You're getting better. The number of people who love you has increased exponentially with the addition of Miss Wallace." He chucked my shoulder. "I'd say you're doing all right."

I pulled my aching body off the erg and gave Dean a hug. "Thank you."

"I aim to please," he said, clapping my back. "You're coming to Orion's party on Friday night, right? After we destroy all foes at the regatta?"

"I thought you said Atlas Hall wasn't your scene."

"This crew has never been better. I'll make an exception if we go 2–0. Just don't bust a gut and puke all over me after the race. As cox, I'm right in the splash zone."

I laughed. "No promises."

We parted ways, and I showered, changed, then started

the long drive to Boston. The euphoria I'd had with Emery the night before began to reappear as I coasted down the highway. Maybe I'd been too rigid in my thinking. Maybe Dad would love a change of scenery, away from painful memories of Mom and her abandonment.

But at the neurology ward, the specialist gave me a grim prognosis: Dad's dementia was progressing rapidly.

"A few weeks at best," Dr. Woodley said, "before he'll need more care than you can give him."

Before he forgets who I am.

He gave me the information for a memory care home in the city, close to MIT, and a new prescription. Dad had more pills now to crowd his medicine cabinet, but none were strong enough to keep his brilliant mind intact. In the car, he was quiet, his gaze on the passing scenery.

I cleared my throat. "Did they tell you what comes next?"

"Yes, son." He smiled thinly, his eyes clear. For now. "It won't be too much longer now."

"Don't say that," I said, my heart aching. "You never know—"

"I know. Time is running out. And I'm so close to my theory. So close. I just need a little more time." He whipped his head to me in a sudden panic. "Don't put me away yet, Xander. Please. Not yet. I just need a few more weeks, and I'll have it."

"It's okay, Dad. I won't, I promise. But…what do you think about leaving New England?"

"When? What for?"

"When it comes time for you to have more help."

I kept my eyes on the road, but from my periphery, he was shaking his head.

"No, I...I can't leave. And our house...that's for you. Our family home. Why?" he demanded suddenly. "What are they telling you? Where am I supposed to go?"

"Nothing, Dad," I said quickly. "It's okay. I was just thinking out loud."

"No, no," he said, shaking his head and running his fingers through his unkempt hair. "I can't. I have to stay close. I have to—"

"Okay," I said soothingly, my heart sinking. "There's a place near MIT for...later. Is that what you want?"

He nodded. "Yes, yes. I can't leave the vicinity, lest she be unable to find me."

"Who?" I asked, a heavy feeling in my gut.

"Your mother," he said.

Fuck.

"I have to stick close. Otherwise, how will she know it's okay to come back?"

"I don't know, Dad," I said. "I don't know."

Chapter 31

EMERY

In English class Monday morning, we finished our lesson on applying the themes of *Romeo and Juliet* to modern life just as the bell rang. I practically jumped out of my seat. I hadn't had a chance to have the girl talk with Harper that was required after a weekend like the one I'd had with Xander.

"Miss Wallace, can you stay a minute?" Ms. Alvarez said sternly.

Harper raised her brows at me. I shrugged back.

"Sure."

When the last student had left, Ms. Alvarez shut the door, and a smile broke out over her face. "UCLA sent me a very large, very thick envelope."

"Oh shit."

I stared as she pulled a manila envelope from her desk

drawer and held it out to me. I took it and was surprised at how heavy it was.

"Go ahead," she said, beaming like a proud mother. "Open it."

"You didn't look and see?"

"This is your moment, Emery. I'm just happy to witness it."

"It could be nothing," I said, tearing the envelope open with shaking fingers. "They might've just felt sorry for me and wrote a really long rejection letter…"

Dear Emery Wallace,

It is my great pleasure to inform you that you have been accepted to the University of California, Los Angeles for the fall semester…

I stopped reading to stare at Ms. Alvarez. "Oh shit. Sorry I keep saying that."

"Perfectly understandable." She came around the desk to hug me. "Congratulations, Emery."

"Oh wow." I sank into the desk in front of hers, the strength having drained out of my legs. I'd done it. I'd rebelled against my father and now a different life was ready to burst forth like a sun on an entirely different horizon.

Thousands of miles away from Xander. After he marries me…

I didn't know it was possible to feel a hundred

emotions—fear, hope, relief, sadness—all at the same time. It left me shell-shocked.

Ms. A drew the rest of the brochures and papers from the envelope. "As I predicted, your tuition assistance is almost nothing. Your federal loans might be restricted too, unless you can separate yourself from your parents' income." She sat down in the desk beside mine. "I know this might seem extreme, but is emancipation an option?"

"No," I said. "But I have…another option. But it's desperately wild and I…I don't want my father to know anything about this."

"He'll have to know eventually," she said gently. "You might benefit from telling him how you feel."

"I will. With prom. Going to UCLA is just a backup plan." I gathered the paperwork and put it back in the envelope. Stuffing it back in—taking it all back—because if my dad caught wind of what I'd done…

"Emery, are you all right?" Ms. Alvarez asked, alarmed now.

"I'm fine. Things just got very real." I pushed the envelope back to Ms. A. "Please keep this for me. I probably won't need it. In fact, I'm sure I won't. My father will see what I'm capable of and it'll be great. Really."

"Emery…"

It was too much. The agony of leaving Xander finally rearing its head and adding to the abject terror of my dad knowing I'd applied somewhere besides Brown. That I had a plan to escape, that I'd marry a Bender to do it…

No! He doesn't have to know. Nothing's happened. Nothing's changed.

I did what I do best: I pushed it all down and forced a smile. "Thank you for your help, Ms. A. I have to go. Thanks again. Thank you so much."

And then I practically ran out the door and straight into Harper.

"What was that all about? You look terrified."

"I'm fine," I said, keeping my voice down as we headed to lunch. "I just…panicked a little."

"Because…?"

"I got into UCLA."

Harper stopped. "That's amazing! Congrats!"

"No, it's…nothing," I said, walking fast.

"Nothing?" Harper hurried to catch up. "Em, talk to me."

We were outside now, and she guided me to a bench near the front stairs. I told her everything that happened with Xander over the weekend.

"It was really perfect, Harper. He was so considerate and generous, but also *so* sexy…" I gave my head a shake. "More than that, we said we loved each other, and I've never been happier."

"That sounds lovely. So what happened?"

"I could tell yesterday morning that it's all starting to take a toll on him. And I just ran out the door because it scares me too. Getting into UCLA is another piece of my dream coming true, but the idea of confronting my dad is terrifying. I keep hoping that he'll come around and let me go to RISD and…"

"And you'll be one big happy family?" Harper shook her head slowly.

"I know," I said with a sigh. "When I think of California, it feels perfect. Except it's exactly where Xander is not."

Harper blew air out her cheeks, then put her arm around me. "I don't know what to tell you, except that you have to be true to yourself. As much as you love Xander, you have to love and honor your own passions and dreams, or you'd just be living half a life. And I know him. He does not want that for you."

I nodded. "He recognized my art even before I did." I inhaled a breath. "But there's still time. I don't have to figure anything out right now."

"You don't have to rock the boat, you mean," Harper said. "Em, you're going to have to confront your father sooner or later."

"Maybe. Maybe not."

"But—"

"Just let me happy a little while longer, okay? Things might all go to shit later, but it's too soon for doomsday." I forced a smile. "The afterglow from my orgasm hasn't even worn off yet."

Harper pursed her lips and recited, "'It was the nightingale, not the lark, that pierced the fearful hollow of thine ear.'"

I recognized the quote from *Romeo and Juliet,* when Juliet tries to convince Romeo that morning hasn't come yet after their first night together. That they still have time before the harsh light of day steals away their happiness.

"Yes," I said. "Exactly."

"Okay, Em." Harper sighed. "Just be careful. We all know how that story ends."

That evening after dinner, my father called me into his study. The days were growing longer, but he still had a fire roaring behind him, casting long shadows.

"Emery," he said. "I have received word from Brown University about your application."

My throat tried to close up and my mouth went dry. "Oh. Okay."

He did not look up from where he was sorting his mail. "You were not accepted. They found you…wanting."

"Oh." Every drop of blood in my body turned to dust. "I-I don't know what to say…"

"I got off the phone with their admissions office this afternoon and it seems that not even a sizable donation from Wallace Industries is enough to make you palatable to them."

They don't take bribes, you mean.

Another storm of relief and fear raged in my guts. "I'm sorry, Daddy. It's the math. I just don't—"

"I trusted you to do all you could to get into Brown, but it's apparent we must now refocus our efforts."

"What does that mean?"

"I don't know yet, Emery," he said, strangely calm as

he regarded me. Then he pulled one of his sudden, disorienting changes of subject. "We are going to have dinner with the Harringtons at the Chart House in Newport on Friday night."

"Oh. There's a party after the regatta that night."

His brows arched, almost amused. "I have yet to decide how you're going to make it up to the family for this humiliation but allowing you to attend a party is not on the list."

That stung and tears pricked my eyes. "Can I still go to the regatta?"

"Our reservation is at 8:00 p.m. So long as you're prepared to leave here at 7:45, I don't see why not."

"Okay. Thank you." I started to go, then stopped. "I'm sorry that I let you down. But just wait until you see what I'm doing with the prom. Honestly, it's coming together so beautifully—"

"I'm sure it is. That'll do, Emery."

I walked out and shut the door behind me. My father had said some horrible things, but he didn't seem furious. He didn't threaten to kick me out of the house. A new kind of hope bloomed in me. Maybe now that Brown wasn't going to happen, he'd finally see I was made for something else. Something just as good; he just needed to experience it firsthand.

I exhaled a shaky breath. I still had a chance.

Friday afternoon, I joined the entire Academy at the

marina to watch our Royal Pride rowing crew take on three different schools in half a dozen different races. Xander's race, the men's eight, was the big one. I was no longer on the dance team, cheering from the dock. Instead, I hugged Harper's arm on the bleachers, waiting for the boats to come from around the bend in the two thousand meter. The marina was packed with people from the different schools, colorful flags were strung up at the dock, and different boats—singles, pairs, and fours—raced in the clear smooth water in front of us. CHA had won every race and now it was up to my boyfriend and his crew to make it a sweep.

"You look positively radiant," Harper said. "What gives?"

It had been a hectic week, both Harper and Xander involved in their own activities—her preparing for the recital, him for this race. I'd hardly seen either one and was practically bursting with happiness.

"I didn't get into Brown. Isn't that great?"

"Uh, congrats? Wait, did your dad flip his lid?"

"That's the best part," I said, my eyes scanning the water, waiting. "He didn't seem all that pissed. I think maybe he's coming around."

"Or he's got a plan B. Em, are you sure—?"

"Here they come!"

The entire crowd on the bleachers got to its feet, cheering on their guys, while the teams on the dock whooped and hollered. I watched with my heart in my throat as Xander and his crew came around the bend, the boats cutting through the water like arrows. Unlike last time, this race wasn't a sure thing. Our team, in gold and black, was fighting for their lives, wedged between New Haven Prep and Provincetown Academy.

My lips parted at the sight of Xander, clad in the unisuit that left no part of his perfect physique in question, setting the pace for his crew with brutal, exacting form. Each guy wore iridescent sunglasses, their mouths sucking air and blowing out with every row, matching his pace, synchronized as if they were one body. Xander's grimace of determination was like the one he'd worn in bed the other night, his body moving back and forth...

"Girl..." Harper admonished—the lust must've been all over my face.

"I know, but can you blame me?"

Her gaze went back to the boys. "Actually, no, I can't."

The crowd grew louder as the racers drew closer to the finish line. Harper and I jumped up and down, the electricity in the stands infectious, zipping through all of us. The Royal Pride boat, with Rhett at the bow, inched ahead. And then again. Then New Haven Prep closed the distance a second later.

"*Pull*," Dean bellowed, his commands blending in with the other coxswains, the cheers, and the rowdy teammates on the dock.

Then Xander, directly in front of Dean, *snarled*.

"Oh my God." I gripped Harper's arm as my knees went weak. I knew Xander was reaching down deep for something more—everything he had to give. And then their boat pulled ahead another half foot, then fell back. The crowd went insane; I was screaming so loud…and then they crossed the line ahead of the other two boats by inches.

"They won." I grabbed Harper by the shoulders. "They won!"

Our crowd went wild, rushing the dock, while the other school's fans clapped and congratulated one another on an exciting race. Harper and I joined the crowd running to the crew as their boats were pulled ashore. Every rower was exhausted but happy, slumped over and patting one another on the back.

They trudged out of the waist-deep water at the shore as girlfriends, friends, and family flew at them, hugging and snapping pictures. I watched from a distance, my hands clasped in front of me to keep them to myself, because no one was supposed to know I was with Xander. He was congratulated heartily by his coaches, Dean, and Harper, but he had no family watching. No one to fly at him and hug him and tell him that what he'd done was incredible.

The *wrongness* of leaving him alone in this victory—in hiding us at all—swept through me like wildfire, burning up all my hesitation. I ran, pushing through the crowd, and called his name.

He stood with his hands on his thighs, bent over, still trying to catch his breath. He spotted me just in time to catch me as I flew into his arms and kissed him.

"What are you doing?" he asked breathlessly, a shocked smile on his tired, handsome face.

"What I should have done months ago," I said. "I love you. I love you so much. I can't believe you did that. That was one the best things I've ever seen."

Xander's expression was heartbreakingly happy. He wrapped me in his arms and spun me around, as if now he was allowed to feel every ounce of victory.

"I love you," he said, and kissed me and I could've sworn the crowd was cheering just for us.

Chapter 32

XANDER

The Academy locker room was loud with celebration as we changed out of our racing gear. Coach Daniels huddled us up to congratulate us, actual tears in his eyes, then released us to change and celebrate at Orion's party.

Dean approached and leaned against my locker. "I just want to personally thank you for not puking on me. Especially during the final hundred meters. Damn, that was insane."

"Insane is right!" Suddenly I was engulfed in Orion's embrace. "I've said it before, but Ford, you're a fucking madman! And the best bloody stroke seat we've ever had."

I winced, knowing Rhett was a few feet away. Orion read my expression.

"Nah, Calloway was made for bow, aren't you, mate?"

Rhett, drawing on his jacket, sneered in an

approximation of a smile. He spoke to Orion, but his black-eyed gaze was on me. "Been rowing stroke my whole life, but…sure. Anything for the team."

Orion scoffed. "Don't mind the Count; he woke up on the wrong side of the coffin this morning." He slung his other arm around Dean. "And you, my favorite coxy. A genius, Yearwood. You're both coming to my party, yeah?"

"Wouldn't miss it," Dean said.

Orion wagged his eyebrows at me. "How about it, Ford? Going to bring Miss Emery, I presume?"

I felt my cheeks redden. "It would appear that way."

Orion cackled. "It would indeed. She's not subtle, that girl. See you tonight!"

He joined the other guys, still rowdy with adrenaline and victory.

"Never in the history of the Math & Physics Club has a member climbed the social ladder so high, so fast." Dean pretended to wipe a tear from his eye. "I'm so proud of you."

"Says the most popular guy in school."

"Not remotely true, but I'll take it." He grinned. "See you tonight, my friend."

I couldn't stop smiling either. "I'll see you tonight."

In the parking lot, the last spectators were driving off and the buses from other schools lumbering out. Emery was waiting for me at my Buick. She threw her arms around me again and gave me a long kiss, her mouth warm and sweet on mine.

"Congratulations, again," she said. "That was amazing.

And watching you row..." She bit her lower lip. "Forgive me for objectifying you, but those unisuits don't make it easy on a gal."

I chuckled and pulled her close. "It's been a long week. I've missed you."

"Me too."

"We have time before Orion's party," I began. "If you're free...?"

"I can't. And I can't go to the party either." Emery glanced away. "I have some news. I've been sitting on it for days, but I wanted to tell you in person."

A sense of foreboding tickled the back of my neck. "What is it?"

She heaved a breath and put on a smile. "I got into UCLA."

"Oh," I said as something inside me deflated. "That's... that's great, Em. Congratulations."

"Xander..."

"It's fine," I said, cutting her off. "It's what's supposed to happen. You have to get away from your terrible fucking father, and I have to help you. Which means we should get..."

Married.

The word hung in the air between us like a coin that's flipped but hasn't landed. A superposition of two states: love and happiness...or separation and goodbye.

"We don't have to do anything right now," Emery said quickly. "It's just a backup plan, remember?"

I nodded. But our "backup plan" had been formulated

before we were together. Before there were feelings admitted and words said that could not be unsaid. Now...

Emery read my expression and said with forced brightness, "It was a wild idea, and I'm probably too chickenshit to pull the trigger anyway."

"But, Em, you have to get to UCLA, far from your father's reach, and live your own life," I said, hating each word but knowing they were true. *Because* they were true.

"I know but also...Brown rejected me."

I took a step back. "Oh shit. Really?"

Her head bobbed. "But my father wasn't all that pissed. I think, maybe, it'll be okay. Everything will be okay."

Her eyes were blue-green pools of love and hope and fear. Fear of confronting her father and still hoping to keep some semblance of a family. To hold everyone together. Despite my hatred for Grayson Wallace, I understood why Emery couldn't let go. When my mother walked out the door that long-ago morning, I hadn't moved. Hadn't said a word. Maybe in some alternate universe, there's a little boy who called out to her and she stopped. A world in which she realized what she was doing and tried to make it work. One in which she stayed.

But it wasn't mine because I hadn't tried. Emery, at least, was trying.

"I have to go," Emery said. "My punishment is a stuffy dinner with the new senator and his family. I'll call you when it's over, and you can tell me everything that went down at the party. Okay?"

"Okay," I said, and kissed her softly.

She gave me her pinky wave and headed to her car as twilight deepened. I drove home feeling as if I were clinging to her hope with both hands, only I knew there was nothing there to keep us from falling.

Our little house was dark; the new medication they'd given my dad made him sleep for upwards of fourteen hours a day. Which was helpful, in a terrible way, since he'd taken to wandering outside lately. Twice, I'd caught him down the road as I drove back from school. The days of my Experiment were numbered, and soon I wouldn't be able to take care of him at all.

I stood in our tidy living room—we had kept Emery's rearrangement of the furniture—and glanced with apprehension at my dad's desk. The cyclone of papers with his equations on them, all reaching into infinity for the ultimate solution.

"The answer to life, the universe, and everything," I muttered.

I tried to harness some of Emery's optimism. Maybe Dad was close. Maybe he'd solve it before disease stole his mind, and he'd be famous. Rich. The most celebrated physicist on the planet. Then I could steal Emery away from her father and pay for RISD. We could be together…

On leaden feet, I crossed the room and turned on the desk light over my father's work, where equations—chains of factors—were scribbled across every page. For the first time, I picked one up and examined it. Immediately, tears blurred my vision. I blinked them back and took up another page. And another.

"Of course," I murmured. "The simplest solution is usually correct."

The pages were covered in gibberish. Algebraic nonsense. Streams of consciousness. Rambling theories that devolved into nothing, or strings of words, or my mother's name, over and over…

I let the papers fall. I hadn't known, but I'd always known. My father's work was another superposition that collapsed under my observation. I was losing him, and so I had to lose Emery. At the very best, I was facing a long separation from her—years even—until my father perished from his disease, because I *would not* do what my mother did and leave him.

But the only thing I had to do tonight was get good and drunk.

Orion had taken over the enormous courtyard in the castle-like "dorm" of Atlas Hall. He was a Mercer, one of the Big Five families that funded the Academy, and I could see his family's money everywhere I turned.

The fountain in the center was lit up with changing-color lights. Rec rooms led into the courtyard, where tables of food and drink lined one side, and a DJ and dance floor took up the rest.

Both the indoor and outdoor spaces were crowded with people by the time I got there, the music loud and thumping, with a hundred laughing conversations thrumming beneath it. Students sat and talked on the couches or made out in dark corners. I spotted my rowing crew standing around a keg, Tucker passing around a flask while Orion kept the punch bowls filled with vodka.

I strode up to my team, plucked the flask from Tucker's hand, and drained it. Whiskey burned a path to my gut, then headed straight to my head, instantly making the world a more palatable place to be.

I handed it back. "Thanks. I needed that."

The guys all stared a moment and then broke out in shocked cheers and bellows. Only Rhett stayed apart, his gaze as cool as ever. Did I give a shit? No, I did not.

Thank you, whiskey.

"Ford, you're a goddamn legend!" Tucker roared, laughing, as if we hadn't spent the year trading punches. "This is the best fucking crew in CHA history!"

He lifted his now-empty flask in a toast. Another cheer went up amid sprays of beer and punch, and I was engulfed in heavy hugs or pounding on the back. The whiskey was already doing its job, making the night murky, banishing all the pain somewhere I didn't have to look at it for a while.

Someone put a red plastic cup in my hand. I downed the entire vodka-punch drink in one go and took another. Then another. Then I grabbed a fourth and wandered the party, blissfully free of *thinking* so goddamn much. My mind, always analyzing, observing, calculating…the alcohol made that impossible.

Time became slippery as I slid into random conversations with random people, the night taking on a strange, carnival-like atmosphere, with each part of the party like a different sideshow. I even thought I saw Harper and Orion having a heated conversation before she stormed away, angrily wiping tears.

I frowned and started after her, but someone grabbed my arm.

"Hey, you're that genius, right?" a guy asked, standing with a group of friends.

"Yep," I said. "I'm a fucking genius. Which is why I'm so obviously winning at life."

He and his friends laughed. "Can you do a trick? Like, demonstrate?"

"Pfft, I don't do *tricks*. But wanna hear a joke?" I endeavored to keep from slurring, but my mouth wouldn't cooperate. "A police officer pulls Erwin Schrödinger over for speeding. The cop is suspicious, so he checks the trunk. He says to Schrödinger, 'Hey! Do you know you have a dead cat in here?' And Schrödinger says, 'Well, I do now!'"

The group gave me pitying looks and snickers. "Uh, sure. Good one, man."

I flapped a hand at them and wandered away. "Emery would've loved that joke," I muttered petulantly, and then sadness whacked me right in the chest.

Where was Emery? At some stupid dinner with her horrible father, who was probably being just nice enough to make her believe he saw how fucking beautiful and perfect and talented she was. That was never going to happen. But *I* saw her, so it was up to me to help make her dreams come true. Me. The one who wanted to keep her forever was the one who had to get her to a galaxy far, far away.

"How's that for a fucking paradox?" I said to no one.

I spotted Dean in the rec room, talking with Rhett, and was overcome with the need to pour my guts out to my best friend. Dean would understand. He would help me. Fuck, I loved that guy. One of the best people…

I staggered closer. They both looked around surreptitiously, then Rhett put something in Dean's hand. Dean pocketed whatever it was, and they went their separate ways, both melting into the crowd.

"Hey!" I cried, but the floor was tilting out from under me. I sat down heavily into a chair—unoccupied, luckily—and held my face in my hands. The room was spinning, and I needed it to stop. Something wasn't right.

"*Nothing* is right," I corrected, and lay back in the chair because my head was too heavy to hold up anymore and if I didn't close my eyes, I was going to puke. On Dean? No, I promised him I wouldn't. Where was he, anyway…?

My thoughts broke apart and I fell into a strange, drunken blackness—not awake but not unconscious either. Music and voices created a wall of sound around me, and I tucked myself into the dark to wait until I could move again.

It felt like minutes but was more likely an hour later when a scream pierced the blackness. I bolted upright, the shock sobering me slightly, and shot to my feet. A crowd had formed in the corner of the rec room and a girl was screaming and screaming…

Dread sank sharp teeth into me as I shoved people aside, and then a strangled cry tore out of my throat. Sierra Hart was kneeling on the floor in a tight blue dress. Dean was lying on his back, his head in her lap, mouth ajar, eyes staring at nothing.

Terror whipped my sluggish, drunken muscles and I staggered to Dean and fell to my knees just as Orion burst through the crowd. He pushed Sierra aside and knelt to do chest compressions on my best friend. I watched, stupefied, as his mouth formed the words: *Call an ambulance!* But no sound came out.

Orion was shouting for help, and Sierra was still screaming, but I could hear nothing but my own blood rushing in my head and see nothing but Dean's staring eyes. Finally, I broke free from the terror and grabbed his jaw.

"Dean, wake up." I blew air into his mouth, dizzy with alcohol and abject dread. "Wake up, Dean, this isn't fucking funny. Please…"

Orion's eyes—stricken and tear-filled—met mine. He never stopped his compressions but shook his head, and a hollow cry ripped out of me.

"*No!*" I slapped Dean so he'd wake up and feel hurt that I'd hit him like that. But he didn't react. Didn't move at all.

Because he's not here anymore…

I blew into his slack mouth. Orion pressed on his chest until finally EMTs arrived and took over. Then Harper was in my arms, clinging to me, sobbing into my shirt because nothing they did was working. Because it was too late.

Because Dean was dead.

Chapter 33

EMERY

"Emery."

"Hm?" I blinked out of my thoughts, where I'd been in California, taking classes at UCLA and then coming home to the little apartment I shared with Xander...

My mother touched my arm. "We're being seated now."

The hostess smiled at our party, a pile of menus in her arms. "If you'll please follow me."

"Senator," my dad said, gesturing. "After you."

Mom, Dad, and I followed Charles Harrington, his wife Shar, and their son Colton through the elegant restaurant that overlooked the bay.

My father leaned into me. "I would like you to make Colton feel welcome tonight."

I frowned. "How, exactly?"

"Listen attentively, don't talk too much, and smile. This is an important dinner."

"It is? Why?"

But he didn't answer. We'd come to a round table in the corner of the restaurant. A prime location next to the tall, floor-to-ceiling windows that gave us a panoramic view. Black water glittered with lights from the boats sailing at night.

I smoothed my pink dress and sat down beside Colton, a pale, dark-haired, gray-eyed guy, a few inches taller than me, whose smug smirk seemed glued on.

If mansplaining were a facial expression…

"Well, this is just lovely, Grayson," Charles Harrington said. He was tall, imposing, with a shock of gray hair. He turned to his wife. "Don't you think so, Shar?"

"Newport is lovely, but I prefer DC." Mrs. Harrington had dark brown eyes, and a fashionable streak of silver in her chestnut hair. She reached to touch my mother's arm. "Cassandra, we must have you down to for a luncheon sometime."

My mother smiled tightly and reached for the wine list. "We must."

When Mom didn't elaborate or engage in the small talk, Dad cleared his throat. "I understand you're something of newlyweds."

The senator covered his wife's hand with his and chuckled. "Not quite but fairly new. Three years ago, now. We met at a fundraiser in DC. She'd just come back from France, and I snatched her up before she could fly off again."

Mrs. Harrington shifted uncomfortably. "I'm sure they don't want to hear our story, Charles."

The waiter took our drink order—everyone had a cocktail or wine, while I had a Diet Coke. My mother had gone silent; I felt my father's pointed stare to continue the conversation.

I turned to Colton beside me. "Did you go to Castle Hill Academy for high school?"

Six years ago?

Colton scoffed. "Definitely not. I attended Groton in Connecticut, then went on to Harvard, where I have graduate and postgraduate degrees in socioeconomics, information systems, and analytics."

"Oh. Cool."

Job done. I picked up my menu, perused the list of seafood dishes, and wished I was at the CHA party, dancing and celebrating with Xander. But immediately, I felt my dad's glare on me again and so I put on a pretty smile for Colton.

"So, what do you do with all those degrees?"

He leaned back, sipping a gin and tonic. "Pragmatically speaking, I'm working on building another startup in the healthcare sector, but my real work is much more forward-thinking. Let me ask you a question, Emery. Do you know why our civilization is in danger of going extinct?"

"Global warming?"

"*Wrong*," he said, relishing my wrongness. "The greatest existential threat to developed countries is underpopulation. Did you know that birthrates have plummeted over the last quarter century?"

"I did not know that," I said into my soda.

"It's true. The working class is aging out, and there are not enough younger workers to sustain the industry at its current levels. I'm part of a global movement to save humanity. We seek to restore population levels and increase the size of the American household, otherwise, we're facing complete societal collapse."

"That sounds…bad."

Shoot me now.

"Colton is very fervent about this subject, aren't you, son?" Senator Harrington said proudly.

"Well, obviously, father," Colton replied. "It's imperative we act now before it's too late."

"And what did you have in mind?" My mother carefully raised her glass of wine to her lips. "How do we solve this 'existential threat?'"

"Cassandra," my dad intoned.

"I'm so glad you asked, Mrs. Wallace," Colton said. "It will take a concerted effort to get our movement's message out, but we can all do our part at home. I plan on marrying soon, for instance, and I expect my wife to bear me between six and eight children, at a minimum."

"At a minimum?" I started to laugh and then saw he was serious. Worse, my dad was listening intently and nodding.

My smile collapsed, and I saw my mother's eyes flare, then dart to me. Her gaze caught and held, and then the conversation moved on to politics, business, and what Senator Harrington was going to do for Wallace Industries, and how much money Wallace Industries would donate to the senator's PAC in return. All of these coded deals and bribes relayed under niceties, nods, and knowing looks.

My dinner arrived—a perfectly grilled halibut—and I could hardly touch it. I itched to find my phone and check in with Xander.

He must be having a better time than I am.

The meal ended and while the parents perused dessert menus and aperitifs, Colton leaned into me.

"It's a beautiful night out. Would you care to take a walk along the marina, Emery?"

I stiffened. "Oh, I'm fine, thanks."

My father cleared his throat. "That's a wonderful idea. You two go ahead, and we'll order a lava cake for you, Emery." He turned to the table. "It was her *eighteenth* birthday last week."

Oh my fucking God...

Colton slid my chair back for me. I rose on stiff legs, taking my jacket and handbag with me. We stepped out along the walk beside the dock. Rocks abutted the water, which was fenced off with small wooden posts with iron chains strung between them. The harbor was full of sailboats, their sails taken in, bobbing gently on the water.

Colton strolled beside me, his hands in his pockets. "Emery, I have to say, you are quite a lovely young woman."

"Thank you. Your parents seem...nice," I said, for lack of something better.

"Shar is my stepmother," he said with a small sneer. "She claims she's never previously married, no children. A pity, but now it's too late."

"Oh. Right."

Gee, that's not a creepy thing to say or anything.

Colton brightened. "I would very much like to see you again, Emery. Perhaps take you to dinner—"

"I think I hear my phone ringing. Vibrating, I mean, on silent. Let me just…"

I fished my phone out of my bag and turned my back on Colton. I'd intended to call Xander or Harper to save me but stopped, shocked to see I had dozens of missed calls from Harper and twice as many texts from friends and people from school: Delilah, Sierra, Elowen…all of them peppered with exclamation marks. I opened one at random from Delilah.

Where are you? OMG Did you hear??? Dean OD'd!

The blood drained from my face, and the phone in my hand began to shake. It wasn't real. It couldn't be real…

I hit call and Delilah answered immediately, sobbing over a backdrop of chaotic noise.

"Emery!" she cried. "Oh my God, it's so terrible. Dean Yearwood. He overdosed at the Atlas party. I'm here now. It's just madness. They think it was fentanyl, but I don't know. I don't know—"

"Wait, slow down," I said, my heart pounding hard. "Dean OD'd? He's okay, though, right? He's okay?"

"No, he's not okay, Em," Delilah wailed. "He *died.*

They just took him away in the ambulance in one of those black body bags…"

My vision blurred, and I staggered back. "Oh, no."

Colton peeked his head into my line of vision. "Everything okay?"

I stared at him in shocked horror, unable to speak.

Xander.

"Delilah," I cried, clutching the phone to my ear. "Where is Xander?"

"He was here. He tried to do CPR with Orion, but it was too late. I don't know where he went." She said something else, but it was lost in her sobs.

I hung up the phone and tried Xander. It went straight to voicemail. I tried Harper and got her message too. My parents and the Harringtons were suddenly there, everyone staring at me.

"Emery?" Mom rushed to me. "Are you all right?"

"I have to go. I have to…I have to go to school."

My father frowned. "Now? What's happened?"

"Dean's dead," I said, the words sounding obscene and wrong. "He's dead and I have to go…"

Abruptly, my father ushered the Harringtons away; I could hear him making some sort of excuse for me, pleasantries and niceties, while I sank onto a bench.

"Mom…?"

She sat down beside me, taking my hand awkwardly. "Who is this boy, Dean?"

"He's a friend. He's Xander's best friend." I gripped her arms in a panic. "I have to get to Xander—"

"Shhh," she said quickly and pulled me close as Dad rejoined us. I held on, the shock giving way and the tears flooding out.

"What on earth is going on?"

"We have to get her home. Now." Mom pulled back to hold my face, her gaze piercing mine. "We're going home now, okay?"

"Terrible end to an otherwise lovely evening," my dad grumbled, while all I could think about was Xander, and Dean's rowing crew, and the sweet kids from the Math & Physics Club—and his parents. Dean's *mother*, getting the news tonight…

I cried in my own mother's lap all the way home. Finally, alone in my room, I pulled myself together and tried Xander again. No answer. I tried Harper, and she picked up.

"Oh, Em, it's fucking awful," she cried.

"I'm so sorry, Harper," I cried with her. "What happened? Are you okay?"

"No. I don't know what to do or how to feel. Because I'm not *supposed* to have to feel this, you know? He's not *supposed* to be gone."

"I know. I wish I had been there for you."

"No, you don't. I wouldn't wish it on anyone. And oh, God, Em. Xander…"

My heart dropped. "Tell me."

"He was out of his mind. Drunk, I think, and so distraught. He kept saying he was going to kill Rhett. That Rhett's a murderer. I don't know what he saw or what he told the police but…God, I just can't believe it."

"Do you want me to come over?"

"No, go to Xander, if you can. He's in a bad way, Em. Real bad."

"Where is he now?"

"Some guys from the crew took him home."

"Okay, I'll try to sneak out. And Harper." Tears flooded my eyes. "I'm so sorry. I know you and Dean were close."

"He was one of my best friends," she said. "I just…I have to go."

She hung up, and I wished I could split myself in two and be with her and Xander both. But getting out to see even one of them was going to be risky. I changed out of my pink dress and into jeans, sneakers, and a T-shirt and hoodie.

I exited my room just as my mother came out of hers, as if she'd been waiting for me. Without a word, she walked down the stairs with me into the kitchen, where my father was making himself a cup of tea.

He looked me up and down. "Where are you going?"

"She's going to see her friend," Mom said.

"Harper," I said faintly. "Dean was…very special to her."

"What happened to this Dean? Wait, isn't he the coxswain for Tucker's crew?"

He was…

I nodded. "I have to go."

To my shock, my mother threw her arms around me. "You drive safely and be back at a reasonable hour."

I nodded and hurried out before my dad could say a word.

I drove as fast as I dared and got to Xander's house just after eleven. My headlights splashed his front door. He was sitting on the stoop, head down, arms dangling off his knees.

I shut off the engine and hurried to him. "Xander…"

He looked up at me, the porch light casting shadows over his face. Haggard, bloodshot, tear streaked. I sat beside him, put my arms around him, smelled the alcohol on his breath. I would've given anything to make him stop hurting, but there was nothing that was going to make this better. The world had shattered and become impossibly broken. No amount of soft words was going to put it back together.

"Rhett killed him," Xander said dully. "He gave him a pill, Dean took it, and it killed him. And I don't think it was the first time, and I…I didn't stop it. I got drunk, and I didn't stop it…"

"Xander, it's not your fault."

He looked at me, confused. Incredulous. "It doesn't make any fucking sense. *Him*? Dean fucking Yearwood? He's better than every single one of those fucking pretentious pricks—" He bit off his words and sucked in deep breaths.

"I know," I said. "I know this is hard—"

"No, you don't know," he snapped, tearing off the porch and staggering a few steps away. "You don't know because if you did know, you'd stay."

I reared back. "What…?"

"You're holding onto a lie, Emery," he said. "A stupid idea that prom is going to fix anything."

"My design is stupid?" I asked in a soft voice.

"No, your design is going to be extraordinary, but they're too fucking stupid to see it. Don't you get it? They don't see you and you don't see them. It's like a selective hereditary blindness, running rampant in the Wallace DNA."

"I know you're hurting right now, Xander, but—"

"I'm just telling you the truth. The facts. Because facts and evidence are how we predict what will happen next. Not magical thinking. Not…*hope*."

He's drunk, that's all, I thought. *He's drunk and he's suffered a terrible loss.*

I got to my feet while Xander turned his back to me, hands on his hips. I approached him slowly, reached for his arm, then pulled at the lapel of his jacket. One slight tug toward me, and a sob tore out of him. He wrapped me in his arms, his body is shaking, I held him as best I could, my own tears soaking into his shirt. He made fists in my hair and my sweatshirt, then abruptly staggered back. He tore his glasses off with one hand and wiped his eyes in the crook of his arm.

"Do you know what he told me?" Xander said. "The other day, Dean said, 'Put your heart out in the world and see what happens.' So I did. And this is what happened. I lost him. And my dad is really sick. I'm losing him too. My mother and Dean and my father…" He looked up at me with tears in his eyes. "And you. Everybody I love…"

"No…"

"*Yes*. You need to marry me so that you can leave me." He snorted a terrible laugh. "I'm such a fucking idiot."

I shook my head, tears falling down my cheeks. "Xander, wait…"

"Please just go, Emery. I need to go to sleep and not feel or think about anything for a little while. I'm sorry… sorry."

He staggered back into the house, and I stood for a long moment in the front yard, alone. Then I drove back home.

Chapter 34

EMERY

The morning of Dean Yearwood's funeral dawned bright and warm. A beautiful day that didn't match the sorrow of the hundreds of people who turned up at St. Catherine's Catholic Church. I thought the brilliant weather was fitting in a terrible sort of way. Dean had been a literal ray of sunshine wherever he went, and I had to think he was smiling down on us, trying to tell us not to be so sad.

The eulogies were all of the same theme: how Dean was truly good a person, how exceptionally kind and funny he was, and how he always had a smile for everyone. Missing, I thought, was any idea why he would take something that stole him away from us. What pressures he might have been facing or what unseen battles he'd been waging, alone.

Finally, toward the end of the service, Xander took the podium.

"Everybody loved Dean," he began, his voice hoarse. "This church can't hold all the people who loved him. And it wasn't just his charisma or humor. It's because he loved everybody. He had the rare ability to see the best in people without judgment. He accepted them. I don't have that ability. Most of us don't. But we all felt it from him. We loved him because it's extraordinary to be seen like that. And now, to lose that…"

He stopped, tears streaming under his glasses, his hands clenched on the lectern.

"If there's a point to any of this, maybe it's to follow Dean's example. To love people while they're here and not wait to understand the depth of them only when they're gone. It's a terrible lesson but maybe the only way we'll learn." Xander swallowed hard and looked at the coffin draped in white. "I'll try, Dean. I promise."

I walked with Harper from the church to the graveside service. Dean's mother and father—her in a faded black dress, him in a shabby dark blue suit—sat on the front row, both looking shell-shocked and frail. Father Doyle gave the service, punctuated by the audience's sniffles and muffled sobs. The entire school had come—the entire town, even.

"So many people," Harper murmured, gazing around at the crowd. "So many…"

My gaze found Xander, standing with his crew in the front. They were all there except for Rhett. I didn't have all the details, but the police had spoken to him that night based on what Xander had seen, and nothing conclusive came of it. Rhett's father was CEO of LaneBreak Records; I guessed he'd pulled every string he had to make sure "inconclusive" was as far as any investigation got. Even so, Rhett was wisely staying away.

Throughout the service, my gaze strayed to Xander. He kept his head down, hands clasped in front of him. He had been a pallbearer at the church with the crew, hoisting the coffin onto his shoulders. He'd looked so stoic but so walled off too.

He doesn't want to hurt anymore.

I dabbed my eyes, and the movement caught his attention. He looked up at me, his mask cracking for a moment, and the pain spilled out. Then he looked away. The service ended, and I lost him in the crowd, finding him again only when he was long gone, walking to his car, alone.

"Are you going to the reception?" Harper asked. "I don't know if I can stand it, but I think I will. I need to talk to his parents. I need to tell them…" Tears filled her eyes, and she wiped them away. "Will you come with me?"

"Of course." I gave her arm a squeeze. "I'm not going anywhere."

She smiled gratefully, and then a shadow fell over us.

"Hey," Tucker said. "Can I talk to you, Em?"

The last time I'd spoken to Tucker was back in

November. He'd sent me an apologetic text for leaving me in the rain. I suspected Xander was behind that, but he refused to confess if he was.

"Um, sure." I stepped aside with Tucker as mourners ambled around us. "I'm very sorry about Dean. He was one of the best."

"Yeah," Tucker said gruffly. "Yeah, he was." He looked terrible, his eyes red-rimmed and shadowed. He cleared the emotion out of his throat. "So listen, Em, has your dad brought around the Harringtons? The new senator?"

I nodded. "We had dinner with them the same night as…the same night. The son is a real creep."

"He's a lot worse than that," Tucker said. "Colton has a podcast where he talks about how women being in the workforce has destroyed society and how we need to get back to the 'pre–birth control' era. Really weird shit."

I smiled wanly. "I didn't take you for a feminist."

Tucker wasn't smiling. "I'm serious, Em. He's one of those bitter little fuckers who hates women because he can't get laid. And based on my experience, your dad isn't going to give a shit about that when it comes to getting what he wants."

My face paled. "No, I can't believe he'd—"

"Pawn you off for profit?" Tucker shook his head. "Just be careful, okay?"

I nodded faintly. "Okay. Thank you."

Tucker hesitated a moment and then bent to give me an awkward hug just as Elowen appeared. She gave me a pitying look, linked her arm in his, and led him away.

After the reception in the church parish hall, Harper said she wasn't feeling well and went home. It was obvious Xander wanted some space, so I drove home, too, with a new sense of dread in my gut. My dad had gone from demanding I go to college to not talking about it at all. And the night at the Chart House…

This is a very important dinner…

I shivered and went to the side door. I heard the shouting before I even stepped inside. Jack's bellows and my father's sharp exclamations. Dad hardly ever raised his voice, which made it more frightening. In the kitchen, Belinda was stirring something in a bowl and crying.

"Oh, Miss Emery…"

"What's happening?"

I raced to the living room, where Mom was standing between Jack and my father. Jack—still in all black—had a duffel bag thrown over his shoulder and one finger stabbing the air at my dad.

"*I'm* the degenerate?" Jack screamed. "You're the one who killed your son! You're the one who has to live with what you've done for the rest of your miserable life!"

"Put that bag down," Dad shouted. "You are not to leave this house with one item. Everything you own belongs to me."

"Bullshit!" Jack cried. "This is my bag. I paid for everything in it myself and you know what? It doesn't matter how much stuff you hoard, or how much money you make, it will never bring him back!"

"Jack, please," Mom begged. Then she saw me. "Emery..."

Jack spun around. "I'm done, Emery. I'm getting out. And if you're smart, you will too."

My gaze went between them. "What? No, Daddy, don't kick him out—"

"Kick me out?" Jack snarled. "I wouldn't stay if you *paid* me."

"Never mind, Emery, let him go," Dad said. "If he wants to walk away from millions—no, billions—then that's his foolish mistake to make."

"Is that how much Grant cost?" Jack cried, his voice breaking. He turned to me. "You know he didn't just happen to *walk* in front of a train, right?"

My mother sank into a chair. "Jack, don't."

"All that bullshit they've been feeding us for years. He didn't *have his fucking music on too loudly* and then *accidentally* step in front of anything. He did it on purpose."

I felt as if the floor was falling out beneath me. "What...?"

"You shut your mouth," Dad bellowed, his face red.

"Grant killed himself," Jack cried, "rather than spend one more fucking minute trapped in the box you locked him in."

But I'd always known, somehow. I just didn't want to look at it. I didn't want to believe. I shook my head, tears falling. "No..."

"*Yes*," Jack said, tears streaking his own cheeks. "That's what happens if you step out of line. If you want something for yourself. Emery, come with me. Walk out the door right now."

"I-I can't. Where…?"

"Do not move, Emery," Dad said. "She is not as stupid as you, Jack. She is a young girl who will not survive on her own."

Colin appeared at the door. "Time to go, Mr. Jack," he intoned.

Jack moved toward the front door. "Last chance, Em. Come with me."

"Wh-where are you going?"

"He doesn't know," Dad said, calmer now. "He has no plan. No future. He's going to live on the streets, giving blowjobs for five dollars apiece. Is that what you want, Emery?"

I didn't know what I wanted, but it wasn't this. I wanted Jack to stay. I wanted my mother to stop crying and my father to stop shouting. I wanted us to be happy, and it was slipping through my fingers. And it hurt, almost more than anything else, to know that I wasn't enough to hold us together.

Jack shook his head, his voice low. "You're going to regret it, Em. He'll give you millions, but that'll be nothing compared to what it'll cost you."

Then he walked out, the door slammed, and then the only sound was my mother's sobs.

Chapter 35

XANDER

A FEW DAYS AFTER THE FUNERAL, I TRUDGED DOWN TO THE Academy marina for row practice. The season's last regatta was coming up. I couldn't have cared less. But since Dean's death, my body felt hijacked, alternating between shocked numbness and crippling grief. Going to school full time no longer made any sense, but I could lose myself in the physical mechanics of rowing, even for an hour or two.

But as soon as I arrived at the dock where the coaches and the men's eight were gathered, I realized just how slow my thinking had been. Rhett Calloway stood with Tucker, apart from the others but dressed in his workout gear, the same as the rest of us.

They both looked at me warily. I stared back, trying to make sense of what I was seeing. Then Orion was there, turning me away as Coach Daniels gathered us around.

Coach clapped his hands without enthusiasm, going through the motions. "I know this is going to be a tough day. We've lost one of our own, and as hard as it is…" He broke off, then cleared his throat. "We have a season to finish, and I'd like to think that Dean would want us to finish strong. To make him proud."

The icy cold numbness wrapped around me started to crack. We all shuffled to the shell, and I climbed in at stroke seat. The rest of the guys followed, Rhett taking his seat at the bow. I gripped the oar in my hands, the rubber, textured handle digging into my palms. The boat gave a final sway—the cox taking his seat—and I raised my eyes, expecting to see Dean's green ones looking back, that familiar grin on his face. A wink and a smile and he'd murmur, "Give 'em hell, my friend."

A stranger stared back. One of the guys who rowed quads. It wasn't Dean. It would never be Dean again.

And then the numbness broke off completely and fell away. Rhett Calloway was behind me, ready to row, his privilege sparing him from consequences. The whole team, this entire fucking school, needed the win more than it needed the truth.

"Jesus fucking Christ."

I tossed the oar aside and climbed out of the boat. I sloshed through waist-deep water to the shore.

Coach Daniels held out a hand as I passed him. "Now, hold on, son…"

"Don't fucking touch me."

"Xander, wait," Orion caught up to me, his eyes shining. "Talk to me…"

I spun around, and behind Orion was Rhett. A white-hot rage fell over me, and I surged forward with a splash of water.

"He killed Dean," I said, my voice hollow. Then the truth of it found me, and I wanted to scream. I leveled a finger at Rhett, my voice rising. "He sold him some poison with no fucking thought to the consequences, and we're all just going to pretend like nothing happened? Business as fucking usual?"

"Now, hold on, man," I heard Tucker say while Rhett bowed his head and looked away.

It took both Orion and Coach Daniels to hold me back, both speaking soothing words, my eyes blinded by tears. For a few moments, there was chaos, and then I stopped fighting.

"Get off me," I snarled, and tore away from Orion and Coach. They made a wall between me and Rhett, but the rage had drained out, leaving only grief and disgust.

"What the fuck is wrong with you?" I demanded of the crew. The coaches. The whole fucking school. "Did he mean *nothing* to you? Whatever it takes, huh? Win at all costs. Put him back on the boat like nothing happened. As if Dean were never here at all."

"Now, son—" Coach began.

"I'm not your son. I'm not on this team. I'm done. Done with this fucking place."

I sloshed through the water up onto the shore, hollowed

out by grief—that horrible sick feeling of nothingness. Absence. There had been someone there—a whole person—and now there wasn't. Echoes of my mother's abandonment. Of my father's illness. And Emery…

And what was it all for? Opening myself up had been such a mistake. I'd been better off as a loner with no friends. Safer in science, studying the cold vastness of space, where all of this hurt was theoretically meaningless. A Planck length of insignificance, 10^{-35} in size, which is as close to nothing as you can get.

In the locker room, I changed, and then I drove away from Castle Hill Academy for the last time.

The Experiment was over. Result: complete and utter failure.

I drove home under a gray sky through the forest-like Bend and turned onto my street. A lone figure walked along the edge, dressed in pajamas. Bare feet. Hair askew.

"Oh, fuck."

I pulled over and jumped out. "Dad. Hey, Dad…"

He looked up blearily, confused. "It seems I've lost my button. Have you seen my button?"

"Yeah," I said thickly. "I know exactly where it is. Come with me and I'll show you."

I drove my father home and guided him to his bed.

"Sharon, Xander will be home soon," he said as he laid his head on the pillow. "Let's not fight, all right? I don't want him to hear it. He's so sensitive."

I tucked him in, my heart heavy as I shut the door behind me. The time had come where what I could give my father and what he needed were diverging.

An hour later, I hung up the phone with Willow Glen Memory Care in Boston and set it on the kitchen table, strewn with invoices and bank statements. My laptop was open to our savings account. The idea of putting my father somewhere cheap was abhorrent. Willow Glen wasn't cheap, but they had space for him. Now I just had to pay for it.

I put my head in my hands as a soft knock came at the door.

Emery stood on my porch, the falling twilight lining her in copper and gold. Tears streamed down her cheeks. She looked as if she hadn't slept in days.

"Hi," she said in a watery voice.

"Hi."

Her head bowed, and in two strides, I was holding her. She clung to me, her small body shaking with sobs.

"He killed himself," she said into my sweater. "Grant. It wasn't an accident. Jack told me, and now Jack's gone too. He took his stuff, and he walked out and…"

Jesus, it doesn't stop.

Emery's words were lost in a flood of tears. I pulled her close, wishing I could somehow tuck her away inside my bones and keep her safe.

There is a way.

"Emery…"

She looked up at me. "I know this isn't what you want.

I don't want it, either. Not like this. But now my dad's talking about the new senator's son. He's older and wants to marry someone young and start having lots of babies right away."

"Fucking hell…"

For a moment, I couldn't see beyond the red haze that descended at the idea of another man touching her, using her, ignorant to all that she was—*with* her father's blessing. But he couldn't marry her off if she was already married.

I led her inside and sat with her on the couch.

"Where's your dad?" she asked.

"Sleeping," I said. "He sleeps a lot now, and whenever he wakes up, there's less of him than there was before."

"I'm so sorry, Xander."

"He doesn't want to leave this house. He throws a fit whenever I bring it up. He says he's waiting for my mother to come back. I'm going to have to move him soon, and it's going to be fucking awful."

"I know," she said. "You have to keep him close."

"And you have to get away. You know that, right?"

She nodded and rested her head against my chest, and for a long while, we sat in the falling light. I'd thought she'd fallen asleep when she stirred.

"Your eulogy was beautiful."

"I'm trying to live up to it," I said. "Like you. You're trying to see the best in your family. But Emery…"

"I know," she said, curling into me. "But I'm scared, Xander."

"Me too." I stroked her hair. "Me too."

LITTLE PIECES OF LIGHT

The following Saturday, Orion and I met Emery and Harper at Providence City Hall. Rhode Island had no waiting period for a marriage license. We applied, were approved, and then waited our turn for a judge to officiate.

Emery wore a simple dress of pale pink, her hair flowing in soft waves around her shoulders. Harper acted as her bridesmaid and witness. Orion stood in for Dean, who would have been my best man. Wracked by grief and guilt, he wouldn't stop blaming himself for throwing that party. Something had transpired between him and Harper, too, though neither would say what it was, nor even speak to each other. The four of us passed heavy glances around at what had to be the most depressing wedding in a decade.

The officiate didn't seem to notice. He said in a bored tone, "Do you, Emery, take Alexander Ford to be your lawfully wedded husband, to love and to cherish, all the days of your life?"

Emery's eyes met mine—blue-green oceans of love and tears. "I do."

"And do you, Alexander, take Emery Wallace to be your lawfully wedded wife, to love and to cherish, all the days of your life?"

"I do," I said, and the worst part was, I meant it with all my fucking heart.

We had no rings. No vows beyond the boilerplate language, and soon, it was over.

"I now pronounce you husband and wife. You may kiss the bride."

We moved closer, and I cupped her face in my hand, her tears spilling down to my fingers. I kissed Emery softly and she returned my kiss, pressing into it urgently before breaking away and crying into my suit jacket.

Back in Castle Hill, she and I drove to my house, where her car waited. It was not yet four in the afternoon. The days were getting longer, the light more golden.

"Do you have to go home?" I asked in a low voice.

"No," she said. "Not yet."

We reached for each other at the same time, with the same desperate urgency. Bruising, devouring kisses, hands in hair and tugging at clothing. We made it inside, to my loft, and stripped each other naked, leaving nothing but the locket around her neck, glinting gold against her skin. We lay down together, and wordlessly, she reached into the nightstand for a condom. She tore it open, then rolled onto her back and put it on me.

"Emery…"

She didn't say a word but pulled at my shoulders until I was on top of her, then between her legs, then sinking inside her. The tight feel of her around me caused an automatic chain reaction of need—synapses firing and sensations flooding me, erasing my thinking mind.

Emery nodded as if answering some unspoken hesitation and lifted her hips to mine. Christ, she was too beautiful. Too soft beneath me and wanting me; I could feel it in every touch, every breath. Our bodies were entwined, *entangled*—one responding to the other in an instantaneous give and take. I became delirious with her, and from that delirium, a sudden, primal need began to grow in me. A need to take. To keep. To mark her as mine. Our separation grew more imminent with every passing day, and my love for her was also entangled with a possessive greed. The pain was too much. Too hard to take, and so I took her instead, as if I could impale her to my bed. To shield her with my body from whatever cruel hand wanted to steal her away.

Emery cried out in ecstasy, her exquisite face contorted, riding the crest of the pleasure as if it were agony.

It is agony, I thought brokenly. *To lose her…*

"Now you," she breathed.

She melted beneath me. Her eyes glassy and dark and heated with permission to take her until I was spent. My body obeyed. I lost myself in her until I couldn't hold on any longer. I emptied myself into her, turned myself inside out for her. Only her, this girl I'd loved from afar for seven years and loved right now with everything I had.

For a long while, we stayed locked together, breathing as one. Her fingers were in my hair, her arms wrapped around me, holding me. I felt melded to her so completely that it seemed impossible that we wouldn't always have this.

This…

This was all I wanted. Her. Eighteen or eighty, I knew I'd never want anyone but Emery.

My wife…

Part V

*I must be gone and live,
or stay and die.*
—William Shakespeare,
Romeo and Juliet

Part V

Chapter 36

EMERY

MAY

THURSDAY MORNING BEFORE CLASS, I LAID MY PROM DRESS out on my bed. Again. I couldn't stop looking at it, though it created such a bittersweet ache in my heart. It was white with a heart-shaped bodice, full-skirted but shorter in the front and longer in the back so as not to swamp my short frame. It wasn't designer label or fashionable like the other girls' dresses would be. But I'd taken some clothes to consignment and made a trade for it, so it felt like mine.

I kept imagining how I'd look in it, wanting to be beautiful for Xander, and standing next to him in his black tux. He'd be so handsome for our photos.

The closest thing we'll have to wedding photos.

I wasn't supposed to be thinking like that. It was a paper marriage only, designed to help me escape after graduation. But my heart wouldn't stop replaying our wedding, terribly short and sad and real—when it wasn't supposed to be real.

I brushed the thoughts away and got ready for school. The end of the year—and prom—had raced up to me so fast. Since the funeral, Delilah and I had thrown ourselves into the work, turning the Castle Hill Country Club ballroom into an elegant, black-and-white wonderland filled with sparkle and light. I should've been excited, but instead all I could think about was how it might be my last night with Xander for a very long time.

At the Academy, I met Delilah and Harper at our usual spot at midmorning break under the willow tree outside.

"We're in really good shape for Saturday night," Delilah said, consulting her iPad. "We just need to put on the finishing touches. Oh my gosh, it's going to be so beautiful."

Delilah was working in overdrive to keep our spirits up. I was a ball of anxious nerves thinking I might have to tell my parents I was leaving, while some light had gone out of Harper's eyes since Dean died, and I didn't know if it was ever coming back. The mood of the entire school was muted now, even on the sunniest of days. Dean's absence was palpable and made the Academy, even with all its pomp and glamour, feel empty. A missing piece it couldn't afford to lose.

"Are you going to prom, Harper?" Delilah asked.

I looked at her, curious about that myself. She hadn't confided in me about whatever was happening with her and Orion, but it didn't seem good.

"Doubtful," she said. "But I'll peek in to see what you

guys have done. Are your parents going to see the result of all your hard work and artistry, Em?"

"I don't know. I can't get as straight answer from them, so maybe that's my answer."

I didn't add that there was still a part of me that wanted desperately for my father to see it and be proud. To spare me from having to walk out the door and be disowned, like Jack. But the stage was set. All that was left was for me to pull the trigger.

And leave Xander. My husband...

Harper and I parted ways with Delilah and headed to English.

"How are things with Xander?" Harper asked, as if reading my mind.

"We're in a superposition," I said wanly. "Really wonderful and really terrible. He's so good, Harper. He's struggling to take care of his father, and he's devastated about Dean. And now—barring a miracle—I'm leaving too. I'm just afraid that..."

"What?"

"He's lost so much, been hurt so many times... I'm afraid that when all is said and done, I'm not going to see him again."

"Why?" Harper frowned. "I can't believe that. He loves you."

I nodded. "And I love him, but..."

There are limits. That's what he'd told me. He had his math and his science, where he found security in the exactness, but now he was drowning.

"Maybe I should just forget California."

Harper gave me a look. "Are you saying that because it feels right or because it's easier?"

We'd arrived to our class, and I was spared from having to answer. At the very end of the period, Ms. Alvarez handed back our papers on *Romeo and Juliet*. She'd printed them out to grade them, preferring to use an actual red pen for corrections and edits.

"All in all, I'm very impressed with your analyses," she said, strolling the aisles. "A testament to Shakespeare's talent that his work still resonates in our day-to-day lives as strongly as it does."

She stopped beside my desk and set my paper face down with a concerned look. I curled the top of the paper over.

A+, but then underneath she had written *Please see me after class*.

"I'll meet you at lunch," I told Harper as the bell rang.

Ms. A shut the door after the last student left. "I'm happy to report that your UCLA financial aid package is wonderfully substantial, with more grants than loans and a small stipend for housing."

A strange mixture of dread and relief flooded me. "Wow. It's really happening, isn't it?"

"Looks like you should have the money at the end of the summer." She lowered her voice. "You accomplished what you needed to, Emery. You're free to pursue your dreams with almost full autonomy."

I swallowed hard. "Great. Thank you."

"It's hard, isn't it? Such a big leap."

I nodded. "I know it's what I have to do to, but the finality of it and how my dad will react... It makes me nervous."

"You don't look nervous, Emery, you look terrified. And the fact that you had to go to such extremes is a worrying sign." She crossed her arms and leaned against her desk. "In your paper, you wrote about the pressure Juliet was under to please her father. How furious he'd been and the names he called her when he learned of *her* secret marriage. Baggage. Disobedient. How he'd been prepared to disown her completely and how powerless she was, caught between her love and her loyalty to her family."

"Not very subtle, right?" I managed to smile.

Ms. A did not smile back. "I want to tell you something personal, if you don't mind. Before I came to CHA, I was living in Phoenix. I *fled* to Rhode Island, clear across the country, to escape an abusive marriage. He didn't hit me, but he took great care to ensure I felt worthless, scared, and doubtful of my ability to take care of myself. I was a grown woman, and it took me years to find the courage to leave. You're only eighteen, and it breaks my heart that you face this kind of abuse from a person who is supposed to love you unconditionally."

I felt tears stinging my eyes. "Thank you for sharing that with me. It helps to know that I'm not crazy for being scared or for feeling stupid that I still want to keep *some* connection to my family."

"That's a natural instinct, even if it's ultimately harmful." She cocked her head. "Can your mother help at all? And what about Xander? Is this a favor he did for you, or is it something more?"

"It started out as a favor, but now it's so much more. It was supposed to be my ticket out of Rhode Island but I...I love him. I love him so much, so another part of me says I should forget UCLA and go with him to Boston. But..."

"But?"

"It doesn't feel right. I can't explain why. I want to be with Xander more than anything, but whenever I think of Boston, I get a tight feeling in my stomach. My dad has offices there. My mom goes to Boston just to have *lunch*. But when I think of UCLA, I feel like I can breathe." I shook my head miserably. "Xander understands that; he knew it before I did. But at the same time, I know it hurts him. It hurts him a lot. He thinks if we try a long-distance relationship, it won't last."

Ms. Alvarez nodded. "Life is messy and complicated, and sometimes it seems so murky, you can't see your way through. That's what your internal compass is there for. To guide you to what's right, even if what's right is the hardest thing."

"It's so hard," I said. "Leaving my family. And Xander. I'm terrified. But I'm also terrified about what happens to me if I stay."

She smiled sadly. "I think that's your answer."

"Thank you so much for everything—"

A knock came at the door, and the president of the

Academy's secretary popped her head in. "Dr. Sterling would like to see both of you in his office."

Ms. A and I exchanged glances.

"Both of us?"

"Both of you."

The knot of dread in my stomach tightened as we walked the halls to the uppermost level of the school, where the president's office was located, overlooking the marina. Reed Sterling sat behind his desk, an imposing man with gray hair and a sharp suit. At the window, his back to us, stood my father.

Oh no...

Dr. Sterling rose as we came in. "Ms. Alvarez, Miss Wallace, please have a seat."

There were three chairs in front of Dr. Sterling's desk. Ms. A took one, I took the middle, and my father, without a word, sat beside me. I glanced sideways, but his face was impassive as always. Unreadable.

Dr. Sterling sat and folded his hands on his desk. Behind him, framed degrees and a dozen awards and letters of recognition filled the wall. "Mr. Wallace has brought to my attention that you, Alicia, have facilitated an application for Emery to a university in California."

Ms. Alvarez's face was pale, but she set up straight.

"No!" I exclaimed before she could speak. "She didn't do anything. It was my idea—"

"It's all right, Emery," she said with a reassuring smile. "Yes. I arranged for her to apply and was so very proud when I learned she'd been accepted."

"I do not appreciate this betrayal," my father said. "I expend a great deal of money so that this school maintains its high standards. I do not expect to be stabbed in the back by its faculty."

I shook my head. "That's not what—"

"*Be silent,* Emery."

"This is a very serious matter," Dr. Sterling said. "We cannot have teachers superseding the wishes of our parents. Ms. Alvarez, as you are a new teacher without tenure, we feel it is appropriate that you finish out the remaining days of this school year. You will not be invited back for the next."

"No!" I cried. "Please don't do this. It was all my fault—"

"It's all right," she said. "I knew the risks and would happily do it again."

"That will do, Alicia," Dr. Sterling said. "You may go."

I could hardly meet her eyes, shame and regret burning my face in icy hot tingles.

She smiled delicately and touched my hand. "Be brave, Emery. Be brave."

I wasn't allowed to finish out the day; instead, my father walked me to his car. Colin held open the door, tall and imposing, saying nothing.

"You've been quite busy," my father said after a long silence.

"My prom design is complicated," I said dully.

"I meant this little stunt about applying to UCLA. Not to mention, I ran into Joe Berger from the county clerk's office in Providence today. He said something very interesting to me. He said congratulations. I asked him what for, and do you know what he said?"

My heart thumped so hard I could barely breathe, and my hands went cold in my lap.

"He replied, 'On your daughter's marriage, of course.'"

Oh God…

"Apparently, an Emery Wallace married an Alexander Ford several weeks ago. I could not quite believe what he was telling me. I told him it must've been a mistake, because that's what it is. A terrible, terrible mistake."

"It's not a mistake," I managed through numb lips. "I love Xander, and I'm going to California."

"You're doing no such thing," Dad said, unbothered. "Emery, you're a young and foolish little girl who doesn't know what the world is like. But I do. It is a game that must be played to win, because the moment you take your eyes off the board, it swoops in with an iron mallet and crushes you. I am providing protection. Something young Mr. Ford could never do."

"That's not true. He's a genius with a bright future, and he's kind and good…and he loves me."

"And he's willing to up and leave for California too?"

"Well…no. He can't. At least not yet, or maybe—"

"Of course not. You've been duped. He is the poor son of a weak-minded person. The son of an enemy, no less, who cost me twenty million dollars in regulatory fees and now has the *audacity* to marry my daughter in secret, like a thief in the night, taking what does not belong to him."

"That's not…that's not what happened," I said, my tongue tying like it always did when I tried to stand up to my father. Anger and frustration turning to tears that he read as hysteria. An overemotional girl who didn't know what she wanted. "You don't understand. Xander is—"

"I'm going to say this one time, and one time only, Emery. You are never to see that boy again. Next week we'll go back to the courthouse and get that ridiculous marriage annulled and restore some sanity and common sense to our household."

"No," I said faintly, feeling as if I were clinging to the edge of a cliff. "No, we're going to prom together—"

"You're not going to prom. Senator Harrington and his family are coming over for a little cocktail party Saturday night."

"What? You're not coming to see…?"

I stared, the words trailing off. The flame of hope that had kept me going through so many cold years was finally sputtering out. For a long moment, I sat in numb shock, until my father, his eyes on the scenery flying by outside the window, spoke in a matter-of-fact tone.

"I understand that Xander has made some serious accusations against RJ Calloway's boy, Rhett, concerning that young man's death."

I swiveled my head. "What…?"

"RJ is a good friend of mine, and Rhett has a promising future that Xander is threatening with his baseless accusations. A defamation suit for attempting to ruin Rhett's reputation wouldn't be unreasonable."

My heartbeat thrashed in my ears. "No, you can't. It wouldn't work. Xander didn't do anything wrong."

"That would be up to the courts to decide. And it would be up to Xander to defend himself. Court fees, lawyer fees…it can all be so time-consuming and expensive. Ruinous, even. Especially for someone struggling to find decent residential care for an ailing parent."

"*Why?*" I cried. "Why would you do that?"

"I was lax with Jack," he said. "I won't make the same mistake with you. I'm not going to let you throw your life away like he has. If I have to tighten the lead, so be it."

My father turned his head to me, his blue eyes seeming to pierce straight into my heart.

"One phone call, Emery," he said, the threat heavy in his mild voice. "One phone call is all it will take. Do you understand?"

The cliff crumbled away. "I do."

Chapter 37

XANDER

Early Saturday morning, I laid out my rented tux for prom on my bed and set the plastic container with Emery's corsage beside it. For the hundredth time I checked my phone. She hadn't returned any of my texts, and all of the dozen calls I'd made to her in the past two days had gone to voicemail. Now that I'd walked away from CHA, I couldn't see her every day, and I missed her.

I miss my wife.

It was a bad idea, to refer to Emery that way, even in my mind, but I couldn't seem to stop doing it. Like poking a wound over and over again so that it never heals. I'd vowed to never use it as an emotional weapon against her, to make her feel pressured or guilty, but I'd also vowed to love her forever, because I did. Another paradox—I loved my wife but wouldn't call her that *because* I loved her.

I shot a text to Harper. Any word from Emery?

The reply came quick. No. Her dad showed up at school two days ago, and I haven't heard from her since. I'm sorry! I should have texted you ASAP, but I wasn't thinking.

Her dad. Of course.

It's okay. I'll try again.
Hold on....

I waited a minute and then Harper came back.

Delilah says they're at the CC setting up for prom. I eased a sigh of relief until she texted again. But she says Em isn't going???

My heart—this battered, bruised thing in my chest—became heavy with new anxiety.

I texted Harper. Heading over now.

On my way downstairs I checked on my dad in his room. Though it was early morning, he was awake, the glare of the TV casting a blue glow over his dull features. He'd lost so much weight, so much light from his eyes. The dementia that laid waste to his mind revealed itself in the wasting away of his body too.

"I'll be right back, Dad," I said. "Don't go anywhere."

"Hm? Tell your mother she's late, and we're going to start dinner without her."

"I will."

And before I left, I double-checked that I'd flipped off the circuit breaker for the oven and that the gas to the stove was shut off. No more 3:00 a.m. breakfasts. No more piano. No more equations...

I jumped in the car, exchanging my concern for my father for a pang of dread for Emery. She'd been working on bringing her vision to life for months. Prom was her dream, and that bastard of a father was somehow stealing that from her too.

I screeched into the country club parking lot a little after nine in the morning and climbed out just in time to see Emery coming out of the front door. She wore jeans and a T-shirt, and her hair was pulled in a messy ponytail. Her eyes were red-rimmed and widened in fear when she saw me.

"Xander?" She glanced around quickly. "What are you doing here?"

"You haven't answered my calls or texts, and Harper says you're not going to the prom tonight?"

Emery stiffened. "No, I'm not."

"Were you going to tell me?"

"Yes...I...I'm sorry. But I have to go. If he sees you here..."

I gritted my teeth. "What happened? What did he do now? What did he tell you?"

"It doesn't matter," she said, her eyes filling. "You need to leave."

"No," I said. "He can't do this to you. Whatever it is he told you, it's a lie."

"You don't know him, Xander," she said brokenly. "You don't know who he knows and what he can do. Please, just go home." Emery glanced around fearfully, then lowered her voice. "But your dad, Xander. Get him somewhere safe, okay? I have to go."

She started past me and I followed, walking with her as she hurried to her car.

"Wait, what about you? Look, I'm sorry I've been distant. I've been so fucking sad about Dean and stupid with old hurt from my mother leaving. I've been thinking in binary, as if there is only you in California and me here because I didn't think I could survive another hit. But I—"

"I'm not going to California," she said. "I ruined my teacher's life. I'm not going to ruin yours too."

"What? I-I don't understand. What did he say to you? Emery...*what did he say?*"

"It's too late, Xander!" she cried suddenly, then heaved a breath. "It's too late," she repeated, calmer now. Resigned. "I can't do this anymore."

I can't do this anymore. My mother's parting words.

"So that's it?" I demanded, a hot, ugly feeling unspooling in my gut. "You're just going to give in? Walk away? You're not going to fight for us?"

"Yes."

"*Why?*"

"Because I'm tired of fighting. I'm so tired of...not being enough. For anyone. You, him, myself..."

"I don't know what that means," I said, something like panic rising in me. "Did I do something wrong? I thought you had a plan—"

"Plans change," she said. "Don't look at me like that.

I can't, Xander." She straightened, jutted out her chin. "This is what I want."

"No, it's not. I don't believe that."

Her eyes flashed. "So now you're going to tell me how I feel too? Like I don't have enough of that already?"

"No, that's not what I meant." I ran a hand through my hair. "Em…what about us?"

"It just got too difficult," Emery said, her lip quivering. She glanced around a final time, then threw her arms around me. "I'm sorry," she breathed into my neck, her tears hot on my skin. "But he's going to win. He always does."

Then she got into her car and drove away.

I stood in the parking for a good while, Emery's absence another black hole opening under my feet. A different version of the same rejection that had wounded me since I was ten years old, compounded by loss and death, until I was numb with it.

With automatic movements, I drove toward home, her words filtering through my breaking heart.

Get him somewhere safe.

Her father must've threatened my dad, somehow. She was trying to save me, maybe, by sacrificing herself. By sacrificing us. But there had been defeat in Emery's eyes, too. And terror. Her father had been making her doubt herself for years, withholding love and affection and only doling it out in little bits, just enough to keep her confused and hoping that one day he'd see her…

And now she's giving up.

So lost in my thoughts, I almost didn't see him until it was too late. I slammed on the brakes, narrowly avoiding hitting my father, who was wandering across the street in the wooden seclusion of the Bend.

"No," I murmured in a cold sweat, my heart pounding. "Not again. Not now."

My father had stopped to stare at nothing. Behind him, a dozen yards away, was our house. His beloved house that he'd refused to leave. It was in relatively good condition, I thought. Close to the bay, some developer might want it. To tear down and build something bigger.

Get him somewhere safe...

I got out of the car and gently helped my dad, still in his pajamas, into the passenger seat. "Where are we going?" he demanded, loud and suddenly angry.

"We're going to Boston."

"Why?" he asked, suspicious. Confused.

I didn't answer, and in another minute, he forgot he asked.

It took an hour and a half to drive to Willow Glen Memory Care in Boston. My father spent the drive alternating between watching the scenery fly by and sleeping. Sometimes, he muttered to himself, and I wished with all my heart he'd talk to me about some complex theory, that he'd speak to me in the difficult language of physics, our native tongue. But by the time I helped him out of the car, I would've been happy if he'd just remembered my name.

At reception, I sat him down in a chair and brought him a cup of water, but his hands were trembling too much to hold it.

"Ah, yes, Xander. We spoke on the phone," the woman behind the desk said. Her name tag read *Joanne*. "We have the room for him, but there was the matter of Medicare not covering the full annual residency fee."

"I know, but I'll have it. I have enough for one year, and I'll make up the rest after that. I just need the time to sell our house."

She looked at me sympathetically. "I'm sorry this is so rough for you. But he'll have excellent care here."

"Thank you."

The intake process took hours, and by the time my father was situated in his room, twilight was falling. I sat at his bedside, surveying the space. It made me think of a dorm. Besides the bed, it had a TV, dresser, small table and chair, and an adjoining bathroom. It was neat and tidy and pastel, nothing like our dark, ramshackle—yet cozy—house. The drive had exhausted him, or maybe it was just the illness working to steal him away.

My father stared blankly at a TV show, then swiveled his head to me.

"What are you still doing here?"

"This is your first night. I don't want you to be alone." I swallowed hard. "I can't leave you, Dad."

"I'm leaving you." He nodded, his eyes back on the TV. "It won't be long now."

"What do you mean?"

But he didn't seem to hear me.

"I worry about him," he said after a minute.

"Who?"

"My son, Xander. He wants to protect me. Or redeem my reputation. Pfft. He doesn't know that I know, but I know."

"What do you know?" I asked, barely daring to breathe. This was the most he'd spoken to me in weeks.

He didn't reply but had gone blank again. I rubbed my aching eyes and thought about getting something from the vending machine. I hadn't eaten all day—

"Physics is a terrible science," he said suddenly. "Stephen Hawking tried to warn us. He said if we discover a Theory of Everything, we will know the mind of God. But why would we want to do that?"

"I'm not sure I'm following you, Dad," I said slowly, carefully, not wanting to lose him again. As if his lucidity was a flighty bird I might scare off.

"Xander studies black holes, but here's something to understand about that," Dad stated. "No matter what is pulled inside, it can never die. Do you know that?"

"That could be true," I said. "If what happens in a black hole follows the Law of Conservation of Energy."

"Hmph. You sound like my son. All science, no magic."

I gave a start. "What did you say?"

But again, he didn't seem to hear me. "Energy cannot be destroyed, only changed from one form to another. Nothing is final. Not even death. But what happens then?

That's the mystery. It's what makes life worth living. If we solved the mystery, what would be the point?"

"We'd know what was coming," I said gruffly. "We could be prepared…"

"Nothing prepares you. The joy, the hurt…" He went away again, then came back. "I'm very proud of him. He's a good boy, my Xander. A young man, now. He's going to be with his love. Beautiful girl, she is, inside and out. But I have to stay here and wait. I'm staying right here until she comes back."

"Who?"

"My wife."

"Dad, no—"

"Tell Xander to remember his Goethe," Dad said, eyes drifting closed, voice heavy with sleep. "'You will never know another's heart unless you are prepared to give yours too.' He needs to put his heart in that girl's hands and trust her not to drop it. She might, and that'll hurt—but it's a beautiful hurt, the best kind. And if she holds it tight and gives hers in return…what's better than that?"

"I can't think of anything," I managed.

"Go to your girl, Xander," he said.

I whipped my head up; he was speaking right to me.

"Go to her, and love her," he said with a smile. "And don't let her go."

Chapter 38

EMERY

I WATCHED WITH A KIND OF DETACHED FASCINATION AS CATERers scuttled around the house, helping Belinda prepare for Senator Harrington and his family. The day was sliding away, getting closer to 7:00 p.m., when Academy students would be filing into the Castle Hill Country Club for senior prom.

Absently, I checked my phone. There were missed calls and texts from Harper and Delilah, but nothing new from Xander. I'd seen his face when I told him I couldn't do it anymore. The hurt and betrayal. His broken heart. I'd done what I'd set out to do, and that was to drive him away. Use his old wounds as new weapons. It had killed me to do it—another little piece of myself broken off and given to my father—but it was the only way to protect Xander, even if he hated me for it. It was the only way to keep my dad from slamming his heavy mallet of money and influence down on them. If I stayed quiet and did what he wanted…

But I had to hope Xander heard my warning to get his father somewhere safe.

At six o'clock, I showered and changed into a little black dress. My prom dress was still on my bed; I hadn't put it away. I couldn't stand the thought of shutting it up in the closet, never to be worn. Not yet.

I did my hair, applied my makeup, and came downstairs, where my father was signing for a flower delivery. He spotted me and his eyes lit up.

"Emery, you look beautiful."

He kissed my cheek, smiling. Proud. I had the terrible thought that it was safer here when he was happy. Xander was safe. And his dad. Maybe I would be too, if I went back to how it had been these past few years. Things had been simpler then, before Xander. Before I loved him.

But I've always loved him…

My mother appeared at the top of the stairs wearing a silk robe, her hair mussed as if she'd just woken up.

"Cassandra, the Harringtons will be here in twenty minutes," my father said. "Get dressed, for God's sake." He turned to me and took my hands in his. "Emery, tonight is very important."

"Okay. Why?"

"The Senator and I are close to a deal that could mean hundreds of millions more to our bottom line. It's imperative that he leave tonight with a favorable view. To that end, I want you to keep an open mind."

"About?"

"Colton has asked for my blessing to court you."

"To *court* me?"

"Yes. With an eye toward marriage. I thought that very old-fashioned and gentlemanly of him."

"And you said yes," I murmured, my hands going cold. "Colton can court me and someday we'll get married."

"Let's not jump to conclusions, Emery," my father said, exasperated. "It's a wonderful gesture and a lovely way to get to know him."

I stared, incredulous, as alarm bells sounded in my heart. "I'm already married," I blurted.

My father's expression darkened. "We're not to talk about that to the Harringtons. Not one word, do you understand? That was a foolish, impulsive thing you did, and we're going to undo it next week."

My gaze drifted to our front door.

Why? Expecting Xander to bust through it on a white horse and rescue you?

No one was coming. I was trapped in this quagmire and would either drown or haul myself out. Fear gripped me. Paralyzed me. I couldn't stay but leaving meant exile. Danger to Xander. I'd stood frozen for what felt like forever when my mother called me from the top of the stairs.

"Emery, can you help me with my dress?"

I nodded absently and followed her into her bedroom, which had once been a large guest room. She'd taken it over after Grant died, and it had become another room Jack and I rarely ventured into. It was dim, the curtains closed, the bed unmade. Prescription medication bottles and wine glasses littered the nightstand, and the air was tinged with perfume and stale wine.

"Please, sit."

I sat on the edge of the bed and watched her go to her closet. She came back with a small wooden box—blond oak with flowers carved into the top. She sat beside me, the box in her lap, grief etched on her face and fear in her eyes. I felt tension in her thin body like an electric current.

"I'm sorry, Emery. I'm sorry so for many things… hundreds of things, going back years. I failed all my children, Grant especially." Her breath shook. "I failed him in the worst, most final way."

I stared, hearing my brother's name on her lips for the first time since he died.

"And I failed you." She turned to me, her eyes red-rimmed and shining. "When you were born, I felt like I could see the future—your father's plans, even if I didn't know the details. I tried to protect you because you were this ball of sunshine and joy. You loved to dance and hugged every stranger. I'd been like that once too, before I married your father."

"Mom, why are you telling me this?"

"Because Emery, your happiness, your joy…it was almost too beautiful to witness. So when these arrived for you, I hid them away."

My mother opened the box. A small sound escaped me. Inside was a stack of torn-open letters, bound with string. She placed them in my lap. Tears filled my eyes as I read my name in neat, boyish handwriting, and my fingers trembled as I pulled the first letter from its envelope.

Dear Emery,

Hello! This is Xander. We met at the park two days ago, and I wanted to write right away so that you know that I remembered your address and so you don't think I've forgotten you…

A sob tore out of me. I rifled through the envelopes—there were at least thirty—my name and address on the front written in neater and more precise handwriting as Xander grew older.

I whipped my head up, tears streaming, to see my mother's eyes spilling over too.

"You had them this whole time?" I choked.

She nodded. "I knew—from the very first letter—that this boy was special. Whoever he was, you had connected very deeply. Even after the terrible news about Grant, you had a different kind of happiness glowing in you, and it broke my heart to hear you ask your father if you had any mail."

I shook my head, shielding the letters from my tears. "God, Mom. I wanted these so bad. Why did you keep them from me?"

"I became certain you and Xander had something precious your father would destroy. He would crush your happiness. I couldn't stand the thought of him ruining whatever might happen with you and this boy. Because he would. I thought if I ended it quickly and silently, it wouldn't hurt you so much. But when you began dating Tucker Hill, I knew I'd made a terrible mistake." She glanced at the letters in my hand. "I almost threw them away, but I couldn't absolve myself by pretending they never existed. And then Xander came back."

I nodded, remembering seeing him on the Academy stairs in September. How my heart suddenly felt like it was beating again.

"He came back, and you came back to life," Mom said. "Your light was so bright, Emery..." She took a shaky breath. "I failed to protect Grant—I'll never forgive myself for that. Then Jack left, and I watched it happen as if I were outside myself. Now that man and his terrible son are coming, and I can't let your father steal your light too."

"Why is he like this?" I whispered. "What happened to him?"

"There was no love in his childhood home. Your grandfather taught Grayson that winning at any cost was the only way to stay safe. To be strong. Then Grant died, and any humanity your father had left died too. Because losing a child cuts into your soul, and he couldn't face the grief or the mistakes he'd made along the way." She took my hand. "I failed to protect my sons, but I won't fail you, not anymore. These letters are to remind you of who you are, how loved you are, and why you must preserve your generous heart, Emery. It's the best gift you can give the world."

"I'm scared."

"I know. I wish I could help you but I—"

"But you're trapped too."

She nodded. "It's no more than I deserve."

"Mom, no—"

"What is going on here?"

My father stood at the door, his hard eyes going between me and my mother. I looked down at the stack of letters and then held them to my heart. I inhaled deeply, as if I could absorb Xander's words and fortify myself with them. I loved him with all my heart. Great, infinite waves that could never die.

I stood up and faced my father. "I'm leaving."

He gave a start. "Nonsense. The Harringtons will be here any minute. Colton will want to—"

"*I'm leaving*," I said, louder. "I'm sorry to wreck your plans, but I'm not staying in this house a minute more."

"Don't be ridiculous." Dad stopped, finally understanding. "Leaving for what? That boy? Your *husband*? He's not even here. He abandoned you. One little threat, that's all it took for him to go running—"

"It doesn't matter. I'm doing this for me."

"Tonight? Alone and out in the cold? Because that's exactly where you'll be if you walk out this door. You'll have nothing."

"That's not true," I said. "I'll have me."

My dad stuttered, impotent with rage. He leveled a finger at my mother. "What did you tell her?"

"The truth," my mother said. "I am living the life you want for her, and I will not condemn her to it."

"*Condemn*," my father spat. "Condemn her to decades of luxury, free of want and worry for the rest of her life?"

"I want more than that," I said. "I *am* more than that."

"And where will you go? You'll take nothing from this house."

"I don't need or want anything from you ever again."

My father trembled with fury, but I could see the fear in his eyes too. Fear for the hundreds of millions he stood to lose, and not one thought spared for his children.

"All three of us, Daddy," I said. "You've lost all three of us, and you still don't get it." I turned to my mother. "Come on, Mom. You can leave too."

She shook her head. "Grant isn't coming back."

"But, Mom—"

"Go, Emery. It's your time."

I clutched Xander's letters to my chest. My father stood in the door, not quite blocking the way but enough. My heart pounded and my breath wouldn't go past my throat, but I took a step. Then another, until I was nearly past him.

He grabbed my arm, like a snake striking, his fingers digging into my flesh. "I'm not let you do this. I refuse—"

"You don't have a say. I know you hate that, but there's nothing you can do." I shook my head. "Some part of me will always love you. But mostly, I just feel sorry for you."

His eyes flared, and then his free hand whipped up and lit my cheek on fire with the sudden, stinging pain of a slap. I turned my head back to stare at him, my face aflame.

And then I slapped him back.

The shock of it, more than the pain, stunned him. His fingers around my arm loosened, and I broke free.

"Goodbye, Daddy," I whispered.

I twisted out of his grip and then I ran. Down the stairs and out the front door. Nowhere to go, no money, no idea what came next. The Harringtons' black sedan was pulling into the drive, and an exhilarated laugh burst out of me. I must've looked like I was running from a fire, running in a dress and heels, with only a stack of letters to my name.

That's all I need.

Night was falling. I ran until I couldn't, and then I walked until I found myself at Brenton Park. The anvil-shaped rock was still there. I sat down, nerves humming, my lungs sucking in the deepest, cleanest breaths of my life, and I read every single one of Xander's letters.

In them, he told me about his life at Langdon School, his worry for his father, and complicated physics questions that fascinated him—as if I were an equal who might understand.

And in each letter, he wondered if I might write back. At first, with curiosity and politeness, then with more and more hurt and confusion as his letters went unanswered.

Under the light of the lone lamppost, I read Xander's words and cried so hard, at times I could hardly see the pages. And then I reached the end. Xander, now fifteen years old, had written to me for the last time.

Dear Emery,

At this point, it's self-flagellation—a kind of sweet torture—to keep writing with no expectation of hearing back. Something has prevented you from receiving my letters, or you have chosen to send them straight to the trash pile. Whatever the reason, I have come to the end of my own capacity for hope.

This will be my last letter.

And because it's my last letter, I feel compelled to write down, in black and white, what I've been too cowardly to express all this time, and that is to say that I love you.

It makes no sense. We were children when we met. We only had a handful of minutes. Scientifically, there is no justification for why I should feel like I do. It is not my nature to romanticize my way into loving a stranger, and it doesn't seem possible that my bitter heart crafted these feelings from scratch. At first, I wondered if it was the comfort you gave me (which was quite a lot). Of all the kids at the park that evening, you chose to sit with the sad boy who'd lost his mother. You made me feel less alone at a time when I had never felt lonelier.

But it's not gratitude for your compassion that compels me to love you. Instead, I worry that it's something unexplainable. Something fantastical or magical that I can't sort out, even with my "genius" brain working overtime. I have no rational explanation.

Nevertheless, I am in love with you. Irrevocably. Some part of me recognized a part of you that day—as if I had found a missing piece of myself. But I have lost it again, so I have to stop writing now, though I'm quite sure I'll never stop loving you.

I hope that your life is full of beauty and joy—as much as you are yourself—and I hope, too, that you somehow know I kept my promise.

I did not forget you.
I never could. I never will.
I will love you forever.

Yours,
Xander

A sob tore out of me. I held the letter to my heart and cried tears of joy that this boy loved me, and I loved him. No matter what happened next, I knew I was going to be okay because my heart was intact. I was alive in the world but fully myself, and that was all that mattered.

I heaved several deep, shaking breaths. My phone was at the house. I had no way to call anyone. Nothing to do but start walking.

"Emery?"

My head whipped up. Xander stood in the yellow glow of the lamp in his usual jeans and jacket. His eyes behind his glasses, red and shining.

"Emery," he said again, his voice a croak. "What happened? I went by your house, and Belinda said you'd left. That you ran out the door."

"I did. I had to. He was going to try to marry me off to that creep." I held his letters tightly to me. "What are you doing here?"

"I was looking for you. I—" Xander hung his head. "My dad isn't doing well. I don't think he's going to… be around much longer. I'm going to sell the house to help pay for the home, but anything after that, I'm giving to you. And the tutoring money. I still have it. I'll give that to you too, so you can make a fresh start in California—"

I tore off the rock, letters fluttering to the ground, and threw my arms around him. I buried my face in the warm skin of his neck.

I'll never let go…

"How are you forgiving me?" he asked against my hair.

"Forgiving you?"

"You were trying to save me. To push me away to keep me safe, and, like a fool, I took the bait. I left you. Now you're out here in the dark, alone…"

"I had to do it alone. I had to walk away with no hope or promise that anything could save me but me." I pulled away to hold his face. "You were exactly where you needed to be. With your father, right?"

He nodded. "He's safe now. In Boston. They can give him the care I can't."

"You did so good for so long, Xander."

His gaze was soft and warm...then sharpened on the left side of my face. "Emery..."

"I'm okay."

"He hit you."

"Yes, but I hit him back," I said, my voice watery. "It was terrible and awful but kind of freeing too. Like something breaking between us forever."

Xander's mouth was drawn down in anger and he pulled me to him again, holding me fiercely. "I'm so sorry you had to go through that."

"I have something to show you." I led him by the hand to our rock and swept up the letters. "Look."

He slowly took them from me. "How...? Where...?"

"My mother had them. All this time. She thought she was protecting me, as if she could stop me from loving you, somehow. She was wrong."

Xander sat down on the rock and I sat beside him. "Did you...?"

I nodded, tears in my eyes. "I read every single one, and they're so beautiful, Xander. It hurt to see how much it hurt you to hear nothing back, but you still said you loved me."

He looked to me. "I always will."

I smiled, my tears spilling over. "Can you kiss me now? I could really use a kiss."

Xander cupped my face in his hands and brought his lips to mine. My eyes fell shut as the purest relief and love infused me. His mouth was warm and soft, and I opened mine to let him in. His gentle tongue tasted every part of me. And I kissed him back, his own taste and scent so familiar now, seemingly made just for me.

His lips retreated, but he kept holding my face, his eyes drinking me in. "Sometimes I can't believe you're real."

"I'm right here."

"And I'm not letting you go again."

"Good thing, seeing as how we're legally bound in holy matrimony," I teased, happiness coming out of my pores.

He smiled but his gaze was intent as he glanced at his watch. "We still have time."

"For what?"

"Prom."

I gave a little laugh. "Are you being serious? No…it's too late."

"It's not too late. It's not even eight. We can make it." He pulled me in close for a moment. "You are so brave, Emery. You did an amazing thing tonight. You deserve to be celebrated." He took my hand and helped me off our rock, then stopped. "Wait, your dress."

"It's at my house." I glanced down at the black cocktail dress I was wearing. "The theme is Black-and-White Ball. This isn't a ballgown, but it works."

"You bought that dress with your own money. You should be able to take what's yours."

"He won't let me take it," I said. "And going back…?"

"I'll get it. You don't have to step one foot in there."

"But Xander, the Harringtons are there. And my dad will call the police, or I don't know what."

"I don't care."

"It would be the worst capper to this night if you got arrested for trespassing. But I can go in," I said, contemplating. "There's something else I want to get. It's important, actually. I'll sneak in through the kitchen. Belinda will help."

"No, Em, wait." Xander was shaking his head. "I didn't think this through. It's a bad idea. You look beautiful just as you are. I can't let you walk back into the lion's den."

"I want to do this," I said. "Grayson can't lock me in, and he won't want to cause a scene in front of the Harringtons. It'll be okay. More than okay. Because I know I can leave." I smiled sadly. "The cell door was locked from the inside the whole time." I kissed Xander's dubious expression. "I want the dress, but there's something I need more."

Reluctantly, Xander drove me back to the house. I thought I'd be scared, but I wasn't the same girl who'd walked out earlier that night. My father had been a monster in my mind but was only a small, petty man in reality. And I was only taking what was mine.

And one more thing. An artifact...

"Oh, Miss Emery!" Belinda whispered when we knocked at the side door. "I'm so happy to see you." She glanced at Xander behind me, tears in her eyes. "Oh, sweet boy, you found her."

I hugged her tight. "I'm just grabbing a few things. Where are they?"

"In the study," she said, letting us in. "Mr. Wallace is entertaining the senator and his family."

"Business as usual," I said. "I'll be right back."

"I'll be right here," Xander said.

The kitchen was on the opposite side of the foyer from the study, and the study door was closed. I could hear voices on the other side. The clink of cocktail glasses. I wondered what my father had told the Harringtons about my whereabouts but decided it didn't matter. Nothing he thought would matter ever again.

What I did not count on was for Colin to be posted at the front door.

I'd started up the stairs when I heard his deep voice behind me. "Miss Emery."

I froze and turned. I had never really considered Colin, who was Dad's bodyguard as much as his driver, a threat until now. He was in his mid-forties and stood over six feet tall. His steel blue eyes bored into mine.

"I'm just grabbing something that belongs to me."

"I'll just have to check with your father." Colin didn't take his gaze off me. "*Mr. Wallace*," he called in a deep, commanding tone.

My father emerged from the study. He saw me and quickly closed the door behind him. "Have you come to your senses, then?"

"I'm just getting something that belongs to me, and then you'll never see me again."

"That is not how this works. You're either here or you're not." Dad gave a nod. "Colin."

Colin strode toward me, and for a second, I was torn between running up the stairs or running back the way I'd come. My hesitation gave Colin an opening. He clamped a hand on my arm, his grip like a vise.

"Let go of me!" I shouted. "Let…go!"

Suddenly, Xander was there, prying Colin's fingers off my arm and giving him a rough shove backward, making him stumble. Then Xander moved to stand between us and spoke in a low, dangerous tone that I'd never heard before. "Touch my wife again and I'll break your fingers."

My wife…

Xander crossed his arms, his feet planted firmly in place at the bottom of the stairs, like a sentry standing guard. Without looking at me, he said, "Go get your dress."

"Don't move, Emery, or I'll have him arrested," Grayson said. "I'll have Calloway sue you for defamation. For trying to blame his son for your degenerate friend's drug overdose."

Xander tensed but said nothing.

"Do you hear me, boy? Get out of my house. Colin?"

Colin lunged forward, gripping Xander by the jacket with both hands.

"No! Stop it!" I tried to push between them. "Don't touch him!"

The study door opened. "Grayson? What on earth…?"

My mother and the Harringtons poured out of the study. Upon seeing them, Xander froze. He broke away from Colin with a hard jolt and stared, the blood draining from his face.

Mrs. Harrington stared back, white as a sheet. The entire room stilled as the very air seemed to tense and crackle.

Xander took a shaking breath. "Mom?"

I gasped. Shar Harrington was wearing the exact same expression on her face as Xander. Her son. I could see the resemblance now—most notably in her rich brown eyes that matched Xander's left.

"Mom?" Xander said again, his brows furrowed as if he were trying to work out the solution to a problem that had plagued him his entire life.

Charles looked between them, studying the resemblance. "Shar?"

She stared a moment more, then shook her head. "I-I don't know what he's talking about."

"What is going on here?" Grayson demanded.

"N-nothing," Mrs. Harrington stammered. "There's been a mistake."

"A mistake," Xander repeated, his jaw working.

Colton narrowed his eyes. "Why is this guy saying you're his mother?"

"Because she is," Xander said. "Shar, now? It was Sharon. Sharon Ford."

Mrs. Harrington scoffed. "I don't know what this is about, but I will not stand for it another minute." She gave Xander a final, lingering glance and then strode out the door.

Charles Harrington turned on my father. "I don't know what kind of madhouse you're running here, Grayson, but this is unacceptable. Come on, Colton."

Colton gave us a parting sneer, and then they were gone.

Xander stared after her—his mother, after all this time—and my heart broke.

"Go to her," I whispered to him from the step behind. "Talk to her and…and get some answers."

Xander inhaled and let it out slowly. "No. I'm not leaving you." He glanced from my dad to Colin. "I'm not leaving you with them ever again."

"But, Xander…"

"Emery." He turned, his expression a mix of heartbreak and love. "Go get your dress. I'll be right here."

Tears flooded my eyes for the hundredth time that night. I ran up the stairs to my room and grabbed my dress that was still on the bed on its hanger. Then I ran to Grant's room and plucked *A Prayer for Owen Meany* from his bookshelf and hugged it to my chest.

"Come on, Grant," I whispered. "We're getting out of here."

Leaving his door wide open, I ran back down the stairs.

No one had moved. Colin seemed to be waiting for orders. Grayson gaped at the open front door. My mother smiled at me, and I hugged her as best I could with my dress tucked under my arm.

"It's not too late," I whispered. "It's never too late."

"Maybe. Someday," she said. "Go."

Then I took Xander's hand, and we walked past my father out the front door.

Chapter 39

EMERY

Xander drove in silence back to his house. He pulled the car into the drive and sat for a long moment, gripping the wheel.

My throat felt thick. "Xander…"

"A thousand times, I imagined what it would be like if I saw my mother again," he said gruffly. "A universe of possibilities for how she might react or what she would say. In some scenarios, she was sad and remorseful. In others—when I was feeling angry and vengeful—she was broken, pleading to come back on her hands and knees. I even imagined some where she was cool and indifferent. But not once did I imagine she'd deny I was her son."

He bowed his head, and I scooted closer in the front seat, put my arms around his shaking shoulders. "I'm so sorry. We shouldn't have gone back."

"No, I'm glad we did." He took off his glasses and wiped his eyes in the crook of his arm. "For you and for me. I needed to know and now I know. The mystery is solved. Like getting the letters back. We can't change what happened, but there's tremendous relief in closing the circle, once and for all…"

I nodded. "I know."

He touched his fingers to my chin. "Come on. We're running out of time."

"Are you sure you want to do this?" I asked softly. "Xander, we don't have to go."

"Yes, we do," he said. "We absolutely do. I can't think of a better way to end this night than spending it with you, surrounded by your creativity. I'm sure you made that place more beautiful than it's ever been."

"Only if this is what you want."

"It's exactly what I want. But what about you, Em? Are you okay?"

I smiled. "I'm sure it hasn't hit me yet. But I know in my heart I did the right thing, even if it hurts. And that counts for a lot."

Inside, the house was dark and empty. I waited in Xander's room while he changed, then I went to the bathroom to change into my white dress. I had no makeup—I'd cried it all off—and my hair hung limply around my shoulders, but when I stepped out of the bathroom, Xander's hand went to his heart.

"I've never seen anything more beautiful than you," he said, slipping a corsage over my wrist.

"Thank you," I said. "And Xander, you're…"

He was simply devastating with his hair slicked back and the black tux fitting his lean, muscled form to perfection. I was overcome with a sense of pride that he was mine.

"We have to hurry," he said. "Let me put my contacts in."

"Why?"

He stopped. "I thought you would want me to."

"Absolutely not. I love you just as you are: my super genius in an athlete's body." I heaved a sigh. "It's a lot to deal with, but I'm doing my best."

He chuckled. "If you insist."

We drove to the country club and pulled up to the valet. Xander tensed beside me. "The Buick isn't quite a stretch limo…"

"I don't want a limo. Everything is perfect." I raised a brow. "And maybe I should remind you that as of tonight, I own literally nothing but this dress, a book, and a stack of letters. I'm not in a position to be picky about transportation."

He laughed and regarded me. "You're radiant."

I kissed him softly. "That's because I'm so happy."

It was a little after nine o'clock when we stepped through the front doors. I tucked my hand in the crook of Xander's elbow, his left hand covering mine. He stopped short when we stepped inside. The prom was still in full swing with Academy students dressed in their finest. I watched Xander, my heart in my throat as he took in the decor: the black balloons that looked like glass orbs, the clear lighted balls that bobbed between tables set with elaborate centerpieces.

"Jesus, Emery," he said. "I knew it would be amazing. I couldn't have imagined this."

"Turned out pretty good, I think."

"Good?" He gazed down at me and started to speak, but I shook my head.

"How you're looking at me right now…like you really see me? That's the best compliment. That's all I've ever wanted."

"I see you Emery," he said. "And I pity anyone who can't."

I reached up to touch his cheek. "I feel sorry for your mom. What a treasure she had that she let slip through her fingers."

Xander cleared his throat and blinked hard. "Will you dance with me?"

"I'd love to."

We made it exactly three steps.

"Emery! Xander! Oh my God!"

Delilah, in a black dress, raced at me and engulfed me in a hug. "You look so beautiful! And Xander…" She hugged him too. "I'm so glad you made it. You told me that you weren't going to make it, and I was so sad. But now I'm so glad! I mean, look at it, Em! Come see the centerpieces in this light…"

"Wait," I said. "I don't have a phone. Is Harper here? Have you heard from her?"

"She was here earlier. Just to see, she said. Haven't seen her since. Orion's not here either…" Delilah shook her head. "Nope, I am done gossiping. Come on. We have to tell everyone you're here."

"No, we don't—"

Delilah led us through the ballroom, past the drink and food stations, to the crowded dance floor. Tucker and Elowen were wrapped in each other's arms, his hand on her ass, a satisfied smile on her face.

Delilah ran ahead to the DJ booth and the music suddenly stopped.

"Everybody, everybody," she said into the microphone. "I just want to interrupt really quick to say, on behalf of the prom committee, welcome to your senior prom!"

The room broke out in cheers and applause, and once the crowd quieted, she said, "I'd also like to recognize Emery Wallace, whose vision and artistry made all of this possible!"

"Oh, Delilah," I murmured as the room erupted again, everyone turning their smiling faces toward me and Xander.

"Soak it up," Xander said in my ear. "You made this happen for them."

Delilah relinquished the mic and then "She Will Be Loved" played over the sound system. Couples moved together, and Xander took my hand and held it against his heart, his other wrapping around my waist and pulling me close. He drew me into his space, his warmth, and the hard, protective strength of his body. He was my sanctuary, a place where I knew I'd be safe forever and where he would be safe with me. After all his hurts, he trusted me with his heart, and I vowed to keep it close to mine, always.

"It's been quite an eventful evening," I said.

He sniffed a laugh. "You can say that again."

I glanced up at him. "You called me your wife tonight."

"Yeah, sorry about that. It just slipped out."

"Don't be sorry," I said. "There's no use fighting what we are to each other, right?"

He shook his head. "And I don't want to anyway."

"Neither do I."

He brought his hand to my face, his thumb brushing over my lips. "I love you, Emery. You make me believe in magic."

I smiled, my heart full. "I love you, Xander. In this universe and in all the rest."

———

When prom was over, we went home to Xander's place.

"This is your house now too," he said fiercely. "Whatever I have is yours. Whatever happens to you, happens to me."

In his room, I stood with my back to him while he unzipped my dress. It fell in a puddle at my feet, and then he unhooked my bra and let that fall, too. He took off his clothes, down to his boxers, and the gravity of the night hit us at the same time, pulling us down with exhaustion. Xander stood for a moment, his skin warm against mine, his hands touching my cheek.

That's my husband, I thought, the purest joy sweeping through me. We then lay down together, kissing and holding each other. I took his glasses off and set them on the nightstand, then tangled my fingers in his hair.

"My beautiful boy with the mismatched eyes," I murmured.

He kissed me. "Forever and always."

My heart sang because I knew in that moment that as long as I was with Xander, I was home.

Chapter 40

XANDER

JULY

Cassidy's was bustling with the tail end of an afternoon lunch rush. I watched Emery glide between tables, her arms laden with food, talking and laughing with her customers. Her financial aid package had come in, but as soon as school ended, she began working at the diner, making her own money. I'd never seen her happier.

Across from me, Harper sipped her chocolate shake. She'd left town for a few weeks after graduation, but in typical Harper fashion, she hadn't given us many details. She looked happy, though, and that made me happy.

"It's been quite a year, hasn't it?" Harper said.

I nodded. "Yes, yes it has."

"And quite a summer. I need to get caught up." Harper raised her brows. "So. California?"

"It seems that way," I said with a smile, watching Emery laugh with one of her patrons.

In three days, she and I would drive west to California, where Emery would attend UCLA and I'd go to Caltech for my doctorate. It wasn't the life I'd meticulously planned, but Dean had been right—good things had a way of working themselves out.

Harper's voice turned gentle. "Emery told me about your mom. Are you okay?"

I toyed with my coffee mug. Seeing my mother after nearly eight years felt like being punched in the face, stomach, and heart, all at the same time. A ghost from my past had reappeared right in front of me, then vanished all over again.

"I have some closure," I told Harper. "Maybe not the kind I wanted, but the kind I expected."

"I'm so sorry." She gave my hand a squeeze. "Do you ever think about reaching out to her? Now that you know her secret identity?"

"No," I said. "She made it clear she's closed that chapter in her life, so I will too."

It sounded so simple to say it, but the emotions involved were too complex for a loud diner at lunch rush. I couldn't move on, but I could move through, and that had to be enough for now.

Emery scooted into the booth beside me. "Last check is dropped." She slung her arm around my neck and planted a long kiss on my cheek, lingering there, then gazing at me as if she hadn't seen me in weeks.

"Girl," Harper said, rolling her eyes.

"I can't help it," Emery said. "Look at his face."

I took a sip of cold water. All it took was one touch or one kiss from Emery, and my blood heated. We'd spent many afternoons in my house—our house—wrapped up in each other, sweaty and curled around each other...

Emery turned her high-wattage smile on her friend. "Harper, did Xander tell you about his offer from Caltech?"

"No," she said, giving me a look. "I'm still getting caught up, but he's also ridiculously modest. Tell me."

Emery was practically bouncing out of her chair. "Apparently, Caltech and MIT have this huge rivalry. Like, legendary. When Caltech found out that Xander wanted to turn down MIT's offer, Caltech lost its mind. They offered him a full scholarship, plus a living stipend and married couples' housing on campus."

"Congratulations," Harper said. "Though I'm not surprised. I *am* surprised that you guys are finally admitting that you're married."

"We'll just be living together," Emery said, unable to keep from beaming. "But also, completely and utterly legally bound to each other."

I laughed. Emery and I had made a plan—another set of vows—to not refer to ourselves as married or use matrimonial language like "wife" or "husband" for five years. To allow us time to be together, live together, and just enjoy being together without so much pressure, so young.

But we hadn't even left Rhode Island, and the five-year plan was already hanging by a thread. Emery had correctly identified us as entangled months ago. Entwined on a level that defied understanding. She was mine and I was hers, and no amount of postponing or pretending could change that.

Harper smiled mischievously. "You know who else went to Caltech?"

She and Emery burst out at the same time, "Sheldon Cooper!"

I rolled my eyes. "Here we go."

Emery kissed my cheek again. "Spoiler alert: Sheldon also won the Nobel Prize. Just saying." From inside her apron, her phone buzzed. She read the text and smiled. "It's Jack. He says he wishes he could be here to see us off, but he's stuck in New York City with his boyfriend and can't get make it." She tapped a response and put her phone away. "He's so happy, which makes me so happy."

"What about your mom?" Harper asked. "How's she doing?"

Emery's smile dimmed. Her mother had come to see her and Jack graduate, before Jack moved to New York, but it had been a short, tense visit. She smuggled Emery her phone and some of her belongings and rushed back home after.

"She's okay, I guess," Emery replied. "A little healthier, maybe, but still blaming herself for Grant. I don't know if she'll ever forgive herself. But I have to trust she'll do what she can when she's ready and give her all my love and support in the meantime."

"And not to bring up the bad shit, but what about your dad?" Harper asked. "Have you talked to him at all?"

"No," Emery said. "My therapist and I have decided that's a bad idea, to say the least. I'm learning to let go of my notion of what—and who—makes up a family. Someone once told me that if the actual family is hurtful or toxic or abusive…" She smiled wanly. "Then it's okay to make a better one."

I took Emery's hand in mine, my throat tight. From the outside, it had been so easy to see how terrible her home life had been, but it was all she'd known. And her loving heart wanted—more than anything—to keep everyone together and to try to make something beautiful out of something that was irrevocably broken. I'd never stop telling her how damn proud I was of her for working to heal while keeping her heart open.

I see you, Emery. I see all of you.

And as if she could hear my thoughts, she turned to me, eyes glistening. "Love you."

"Love you, Em."

Harper coughed. "Maybe I'll leave you…"

"No, stay!" Emery laughed, grabbing her hand. "I want to hear about you. For instance, where the hell have you been?"

Before Harper could say a word, Delilah Winslow slid into the booth, her dark eyes lit with conspiratorial excitement.

"Okay, I know—no more gossip, but this is kind of important. For you especially, Xander." She leaned in, drawing us all closer. "Apparently, RJ Calloway was making noise about suing anyone who accused Rhett of dealing drugs."

"Yes, I heard," I said darkly.

"But Sierra had a sit-down with the police a few days ago—apparently she knew more than we thought—and now the Calloways are settling out of court with Dean's family."

"Oh shit," Emery breathed. "Really?"

Delilah nodded. "Rhett pled no contest to some lesser charge, and they paid the Yearwoods an 'undisclosed' amount of money." She leaned in closer. "Sierra told me it's twenty million."

Harper and Emery looked shocked and relieved, but I felt sick. Since Dean's death, it had come out that the Yearwoods were on the brink of bankruptcy. Even homelessness. Dean had been keeping a 4.0 GPA, coxing for the crew, and working two jobs trying to keep them afloat. He'd been awarded a full scholarship to Yale and would've been premed, but the long hours and stress had gotten to him. Rhett had been supplying him with Adderall to keep up, but that night Dean had wanted something "fun." Rhett had obliged, but the pill had been unknowingly laced with fentanyl. One dose—one bad pill—and that's all it had taken to steal one of the best people away forever.

"I'm glad the Yearwoods don't have to struggle anymore," I said. "But Dean was worth more than twenty million. He was priceless."

The table grew quiet—an impromptu moment of silence for our friend—and then Delilah cleared her throat.

"I can't stay." She glanced between Harper and Emery. "We're still on for tomorrow night?"

"What's tomorrow night?" I asked.

"We're having a sleepover," Emery said. "A real, honest-to-God, girls-only sleepover."

"Em's never had one," Delilah said. "We can't let her leave without spending one night, braiding hair, eating junk, and talking about boys."

"Namely you," Emery said in my ear and kissed my cheek. "They're going to be so sick of me talking about how amazing you are."

"Too late," Harper said.

Emery's break ended, and I hugged the girls goodbye, Harper the longest.

"Take care of our Em, okay?" she whispered. "And let her take care of you."

"I'm going to miss you," I said gruffly. "You and Dean were my first real friends. Leaving you sort of feels like leaving him all over again."

"Grief is strange that way," she said. "I feel the same, now that you're going. But I'll be out to visit you soon. You're both stuck with me."

"We'd better be."

I waited in the parking lot until Emery came out, carrying a to-go back in her hand. She climbed into the Buick's passenger seat. "It'll be cold by the time we get there, but he loves the fries so much."

"He does." I leaned over and kissed her. "I love you so much."

"Me too," she said. "And if I haven't told you enough already, I'm so grateful that you're willing to move to California with me. I feel almost selfishly happy when MIT had been your dream…"

"I have a new dream," I said. "And it's better for him."

"Are you sure?"

"I'm sure."

We drove to Boston as the brilliant July sun was just starting to sink. At Willow Glen, Dad was in his chair by the window with a view of the gardens below. Emery went to him with her bag of food while I talked to his primary doctor. All the doubts I couldn't tell Emery, I said to him.

"Am I making a mistake?" I asked Dr. Wilbur. "Dad told me he wanted to stay. But…"

Dr. Wilbur smiled gently, his bald head gleaming in the hallway light. "Your father is in severe cognitive decline, Xander. Most days he doesn't know where he is at all. And while I know you want to grant him as much agency as you can, being with him is the best gift you can give. If that means taking him to California, then so be it."

The words were reassuring, but somewhere, below the damaged brain tissues and failing neurons, he was still himself. I hated to think I was doing something he didn't want or that I was abandoning his legacy by leaving MIT.

Dr. Wilbur read my skepticism. "Talk to him. Tell him how you feel, but I think being with you is more important than anything else." He smiled gently. "Your father is a kind man and very joyful. One of my favorite patients, if I'm being honest. I hate to see him go."

"And he's okay to make the trip?"

"He'll be fine. I promise."

I heaved a breath. "Thank you."

Inside the room, Emery had set up a tray for Dad and put the food in easy reach. He picked at fry, a smile on his lips. At this stage, he had difficulty speaking, and he was losing the ability to feed himself, too.

"Can I sit, Em? I need to tell him."

"Of course." She kissed my dad's cheek. "I'll get coffee."

I sat down in the chair she vacated. "Hey, Dad, I need to ask you something. It's pretty important."

His blue eyes—blue like one of mine—stared into the garden, seeing it but not taking it in.

"We're going to move to California. The three of us. Emery, me, and you. Emery is going to go to UCLA and I'm going to Caltech. They gave me quite a nice package. She and I are leaving in a few days, and once we're there, I'm going to find you a home close to us so we can see you all the time."

He said nothing, didn't react, and maybe it was my imagination, but it seemed like my words might have filtered in because he turned his head slightly to me.

"Einstein," he whispered, the name mangled but clear.

I smiled, tears pricking my eyes. "That's right. I'm going to take you to the Athenaeum at Caltech, where Einstein stayed in the 1930s. We're going to see where he worked and gave lectures. How does that sound?"

Dad's gaze went back to the garden, but I could have sworn he smiled at that.

I hadn't told him that I'd seen my mother at the Wallace house all those weeks ago. I didn't know how much—if anything—he could understand, but I knew she wasn't coming back. And part of what fueled my taking Dad to California was so he wouldn't have to sit and wait for someone who pretended he'd never been part of her life. He deserved more than that, and maybe I did too.

Emery came back. "Everything okay?"

I nodded. "It's just…a lot."

"I know."

She put her arms around me, and I let her love and light seep into me, comfort me. "I need a minute."

"Of course."

I went to the adjoining bathroom and set my glasses on the sink, then splashed cold water on my face. In the mirror's reflection, under the harsh fluorescent lighting, the color differentials in my eyes were stark. The blue very blue, and the brown very brown. One from him, one from her. Mom was part of my life, my history, and I'd hated seeing that fact staring at me in the face every time I looked in a mirror.

Emery had once told me it was conflicting forces inside me, which I'd dismissed with my usual scientific disdain. But as usual, she was right. Emery's explanations of life, the variability of it, added so much richness to my world. She was destiny, hope, and love to my science and skepticism. Without her generous heart, I'd have remained trapped behind my rigid walls of math and science, trying to keep myself safe from the unpredictability of life. I may have helped her escape her prison, but she unlocked the door to mine.

I stepped back into the room. Emery was in the chair beside my dad again, holding his hand and chatting with him about the light falling over the trees and giving names to the different colors of the sunset.

She had once jokingly said she'd solved the unified Theory of Everything, but I think she had. Like light, everyone was made up of both particles and waves. We thought ourselves to be individual pieces, bumping into each other, creating causes and effects in our own little spheres. But it was also true we belonged to a greater, infinite wave. Connected. Vital. The cosmos was so vast we couldn't comprehend it, but each one of us was integral to the whole at the same time.

And that idea, more than anything else, made me feel like I wasn't alone.

She gave that to me.

I gazed at Emery, thinking I had never loved anything more in my life.

She turned and smiled back at me. "I love you too."

Epilogue

EMERY, FIVE YEARS LATER

*The cosmos is within us.
We are made of star-stuff.
We are a way for the
universe to know itself.* ✧
—Carl Sagan

"We made it," I thought, smiling to myself. I tugged my silky robe tighter and sipped from my flute of champagne.

Not that I had any doubts, but our five-year plan had run its course, and now we were having a real wedding to replace the sad little ceremony we'd had in Providence. But we'd already been living in a real marriage for the past five years; there was no point in pretending this wasn't forever.

Harper, my maid of honor, sat beside me in the elegant, sun-filled bridal suite at the Storrier Sterns Japanese Garden in Pasadena, not far from our little apartment. Xander had wanted the venue.

"Because it reminds me of your room in your house in Castle Hill, with the cherry blossom tree you painted with your own hand," he'd said. "You made an oasis for yourself out of your artistry. I know the memories there weren't worth keeping, but I think it's important to honor that part of you, Emery. The part that never gave up."

As if it were possible to love him more…

I glanced around the bridal suite and wondered if it were possible to love anyone more than the women in the room, either.

"Are you nervous?" Harper asked, gorgeous in her emerald-green dress.

"About marrying Xander?" I teased. "Been there, done that."

She laughed. "I meant about returning to the east coast."

After I graduated UCLA armed with a degree in architectural and urban design and an interior design certificate I started my own business. I didn't have a storefront but worked remotely and already business was good. Xander graduated from Caltech with PhDs in quantum physics and astrophysics. Before the ink was dry on his diplomas, he was offered a position doing research with the Event Horizon Telescope in Massachusetts, which worked out of the Harvard-Smithsonian Center for Astrophysics, where he'd be teaching as an adjunct professor.

My business was mobile. I could do it from anywhere, so there was no way I could let him turn it down.

But I knew why Harper was asking. Massachusetts bumped elbows with Rhode Island, but I was no longer the scared girl I had been back in Castle Hill. I wasn't about to let old fears or pain stop either one of us from achieving our dreams. We'd both been working so hard, saving money for the move, and setting aside enough to throw a big wedding to celebrate us before a much-needed honeymoon in Costa Rica.

"I'm not nervous about that," I said, and smiled at my mother as she joined us. "I'll be closer to Mom now."

She smiled back, looking regal in her pale green, mother-of-the-bride dress. Her cheeks had more color, and she had more weight on her bones since divorcing my dad two years ago. She took him for half of everything he owned…not that it mattered. His business was booming, but he had no one to share it with. He sat on top of his mountain of gold alone.

To me, that was a fate worse than financial ruin.

"Em, isn't it time to put on your dress?" Delilah cooed from the other side of the bridal suite, where my simple but elegant dress was waiting. She stood with Christina and Chloe, my UCLA BFFs, and Alicia Alvarez.

After Ms. Alvarez was fired from Castle Hill Academy, she took another job in Virginia and quickly rose in the ranks to administrator. I don't think she ever belonged in a place like CHA. Or maybe they needed her more than they knew and had stupidly let her slip away.

She joined us and clinked her champagne flute to mine. "Put on that dress, sweetheart. We're all dying to see it."

"I will," I said. "I just want to take in this moment a little longer."

The women in my suite were my favorite people…but for my other favorite person across the hall, getting ready with his groomsmen: Orion, Kevin Huang, and his best buddies from Caltech: Quinton and Kieran. I loved all of Xander's friends as if they were my own brothers.

And Jack, my own brother.

He was one of Xander's groomsmen too.

I smiled. Today would've been perfect but for two missing pieces: Xander's father had passed away six months after we arrived in California. They'd been happy ones; he smiled a lot and seemed to enjoy himself when Xander had wheeled him through the Athenaeum, pointing out different Einstein artifacts. The light in his eyes had never been brighter.

Xander had taken his ashes to the Bend alone and scattered them in the bay.

"It was his favorite place," Xander had said. "He'll be close to Dean there."

Dean, of course, was the other missing piece. But the sun was brilliant on this June day, just as it had been at his funeral.

They're both still with us—little pieces of light that go on forever…

After more prodding from Delilah, I got up to put on my dress with Alicia's help.

"I'm so proud of you, Emery," she said. "And so very happy."

"None of this would've happened if you hadn't helped me, Ms. A. You gave me the courage."

She shook her head. "I didn't do anything. You walked through the door on your own."

"But you held it open for me." I put my arms around her. "Thank you."

She held me tight as a knock came at the door. Delilah answered.

"Xander! You can't see the bride before the wedding!"

I laughed while the ladies formed a barrier at the door.

"I know," Xander said. "I'm sorry to break tradition, but this is vitally important."

"It's okay," I said. "I'm not in my dress yet, and that's the bad-luck part, I think."

"Yes, that's the exception to the rule." Xander sounded mischievous. "Five minutes, that's all I need."

The ladies filed out and I tightened my robe around me. Xander was beautifully handsome in his tux, a yellow daffodil in his lapel that matched those in my bouquet.

"What are you up to?" I asked. "This is highly unorthodox."

"I know but we're doing this right today, aren't we? Making up for that terrible ceremony in Providence?"

"It wasn't all bad," I said with a smile. "Is now a good time to confess I've been calling you my husband in my mind and heart for the past five years?"

His grin softened. "What a coincidence. Because I've been calling you my wife since the day I sent that text offering to marry you."

"Oh, Xander…"

"But back to the matter at hand. That day in Providence, we had nothing. No dress. No real vows. And no ring."

"Well, it was kind of an emergency—" I gasped as

Xander went down on one knee and pulled a small black velvet box from his pocket. "What are you doing?"

"I don't want to skip any steps or leave anything undone," he said, his blue and brown eyes so intent on mine, so full of love. "I want to give you everything you deserve, Emery. And that's the entire damn world. Because that's what you've given me. You've shown me that life is so much more than the facts and the science I built it on. I think I somehow always knew that and that's why I kept looking to the stars. And then I found you."

"Xander…" I inhaled a shaky breath.

He opened the box to reveal a round-cut diamond solitaire with five little diamonds surrounding it. A star, glittering in the sunlight.

"Emery, will you marry me…within the next ten to fifteen minutes?"

A joyful laugh burst out of me. "Yes. Yes, Xander, I will marry you. Again. A million times."

He slipped the ring on my finger, and I kissed him with my entire heart and soul, this man who I've loved in a hundred lifetimes.

"You know what I think?" I said. "We meet in all universes, and we get married in every single one."

Xander smiled, brushing hair from my face. "I think you're right."

XANDER, THREE YEARS LATER

I stood before the whiteboard in one of the many lecture halls at Harvard. One half was covered in equations, the other in my crude rendition of a black hole—a black orb with a ring of light around it, like one of Saturn's rings—emitting little particles of radiation.

I should've hired Emery to draw this for me.

I smiled to myself as three hundred pairs of eyes—my Introduction to Astrophysics class—listened attentively. My "day job" that paid most of the bills while working at my dream job: researching black holes with the Event Horizon Telescope team.

But being surrounded by students who were as eager as me to unravel the mysteries of the cosmos was more rewarding than I thought possible.

"In 1974, Stephen Hawking offered his groundbreaking theory that reshaped our understanding of black holes. His 'Hawking radiation' suggests that black holes are not entirely black; instead, they emit faint radiation near the event horizon, which means black holes are actually decaying or breaking down over time. Lots of time. This leads to an information paradox. Can anyone tell me why?"

Hands went up. I picked a young woman in the front row.

"Because quantum mechanics says that information can't be destroyed. So if the black hole is breaking down, what happened to everything it sucked in?" she asked. "Where did all that light go?"

"Exactly," I said. "Where did all the light go?"

I paused, my thoughts going inexplicably to Dean

Yearwood. I smiled and was suddenly back in a shell with sunlight glinting off the water, an oar in my hands and my friend sitting in front of me, wearing that grin of his…

I cleared my throat and came back to the lecture hall.

"Hawking's theory suggests that even in a black hole, light can never be destroyed. No matter how dark things get, it's still with us. Always."

"Wow, Dr. Ford," one student said with a grin. "Almost sounds like you're not talking about science anymore."

I caught sight of Emery standing at the top of the lecture hall, leaning in the door.

"A wise woman once told me too much science and not enough imagination isn't good for the soul," I said, earning some laughs. I checked my watch. "Time's up. I'll see you all next week."

The students shuffled out. With my heart pounding, I strode up the walk of the huge lecture hall and met Emery at the door. I kissed her hello so I wouldn't blurt out the secret I'd been walking around with for a week.

"Wow, that was quite a greeting," she said when we broke our kiss. "Better be careful or else I'll want to tear your clothes off right here in front of all your students."

I felt heat climb up to my ears and she touched my cheek.

"I love how you blush, but I can't help it," she said. "You're just so sexy, the way you talk about radiation and paradoxes and…flux capacitors."

"Come again?"

She laughed. "I'll never understand how you can

simultaneously be one of the smartest people on the planet but still haven't seen *Back to the Future*."

"I'm still getting caught up. Why are you here? Not that I'm complaining."

"Oh, I have my reasons. You look very happy, by the way," she said, suddenly looking nervous. "You didn't hear…? I mean…"

"Hear what?"

"Nothing!" She took my hand, pulling me down the hallway, deeper into the Jefferson Building.

"The parking lot's the other way," I said. My good news wanted to burst out of me, but my wife's face when she saw it firsthand would be a million times better.

"In a second, in a second," Emery was saying. I noticed a group of my students behind me smiling and whispering.

"Where are we going?"

"Geez, so many questions, Alexander."

I chuckled, thinking back to that day so long ago when I sat on that rock while this beautiful girl peppered me with more questions than I've ever been asked in my entire life. More students had gathered, as well as faculty and colleagues of mine. A large crowd now walked behind us.

"What in the world is going on?"

We'd come to a *T* in the hallway. Emery was breathless now, her cheeks flushed. "Take off your glasses."

Before I could move, she took them off for me and put them in my hands, then craned up on her tiptoes to cover my eyes. "It's just around the corner."

"What is?" I asked, taking shuffling steps forward. "My birthday is still in November, right?"

A few more steps, and she let go of my eyes. "Xander, look."

I blinked, put my glasses back on, and looked up. Immediately, my gaze was flooded with tears and my heart felt too big for my chest.

"Emery…" I said gruffly. "Is this real?"

"It's real, baby. His legacy. It will never be forgotten. *He* will never be forgotten."

I nodded, holding her hand tightly. The entrance to the wing that led to the research labs now read Dr. Russell J. Ford Hall.

All around us, the crowd burst into applause and cheers that resonated down the halls. Beside me, Emery wasn't bothering to conceal her tears. One of my colleagues, Dr. Granger, the head of the physics department, was suddenly there, shaking my hand. "Congratulations, son."

I stared back. "How…?"

"Your father's work in photoelectron spectroscopy was groundbreaking and caused a chain reaction of further discoveries that we're still making to this day."

"I thought…I thought he'd been forgotten," I said, my voice wavering.

"Impossible," Dr. Granger said. "And if I may say, I think he'd be very proud of you."

I clenched my jaw, trying to hold it together. "I hope so." I glanced down at Emery. "How long has this been planned?"

"Months," she said, wiping her eyes. "And can we just appreciate for a second how hard it was for me to keep this a secret?"

I wrapped her in my arms and kissed the top of her head. "Thank you."

"This wasn't me. I had nothing to do with it—"

"Everything good in my life can be traced back to meeting you."

Her smile was radiant. "I feel the same. Because we're entangled. That's some science I understand."

"It's not science, it's magic," I said. "Come on. I want to show you something."

We drove through Cambridge in our newish car to a little two-bedroom Victorian house not too far from Harvard. It had a drafting room, filled with sunlight, that was perfect for Emery to run her design business from. We'd put an offer on it three weeks ago, but our realtor had said interest was high, and chances were slim.

I parked in front, and Emery's eyes widened. "Xander…" she said slowly. "Why are we here?"

"Because this morning, before my lecture, I picked these up." I fished the keys out of my jacket pocket and handed them to her. "It's all yours, baby."

"What? I…I thought we didn't have a shot. I thought there was a lot of interest."

"I think they liked you the most."

The owners had loved the house but had outgrown it. They'd wanted it to go to someone they felt would take care of it. So I'd written them a letter about Emery—who she was, and how she'd do more than take care of their house. Writing about my amazing wife was all it took.

Because it's impossible not to fall in love with her.

She glanced up at me. "Are you saying…?"

"Welcome home, Em."

"Oh my God!" She threw her arms around my neck, then scrambled out of the car and ran up the steps to the house. "My hands are shaking. I can't…"

I took the keys from her and unlocked the door. We stepped inside the cozy little house, empty now and in need of some light and life.

"Xander, I can't believe this…"

"Believe it, baby. I can't wait to see what you do with the place."

Emery's head whipped up to me. "What do you mean?"

"I mean what I said: It's all yours. To design and make it as beautiful as you want."

"You want me to design the whole thing?"

"Well, I can help with the handiwork, but yes," I said, chuckling. "Have at it. I trust you, and I know you're going to make it perfect."

"The things I'm going to do to this place…"

We moved through the living room, to the kitchen, to the guest bedroom, Emery's eyes already full of ideas.

I opened the door to the second bedroom and wrinkled my nose at the dust. "We should show our friends before and after photos of the guest room so they appreciate your hard work."

"Ummm, about that." Emery bit her lower lip, her eyes twinkling. "Our friends are going to have to sleep on the couch."

"Why is that?"

"Because this is the baby's room."

Now it was my turn to stare. "Emery…?"

"I took a test this morning…"

I was truly afraid I might pass out from all the joy this day was bringing. We'd been trying for a year to get pregnant and had started to worry. We'd been about to investigate fertility options despite our concerns that it'd be too expensive, but now…

"Are you sure?"

"I'm sure. You're going to be a daddy."

"Oh my God." I cupped her face in my hands. "And you're going to be a mom. The best mom."

She nodded. "We will be everything to this baby that we never had."

Emery was right. She would make a remarkable mother, and I'd do nothing but my best to be the most caring father for this baby that I was in love with already.

"I love you," I whispered. "So much."

"I love you, Xander." She gave a tearful laugh. "We came a long way, but we made it, didn't we?"

I nodded. "Yes, baby. We sure did."

The End

Read on for a peek at another emotional YA romance by Emma Scott, *The Girl in the Love Song*

I

Dear Diary,

The first thing you should know about me, since we're going to be friends, is that my name is Violet McNamara, and I'm thirteen years old. Today is my birthday, and you are one of my presents. Mom gave you to me because I'm on the "cusp of womanhood"—insert major eye roll—and said I might want to write down my emotions. She says they're bound to get "dramatic" at this age, and writing them out can help keep them from burrowing deep and then spewing out later.

That's ironic. Lately, she and Dad have been spewing out their dramatic emotions, screaming constantly at each other. Maybe.

> they need a diary too. Maybe that's what I'll get them for their anniversary next month. If they make it that far. I don't know what happened. We were all so happy, and then it started to dissolve, piece by piece.
>
> God, they're screaming right now. This house is huge, yet they fill it up with their rage. Where did it come from??? Makes my stomach feel weird, and I just want it to stop.
>
> Happy birthday to me.

I set my pen down and put my headphones on. Absofacto blared in my ears, drowning out Mom's and Dad's raised voices. A shattering of glass broke through my music. I flinched, my heart jumping in my chest, and a teardrop smeared the ink on my first diary entry. I carefully dabbed it away, turned up the music, and waited for the storm to pass.

> They're done now, but God, one of them smashed something. Mom probably. That's the second time that's happened. Things are getting worse. Just two weeks ago, they were still sleeping in the same bed, and now Mom's taken over the bedroom and Dad's in the den.
>
> Maybe it's a phase. Maybe if I work hard enough and make them proud of me, they'll be happy again, and everything can go back

to the way it was. I'm going to be a doctor. A surgeon. Someone who puts broken things back together. Maybe I'll start with them, ha ha.

Anyway, I don't want to write more about what's happening to this family. I'll write about something better. Namely, River Whitmore. <3

It's probably every cliché multiplied by a million to fill a diary with thoughts about boys, but I've had a crush on River since forever. But if you saw him, Diary, you'd understand. He's like a thirteen-year-old Henry Cavill, only not British. You can tell he's going to be big and muscular and sexy when he's older. (OMG I can't believe I wrote that!)

ANYWAY, his dad owns Whitmore's Auto Body shop, and River helps out there in the summer. When Dad takes the Jag in for any work, I tag along, even though I always clam up around River. Another cliché: the nerdy girl and the popular jock who doesn't know she exists. He's a star football player who's going to keep playing quarterback all through high school and then in college, or maybe he'll go straight to the NFL.

That's what his dad is always saying, anyway.

> As for me, UCSC is my dream school. Santa Cruz is so beautiful. I can't imagine living anywhere else. I'll eventually have to leave for med school, of course, which will be hard since specializing in general surgery means years of study. And a crap ton of student loan debt. But get this: for my last birthday, Mom and Dad said they'd pay for all of it!!!
>
> I was over-the-moon happy when they told me. Grateful beyond words and glad because I could stay close to them. Only now it feels like our happy life was temporary, and it's all falling apart. I don't know what happened to them. Something money-related, I think. (See? Money can really suck.)
>
> Anyway, I~

My pen scratched at the paper as a sudden silence jarred me. There was a trellis on the wall outside my second-story bedroom, and a bunch of frogs that lived in the leafy vines had just gone quiet. Sometimes, I'd imagine River Whitmore climbing the trellis to rescue me from my parents and their disintegrating marriage, but it would also make a perfect ladder for an intruder. I snapped off my desk lamp and sank back into the darkness of my room, breath held.

Slowly, the frogs started up again.

I pushed my glasses higher up on my nose and looked

out my window over the darkened Pogonip forest of redwood and oak that bordered our backyard, then leaned over my desk and peered down.

There was a kid. A boy.

He looked about my age, though it was hard to tell only by the light of the moon hanging fatly in the sky. He had longish brown hair, and his shoulders were hunched into a dark jacket. The boy paced a small circle in frustration, as if he'd come to a dead end—my house—and didn't know where else to go.

I glanced at my clock; it was nearly ten.

Why is he out here? Alone?

The boy slumped against the wall beneath me, next to one of the coiled hoses hanging off its faucet. The frogs went quiet again as he slid down to sit on his butt. He drew his legs up, dangled his wrists off his bent knees, and hung his head. I wondered if he was going to sleep like that.

I ran my tongue over my braces, thinking. Should I call Dad? The police? But that would get the boy in trouble, and he looked like he was already having a crappy day.

I lifted my window, and warm June air wafted in. Wood scraped wood, and the boy's head shot up. Moonlight fell over his face, and I sucked in a little breath.

He's beautiful.

What a random, silly thought. Boys aren't *beautiful*. None that I knew. Not even River, who was more dashingly handsome. Before I could debate this issue with myself further, the boy scrambled to his feet, ready to run.

"Wait, don't go!" I called in a hissing whisper, shocking

him and myself in the process. I don't know what prompted me to stop him or why. It just popped out, like I couldn't help myself. Like it'd be a mistake to let him go.

The boy stopped at the edge of the boundary where the path became forest. I lifted the sash higher so I could lean over and rest my arms on the sill.

"What are you doing out here?" I whisper-shouted.

"Nothing."

"You came out of the woods?"

"Yeah. So?"

"Well, it's trespassing for one. This is private property. You shouldn't be here."

They were always saying that on TV. Sounded good then.

The boy scowled. "You just told me not to go."

"Because I wondered what the heck you were doing. It's late."

"I was just…taking a walk."

"Where do you live?"

"Nowhere. I don't know. Someone's going to hear us."

"Nah. Our neighbors are pretty far." I sucked on my braces again. "But this whispering sucks. I'll come down."

"Why?"

"To talk better," I said and wondered if turning thirteen had magically erased some of my shyness.

Or maybe it's just this boy.

"You don't know me," he said. "I could be dangerous."

"Are you?"

He thought for a second. "Maybe."

I pursed my lips. "Are you going to hurt me if I come down there?"

"*No*," he said, irritated. "But you shouldn't be taking chances."

"Just stay put."

I was in my pajamas—leggings with a slouchy UCSC sweatshirt over them. I grabbed my Converse shoes from the closet of my super neat room and slipped them over my socks.

I stuck my head out the window again. The boy was still there.

"Be right down."

I sounded as if I climbed down the trellis on the regular. I wasn't the sneaking-out-at-night type of kid, but I was surprising myself right and left that night. I tucked my dark hair out of my way, climbed up onto my desk, and then stuck one foot out onto the ledge.

"Don't," the boy said from below. "You're gonna fall."

"I will not," I said and carefully found my grip on the inside of the window ledge with my hands while my right foot snaked out for a rung on the trellis.

"How do you know it'll hold?" the boy called up.

I had no idea if it would hold, but I'd already left the safety of the window ledge for the thinner, wooden crisscrosses of the trellis. I brushed vines out of my way and climbed slowly down, making sure to take my time, to find each foothold. Then I plopped to the ground and dusted my hands together.

"See? Stronger than it looks," I said.

The boy glowered. "You could've been hurt."

"Why do you care?"

"I...I don't. Just saying."

He jammed his hands in his jacket pockets and flipped a lock of hair out of his eyes. He had beautiful eyes—blue like topaz. Up close, I could see his jeans had holes in them and not because that was the style. His jacket was worn at the elbows, and his hiking boots were scuffed, the laces held together by knots. A ratty old blue backpack hung off his shoulders.

But he was even better looking than I imagined from that first glimpse, though in a totally different way than River. This boy had a softer face somehow. Still manly—I imagined he'd grow up to be very handsome. His eyebrows were thick but not too thick and looked perpetually knitted together with worry. He had a nice nose, and his mouth was pretty perfect. I actually had no idea what a "perfect" mouth looked like on a boy, except that this boy had one.

We stood for a few quiet moments, taking each other in. The boy's eyes swept over me, and I wondered if he was taking inventory of me the same way I had of him. Normally, I'd have been self-conscious about my glasses, my braces, and my boobs that were growing in faster than I was ready for. I had no feature that anyone would call perfect, yet somehow, it was okay to be standing there in the dark with him.

"So...I'm Violet."

"Miller."

"Miller is your first name?"

"Yeah. So?"

"It's usually a last name."

"Violet is usually a color."

"It's still a name."

Now that we weren't whispering, I noticed Miller's voice had pretty much already changed. Deepening but without that squeak to it, like poor Benji Pelcher, who sounded like he took hits off helium balloons. Miller had a nice voice. Low and kind of scratchy.

"Well?" Miller asked. "What do you want?"

I cocked my head at him. "You're awfully grouchy."

"Maybe I have a reason to be."

"Which is?"

"None of your business." He glanced around at the darkened forest behind him. "I should get back."

He said it with a kind of sadness. The giving-up kind. Like he would rather do anything other than go back.

So don't let him go.

I softened my tone. "Can you at least tell me what you're doing out here?"

"I told you. Taking a walk."

"In a dark forest at night? Do you live nearby? I've never seen you before."

"We just moved. Me and my mom."

"Cool. Then we're neighbors."

Miller jerked his chin at my house. "I don't live in a house like that."

The bitterness in his voice was so strong, I could practically taste it.

"Won't your mom worry you're out here?"

"She's at work."

"Oh."

I didn't know any parents who worked at night in my neighborhood, unless they were in tech like my dad. He spent late hours at his computer, but I doubted that Miller's mom was working late at InoDyne or one of the other big places near the university.

Most tech kids could afford shoelaces.

A silence fell, and Miller kicked at the dirt with his boot, hands still jammed in his jacket pockets, eyes on the ground, as if waiting for something to happen next. Frogs chirped, and the forest breathed behind him.

"So you're new here?"

He nodded.

"I go to Coastline Middle."

"I'll go there too."

"Cool. Maybe we'll have some of the same classes."

Maybe we can be friends.

"Maybe." He glanced up at my house, a longing expression on his face.

"Why do you keep staring at my house?"

"I'm not. It's just…big."

"It's all right." I slumped down against the wall like he had earlier.

He smirked and sat beside me. "What's wrong with it? Not enough butlers?"

"Ha ha. The house is fine. It was perfect, actually."

"And now it's not?"

"My parents aren't happy lately."

"Whose are?" Miller tossed a pebble into the dark.

"Yeah, but I mean, they're *a lot* unhappy. Like screaming matches and throwing things. Never mind." My cheeks burned. Why did I say that?

But Miller's eyes widened in alarm. "They throw things? At you?"

"No, it was just the one time," I said quickly. "Maybe twice, but that's it. No big deal." I cleared my throat. "All parents fight, right?"

"I wouldn't know. My dad died a few months ago," he said, looking away. "Just me and Mom now."

"Oh my God, I'm so sorry," I said softly. "That's got to be hard."

"What do you know about it?" Miller asked with sudden tightness in his voice. "At least you can live here. At least if your parents start shouting, you probably have a big cushy room to hide out in instead of…"

"Instead of what?"

"Nothing."

Another silence fell. Miller's stomach growled, and he quickly tried to cover up the sound by scuffing his boots.

He started to rise. "I gotta go."

But I didn't want him to go.

"Today is my birthday," I said.

Miller froze and then sat back down. "Yeah?"

"Yeah. I'm thirteen. You?"

"Fourteen in January. You had a big party, I suppose."

"No. My friend Shiloh and I saw a movie, and then my parents bought me a cake. I only ate one piece, and I don't think Mom and Dad had any. There's a lot left. Do you want some?"

Miller's narrow shoulders rose and fell.

"It's going to go to waste if we don't eat it," I said. "And there's nothing sadder than a birthday cake with only one piece cut out."

"I can think of a hundred things sadder," Miller said. "But yeah, I could eat some cake."

"Great." I got to my feet and swiped dirt off my butt. "Let's go."

"Into your house? What about your parents?"

"It's safe in my room. Dad sleeps in the den now. Mom will be in her room, but she never checks on me. Like, ever."

Miller frowned. "You're gonna let me hang out in your bedroom?"

I started to climb back up the trellis. "Yes. I never do anything I'm not supposed to, but today's my birthday, and they screamed at each other on my birthday, so here we are." I peered over my shoulder down to him. "Are you coming or not?"

"I guess."

"So come on."

I climbed back into my room, and Miller followed. I moved the lamp to make room for him as he crawled across my desk and gracefully jumped down.

"Now we know the trellis can hold both of us," I said.

Not sure why I felt that was important, except that something told me, even then, that this wasn't going to be the last time Miller came up to my room.

But having him there, up close and in the light of my desk lamp, my insides felt funny. A little bit scared, a little bit nervous, a little bit excited. He was taller than me by a few inches, and his blue eyes looked miles deep. Filled with thoughts and a heaviness I didn't see in any kid I knew, except maybe my best friend, Shiloh.

He saw me watching him and how my hands were clutched together in front of me.

"What?" he asked warily.

"I don't know," I said, pushing my glasses up and fidgeting with a lock of my black hair. "Now that you're up here, it's a little…different."

"I'm not going to steal anything. And I won't hurt you, Violet. I never would. But I'll go if you want."

"I don't want you to go."

Miller's brows unfurrowed for a moment, softening his entire face, and his bunched shoulders loosened.

"Okay," he said roughly. "I'll stay."

My heart squeezed with a little ache at how grateful he sounded. Like he wasn't used to being wanted around maybe.

He looked away from me—I was probably staring—to take in my impeccably neat room with its queen-size bed and white ruffled comforter. Bookshelves took up the wall facing the window, and posters of Michelle Obama, Ruth

Bader Ginsburg, and the soccer player Megan Rapinoe were on the others.

"Don't all girls cover their walls with movie or rock stars?"

"Yes, because *all* girls are exactly the same," I said with a grin. "These are my inspirations. Michelle reminds me to stay classy, Ruth keeps me honest, and Megan pushes me to do my best. I play soccer too."

"Cool." Miller's eyes widened, taking in my en suite bathroom. "You have your own bathroom? Wow. Okay." He gave his head a disbelieving shake. He looked almost mad.

"Okay, so, um, hang tight," I said. "I'll go get the cake."

I left Miller in my room and shut the door quietly behind me, then crept along the long hallway, passing guest rooms and bathrooms, toward the staircase. My nervousness tried to creep back in.

It's a little bit crazy to let a perfect stranger into our house. You know that, right?

But I was a straight-A student, and teachers were always telling me how smart I was, how I had a knack for remembering facts. And the fact was Miller had shown concern for my safety no less than three times in our short conversation. His grouchiness came from suspicion, like he couldn't figure out why I was being nice to him.

Because he's not used to people being nice to him. Or bedrooms with attached bathrooms.

In our huge, granite-and-stainless-steel kitchen, I took

the birthday cake box out of the fridge. The sound of Miller's growling stomach echoed in my head, so I filled a Trader Joe's shopping bag with paper plates, a bag of tortilla chips, a jar of salsa, two cans of Coke, forks, and napkins. I slung the bag on my shoulder, carried the cake box with both hands, and snuck back upstairs.

I fumbled my bedroom door open. Miller was gone.

"Crap." My shoulders slumped with disappointment that bit harder than I expected. Then I nearly dropped the cake box when Miller appeared from my walk-in closet.

"Wasn't sure if it was you," he said.

"I thought you bailed on me."

"Still here." He eyed my grocery bag, and his voice tightened. "What's all that?"

"Food. I've been studying all night—"

"You study in the summer?"

"Yes. I take high school prep classes. I'm going to be a doctor someday. A surgeon. That takes years of school and training, so I'm trying to get ahead."

"Oh. Cool."

"So I was studying, and it made me hungrier than I realized. It's not much. Just chips and salsa and soda. Plus birthday cake. Not exactly *Health Food Weekly*'s snacks of choice…"

Miller said nothing, and I sensed that he was too smart to fall for my thinly disguised charity. His hunger must've overcome his pride though, because he didn't argue but let me set up our small picnic on the floor, shielded by the bed should a parental unit walk in.

I sat against the wall while Miller sat perpendicular to me, against my bed, his long legs in front of him. I laid out the food, and we ate and talked about some of the kids at school he'd meet.

"The captain of the youth football team is the quarterback, River Whitmore," I said and immediately wished I hadn't made him my opener. My face flushed red. "Do you play football?"

"No."

"Um, yeah, so he's the quarterback."

"You said that already." Miller's sharp gaze slid to me then away. "You like him."

"*What?*" I practically shrieked, then lowered my voice. "No, I… Why do you think that?"

"Because of how you said his name. And your face got all red. Is he your boyfriend?"

"Hardly. I mean, look at me."

"I am looking at you."

And he did. His blue topaz eyes were on me, not just observing but *seeing* me. I felt as if the deepest secrets of my heart were painted all over my face. Warmth swept over my skin, and I had to look away.

"You know how it is," I said. "I'm a geek, and he's a football god. He doesn't know I exist. But we've been in school together since kindergarten and I… I don't know. I can't remember a time when I didn't have a crush on him." I smacked both hands to my cheeks. "I can't believe I just told you all that. Please *do not* tell anyone when school starts. I'll be mortified."

Miller looked away and reached for his soda. "I'll forget you even mentioned it."

"Right, so…anyway, you'll also meet Shiloh. She's super smart and sarcastic. And beautiful too. She looks a lot like Zoë Kravitz. She's my best friend. My *only* friend."

"I got none. You're doing all right."

"Yeah, but you just moved here. I've lived here my whole life." I brushed a lock of hair behind my ear. "But you and me—we're friends now, right? Let's exchange phone numbers! So we can text." I grabbed mine from off the bed. "Holy crap, it'll be so cool to get a text and not automatically know it's Shiloh."

"I don't have a cell phone," Miller said, brushing his hands off on his torn jeans, not looking at me.

"Oh. Wait, really?" I let my phone drop in my lap. "How do you survive?"

"If you have to live without something, you just do."

"I can't imagine it."

He scowled. "I'll bet."

"Hey…"

"Well? Didn't you just say you couldn't imagine it?"

"Yes, but that's not fair to—"

"Fair?" Miller scoffed. "You have no idea about fair."

"Why are you getting mad at me?"

He opened his mouth, then snapped it shut. "I'm not."

I let a few seconds go, then glanced up at him. "It's okay. You can tell me stuff. If you want."

"What kind of stuff?"

"Any kind."

Like where you live.

"We just met," Miller said. "And you're a girl."

"So?"

"So. Guys don't talk about stuff with girls. They talk with other guys."

"Friends talk to each other, remember? And besides…" I made a show of looking around and then peeked under the bed. "No guys here."

He snorted a laugh. "God, you're a dork. But kind of brave too."

"You think I'm brave?"

He nodded.

My cheeks felt warm. "No one's ever called me brave before."

A small smile flickered over his lips as our eyes met. The air between us seemed to soften and grow still. Kind of perfect, just sitting there with this boy on my birthday.

Then my mom threw open her bedroom door from down the hall with a *bang*, and her footsteps thumped down the stairs.

I flinched, and then Miller and I froze. A few minutes later, her voice rose, and my father answered, both of them growing louder and louder until they were in a full-blown shouting match. I could feel Miller watching me, and my face burned. My stomach tightened into knots around all the food I'd just eaten, making me feel sick.

"I can't believe it!" Mom screamed from below. "Another one, Vince? How many more?"

"Jesus Christ, it's after ten at night. Get off my back, Lynn!"

Their words became indistinct—Mom probably chasing Dad deeper into the house, waving some papers at him like I'd seen her do.

Humiliation burned right through the center of me. I drew my knees up and covered my ears, wishing they'd both drop dead.

The green scent of pine needles and the spicy bite of salsa wafted over me. I peeked one eye open. Miller had moved to sit beside me. He didn't put his arm around me but sat close enough that we were touching. Shoulder to shoulder. Making contact. Letting me know he was there.

I leaned over, tipping into him, and we listened until my parents' blowup faded out. Mom's footsteps thumped back upstairs. Her door slammed. Below, the den door slammed too, and silence descended.

"They fight a lot?" Miller asked in a quiet voice.

I nodded against the worn material of his jacket. "They used to love each other, and now they hate each other. I feel like I was in a simulation of the perfect family, but there's a glitch in the programming."

"Why don't they just get divorced?"

"I think there's some kind of money situation. They don't tell me anything, but I know they can't split up until it's fixed." My eyes stung. "But I keep hoping the money situation will sort itself out and it'll fix them too."

Miller said nothing, but I felt his shoulder press into me a little more.

"We're friends, Violet," he said finally, looking straight ahead.

"What?"

"You asked…and yeah. We're friends."

I peered up at him, and he looked down at me, and happiness filled in the cold spaces left by my parents' new hatred of each other.

I found a smile. "Ready for cake?"

I cut slices of strawberry cake with vanilla icing, and Miller and I ate and talked some more. I nearly made him spew Coke out his nose laughing, telling him about the time one of the skater dudes, Frankie Dowd, tried to jump his board off the lunch table in the cafeteria and fell, sending trays of food flying into people's laps.

"It set off a food fight," I said. "Oh my God, the principal was *pissed* and tried to give the entire seventh grade detention all at once."

Miller laughed harder. I loved his laugh; it sounded good in his scratchy voice, and his entire face lit up. That stressed-out tension went away, just for a few minutes, and that made me feel like I'd done something even better than giving him food.

We ate until we were stuffed, and Miller heaved a sigh. "Crap, that was good…" A thought seemed to occur to him, and that damn worry swept right back over him again. "I should go."

"You don't have to—"

"Yeah, I do." He got to his feet and shouldered his backpack. "Thanks for the food. And the cake."

"Thanks for eating it with me so I don't feel so pathetic."

"You're not pathetic," Miller said fiercely, then jammed his hands in his pockets. "Do you think maybe I can take another piece with me?"

"Take the whole thing. I don't want it."

"No," he said, his voice low. "I'm not taking your birthday cake. Just one piece. For my mom."

"Oh. Of course." I wrapped a piece of cake in napkins and handed it to him. "Miller?"

"Don't," he said, putting the cake into his backpack.

"How do you know what I was about to say?"

"I know what you're going to ask, but don't bother. Tonight was a good night. I don't want to mess it up."

"Telling me where you live would mess it up?"

"Yeah, it would. Trust me. Might mess *us* up."

"Us?"

"Being friends," he said quickly. "You might not want to be friends with me."

"I doubt that, but okay. I won't bother you about it anymore."

For now.

"Thanks. And thanks for the cake."

"Sure," I said. He started toward the window, and I bit my lip. "See you tomorrow?"

"You want me to come back?" His blue eyes lit up for a quick second, then he offered a careless shrug. "Yeah. Maybe."

I rolled my eyes and clasped my hands in front of me.

"Oooh, *maybe*. So I'll just wait up all night for you, *hoping* and *praying* and *pining* for you to come back."

He laughed a little. "You're so weird."

"And you're grouchy. We sort of fit. Don't we?"

He nodded, his eyes dark in the dimness. "I'll see you tomorrow." He started to climb out the window.

"Hey, wait!" I said, stopping him. "I didn't ask your last name. Is it a *first* name? Ted? John? Oh! Is your name Miller Henry?"

He smirked. "It's Stratton."

"Mine is McNamara. Nice to meet you, Miller Stratton."

He smiled but turned his head away before I could see all of it.

"Happy birthday, Violet."

Oh my God, Diary, that was nuts!!! I just snuck a boy in my room! We talked and ate and laughed, and I feel like I've known him forever. I don't know how else to explain it. Like when I met Shiloh, and we were friends right away. Miller's not like any other boy at school, who makes dumb sex jokes and plays video games all day. He's deep. No, that sounds cheesy. He has depth.

His grouchiness doesn't bother me either, and he didn't mind—too much—that I asked a million questions. Even so, he's still kind of a mystery. Like it could take years to get to know all of him, I think. He wouldn't tell me where he lived. I get the feeling he and his mom are poor, since he was so hungry, and his clothes are in bad shape. But all the houses around here are huge. He can't have walked very far to get here.

I invited him back tomorrow. I hope he comes. I want to give him some more food without making it look like he's my charity case. But mostly, I want to talk to him more. I want to get to know him and let him get to know me. I mean, how often does that happen? Getting to know a brand-new person...that's kind of like opening a birthday present.

Speaking of which, I now have two friends.

Happy birthday to me!

ACKNOWLEDGMENTS

I'm so grateful to so many people, not only those who had a hand in bringing this book to life but those who've been with me on my writing journey from the very beginning.

To my beta readers, MJ, Joanne, Annette, and Terri, thank you for shepherding me through so much writerly angst and encouraging me when Xander and Emery's story seemed so difficult to tell. Love you all for your support, always.

To Summer, Dawn, and Diana—thank you for being the best friends and inspirations a gal could ever want.

So much love and gratitude to my new Bloom family and my agent, Georgana Grinstead, for making my most precious and cherished dreams a reality.

Thank you to my brilliant editor, Shaina, for being as much of a quantum physicist enthusiast as me; it was so gratifying to know Xander and his genius were in good hands.

To my PA, Melissa, for being my right-hand gal but also for literally everything else you do. I will never stop being grateful for you. Love you.

To Robin, who is the reason most of my books make it out of my head and into the world. I'm beyond grateful for your love, encouragement, tireless work, and for putting up with me through every minute of doubt and second-guessing. Thank you for being with me every step of the way.

To Talia and Bill—it's all for you. All my love.

And lastly, I have a deep and abiding love of quantum physics and astrophysics but not the expertise. I would not have been able to create my beloved Xander Ford without the brilliance of actual physicists and scientists who unknowingly had a hand in the writing of this book and to whom I'm so grateful.

References:
In My Time of Dying, Sebastian Junger
When We Cease to Understand the World, Benjamin Labatut
Quantum Physics for Beginners, Into the Light, John Stoddard
Spooky Action at a Distance, George Musser
On The Origin of Time: Stephen Hawking's Final Theory, Thomas Hertog
NASA at science.nasa.gov

ABOUT THE AUTHOR

Emma Scott is a *USA Today* and *Wall Street Journal* bestselling author whose books have been translated into six languages and featured in Buzzfeed, Huffington Post, *New York Daily News*, and *USA Today*'s *Happy Ever After* blog. She writes emotional, character-driven romances in which art and love intertwine to heal and love always wins. If you enjoy emotionally charged stories that rip your heart out and put it back together again with diverse characters and kindhearted heroes, you will enjoy her novels.

Visit: emmascottwrites.com
Subscribe: bit.ly/2nTGLf6
Hang Out: facebook.com/groups/906742879369651
Follow: facebook.com/EmmaScottwrites
Contact: emmascottpromo@gmail.com